Dedication

For

Ada Civitarese Basso

Always in our thoughts
Forever in our hearts
Eternally loved

I would walk a thousand miles
To see your smile and hear your laugh
One more time

Forgiveness
Is the mightiest sword.
Forgiveness of those you fear
Is the highest reward.
When they bruise you with words,
When they make you feel small,
When it's hardest to take,
You must do nothing at all...

Charlotte Bronte
(Jane Eyre)

Acknowledgements

Although writing is a solitary craft, no writer can work in isolation. I owe my deepest gratitude to my family and friends:

To my parents, Ersilia and Dolfino Sichirollo, who have always loved me and taught me the value of family and the beauty of my Italian heritage.

To *The Disorganised Scribblers*, Anita Davison, Lisa Yarde, and Anne Whitfield whose ongoing friendship and encouragement refreshed me every weekend as we Skyped from the four corners of the world to dream, commiserate, and exchange our wisdom. I'm in awe of your talent and blessed to have you in my life. We are proof that an enduring friendship can surpass the miles that separate us.

To N. Gemini Sasson for leading the way into the Indie world and showing us all how a good story, well written, can reach lofty heights.

To the members of the Historical Fiction Writers Critique Group, Cori Van Hausen, Dave Lefurgey, Greg Graham, Miranda Miller, Ursula Thompson, Pamela Maddison, Rosemary Rach, Wally Rabbani, and the many others who lent their patience and experience to my rough first drafts. Your collective advice has made my manuscript much stronger.

To my dear friends Sandra Falconi, Paddy Cush, Ersilia Ward, Laurie Rezanoff, Lisa Yarde, and Colleen MacLellan. Thank you for allowing me to impose upon you for reading the final draft. I am grateful for your scrutiny and input.

To my cousins, the Lanzillotta family, Emilia, Roberto,

Marcus, and Matteo, thank you for allowing me the joy of naming my characters after you. I love you all.

To Sue Sturgeon who delights me each Christmas with a cross-stitch heirloom. I have treasured every one.

To my immediate family, Richard, Amanda, and Genna. The writing world is hard to understand, especially the incessant need to sit before a computer. I appreciate your efforts to understand and to help me achieve my goals.

And last, but never least, to my little grandson, Joey. You are the light of my life, my very favourite boy.

1

Pointe-du-Lac
New France
1702

Fast approaching hooves rumbled against the damp earth of the long, tree-lined dirt road. Emilie Basseaux glanced back at the sound. Two men on horseback cantered towards them. *Mon Dieu, non,* Emilie thought, not them again.

Her heart raced. A momentary lapse distracted her from possible danger. She had allowed her thoughts to wander to her pending nuptials to Robert Lanzille, the miller of Pointe-du-Lac. They would marry in three days. Lost in her daydreams, enjoying the pleasant walk down the shady lane amid towering maple and pine trees, she had lost track of time. Now, Emilie hastened her step, but the two men slowed their horses to a walk beside her. She looked up from beneath the brim of her straw bonnet.

The youthful Seigneur Richard Tonnacour gazed down at Emilie from the lofty perch of his well-muscled black gelding. Impeccably dressed in a dark blue coat, white shirt and hose, tendrils of his brown hair curled onto the nape of his neck below his white wig. Once again, the heated interest in his eyes made her cringe.

Seigneur Richard's presence disturbed the calmness of the day. To Emilie's right, rays of sunlight danced upon the calm waters of Lac Saint Pierre. Upon its serene waters, an Abenaki Indian guide paddled two voyageurs in a fur-laden canoe. To her left, ships with billowed white sails rode the placid waves of the mighty Saint Lawrence River enroute to destinations unknown.

Next to him rode his cousin, Seigneur Pierre Robillard who had been with him yesterday when she encountered them on this very same lane.

Granted the title deed of a vast fief of at least a dozen miles squared with frontage on the great Saint Lawrence River by King Louis of France, Seigneur Richard commanded the fealty of almost all the *habitants* and colony folk. He even owned the mill, which her betrothed, Robert, operated. Emilie's late father, a fur trader, had purchased their home in the village outright, and Emilie and her mother were not under obligation to either of the overlords whose estates bordered each other.

"*Bonjour,*" Seigneur Richard said with a smile. He tipped his tricorne, its ostrich feather dancing in the gentle breeze. His grey eyes roved her body from face to breast to hip and back again.

His blatant attention stirred her annoyance. "*Bonjour,*" she replied, her voice deliberately curt. Common sense told her she should respond, not only because he was the seigneur of Pointe-du-Lac, but also because he was Robert's overlord, and one whom everyone feared. She averted her gaze and refrained from saying anything more in the hopes he would ride away.

"And where might a lovely young woman like you be going at such an odd hour?" The resonance of his deep voice seemed at odds with the tranquility of the day. Everyone feared this man. She frowned and quickened her stride.

"Come, come," he said. "Surely you are not going to ignore me like you did yesterday?"

"I mean no offence to you, *Monsieur,* but I am betrothed and it would set tongues wagging were I to linger in conversation with another man. I'm certain you can understand my wish to preserve my good name and virtue." She met his gaze without wavering.

Rumours of his tyranny and lasciviousness abounded and

Emilie knew that even a brief conversation with the man could tarnish a young woman's reputation.

"Betrothals can be broken."

"Not so, *Monsieur*, especially when one's family and the Church has already given their blessing."

"Ah, but if your destiny should lie in another direction, you would be powerless to avoid it," he said with a grin.

Emilie wiped her sweaty hands against the coarse material of her homespun gown. She disguised her clenched fists in the folds of her gown so that he could not see how his words affected her. "I know well where my destiny lies. It's my own will that keeps me firm upon its path."

Seigneur Pierre chortled. "Have a care, young lady, for a man like my cousin Richard is easily stirred by a spirited woman. Brazenness adds spice to the chase."

His words rang true and Emilie resolved to avoid Seigneur Richard's questions. She could not allow him to goad her into more talk. She must discourage him and send him on his way as politely as possible.

Seigneur Richard cast his cousin a stern glance, turned his attention back to Emilie, and smiled. The sun shone through the leaves behind him, casting an eerie halo around the white wig on his head. "I'm a man who knows well how to carve his own destiny, Mademoiselle Basseaux. It's a rare occasion when I do not succeed. A poor girl like you would do well to remember that, for I have much to offer."

Emilie ignored him, her eyes focused straight ahead as she continued walking, praying for the men to leave.

Undaunted, Seigneur Richard and his cousin followed, but from a greater distance. Their voices drifted to her although she could not make out everything they said. Then she heard Seigneur Pierre bellow out a laugh.

"You shall see, my friend, you shall see," Seigneur Richard

said in a voice clear enough for Emilie to discern the fury within it.

She threw a swift glance back to see him kick his horse into a canter, his face scarlet.

Seigneur Pierre laughed even more and followed.

Emilie watched Seigneur Richard ride away, his hair flowing against the nape of his neck. She expelled a pent-up breath hastened her step.

Emilie fell into her own thoughts, troubled, unable to dispel the bad feeling that arose within her. She prayed that the seigneur's attention meant nothing and that her upcoming wedding would end the man's interest. Judging by the comments she overheard between the two men, however, she sensed more trouble. What form would it take? More importantly, how could she prevent it?

She pondered whether to tell Robert, but decided against it. Robert, her handsome and gallant devotee. His love for her held no bounds, as did hers for him. If he knew of this, Robert would become angry and might confront Seigneur Richard in her defense. That would mean certain trouble because Robert owed his livelihood to Seigneur Richard. He could cast Robert out of his mill and deny him the work in which he took such great pride. What then of their future? *Non*, she could not take any risks. She must find a way to deal with this herself.

A vain hope arose that perhaps her mother could advise her, but she dismissed it almost immediately. Although her mother possessed a shrewd mind, she also had a tendency to over-react and might complicate matters. Emilie knew that once stirred, her mother would be relentless towards finding a resolution. She might even accost Seigneur Richard herself. This too would bring trouble for Robert. *Non*, she must not breathe a word of this to her mother either.

Only one man could help her – Père Marc-Mathieu, the

Jesuit priest who lived on the outskirts of Pointe-du-Lac in a convent with several of his brethren. Revered for his kindness and wisdom, Emilie trusted him to give her sound advice. He had the ability to deal with Seigneur Richard without further agitation or provocation. She would speak to him tomorrow at chapel.

Even though this second encounter with Seigneur Richard disturbed Emilie as much as that of the day before, she was secure in the knowledge that Père Marc-Mathieu would help her put all this trouble to rest. For now, she decided to cast the overlord from her thoughts, dismissing the encounter as the actions of a spoiled man whose opinion of himself was higher than that of those around him. She entered her home with a lighter heart, refusing to allow it to dampen the happiness of her approaching wedding day.

2

Not for a moment did Père Jean Civitelle anticipate trouble as he strolled along a narrow lane, reading his breviary. He shut his book, careful to save his place with his index finger, and clasped both hands behind his back. Eyes downcast, he continued on his walk. A gentle evening breeze billowed his black cassock while he whispered his evening prayers.

At this, his favourite time of day, he glanced to the west where the glow of the setting sun cast a rose-coloured hue over Lac Saint Pierre. A quiet stroll and a few gentle prayers helped soothe him in anticipation of a restful night's sleep. He re-opened his book to read the next psalm.

When he looked up again, he had reached a fork in the lane. The right path ascended to his small parish church and rectory. To the left, another path descended into the centre of the village settlement. Père Jean turned right and heaved a sigh of satisfaction, for he could not recall ever feeling so much at peace. He enjoyed his simple life and unassuming home. Both the small, whitewashed church and the attached two-storey home where he lived had been built of rough-hewn timber from the lands of the seigneury. The parishioners themselves had built it and he cherished it.

He noticed the two men immediately. They stood a little way ahead in his path. The taller of the two cleaned his fingernails with the tip of a knife, his tricorne tilted low over his eyes. His companion, dressed in a brown linen frock coat and breeches stood with arms akimbo in the middle of the lane. They seemed to be waiting for him because the moment he appeared, they exchanged a quick glance, fixed their gazes on him, and blocked the path.

Père Jean kept his book open before him as if reading it, but he watched every move the men made. They advanced towards him. A knot formed in his stomach. Had he offended some great man, some vindictive parishioner? He could think of no reason for these two men to seek him out. The closer they came, the more they narrowed their eyes.

He slid two fingers beneath his collar and ran them round his neck. Père Jean glanced behind him, but the lane was deserted. He looked left towards the settlement, but no one stirred there. What could he do? Turn back? It was too late. Should he run? It would make him look cowardly or appear as if he had something to hide. Besides, his cassock would impede him. Since he could not escape the danger, he had no choice but to confront it. He broke out in a cold sweat and swallowed, his mouth and throat were parched. The grip on his book tightened as he drew nearer to the strangers. He recited a verse in a louder tone and composed his face into a tranquil, careless expression. When the two men came to a stop before him, it took nearly all of his effort to smile.

"Père Jean!" The tallest of the two stepped into his path and peered at him with dark, close-set eyes. He chewed on a long blade of straw.

The priest raised his eyes from the breviary and held it open in both hands. "Yes. I am he. Who are you and what can I do for you this fine evening?"

The tall man glared at him as if he had caught a criminal committing a grievous offence. "Tomorrow you plan to wed Robert Lanzille and Emilie Basseaux?"

"*Oui*. That is so."

The tall man removed the straw from his mouth. He scowled and his upper lip rose in a sneer. He took a step forward and Père Jean could smell the wine on his breath. "Mark my words well," he said in a deep, authoritative voice. "You will *not* perform that marriage. Not tomorrow. Not ever."

"Gentlemen, you are both men of the world, and know how these things go." Père Jean's voice quivered. "A poor parish priest has nothing to say about it. People make their pledges to each other then come to us to marry them. We priests are servants of the community who serve the needs of our flocks, within the doctrine of the Church, of course." Père Jean swallowed the lump of fear wedged in his throat. "Gentlemen, please be kind and put yourselves in my place. I have no choice; it is my duty, the role of my office. The banns have been read. The families have prepared the celebration. Money has been spent. The entire village is in readiness."

"*Mon* Père," interrupted the shorter of the two men. A false smile belied the grimace on his face. "It's a simple request, one we know little about. A warning from the man we work for. Do you understand?"

"But, gentlemen like you are too just, too reasonable to make such a threat." Père Jean tucked his book and hands into the pocket of his cassock to hide their trembling.

The short man's face reddened and his countenance turned dark. "You are not to perform this marriage. If you do, it will be the last ceremony you will *ever* perform."

"Silence," replied the tall man shaking his head. "*Le bon Père* knows the ways of the world. We are good men. No harm will come to him if he obeys." His right hand rested on the grip of a large knife tucked into his belt. A smile arose on his face. "Our master, Seigneur Richard, sends his kindest respects to you."

The name struck Père Jean like a lightning bolt in a storm. A shiver of fear ran down his spine. "If you could ask him to-"

"There is nothing to ask," the tall man interrupted. His scowl hovered between vulgar and ferocious. "For your own good, whisper not a word about our talk. If you do, you'll suffer the same consequence as if you married the couple." He paused and gave Père Jean a hard stare. "Well, what response does your Reverence wish us to relay to Seigneur Richard?"

"My respects?" Père Jean stammered.

"Be clear, Père Jean," the short man growled.

"I am disposed, uh, always disposed to obedience." Having spoken these words, Père Jean did not know whether he had given a promise or whether he had only paid them homage.

The men seemed to accept it because they both smirked.

"*Bon*. Good evening, Père Jean." The tall man nodded as he and his companion brushed past.

A few moments before, Père Jean would have given almost anything to be rid of the two menaces. Now, he wished to prolong the conversation to convince them to abandon their threat. "Gentlemen," he called out.

They turned around simultaneously.

He opened his mouth to ask them again to reconsider, but his courage failed him. His heart sank. "A good evening to you, too."

The two men turned and ambled away until they were out of

sight.

Père Jean wiped the sweat from his brow then hurried up the path toward his home. He loathed himself for not being born with the heart of a lion. The two men had made him feel like a trapped animal, without claws and without teeth, forced to either fight or be devoured.

He was not born noble, or rich, or courageous. He had gone through life like a fragile piece of earthenware amongst huge chunks of unstable iron. Hence, when his parents had urged him to enter the priesthood, he acquiesced. He had not reflected adequately on the strict vows and many obligations that would forever bind him. Instead, he thought only about the promise of a comfortable, safe life and a profession that would raise him into a powerful, revered class. No level of society completely shelters an individual, so he had been forced to find ways to hide his personal shortcomings.

For safety's sake, he never took risks. When he could not escape opposition, he yielded. If conflict arose from words that resulted in the threat of fists or weapons, he chose neutrality. If forced to choose sides, he always favoured the stronger. He kept a respectful distance from those in power and bore their scorn at his submissive nature in silence. With bows of his head and respectful salutations, he drew smiles from the most haughty and surly whenever he met such people in the street. In this way, he managed to navigate sixty years of life without too many tempests.

However, he had paid a high price. Because he had stretched the limits of his endurance by always yielding to others and swallowing a myriad of bitter retorts in silence, it had affected his health. He suffered from indigestion, constant insomnia, and ailments of the bowel. Tonight, his quiet evening walk had turned into a nightmare. Razor-sharp pains now roiled about in his gut.

The faces of the two men haunted him. He struggled up the path, his chest heaving. Their conversation replayed itself in his mind. The warning from Seigneur Richard, a man known never to have uttered a false threat, made his bowels tighten with fear. Seigneur Richard had seen this parish built and was responsible for all of Pointe-du-Lac. The fidelity of the people to the parish priest was as strong as their loyalty to the seigneur who ranked as their patron and protector. A most delicate balance. Père Jean could ill afford to displease either party. Now he walked a dangerous narrow path from which there was no escape.

These thoughts tossed about in his downcast head. How easy it would be to refuse to marry Robert Lanzille and Emilie Basseaux. Robert would want to know why. What excuse could he give? Outwardly, Robert had a gentle demeanour, but if crossed, what then? Robert passionately loved Emilie, a beautiful and virtuous young woman. A man in love would find another way to marry. Robert would not care about the trouble this might bring upon a poor defenseless priest.

What misfortune! Why had those two frightful men put themselves in his path to interfere with his work? Why did they not approach Robert directly? Oh, why hadn't he suggested they speak to him?

He turned his thoughts to the man who had robbed him of his peace. He knew Seigneur Richard only by sight from chance encounters. He had always paid him humble reverence. It had even fallen upon him to defend the Seigneur against those who, with subdued voice and looks of fear, wished him ill. In every circumstance, he urged them to respect Seigneur Richard. Now he wanted to utter all those hateful epithets he had quelled in others.

Amid such turbulent thoughts, he reached his small church and rectory. After turning the key, he entered and pulled the door shut behind him. He leaned against it, clutching his chest, fighting for each breath.

"Rose!" His anxious voice broke the silence in the still house as he called for his housekeeper. "Rose!"

"I'm coming," Rose huffed from the dining room.

Père Jean crossed the entrance hall and stood in the doorway of the dining room. The comely woman set a flask of his favourite wine in its usual place on the table. Before she could attend him, he rushed into the room, his step unsteady, hands shaking, his breathing hard and fast.

Her mouth fell open. "Mercy! What has happened to you, *mon* Père?" She pulled out an armchair for him.

He slumped into it. "Nothing."

"Nothing! You expect me to believe that when you appear so agitated? Some great misfortune has occurred. What is it? Tell me!"

Père Jean looked up into the face of his housekeeper who had served him for many years. He depended on her for everything. She prepared his meals, washed his clothes, and organized his life. She knew when to obey and when to command. Rose bore his grumblings and fancies, and made him suffer the same when her turn came, which occurred frequently now that she had surpassed the age of forty. She had remained unwed, refusing all offers of marriage because no man met her expectations. Thus, she focused all her attention on Père Jean and her role as his housekeeper.

"Oh, for Heaven's sake! Don't you know by now that when I say 'nothing', it's either nothing, or something I cannot speak about?"

"Not even to me, the one who works like a slave to take care of you? The one who advises you, cooks your meals, fights your battles?" She rested her fists on her ample hips.

"Hold your tongue, woman, and say no more. Give me a glass of wine." He leaned forward and grasped his stomach.

"And you still persist in saying that it is nothing!" Rose grumbled while she filled the glass and held it as if she would relinquish it only in exchange for the secret he kept.

"Give it here." Père Jean took it from her with an unsteady hand. He emptied it, a draught to soothe his rattled nerves.

"Do you intend to force me to ask others what has happened to you?" Rose faced him with arms now crossed beneath her abundant breasts and stared at him, seeking the truth from his eyes.

"Let us not argue. It is my problem, my life!"

"Your life!"

"*Oui*, my life, not yours."

"You know that whenever you've told me anything in confidence, I've never revealed it."

He snorted. "Like the time you-"

"Père Jean," Rose interrupted. "I have been a loyal servant to you, and if I wish to know what ails you, it is because I care, and want to help you, to give you good advice, to comfort you."

He studied her, believing her sincerity. The truth was that he wanted to rid himself of this burdensome secret, but he also knew she had a big mouth, which she opened far too often. However, his desire to unburden himself overcame his reticence. "Well, if you vow never to repeat what I tell you..." he hesitated.

"*Oui, oui,* of course." Rose pulled out a chair and sat.

With many sighs and doleful exclamations, he related the miserable event. When he came to the terrible name, he paused and made Rose make new and more solemn vows of silence.

Satisfied, he inhaled a deep breath. "Seigneur Richard." He sank back in the chair and shook his head.

"Mercy!" exclaimed Rose. "That wretch! What a tyrant! Such a godless man!"

Père Jean glanced about. "Quiet, or do you wish to ruin me

altogether?"

"Why? We're alone." Rose's voice grew even louder. "No one can hear us. What will you do?"

"You see?" exclaimed Père Jean, in an angry tone. "You have no good advice to give me. Instead, you ask me what I shall do, as if you were in this quandary and it was my place to help you."

"But if I give you my poor opinion-"

"Let me hear it," he interrupted.

"Send a letter to Bishop Nicholas de Laval. Everybody says he is a saint, a bold-hearted man who fears no one and who glories in upholding a poor priest against such tyrants. Inform him of what happened."

"Those men intend to kill me and that is your advice? Write a letter? Heaven help me! As if the Bishop can stop Seigneur Richard!"

"Woe to us if those dogs really can bite instead of bark."

"Of course, they bite, woman! They are tyrants who would not hesitate to murder a priest who thwarts their wishes."

"If everyone sees a priest yield to their threats-"

"This isn't the time for foolish words."

"Well, if you don't like my advice, you can worry about it all night long, but don't make yourself ill over it. Eat some supper before you go to bed."

"Think about it? I can think of nothing else. All night long, I shall think of it. Oh why did this happen to me?" Père Jean rose to his feet.

Rose pointed to the warm tourtière on the table.

"Thank you, but I'm not hungry."

She poured some more wine. "Drink. It helps your stomach."

"A strengthener." He accepted the glass, muttering all the way to his bedchamber.

Once inside, he downed the contents, laid on the bed, and stared up at the all too familiar ceiling. He rolled onto his side and punched his pillow. "What is a poor wretch like me to do?"

3

Fretful thoughts kept Père Jean from sleep as he sought a way out of the hateful situation that trapped him. To ignore the threat and perform the marriage meant certain death. If he confided the incident to Robert, together they might find a solution. However, his instincts warned against this. He did not know the young man well enough to predict his reaction. Telling Rose, too, had been a mistake. He prayed she would keep her mouth shut, but doubted it. He could flee, but to where? If he did, he might be forced to tell lies his conscience would not allow. As he tossed, he found flaws with every idea that entered his mind and rejected plan after plan. He needed time; a reprieve of some sort. The answer came to him in a rush. The start of Lent was only two days away and it would last a full two months. An old canon law discouraged priests from performing marriages during this period. If he could delay the wedding by two days, the bride and groom would have no choice but to wait until after Lent. A great deal could change during that time.

He mulled over this new idea with enthusiasm. It might work, even though most people knew that a priest could use discretion in such matters, and depending on the circumstances, overlook the ruling altogether. Robert might or might not know that, but Père Jean's age and experience gave him an advantage over youth, and could help to convince him. Besides, the miller would have no choice in the matter. After all, love might drive Robert, but *he* was fighting to preserve his life. Satisfied at last, Père Jean closed his eyes. Sleep soon overtook him, but it was an uneasy slumber with visions of menacing hoodlums, aggrieved brides and grooms, pistol shots, and copious amounts of blood.

Morning light crept through the closed shutters of his bedroom and he gradually awoke. The usual feelings of comfort and tranquility swept over him, and then the recollection of yesterday's calamity struck him. His eyes sprang open. Reality returned with rude abruptness. Bitter at his horrible circumstances, he rose reluctantly, and commenced his morning ablutions. His mind raced as he reviewed the plan he had formulated in the night. Convinced it would work, he donned his cassock, and went downstairs. He took a seat at the head of the dining room table and tried to compose himself. It was still early and Rose wasn't due for an hour or so. Drumming his fingers on the tabletop, he waited for Robert to arrive for their earlier agreed upon meeting.

4

Robert awoke long before dawn, eager to greet the new day. Today he would wed his true love, Emilie Basseaux, the most beautiful girl in Pointe-du-Lac. With great care, he buttoned his white, long-sleeved shirt and tucked it into his new black breeches. A black silk coat with pleated panels inserted in the side seams, new leather shoes fashioned with silver buckles, and a slate grey tricorne completed his wedding outfit. He whistled light-heartedly as he set out to meet with Père Jean to confirm the details and exact time of the ceremony today.

Pointe-du-Lac was still quiet, although coming awake with activity. His neighbor, a *habitant* woman with ten children, waved as he crossed the street ahead of two Algonquin men who led a train of three horses laden with pelts of beaver. He inhaled the aroma of baking bread emanating from one of the cottages, a rarity due to last year's drought. The shortage of grain had been compounded by the failure of several ships with seeds and supplies failing to make port.

Despite the hardships faced by the people of New France, his heart swelled with pride at the thought that he had milled the grain for that baking bread. Although there had been little grain last harvest, as an unmarried man, he had given his entire share to the more needy families in Pointe-du-Lac. He could not bear the thought of children going hungry and Emilie loved him all the more for it.

Emilie, the one woman who had succeeded in capturing his heart. His love for her was so profound, so enduring. She was as vital to him as the air he breathed and the water he drank. She sustained his life and brought joy when there had been much sadness. He had no family but her, and her mother, Ada, now.

As he walked, he reflected on his life thus far. Although he had never known the identity of his true parents, he came to love the man and woman who had raised him from childhood. But at the age of fifteen, he lost both of them. His adopted father died of apoplexy and his adopted mother died of a fever one year later. An only child, he had been left alone and in despair on the family farm. Ever conscious, and sometimes fearful of Seigneur Richard Tonnacour, Robert had worked hard to maintain the farm and pay the heavy dues he owed. Pleased with his success, Seigneur Richard sent him to work at the mill to apprentice with the aging miller. When the miller became too old, the seigneurial mill passed to him. Although the mill itself was small and poorly built, Robert did his best to crack the wheat into coarse meal and flour. Many now considered him a wealthy man. Even though drought reduced this year's crops, and many had already begun to feel the pinch of hunger, he was not struggling as much and had even put away a small amount of money. From the moment he cast his eyes on Emilie, he knew he would marry her, and saved his money. From the moment he cast his eyes on Emilie, he knew he would marry her, and saved his money. Her beauty, her goodness, and her charismatic personality drew him as a thirsting man is drawn to a mineral spring. Over time, he managed to acquire more than enough money to provide for himself and his bride in the years to come.

Robert knocked on the door of the rectory.

Père Jean himself answered with a strained smile.

Robert smiled. "*Bonjour,* Père Jean. As we agreed, I've come to confirm the hour for the wedding ceremony."

The priest's smile faded. "Come in, Robert, come in." He led him into the dining room and gestured for him to sit. The priest stared back at him with a hesitant, distant demeanour. "Now, what day do you speak of?"

Robert frowned. "What day? Don't you remember, Père? Today is the day."

"Today?" Père Jean frowned. "It is impossible."

"Why, what do you mean? What has happened?" Robert took note of the dark circles beneath the priest's eyes and his pale complexion.

Père Jean took hold of the cross that hung round his pudgy neck and slid it back and forth on its chain. "I'm sorry, uh, I don't feel well."

Robert studied the priest again. He looked tired, but not ill. "A wedding ceremony is brief and not too fatiguing. It won't take long."

Père Jean hesitated. He pulled a handkerchief from the pocket of his cassock and wiped the sweat from his brow. "But-"

"But what, Père?"

"There is a problem."

"A problem? What problem can there be?"

"To understand the difficulties I face, you must put yourself in my place. I am softhearted and struggle to please everyone. If I forget something or fail to do my duty in some way, I am ridiculed."

"But what is the matter?"

"Many formalities are required to perform a marriage."

"*Oui,* I know, for you have burdened me with them during the last few weeks. But I have done all you requested of me, have I not?" Robert's voice rose.

"*Mais oui,* everything is done, on your part. Please, have patience. I have neglected some of my own duties regarding these formalities. We poor priests are caught between a mortar and pestle sometimes. I am sorry."

"Tell me what is needed and I'll do it immediately."

Père Jean swallowed. "Do you know what absolute impediments are?"

Robert shrugged. "What could I know about such things?"

"Then you must have patience and leave it to me because *I* do know."

Robert opened his mouth to speak, but the priest raised his hand to stop him.

"Please, Robert, don't be upset. I'm ready to do all that is required to satisfy you. For now, your life is a good one, it wants for nothing. Besides, the whim of marriage came upon you so suddenly, you can easily wait a little longer."

"Why are you doing this?" Robert's voice erupted.

"It's no fault of mine. I don't make these laws. Before performing a marriage, it is my duty to certify that there is no impediment."

"But what impediment could there be?"

"It is not something that can be easily determined, but I hope it will amount to nothing. But whether the consequence is great or little, I must complete the research."

"I don't understand."

"Nevertheless, I must do my duty."

"But I thought you researched everything already?"

The priest shook his head. "*Non*, not as I must."

"Why did you tell me last week that all was ready if it was not?"

"Now you find fault with my over-kindness. I have done everything, but, now I have learned something more."

This strange discourse baffled Robert. "And what do you wish me to do, Père?"

"Be patient for a few more days, my son. It is not an eternity."

"How many days?"

Père Jean rubbed his chin. "Fifteen days will suffice."

"Fifteen days! *You* chose this day and now that it is here, you tell me I have to wait fifteen more days." Robert's voice rose as he swung his fist through the air in frustration.

Père Jean placed a timid hand on his shoulder. "Don't be angry. I'll try to accomplish everything quickly."

"And Emilie, what must I say to her?"

"That the oversight is entirely mine."

"And what will the people of Pointe-du-Lac say?"

"Tell them that I have made a blunder through haste and oversight. Blame me for it all. Come now, Robert, it is only a little longer that you both have to wait."

"Then will there be no more impediments?"

Père Jean raised his brows and nodded.

Robert sighed. "Very well. I will wait, but before that day, I will return to see you, to make sure." Robert pursed his lips, cast the priest a pointed glare, and departed.

With a heavy heart, Robert walked away to break the news to Emilie. Consumed with frustration, he thought back to the conversation. More and more, it struck him as odd. The priest's reserved demeanour, guarded words, shifting eyes, and the strange and unexpected delay to the nuptials, convinced him Père Jean was hiding something. But what?

About to turn back to confront him again, Robert noticed the priest's housekeeper heading to the rectory.

"Rose," he called out and quickened his pace until he came face to face with her. At his advance, she averted her eyes. "Good morning, Rose. I had hoped to see you at my wedding today, but it has been postponed."

"I'm sorry for you both," Rose looked away in obvious discomfort.

"Can you do something for me? Père Jean has given me a reason, but I don't understand it. Can you explain why he can't marry us today?"

"How should I know?" she shrugged. "I'm only the housekeeper."

He studied her thin face. Above a Roman nose, hazel eyes darted back and forth. She was an efficient woman, known for her baking skills and dedication to Père Jean. Whatever the secret, Robert was determined to draw it from her. "Come, Rose, we have been friends for a long time. Haven't I always saved the best flour for you? Tell me what you know."

"Life is never easy." She bit her bottom lip.

He kept his silence, fixed his gaze on her, and kept it there without wavering.

She looked at the ground and pushed about a pebble before looking up at him. "I can't tell you anything; because I don't know anything. But Père Jean would never mistreat anybody. And it is not his fault."

"Whose fault is it then?" Robert narrowed his gaze.

"I know nothing, but I will tell you this. If he caused any harm, it was accidental, and only because of his good nature." She paused. "There are many evil people in this world, overbearing ruffians, men without conscience."

Robert understood well the meaning behind her words. "Tell me who caused this." He struggled to suppress his agitation.

"You'll never hear it from my mouth. I must go now." She elbowed past him to the priest's house.

Mouth agape, Robert watched her go. She entered through the front gate and disappeared into the garden at the rear of the church.

When she was out of sight, Robert ran back to the front door of the parish house. He entered without a sound. Père Jean sat in an armchair, hunched over the dining room table, his head in his hands, as if he were ill. Robert stepped closer, determined to get a straight answer.

"Robert!" Père Jean glanced up, eyes wide and his voice tremulous.

"Tell me who opposes my marriage to Emilie." Robert glared at him.

The priest turned as pale as milk. He glanced at the door and tried to rise from his chair, but Robert sprang forward, locked the door, and tucked the key in his pocket. "Everybody seems to know my affairs, except me. Who prevented my wedding?"

"Please, don't ask me this."

"I want to know," Robert insisted, laying his hand on the hilt of the small knife he always carried in his pocket. "Tell me!" Robert stepped closer.

"Who told you?"

"No more delays, Père Jean."

"If I tell you, my life is in danger."

"It is my right to know."

"Surely, you do not want to put my life at risk?"

"Tell me." Robert shouted, his patience at an end.

Père Jean wrung his hands. "Swear to me you will not repeat what I tell you to anyone."

"I swear that I will lose control if you don't tell me the name right now."

"Seigneur-" Père Jean sputtered, his face as fearful as if he faced an executioner.

"Seigneur who?" Robert leaned forward, fists clenched behind him. There was only one Seigneur in Pointe-du-Lac, but he wanted to hear the name from the priest's lips.

"Seigneur Richard!"

It took a moment for Robert to absorb the information. "What did he say to you?"

"What did he say?" Père Jean asked. "I wish it never happened." His voice alive with emotion, he told Robert everything. By the time he finished, his face was red and his eyes bulged from their sockets. "There, now you know, Robert. You've treated me badly, a priest, in his own house. In a sacred place! I kept the truth from you for your own good. It's my ruin that you've forced it from my lips. If I perform the marriage, I'm a dead man. Now, you know." He shook his head and scowled. "Open the door and give me my key."

"I'm sorry." Robert spoke softly, but his thoughts yet raged. "Try to understand. What would you have done in my place?" He took the key from his pocket, put it back into the lock, and turned it.

Père Jean came to stand beside him. "Swear to me you won't say or do anything."

Robert looked him in the eye. "I was wrong for accosting you like this and I beg your pardon." He opened the door and prepared to leave.

"You must swear." With a trembling hand, Père Jean seized Robert by the arm.

Robert shook off the priest's hand, walked out the door, and out into the lane. He didn't look back.

5

"Robert! Come back" Père Jean yelled, but Robert had gone.

"Rose!" Père Jean staggered back to his chair in the dining room and slumped into it. Yesterday's scare, the sleeplessness of the night, the hostile conflict with Robert, and his fear for the future, took its toll. He struggled for breath and his body shook with nerves as his bile arose.

At length, he heard Rose enter through the back door. "Rose!" he called out, his voice strained.

She strolled into the room, a basket dangled from her arm filled with last year's carrots.

"You told him!" Père Jean accused.

Her mouth fell open. "I told him nothing."

He shook his head and felt ill. "Lock all the doors and do not step outside for anything. If anyone knocks at the door, answer from the window." He rose, trembling.

"Where are you going?" Rose asked, alarmed.

"To bed with a fever." He ascended the stairs, mumbling as he went, "Oh, what trouble. May God spare me."

6

Robert's mind whirled as he stormed away. Although unsure of what to do, he knew he must act. All his life, he prided himself on his easygoing manner and genial disposition. He loathed violence and abhorred deceit. But today, something awakened deep inside of him – vengeance. Robert would fight to the death for Emilie, whom he loved more than life itself.

Seigneur Richard practically owned him, for no one but a seigneur could own a mill in New France. The man controlled all his work and took more than his allotted share of flour. Now he had reached out with his greedy hand to take Emilie from him and control this part of his life too. Robert's first instinct was to run to Seigneur Richard's house and seize him by the throat and squeeze the life from him, but he remembered that the man's house was well garrisoned, both inside and out. Only close friends, relatives, or servants were permitted entry. He dreamed about taking his musket, hiding behind one of the trees that lined the road to the seigneurial manor house, and waiting for him to appear, unaccompanied, of course. He visualized raising his weapon, taking aim, and firing, and watching the wretch fall to the ground. He would stand above him, look him hard in the eye, then spit in his face, and curse him.

His thoughts then wandered to Emilie, of their promising future, and how eager they had both been for their wedding day to arrive. Any dreams of killing Seigneur Richard evaporated. In its place, came visions of a more pleasant nature. He remembered the goodness of the man and woman who raised him, their love for him and for each other, the faith they instilled in him. His entire life had been righteous, innocent of all crime. How horrified he had been each time he heard of a killing. Remorse for his murderous thoughts washed over him.

What then of Emilie? Now, he must find the words to tell her their wedding was not to be. What should they do? How could they get married, in spite of their sinister adversary? Why had Seigneur Richard done this to them? The only reason he could think of was the man's own desire for Emilie. Was it possible? She had never mentioned Seigneur Richard before, not even in passing. Had Emilie encouraged the man somehow? Robert doubted it. Perhaps she wasn't aware of Seigneur Richard's interest. Could the man have developed his passion without her knowledge? He must have made some advance towards her in order for him to block their wedding.

Embroiled in such thoughts, he arrived at Emilie's house, its whitewashed walls brilliant against the morning sun. A little garden surrounded by a low stone wall separated it from the road.

Robert entered the garden. From an open window came the cheerful sound of women talking and laughing – Emilie's friends had come to dress her for the wedding. He didn't want to draw attention to himself, but he needed to talk to her privately. A small girl, who played in the garden, noticed him, and shrieked, "The bridegroom!"

"Hush, Patrice, hush!" Robert motioned for the child to come close to him. "Go to Emilie, take her aside, and whisper into her ear. Make sure no one hears you. Tell her I'm here and want to speak to her. Tell her to come immediately."

The girl nodded, skipping away to do as he bid.

Through the window, Robert saw Emilie laughing, encircled by her friends. Her luxuriant chestnut hair cascaded down her shoulders and back, glimmering against the morning sun. Lacy pleats of pink flowed from the shoulders of her taupe-colored sack-backed gown. She turned and he caught a glimpse of her beauty; a delicate upturned nose, eyes of the deepest, darkest brown, and round cheeks always ablush. Never had she seemed so far away, so unattainable. Invisible fingers of pain squeezed his heart.

Patrice made her way through the room of women and whispered her little message into Emilie's ear. Robert saw Emilie nod and announce, "I'm going for a moment, but will be back shortly," and she disappeared from view.

Emilie's face beamed with happiness when she stepped through the front door of the house and saw him. It faded the moment she noticed his uneasiness. "Robert, what is the matter?" Lines of worry creased her forehead.

For the first time, he could not help but wonder about

secrets she might be keeping. "It breaks my heart to tell you this, but we can't marry today. Only God knows when we can."

Emilie's face paled. "What do you mean? I don't understand."

As he related the events of the morning, she listened intently. With his every word, she grew ever more silent, her gaze on the ground. When he mentioned Seigneur Richard, she looked up and covered her mouth with her hand.

"Oh, *non*. I feared he would not leave me be!" Her hands shook with emotion.

"You knew of this? Seigneur Richard's intentions?" Robert's gut wrenched. His chest tightened and it became difficult to breathe.

"*Oui*, uh, *non*, oh, I never imagined he would go to these lengths." Her face reddened and she wrung her hands.

Robert took hold of her shoulders. "What happened? Tell me everything."

"Oh, Robert, can't you see I'm upset?" Her pain-glazed eyes glanced about and took in a man who strolled past them and waved and the group of young boys who waited in the lane to follow the bride and groom to the church. "I cannot speak out here. First, let me fetch my mother and send everyone inside the house away. Then we can go inside and I'll tell you both everything at the same time." Her hands shook as she spoke.

Her posture withered when she turned to leave.

"Emilie," Robert called out. He swallowed the lump of pain in his throat. "Why didn't you tell me?" An eternity of hurt lived in his voice.

Emilie turned back and reached out to caress his cheek, her eyes tearful. "Oh, Robert! I love you. I never thought that something so meaningless would come to this."

At that moment, Emilie's mother, Ada appeared at the front door. Without saying a word, Emilie darted past her.

In response to her daughter's abrupt behaviour, Ada's initial smile soured and turned into a scowl directed at Robert. The friends, who had followed Ada to the doorway, now stared at him, mouths agape.

Robert watched as Emilie met the women at the doorway, her back straight, her body motionless. The women faced her in complete silence.

"I'm sorry, but the priest has taken ill and cannot perform the wedding." Emilie's voice trembled. "Please, I must be alone now."

After a long pause, her friends departed, stopping to give her a consoling pat on the back or a sympathetic hug. She bore them all without expression of emotion. Robert's heart lurched at the sight of Emilie's stoicism. He understood her pain. Not only did it show on her face, but her entire appearance seemed to have changed, as he knew his had. The light disappeared from her eyes; disappointment flattened her walk.

He watched the women disperse with a strange detachment. He did not doubt that tongues would wag, and by the end of the day, all of Pointe-du-Lac would be abuzz about the mysterious scandal that prevented the much anticipated wedding. But that mattered little to him now. The only thing that held any importance was Emilie and the dreadful secret she kept from him.

7

After Emilie's friends left, an anxious silence fell over them. Emilie chewed her lower lip fretfully as Ada and Robert gazed at her intently.

Ada frowned. "We'd best talk inside. Come into the kitchen." She led the way and closed the door behind them. "Now, tell me what happened." Her voice sounded shrill with worry.

Robert clenched his fists. “The priest refused to marry us today.”

“Refused?” Ada's mouth fell open. “But why?”

“He's afraid to perform the ceremony because Seigneur Richard threatened to kill him if he did.” Robert cast Emilie a pointed look, but she returned it with a questioning one of her own.

“Seigneur Richard?” Ada's hands trembled as she made the sign of the cross. “*Mère de Crisse,* protect us. I don't understand what Seigneur Richard has to do with us. He owns the land surrounding Pointe-du-Lac, but Emilie and I aren't beholden to him. Before my husband died, may he rest in peace, he bought this house outright, so we do not fall under his rule.” She glanced back and forth between Emilie and Robert.

“I don't understand the seigneur's reasons, but Emilie knows something.” As soon as Robert spoke the words, an anguished pause ensued.

Both Ada and Robert fixed their attention on Emilie. She gathered her courage and composed herself. “I had no idea it would come to this,” she said, her voice barely above a whisper. Her mind raced as she sought words that would explain all and ease the impact.

“What is it? Tell me what happened.” Lines of worry formed on Robert's brow.

Emilie suspected he feared she would utter a secret infidelity of some sort, but she had done nothing wrong, and that realization gave her courage.

Head down with hands balled into fists, Robert waited, his face tense.

Emilie inhaled a deep breath. “A few days ago as I walked home after spinning, Seigneur Richard and his cousin, Pierre Robillard, rode up beside me. Seigneur Richard tried to converse with me, but I did not encourage him. I quickened my pace until I caught up with my companions. The two men spoke to each other, and although I couldn't hear everything they said, I did hear Seigneur Pierre laugh. Then Seigneur Richard said, 'Let us wager on it'. After that, they rode away and I thought nothing more of it."

"That's all?" Robert exhaled and shook feeling back into his hands. The muscles of his face relaxed.

"*Non.* There is more." Emilie could not keep her voice from trembling, for she dreaded his reaction.

Robert pursed his lips and crossed his arms. His eyes never wavered from hers.

Emilie straightened and inhaled a deep breath. "The next day I encountered them again on the same road. Seigneur Richard tried again to engage me in conversation, but I rebuffed him. Seigneur Pierre laughed and Seigneur Richard said, 'You shall see, my friend, you shall see'. This time his voice sounded angry. Afterwards, I became worried, so I went to see Père-"

"You confided this to someone else instead of to me, your own mother?" Ada's displeasure reverberated in her voice.

"I told Père Marc-Mathieu of the Jesuits, *Maman*, the last time we went to chapel." Emilie paused, for she did not want to offend her mother. "While you were speaking with your friend, I confided in him. Afterwards, you were in a hurry to return home, but I prolonged it by talking to everyone we met so that we wouldn't have to walk home alone in case we encountered Seigneur Richard."

At the mention of the Jesuit priest, Emilie noticed the tension in her mother's face fade. She knew her mother respected the Jesuits, especially Père Marc-Mathieu. With little resources, the community of priests had built a stone and timber house and started a school for boys. They farmed too, their stock consisting of several hogs, a pair of asses, a smattering of geese, and numerous varieties of fowl. Almost everyone in Pointe-du-Lac had benefitted from their charity at one time or another.

"It bothers *me* that you didn't tell *me*." Robert's voice vibrated with hurt.

Emilie caressed his face with the back of her fingers. "I didn't want to distress you, especially when there was nothing you or I could have done to prevent his attentions. Besides, I hoped that my obvious attempt to avoid him and our forthcoming marriage would put an end to his vile pursuit of me." She paused. "It meant nothing. That's why I didn't tell you."

"Nothing!" Robert kicked over a chair. "A man accosts my bride and you say it is nothing! Now look what has happened because of it. I could have put a stop to it," he roared. "Now this bastard has spoiled our wedding."

Emilie's eyes widened and she reached out for his arm. "Robert, please, your reaction, that is exactly why," she said in a voice that soothed. "You would have confronted the man. He's dangerous and I don't want you to enter into a dispute with your overlord. It would bode ill for our future."

Robert's posture relaxed. "You're right. I'm sorry I doubted you."

"And I'm sorry this has caused you pain." Emilie reached for his hand.

Robert raised it to his lips for a kiss.

Ada stepped in with a reproachful frown and pulled Emilie's hand away from Robert's. "What advice did Père Marc-Mathieu give you?"

"He told me to hasten the wedding and remain at home. He hoped that if I kept out of sight, Seigneur Richard would lose interest." Emilie turned to Robert. "Oh, Robert, don't you remember when I begged you to set an earlier date for the wedding?" She felt her cheeks redden. "I can imagine what you must have thought of me! But my motives were good. I was acting upon Père Marc-Mathieu's advice. I was certain it would all turn out well. This morning I didn't even think of it, certain our marriage would put a stop to it all."

"*Merde*!" Robert paced the length of the room, his hands clenched into fists. He came to a stop in front of Emilie, his face gentled somewhat. "You did nothing wrong. If only I could save you from all this, I would. You did well not to encourage him. Emilie, I swear I will not let this ruffian harm us."

"*Non*, Robert! You mustn't do anything." Emilie gripped his arms.

"Listen to my daughter, Robert," Ada urged. "She's right."

"Robert, you have a trade, and I could find work. We can move away, far away, beyond Seigneur Richard's reach." Emilie turned to her mother. "*Maman*, you could come with us, too."

Robert shook his head. "How can we go? We're not married. If we leave, we'll never get a certificate of no impediment from the Church. I won't compromise you. *Non*. We must marry first." He glanced at Ada who nodded her approval.

A depressed silence fell over them as each retreated into their thoughts and took a seat at the table.

A small basket filled with the last harvest's carrots rested in the centre of the table.

"That's a lot of carrots," Robert asked puzzled. "What are they for?"

"They are for your wedding. For you to eat. Now what do I do with it all?" Ada shook her head.

"Me? I hate carrots." Robert puckered his face to show his distaste. "What would I want with all those?"

"You are to eat them, of course. Carrots are necessary for men. They're long and hard and the more carrots a man eats, well, the more he will become just like them. You'll need it for your wedding night." To drive her point home, Ada grabbed one in her fist and thrust it from a horizontal to a vertical position.

"And I want a grandchild sooner rather than later." At this, Ada gave first Robert and then Emilie a pointed stare.

Robert opened his mouth to say something, but Emilie stopped him. "Best not to encourage her," she said, casting a stern look at her mother.

The three fell silent again.

Delicious smells emanated from two large pots that boiled away on the stove. The aroma of baking bread wafted from a brick oven in the wall next to the hearth. Emilie hunched her shoulders. Scarce food prepared for the cancelled wedding feast. "*Mon Dieu*, now what do we do? How long must we wait?"

Ada leaned forward and patted her hand. "Perhaps we're making too much of this. Sometimes, things look bleak, but often, they are not as bad as people make out. All we need is advice from someone knowledgeable in these matters. Do as I tell you, Robert. Go to Trois-Riviere. Find Monsieur Antoine Rivet, the magistrate. Tell him what has happened. He is a tall, thin man, bald, with a red nose and a wine-colored mole on his cheek."

Robert nodded. "I've heard of him."

"He will advise you." Ada pointed to the chicken coop visible through the open back door. "Take those four capons to him for payment. Poor creatures. They are the only four that weren't slaughtered for the wedding feast."

"*Non*, there's no need. Keep your capons. I'll pay the man."

Emilie smiled at her mother's generosity in the face of their poverty. After they married, Robert had promised to care for her mother too and they would never have to worry again. She marvelled at this man whom she had come to love so much.

Robert pushed back his chair with a loud scrape against the wood floor and rose to his feet. "I'll go now."

Emilie pressed a hand to her throat. "Good luck, Robert, I hope all goes well."

"I'll return as soon as I can." Robert reached down, took Emilie's hand and kissed it. "I hope to return with good news."

8

Robert hurried to his home behind the seigneurial mill, saddled his horse, a scarcity in New France, and rode with great haste to Trois-Riviere. He asked an old man with a weathered face, who sat outside a small house, to point out where the magistrate lived. The fellow smiled a toothless grin. With gnarled hands, he waved his cane about and directed Robert to the end of the short lane to the last house on the right.

Robert tossed him a gold sou and thanked him before continuing. He arrived at a well-kept stone house with flower boxes in each window and a tidy garden on all sides. A woman peeked out from behind a partially opened shutter on the main floor before the door swung open. She studied him through narrowed eyes.

Robert removed his hat. "Good morning, I wish to see Monsieur Rivet about an important matter."

The woman eyed him suspiciously from head to toe. She had a mole beneath her nose from which grew a long, black hair, which annoyed Robert enough to want to pull it out.

The magistrate shuffled up behind her. "I am Antoine Rivet."

Robert recognized him from the wine-coloured, arrow shaped mole on his cheek. Tall, lanky, and almost emaciated in appearance, the man didn't smile. His nose was indeed a little on the red side, likely from too much wine. Only a few strands of hair stuck to his shiny scalp.

Robert looked into his eyes. "I've come for advice."

"Come in." Rivet waved him into the study.

The room lay in darkness until he swung open the shutters. Large bookcases lined with dusty old books covered one entire wall. In the middle of the room stood an ornate table of dark wood covered with stacks of books and various papers. Two wooden chairs, that looked uncomfortable, faced the desk. On the opposite side stood a large wingchair with a high square back covered with leather and fastened with large nails. Robert noticed some of these had fallen out, letting the leather curl up in places, leaving the corners unencumbered.

The magistrate shut the door and invited Robert to sit. "Tell me about your case, young man."

Robert hesitated before he sat. "It is a matter of utmost gravity and I must ask you to keep it confidential."

"Of course, please proceed," replied the magistrate as he took his own seat at the same moment Robert took his.

Robert turned his tricorne around in his hands. "I want to know, ah, it is a long story."

"Start from the beginning," urged the magistrate.

"Monsieur Rivet, I find myself in an impossible situation and do not know what to say. I want to know-"

Rivet glared at Robert with impatience. "Goodness, you people are all alike. Instead of relating your case, you hesitate and ask questions. Say what you've come to say. I'm a busy man."

"I beg your pardon." Robert cleared his throat, stopped fidgeting, and set his hat on his knee. "I want to know if there's a penalty for threatening a priest and forbidding him to celebrate a marriage."

"Hmm." The magistrate frowned. He pressed his lips together and blew out some air from one side. "This is a serious matter. There *are* laws against such a thing. Let me find it." He leaned forward and hunted through the chaos of books and papers on his desk. "Now where can it be? Magistrates are obliged to have so many things in hand! It must be here somewhere." Turning to the bookcases behind him, he ran his fingers over several volumes. "Ah! Here it is." He pulled out the book and flipped several pages, muttering over some passages, pausing with emphasis upon others. "Here's the section. It reads, "Those who commit tyrannical acts, excite commotions by violence, oppress the weak by compelling them to make hard bargains in purchases, rents...to perform or not to perform marriages." He glanced up at Robert.

"That is exactly my case," said Robert.

"Hmm, I need to find the penalty." His eyes followed each sentence. "Ah, here it is. *A priest who fails to perform that to which he is obliged by his office...*" He glanced up at Robert.

Robert leaned forward, a surge of hope filled him. "It seems as if that law was written specifically for me."

"It seems so. It says here that magistrates shall proceed by fines or imprisonment, according to the persons involved and the circumstances. It's all here." He leaned back and steepled his fingers. "If I am to be your advocate, you must tell me everything and it must be the truth. You must name the person who has wronged you. I suspect he is someone of consequence, and, in that case, it is my duty to speak to him. I won't tell him your name and I will take all necessary measures against him to end the affair in accordance with the law. I've extricated others from worse predicaments and I'll get you out of this difficulty – at a cost, you understand. Once I know who has offended you, I'll know better whether to bargain with him or incriminate him. I know well how to manage these edicts; no one must be guilty, and no one must be innocent. I will clear your name. As to the priest, if he has any discretion, he will keep in the background; if he is a simpleton, well, we can dispose of him. Your case is serious, very serious, but the law is clear."

While the magistrate poured forth his muddled rhapsody, Robert scratched his temple. It seemed the magistrate believed him to be at fault in some way. "Monsieur Rivet, I think you have misunderstood me. I have threatened no one and have never done anything contrary to the law. A crime has been committed against *me* and I seek justice. I'm pleased to know that a law exists to protect me."

"Why are you here then? I don't understand!" The magistrate slapped the desk in frustration. "You are all alike; you don't know how to speak succinctly!"

"I beg your pardon, Monsieur, you didn't give me time." Robert hated that his voice hardened, but he couldn't help it. "Today, I was to have married a young woman. Everything was ready. This morning, the priest refused to marry us. I pressed him until he confessed that he had been forbidden to celebrate our marriage, under pain of death, by a tyrant named Seigneur Richard Tonnacour."

"Richard Tonnacour?" The magistrate raised his brows and the mole on his cheek became even more distorted. His eyes widened and his face reddened. "I cannot take your case. I've nothing more to say to you. Leave now. I do not wish to discuss this any further."

"But I speak the truth and will swear an oath."

"I told you, I will not take your case. I wash my hands of it." He rubbed his hands, one over the other, as if he washed them.

"Please, listen," Robert pleaded as he rose.

The magistrate strode around the table and pushed Robert toward the door. On reaching it, Rivet opened it wide and called out for the servant. "Come and show this man out."

The woman rushed to the front door and held it open. She sneered at Robert as he passed through it.

9

After Emilie and Ada changed out of their wedding finery, they sat at the kitchen table and waited for Robert's return. Ada sighed. “Don't worry, Emilie. Antoine Rivet is a wise magistrate. He'll give Robert good advice, wait and see.”

“Even so, Mother, we must do everything we can too. Père Marc-Mathieu is used to helping people like us. I think we must let him know what has happened and inform him that his advice failed.”

Ada nodded. “You're right, but the Jesuit convent is two miles away and I don't think it's wise for us to leave the house.”

Someone knocked on the door and called out a blessing in a low, but distinct male voice.

Emilie rose to her feet. “Who could it be?” she whispered.

Ada shrugged and motioned for Emilie to hide behind the door. She straightened her gown, inhaled deeply, and swung open the door. A portly Jesuit priest with a stained leather bag slung over his left shoulder stood in the doorway.

“Ah, Père Nicholas,” exclaimed Ada. With his melon shaped face and large, frog-like eyes, his ugliness never ceased to amaze her.

“May the Lord be with you.” He bowed his head, opened the leather bag, and held it out. “I've come to beg for some grain.”

“Emilie, go and fetch some for the good Father,” said Ada.

Emilie turned toward the small door that led to their storage room, but, before entering it, she paused. When the priest wasn't looking, she raised her index finger to her lips to warn her mother to say nothing.

Ada saw the sign, glanced back to Père Nicholas, and gave him her most gracious smile.

“Isn't today the day of Emilie's wedding?” the priest asked. “Something is astir in the neighbourhood. Do you know what has happened?”

Ada shook her head. “Père Jean is ill, and we are obliged to postpone the wedding.” She paused. “How does the collection of grain go in such difficult times?”

The priest shook his head. “Badly, good woman, badly. This is all I've managed to collect today.” He slid the bag from his shoulder and opened it up. “And in order to collect this mighty bounty, I’ve had to knock on ten doors.”

“But there was a drought last year and everyone is struggling. Everything, especially grain, is scarce.”

“And what we must do, good woman, to make better times return, is to give alms.”

Emilie returned, her apron so laden with grain that she struggled to manage it. She held the two corners stretched out at arm's length, while the priest placed his bag on the ground and widened its opening to receive the gift Emilie poured into it.

Ada's brows furrowed and she cast Emilie a reproachful look, but Emilie returned a reassuring smile. The priest broke forth into praises and expressions of gratitude, and replacing his bag on his shoulder, prepared to depart.

“Père Nicholas,” called out Emilie. “I have a boon to ask of you.”

His hand already on the door latch, he turned around to face her. “Most certainly.”

“Please tell Père Marc-Mathieu that we need to speak to him. Ask him to come immediately. My mother and I cannot go to him ourselves.”

Père Nicholas smiled. “Is this all? I shall attend to the matter.”

“I'm grateful to you,” Emilie said as she bowed her head slightly.

He glanced about and spotted the basket on the table. “Are those carrots I see?”

“Why yes, they are,” Ada said.

“Ah, carrots, one of my favourite foods.”

“Wait and I'll give you some.” Ada grabbed the basket and

emptied a few into his bag. “Mind that you don't eat too many. They're not good for priests.”

A puzzled look came over him and he opened his mouth to say something, but Ada interjected and swung open the door. “We shall await Père Marc-Mathieu,” she smiled.

“God bless you, good woman,” said Père Nicholas as he departed.

Emilie and Ada watched from the doorway until he crossed the road and passed out of their sight.

Ada slammed the door. Her face wrinkled into a grimace and turned a bright shade of red. “All that grain! To give so much away when food is so short! You must have given him our entire supply.”

Emilie fisted her hands on her hips. “If we had only given him a handful, he would have continued going door to door asking for grain. Who knows how long it would have taken to fill his bag and return to the convent. Besides, what with chatting here and there, he might have forgotten. This way, he's finished and can attend to my request.”

“You thought wisely,” Ada nodded. “Besides, charity always brings a good reward.”

Emilie grinned. “I'm glad you agree. You've been a wonderful mother who has taught me much.”

Ada blushed. “I may have my flaws, but you're my only child and you must never doubt that I love you.”

Another knock sounded. When Emilie answered it, Robert sauntered in, shoulders slumped, and shaking his head. “What a waste of time that was!” He plunked into a chair and related what transpired with Antoine Rivet.

“But how can that be?” Ada stood with her arms crossed. “My advice was good. Perhaps you did not approach him nicely enough.”

“It doesn't matter,” Emilie interrupted. “Père Marc-Mathieu

will help us."

"In the midst of all this misfortune, I would welcome anyone's help." Robert rapped the tabletop with his fingers. "But if Père Marc-Mathieu fails to find us a remedy, rest assured that *I will* find one."

"Robert, we must be patient and trust Père Marc-Mathieu," Emilie urged.

"I hope so, but one way or another, I will get vengeance – or find someone to get it for me. There must be justice in the end."

Robert grew quiet. Emilie watched him warily, engrossed in her own thoughts and plans as they shared a melancholic lunch together. Even though she loved him for his fierce protection, she needed to keep his anger from surfacing. Attempts at confrontation or vengeance would only worsen their situation.

When they finished, Robert rose and thanked them. "I'd better go. There is much I have to do."

Emilie looked at him, trying to read his thoughts as she walked Robert outside to the gate. "Good-bye," she whispered.

"I'll return soon, Emilie, I promise." he said. "Don't worry; it will all turn out right."

She nodded and gave him a smile. "I hope so."

"Never doubt that I love you."

"I know," she whispered, her eyes never leaving his retreating form until he passed from view.

10

As Robert returned to the mill, his fury mounted. He and Emilie would have been married by now, locked arm-in-arm, heading for their wedding feast. Instead, he was alone. As he made his way home, loneliness gripped him. The same words kept repeating in his mind as he went. *There must be justice in the end. There must be justice in the end.* He seared them onto his heart, resolved to make them come true.

11

The afternoon sun was beginning its descent when Père Marc-Mathieu set out for Emilie and Ada's house. Its rays heated his head and shoulders as he walked. Nothing invigorated him more than a good walk, especially one which would lead to a good deed. Slim and agile, he felt much younger than his fifty years. His greying beard and hair gave him a look of wisdom as opposed to agedness.

As he walked, a soft breeze shook the new leaves on the boughs of the trees. He glanced at the fields on either side of the road; the ploughing and seeding well underway. He hoped this year's grain yield and quality would be better than that of the previous year. The drought had taken a brutal toll upon all of New France; the land, its people, even God's creatures suffered.

People greeted him sadly when they passed. A long cold winter had followed a poor harvest. Food was scarce, but the sight of *habitants* in the field brought renewed hope. As he passed, he waved to a young boy who held a bony cow by a cord around its neck. The young boy smiled and waved back. The child looked about and stopped to pick up something from the ground, likely something edible to appease his hunger.

When Père Nicholas had interrupted his midday meal to bring him the urgent message from Emilie, Père Marc-Mathieu feared some misfortune had befallen her. He abandoned his food and departed. Now, his stomach gnawed with hunger.

Why did he care so much about the young woman? And why did he respond to her summons as promptly as if the Pope had called for him? If someone he did not know had requested his help, he would have attended, but in his own good time. Yet, because it was Emilie, he rushed to her. Why? Because he admired her honesty, her beauty? Yes, even a celibate priest could be attracted to a beautiful woman. After all, he was a normal man, but one strong enough to overcome such urges. No, he admired her faithfulness and charitable heart. Emilie always had a smile and a kind word for everyone. Seigneur Richard posed a great danger to Emilie and he railed at the man's persecution of her. Now he feared his earlier advice for her to keep silent might have brought about some sinister consequence.

Immersed in his thoughts, time passed quickly. Before long, he reached Emilie and Ada's front door and knocked.

"Père Marc-Mathieu! Thank goodness you are here!" exclaimed Ada as soon as she opened it.

He passed over the threshold, and at first glance, knew instinctively that his concerns were justified. He seated himself on a three-legged stool and looked up at Emilie. "Tell me what has happened."

He listened without interruption. Anger heated his cheeks. He raised his eyes to heaven and tapped his shoe impatiently, but managed to curb his tongue until Emilie completed her explanation. He covered his face with his hands. "I am sorry for you both."

"You will help us, Père?" Emilie's, brows rose. "Can you marry us?"

"Even if I wanted to, I could not perform the wedding ceremony. It would not be valid. Only a parish priest can sanction and bless a marriage. Were I to make the attempt, Père Jean could have it repudiated."

Emilie's shoulders sagged. Ada shook her head but remained expressionless.

"But don't despair. Let me think what I can do." He rose and rubbed his chin as he paced the length of the room. The situation was urgent, the problem intricate. Remedies were limited and uncertain, and also dangerous. "I could instill shame into Père Jean by making him see he is failing in his duties, but shame and duty matter little to someone overwhelmed with fear. I could inspire him with fear, but what could scare him more than the threat of murder he already faces? If I inform the Bishop of this matter, I could invoke his authority, but that would require time. And if I did manage to arrange your marriage, would that stop a man like Seigneur Richard? I could engage my brethren, but Seigneur Richard pretends to be a friend to the Jesuits and often donates money. I must proceed with caution or risk making the situation worse."

He ran his hands over the plain rope belt at his waist and tried to consider every possible solution. "I think it would be best to confront Seigneur Richard and dissuade him. Thus, I might discover more about his intentions and could act accordingly."

While he considered the matter, a rap on the door heralded Robert's return.

"Have they told you?" asked Robert, his tone agitated as he pulled out a chair, straddled it, his chest pressing against its back.

Père Marc-Mathieu slumped back on his stool. "*Oui.*"

"How can we put an end to this foolishness?" Robert slammed his hand on the table.

"I'm not certain, but rest assured, I'll do all I can. We must trust in God. He will not forsake us."

Robert's face relaxed. "Thank you. You are renowned for your resourcefulness, but Père Jean and that Monsieur Antoine Rivet-"

"Don't worry about them for now. You'll only become irritated. I repeat what I've said to Emilie and Ada- I will not forsake you."

"Thank goodness you aren't like them, those good-for-nothing imbeciles," Robert said. "I just went to speak to some of my friends to solicit their help against Seigneur Richard, but they turned me down. They always said they would give their lives to defend me, but now that I need them, they refuse to come to my aid." Robert stopped, his hand rose to his mouth.

Emilie and Ada stood with their mouths agape.

Père Marc-Mathieu frowned.

"I meant to say, uh, I do not mean-"

Père Marc-Mathieu narrowed his gaze. "What did you mean to say? You went to solicit help from your friends to threaten Seigneur Richard? To retaliate? Do you want to ruin any chance I have of helping you? Your friends could not have helped you, even if they had been willing. They know Seigneur Richard is not a man to be trifled with. Threats and vengeance will gain you nothing." He grasped Robert's arm and looked at him sternly. "You have to put your trust in me, and in God."

"I do!" Robert slipped his arm from the priest's grasp.

"Very well," Père Marc-Mathieu said. "Promise me you won't attack or provoke anyone and that you'll let me guide you."

Robert looked at his hands. "I promise."

Emilie drew a long breath, as if relieved of a great weight.

"That's wise, Robert," Ada encouraged.

Père Marc-Mathieu rested his hand on Robert's shoulder. "I'll speak to Seigneur Richard right now. If it pleases God to touch his heart, and give force to my words, all is well. But if not, He will show us some other remedy. Meanwhile, try to keep quiet and calm. Avoid gossip, speak to no one, and don't leave this house. I'll return as soon as I can."

Père Marc-Mathieu cut short their words of gratitude and left for the den of the wild beast he had undertaken to tame.

12

On the outskirts of Pointe-du-Lac, the manor house of Seigneur Richard rose like a lone castle. A group of small homes, inhabited by those in service to him, surrounded it. Père Marc-Mathieu noticed muskets, spades, rakes, straw hats, nets, and casks of black powder behind open windows and doors. Blank faces stared back at him. Old men, having lost their teeth, appeared ready at the slightest provocation to snarl back and show their gums. Masculine looking Algonquin women with strong, sinewy arms, who could attack with their hands as well as their sharp tongues, stopped what they were doing to watch him. Even the children who played in the road, displayed an air of defiance in their demeanour.

He ascended a winding footpath to a small, level plot of ground in front of the Seigneur's stone-built, two-story manor house. Except for the trill of a bird in the distance, perfect silence reigned. A gentle breeze swayed the leaves on nearby trees. Two men lay stretched out on benches to the right and left of the front door.

Père Marc-Mathieu hesitated, prepared to wait, but one of the men rose, and gestured for him to come forward. "Père, come. We don't make Jesuits wait. I've sometimes been given shelter by Jesuits when things weren't going so well for me." The man reached for the lion's head knocker and rapped twice. This roused howling hounds inside.

In a few moments an old grumbling servant with a full head of white hair swung open the door. Upon seeing Père Marc-Mathieu, he made a low bow, quieted two mastiffs, and invited him inside. Père Marc-Mathieu entered a narrow corridor and followed the servant, who regarded him with a surprised and respectful look. "Are you not Père Marc-Mathieu?"

"I am."

"You must be here to do some good," the servant sneered. "I suppose good may be done anywhere, even in a place like this."

They continued along the corridor until they reached a closed door. From within came the occasional scrape of cutlery against dishes and discordant voices in heated conversation.

Père Marc-Mathieu suppressed an instinct to withdraw. "I can wait until the meal is over."

The servant swung open the door.

The die was cast. To retreat now would be foolish.

Seigneur Pierre Robillard looked up from his dinner. "Ah, come in."

Seigneur Richard's jaw dropped at his unexpected appearance, but because of his cousin's blunt invitation, Père Marc-Mathieu knew the seigneur had no choice but to permit him to enter.

"Come in, Père, come in." Seigneur Richard put down his fork and wiped his mouth with a cloth.

Père Marc-Mathieu advanced, gave Seigneur Richard a nod, and responded respectfully to the salutations of the other men in the room. Accustomed to fighting for the innocent against the wicked, he stood with an air of security and an undaunted heart. Although eager to plead his case, he experienced horror mingled with compassion for this notorious seigneur. He stood calmly before Seigneur Richard, his mouth salivating in response to the feast on the table before him.

They had just begun to eat their pea soup. Two loaves of bread sat at either end of the long table with wheels of cheese in between. Bowls of buttered beans and roasted potatoes surrounded a venison roast in the centre. Annoyance washed over him at the sight of so much decadence when so many in Pointe-du-Lac went hungry. His own stomach growled with pangs of hunger, but he said nothing.

Seigneur Richard sat in an armchair like Herod on his throne. Used to receiving homage, the man stared at him with a stern expression that prohibited requests, advice, correction, or reproch.

Pierre sat to Richard's right. On the other side of the table sat Monsieur Jacques Gagnon, chief of all magistrates. Opposite him, with an attitude of the purest, most unbounded servility, sat Antoine Rivet with red nose and birthmark. Facing the two cousins were two other guests he didn't recognize. Those two kept their heads down and ate like swines out of a trough.

"Bring the good Father a seat," said Richard.

A servant presented a chair.

Père Marc-Mathieu remained standing and looked pointedly at Richard. "Please forgive my unexpected visit, but I wish to speak to you about a matter of importance."

"Very well, I will be happy to speak to you." He gestured to one of the servants. "But first, bring the Jesuit father something to eat and drink."

Père Marc-Mathieu raised his hand to refuse.

"*Non, non.* Let it never be said that a Jesuit left my house without a full belly or an arrogant creditor without seeing the butt end of my rifle," exclaimed Seigneur Richard.

The men erupted in laughter. A servant brought in a plate, heaped it with food, and presented it to Père Marc-Mathieu who, unwilling to refuse the invitation of the man he wanted to sway, did not hesitate to sit, pour some wine and sip it. Was this not the way that Satan tempted Christ? The loud argument that greeted his arrival had vanished. In its stead, an awkward silence befell the group, interrupted only by the scrape of dishes or cups against the table top.

Père Marc-Mathieu waited, his thoughts focused on the conversation to come. He studied Richard's every move.

Richard glanced at him from time to time, too. Each time

their eyes met, Père Marc-Mathieu forced his expression to remain impassive, but with the deliberate air of someone determined to remain until he had been heard. He knew Richard would gladly send him away to escape any conversation; but dismissing a Jesuit priest without giving him audience would leave a poor impression. He finished his food, drained his glass of wine, and rose from the table. The other guests rose too without ceasing their clamour. "Please excuse us. The good father and I will adjourn into the other room." Richard advanced haughtily towards Père Marc-Mathieu who rose with the other men. "At your command, Père." Seigneur Richard gave a nod of his head, gestured to the door, and led him through to the adjoining room.

13

At a loss for words, Père Marc-Mathieu stared at Richard. He hesitated then reached for his rosary, which hung from the rope around his waist. He held it in his palm as if it could give him strength or endow him with speech.

Seigneur Richard stood with arms crossed in the centre of the room, his expression cold. "So, what is it you want from me, Père?" He enunciated the word 'Père' as if it were dirt in his mouth.

A thousand retorts sprang into Père Marc-Mathieu's mind, but he restrained himself. He thought of Emilie and Robert and their predicament. Best to avoid agitating the situation further, he thought. Instead, he gave Richard a congenial smile. "I seek a boon from you; a deed of mercy." He chose his words prudently, his tone reserved, one of humility. "Two men of unsound character have used your name to torment a poor priest and deter him from performing his duty to wed two innocent persons. In good conscience and honour, you can restore all to order and help the bride and groom who have been so shamefully wronged."

Richard narrowed his eyes. "Do not speak of my conscience unless I ask you to. As to my honour, I alone am its guardian. Anyone who dares tell me what to do offends me."

Père Marc-Mathieu ignored the hostility and remained steadfast. "It was not my intent to offend you. Criticize me, rebuke me, but listen to what I have to say." He reached for the silver cross of his rosary and held it up to Seigneur Richard. "Please perform this small act of justice. Remember that God watches over Emilie and Robert and He hears their prayers."

"The respect I bear for your cassock is great, but if anything could make me ignore you and its reverence, it would be for you to dare tell me what to do in my house."

Heat flooded Père Marc-Mathieu's cheeks, but he remained calm. "I pray you never regret not listening to me. I'm not here to lessen your honour. You have power-"

"When I need to hear a sermon, I go to church." Enmity resounded in Richard's voice. "Do not preach to me in my own house! You treat me as though I were a person of no influence."

Père Marc-Mathieu ignored the remark. "God sent me here to intercede for these innocents."

"I have no idea what you mean. I suppose there must be some young girl you are concerned about. Make confidantes of whom you please, but don't annoy me further. I've had enough of this discussion." Richard moved towards the door.

Père Marc-Mathieu blocked him. "It's true I am concerned for her, but not any more than I am for you. I'll pray for you with my whole heart. Please don't keep a poor innocent in anguish and terror. One word from you can fix everything."

"Since you seem to think I can do so much for this person, and since you are so concerned for her..."

"*Oui*?" Père Marc-Mathieu held his breath.

"Advise her to come here, and put herself under my protection, under my roof. I'll see to her every need. No one will harm her. I am a man of my word."

Père Marc-Mathieu could no longer contain his outrage. All his resolutions for prudence abandoned him. "Your protection!" His indignation burst forth without restraint. He shoved his forefinger into Richard's chest. "You caused this problem. Woe to you for such an outlandish proposal. You have lived up to the rumours of your sinister reputation, but I don't fear you."

Malice twisted Richard's features. "Watch how you speak to me, priest."

"I speak to you as I would to anyone who forsakes God. This young woman is an innocent and under God's protection. I don't need your help to protect her."

"How dare you speak to me like this in my own house!" Richard took a menacing step forward, his fists clenched.

"I pity this house. A curse hangs over it. You'll soon see that the justice of God cannot be restrained by four walls and a handful of armed guards at your gates. Do you think God gave you the right to torment her? Do you think He would not defend her? You have ignored His counsel and mine, and you will be judged for it! Emilie is safe from you. And as for you, I predict that the day will come-"

Richard listened to him with a look of outrage and silent astonishment, but when he heard the beginnings of a curse, a look of fear passed over his face. He seized Père Marc-Mathieu's outstretched arm. "Get out of my sight, you cassocked demon!"

Père Marc-Mathieu kept calm as he yanked his hand free from Richard's grasp.

"Loathsome minion!" Richard shouted. A drop of spit flew from his enraged mouth and landed on Père Marc-Mathieu's cheek.

Although disgusted, he did not wipe his cheek, nor did he

react to the tirade.

Richard jabbed his finger into Père Marc-Mathieu's chest. "A cassock hides your stupidity and cowardice. You need to learn how to speak to a man of means. Get out of my house. Now!" He pointed to a door opposite the one they had entered.

"You will regret this."

"It is you who will regret it, priest."

Père Marc-Mathieu departed, closing the door behind him.

In the corridor stood the same old man who had received him when he arrived. Père Marc-Mathieu realized he must have been eavesdropping. The man raised his index finger to his lips and beckoned for him to follow. He led him through the kitchen to a rear door. "I heard everything and need to speak to you," the aged man whispered.

"Speak up, my good man."

"Not here! It would not go well for me if the seigneur caught me talking to you. I'll stop by the Jesuit convent tomorrow where we can speak privately."

"What is it?"

The old man shrugged. "Something's in the wind, that's for certain. I shall find out what I can. Leave it to me. I see and hear strange things all the time! And I want no part of it."

"God bless you!" Père Marc-Mathieu laid his hand on the servant's head, who, though much older than himself, bent before him with the respect of a son. "God will reward you. I'll await you tomorrow."

"Go and please don't betray me." The old man looked around. "I'll make sure no one is about." He flung open the back door and looked about. "All is clear."

Père Marc-Mathieu grasped the old man's hand. "What's your name?"

"I am Etienne."

"Bless you, Etienne." Père Marc-Mathieu made the sign of

the cross over him and hurried away, pondering what had happened. He had caught the servant listening at his master's door. Was it right to endorse such deviousness? Yet, in this case, might it not be an exception?

He reached the road, glad to have turned his back on Seigneur Richard and his cursed house. He breathed more freely as he hastened down the hill, his face flushed, his thoughts agitated and confused. The old servant's unexpected offer had come as a great relief. It seemed as if Heaven had intervened to help him. From Seigneur Richard's house, too! He never dreamed of such luck and he had experienced little of it in his life.

Life had never been easy, especially in the wilderness of this new world. He came to New France to escape hardship and turmoil, yet he found himself surrounded by it. Born into a noble French family, Père Marc-Mathieu had never known hunger until he arrived here. The youngest of five sons, he had donned the black robes of the Jesuit priesthood after a deadly altercation in the streets of Paris one fateful night. A thief brandishing a knife had accosted him and demanded his money. A scuffle ensued with disastrous results. In defence, he struck a hard punch and the man fell back onto a stone wall, striking his head hard, dying instantly. Horrified at having taken a life, he sought out the man's family to explain what happened and seek forgiveness. Incredibly, they absolved him. But even after he paid all the burial costs and made a generous endowment to the man's parents, he struggled with his conscience; for his lost soul, forever tarnished for having killed a man.

No matter how hard he tried, he could not forgive himself. It was during one of many confessions to his local priest that the idea to join the Order of Jesus came to him. His parents had given him their blessing. For him, a life of servitude brought hope for atonement. He took his vows with a willing heart and soon embarked on a ship headed for New France.

Not once had he regretted it. His work educating young Algonquin boys and preaching the doctrines of the Church to the people of New France brought immense satisfaction and helped ease the guilt of his sin. This past year, however, he had suffered along with everyone else because of the poor harvest and the ships that failed to reach port with much needed food, seeds, and supplies from France. He looked toward the west. Already the setting sun touched the horizon. Though weary after such a nerve-wracking day, he quickened his steps. He must return to Emilie and Robert and relay what happened. Then he must return to the convent before nightfall, before the doors were locked.

14

Anxious for Père Marc-Mathieu's return, Emilie chopped an onion in preparation for dinner while Robert sat at the table. He seemed irresolute and uncomfortable. She had never seen this side of him before, and her heart broke to see him suffer so. Robert was a good man, an honest miller, beloved by all. She loved him with all her heart, but now, all their hopes and dreams had been shattered. How could Robert stand a chance in a battle of wills against someone as wealthy and powerful and corrupt as Seigneur Richard? She prayed Père Marc-Mathieu could somehow resolve this terrible obstruction. The onion burned her eyes and she raised a cloth to her face.

"Don't worry, Emilie," Ada said sympathetically. She sat in a chair next to the hearth while she wound yarn around a reel. "I have an idea," she announced. "I think I've found an answer to all this trouble, perhaps more quickly than Père Marc-Mathieu can."

Emilie lowered the cloth and studied her mother. “How?”

Robert glanced up. “Tell me what I have to do?”

Ada dropped her reel into the basket at her feet and went to sit beside Robert. “If you were married, this problem with Seigneur Richard would be behind us.”

“No doubt,” nodded Robert. “If we were married, we could move to Trois-Riviere, Québec, or Saint-Anne-de-Beaupre where my friend, Bastien, lives. He's wanted me to move there for quite some time. Bastien says the seigneur there is generous and kind. I never listened to him before because my heart was here. But once married, we could all go to live there in peace, out of that villain's reach.”

“*Oui*,” said Emilie agreed, “but how?” She came to sit at the table across from Robert and Ada.

Ada grinned. “Well, it's quite simple.”

“Simple?” Robert stroked his chin.

“*Oui*, if you know how to go about it.” Ada leaned forward. “Listen carefully. I once overheard two priests speaking about an old church law that still exists. It may be obscure, but it's still valid.”

Emilie's spirits lifted and she leaned forward. “Tell us, Mother.”

Ada took hold of her hand. “To solemnize a marriage, a parish priest is necessary, but his consent is not. It is enough for him to be present, as long as the banns have been read, and in your case, they have.”

Robert's face puckered with confusion. “I don't understand.”

“Two witnesses go with you to the priest who must not know you are coming. You have to surprise him; otherwise, he'll evade you. In the priest's presence, you must say, 'this is my wife'. And Emilie, you must say, 'this is my husband'. All must hear you say it clearly. And *voilà*,” she snapped her fingers. “You are considered married. It is as valid and sacred as if the Pope himself blessed it. But be wary, once you speak these words, the priest may become angry, but it will be too late. In the eyes of God and the Church, you will be considered lawfully married."

"Could this be possible?" Emilie exchanged an incredulous look with Robert.

"Of course it's possible!" said Ada. "A friend of mine is living proof of it. She wished to be married against the will of her parents. She and her man did as I described. The priest suspected she might attempt it, so he was careful to avoid her, but they had prepared well and caught the priest at just the right moment. They spoke the words and became man and wife. Never mind that she repented of it the next day. Not enough carrots, I suspect."

Robert rolled his eyes.

"You are certain it can work?" Emilie asked. Could this be the answer to their prayers? She glanced at Robert whose eyes seemed alight with optimism. Why did she not feel the same? Doubt tumbled about in her mind.

"Positive. These marriages are valid, although only those who have met with some obstacle in the ordinary method resort to it. Priests take great care to avoid being surprised by couples accompanied with two or more people."

"It seems too simple to be true!" Robert fixed his eyes on Emilie with a look of imploring expectation.

Emilie glanced away, uncertain.

"Of course it's true!" Ada crossed her arms and leaned back in her chair. "I never lie. If you don't believe me, find your own solution to this mess. I wash my hands of it."

"Please, I meant no offence." Robert reached for Ada's hand. "It seems too easy."

When Ada relaxed, Emilie was relieved to see his words dispel her mother's indignation, yet she still did not understand. "But why didn't Père Marc-Mathieu think of it?"

"Of course he thought of it," Ada said. "Do you think it didn't enter his mind? But he would never tell us about it."

"Why not?" Emilie furrowed her brows. She tensed, fearful she would not like the answer.

"Because the clergy don't approve of this method."

Emilie hesitated, as she came to understand the implications of what they were planning. Such an act was nothing more than a deceitful trick, a lie, a sin.

Robert rubbed his temples. "I still have trouble believing it can be so simple."

Ada shrugged. "I don't understand it either, but it is legitimate."

"If it isn't right, then we shouldn't do it." Emilie stared at her mother. "How can you even suggest it? To be married under deceitful pretenses is a terrible way to start a new life."

"I would never give you advice contrary to God's will," Ada said. "If it were against the wishes of your parents to marry, that would be different, but I approve of your wedding each other. It's that villainous seigneur and our spineless priest who prevents it."

Robert looked at Emilie. "Let's do it."

"Don't speak of this to Père Marc-Mathieu until it's all over," cautioned Ada. "But a marriage is a marriage and what's done is done. Rest assured, afterwards, in his heart, Père Marc-Mathieu will be happy to see you wed." She smiled at Emilie.

"I'm not sure." Emilie stared at the napkin she wrung in her hands.

"Emilie, it's completely lawful," Ada said. "What's there to worry about? First, you must find your witnesses, then you have to find a way to accost Père Jean who is hiding in his house. How will you get in to see him and make him stand still long enough for you to utter the words? I suspect that when he sees you both arrive with two people in tow, he'll flee like the Devil from holy water."

"I think I know a way." In his excitement, Robert struck the table with his clenched fist. Dishes and plates rattled at the blow.

Emilie shook her head. "I don't know. This doesn't seem honest. Père Marc-Mathieu told us if we acted in good faith, God would help us. We should heed that advice. Nothing good can come of something that feels wrong."

"God helps those who help themselves," Ada said. "We'll tell Père Marc-Mathieu about it afterwards. All will be forgiven, you'll see."

"Emilie," Robert said, his voice gentle, pleading. "Don't fail me now. Have we not done everything right so far? By now, we should have been man and wife. The priest fixed the day and hour. It's not our fault if we are forced to use a little cunning. I'll find the witnesses and make a plan and return as soon as I can to explain everything." He gave her an imploring look, and cast Ada a knowing glance before he made a hasty departure.

Emilie shot her mother a glaring look and rose from the table. Lips pursed, she picked up the knife and hacked at the onion as if the knife itself were possessed. She could never give into murderous thoughts or she would be as evil as Seigneur Richard.

15

Trouble had sharpened Robert's wit. His entire life, he had walked a narrow, straightforward path. Now, under such dire circumstances, he had devised a plan for him and Emilie to marry that would impress Satan himself. He refused to allow a man of wealth and power to steal his woman. Regardless of the personal cost, he was determined to defeat Seigneur Richard, even if it took his dying breath.

He walked to the home of his friend, Denis. At his knock, Denis invited him in. The front door opened into a spacious room with a hearth against the far wall. A discolored and worn woolen carpet covered the wooden floor upon which stood a rickety table and chairs made of pine. A huge sideboard rose from the floor towards the low, open-beamed ceiling. Primed and ready for use, a musket with its stock downward rested against the wall near the spinning-wheel in the corner. An array of pots and cracked dishes, poorly made cupboards and drooping shelves, decorated the remaining space.

The sight Robert beheld was one of poverty and it twisted his gut to see such good people endure so much suffering. Denis' wife stood over the fire stirring the contents of a saucepan with a broken rolling-pin. His mother sat at the table, which had seen too many years of use. Four little children stood around, waiting, their eyes fixed on the saucepan. Judging by the size of the pot, it was meager fare for the size of the household- confirmation that the drought had fallen hard upon all of Pointe-du-Lac's families.

Denis was a *habitant* who leased land from Père Jean. Like seigneurs, many priests were also granted seigneurial lands. Robert knew Denis didn't have the money to pay his rent to the priest.

While Robert exchanged salutations with the family, Denis's wife poured the contents of the saucepan into a wooden trencher and set it on the table. It looked like some kind of watery stew.

"Will you share a bowl with us?" Denis's mother asked as she rose to grab another bowl from a nearby shelf.

Robert smiled at the generous offer. *Habitants* never failed to invite a friend to share a meal, even if it was their last mouthful. "Thank you, but I only came to speak to Denis, not to disturb your family. He can dine with me at the inn and we can talk there."

A look of relief passed over everyone's faces at the unexpected invitation. Denis grabbed his tricorne, which hung on a hook behind the door, put it on his head and set off with Robert.

At the inn, they were the only customers. Poverty, exacerbated by drought, kept most of the usual patrons away. They partook of some onion pie with hot pea soup, and after each of them emptied a tankard of ale, Robert addressed Denis. "If you will do me a small favour, I will do you an even greater one."

Denis poured more ale from the pitcher into their tankards and set it down. "I'm listening."

"You owe money to Père Jean for the rent of his fields."

Denis leaned back in his chair. "Now why did you have to remind me about it? You've spoiled my dinner."

"If I remind you of your debt, it's because I intend to give you the means to pay it."

"Really?" Denis's eyebrows rose

"I do." Robert grinned. "Are you pleased?"

"Pleased? I should think so, if only to rid myself of those piercing looks Père Jean gives me every time I encounter him. He reminds me by saying, 'Denis, when will you settle this business?' He chastises me as if I were a child. I want to repay him so that he'll return my wife's gold necklace, which he holds as collateral."

"If you'll do me this favour, Denis, the money is yours."

"With all my heart. Tell me what it is you need me to do."

"But," Robert glanced to the left and right then laid his finger across his lips with emphasis.

"You don't need to tell me. I'll not say a word." With thumb and forefinger, Denis made a twisting motion across his lips.

"Père Jean has made some absurd objections and delays my

marriage. I am told that if Emilie and I go before him with two witnesses, and I say 'this is my wife' and Emilie says 'this is my husband', we will be married."

Denis twisted his tankard. "And you want me to be one of the witnesses?

"*Oui.*"

"And you'll pay me the full amount I owe the priest?"

"Exactly. But we have to find another witness."

"I suggest my brother, Gervaise. You can pay him with something to eat and drink."

Robert nodded. "After Emilie and I are married, we'll bring him here to celebrate with us. But will Gervaise know what to do?"

"I'll prepare him."

"We'll do it tomorrow night as soon as it becomes dark. We can meet on the road to the parish."

"Both of us will be there."

"But," Robert raised his finger to his lips again.

"I know," Denis nodded.

"What if your wife questions you about where you are going, as no doubt she will? What will you tell her?"

Denis frowned. "I'll create some story to put her mind at rest, don't worry."

"Very well," said Robert. "Tomorrow."

Together they left the inn and parted.

16

Emilie remained tight-lipped as she listened to Robert discuss the arrangements he had made for them to wed.

"It sounds like a good plan," Ada said. "But you forgot something."

"What else could there be?" Robert asked.

"Rose! You forgot about Rose! She'll admit Denis and his brother into the house because of the money they owe Père Jean, but you two?" She shook her head. "You'll have to distract her somehow."

"What can we do?" Robert furrowed his brow and stroked his chin.

"I know!" Ada's face brightened. "I'll go with you. I have a secret I can share with Rose. I'll keep her engaged so that she won't see you enter the house."

"Bless you!" Robert kissed Ada on her cheek. "I always knew you were a wise woman."

"But none of this will work unless we can persuade Emilie." Ada turned an admonishing eye to her. "Tell him what you told me when he was away."

Emilia swallowed and gave Robert a long look. "I'm sorry, but I can't go through with it. It's dishonest, a sin."

Robert's mouth fell open as pain glazed his eyes.

Emilie crossed her arms, prepared to stand firm. "In order to do what Mother suggests, we have to be deceitful." Heat spread over her cheeks. "Ah, Robert! What a terrible beginning to our lives together. I want to be your wife, but in the right way, with God on our side, speaking our vows before an altar. We can wait a little longer to be married. Let's leave this to God. He'll help us without having to resort to all these tricks. And why do we have to keep this entire secret from Père Marc-Mathieu?"

They heard a brisk tread outside. An anxious silence fell over them.

"It's probably him. Say nothing about this." Ada gave Emilie a warning glance, straightened her gown, and swung open the door.

17

Before Père Marc-Mathieu could knock, Ada swung open the door. Robert and Emilie stood behind her. At their hopeful gazes, he shook his head. "There is no hope from that man." Although he knew that they had not expected much from his meeting with Seigneur Richard, confirmation of his failure caused their heads to droop and their shoulders to sag. A pang of guilt gripped him for having raised their hopes. How could he, a poor, powerless priest, have thought to deter a wealthy evil-doer like Seigneur Richard?

Anger surfaced in Robert's face. "I want to know what reasons that dog gave for asserting that my bride should not be my wife!" He gnashed his teeth.

"If those who commit injustices were obliged to give us their reasons, the world would not be as bad as it is." Père Marc-Mathieu gave Robert a look of pity.

"He didn't give a reason?" Robert asked through tight lips.

Père Marc-Mathieu shook his head. "He didn't."

Robert ran his hands through his hair, his face red. "But, surely, the fiend said something?"

"I can't repeat it. His words were angry, contentious, and he denied all knowledge of Emilie, yet, I knew my suspicions were well-founded. He insulted me and accused me of offending him. He's an insolent, reprehensible man who believes he can get his way by making threats. He neither mentioned Emilie's name nor your own, Robert, but by the end of our conversation, I understood too well that he is immovable."

He turned to Ada who placed a consoling arm around Emilie. "Don't despair!" He faced Robert. "I understand what you must feel in your heart, but you must be patient. Give God a few days to do his handiwork. I have an idea. I can't tell you anything more now. Come see me at the Jesuit convent tomorrow and I'll explain everything. Or if you can't come, send someone you trust in your place." He glanced out the window. "The sun will set soon and I have to be home before dark. It is our strictest rule. Have faith and courage." He blessed them with the sign of the cross. "*Bonne nuit*."

His heart heavy, Père Marc-Mathieu turned and walked away along a crooked, stony path; a shortcut to the convent. If he didn't arrive soon, he would run the risk of a severe reprimand, or worse, the infliction of a penance, which might prevent him from helping Robert and Emilie in the morning. He must do all he could for them. Besides, Seigneur Richard must be made to see the error of his ways.

18

Emilie watched Père Marc-Mathieu walk away. She returned to the table and sat across from Robert who stared at his hands and cracked his knuckles.

"Did you hear what Père Marc-Mathieu said?" Emilie smiled. She reached over and touched his hand, putting a halt to the annoying sound. "He's found a way to help us. I knew we could trust him. He's a man who, if he promises you ten of something, will bring you a hundred."

"There's no other like him," interrupted Ada as she flopped back into her chair. "But he ought to have said a little more about what he's planning. At the least, he should have taken me aside and told me."

Robert shoved his chair back and rose. "I can't sit around here and do nothing but wait!"

"Have patience." Emilie reached for his hand.

"What are you going to do?" Ada narrowed her gaze.

Robert let go of her hand and clenched and unclenched his

fists. "I'm going to put an end to this right now. Seigneur Richard may have a devil in his soul, but he's made of nothing more than flesh and blood."

"No, Robert, don't do anything!" Emilie rose up and took hold of his hand again.

"Don't say such things, Robert, even in jest," Ada admonished.

"In jest!" Robert leaned over the table and planted his hands before Ada. "I'm not jesting. I'm deadly serious."

"Robert! I've never seen this side of you before." Emilie squeezed his hand, unable to disguise the worry in her voice. Deep in her heart, she sensed he might attract trouble of some sort. Why did men always have this incessant need to take matters into their own hands through violence?

"For Heaven's sake, Robert!" Ada lowered her voice. "It's futile. Seigneur Richard has an army of men and an arsenal of weapons at his beck and call. Stay away from him and let God deal out the justice."

"*Non*, I'll get my own justice! It won't be easy. The ruffian is well-defended, dog that he is! But never mind. With a little patience, I'll free the world from this vermin and everyone will laud me for it."

Emilie stared hard at him. She inhaled a deep breath to calm herself. "Then you don't care about me." She kept her tone resolute while her entire world unravelled before her eyes. If she didn't stop Robert from doing something rash, it would destroy his life and hers too. "I pledged my troth to a good, God-fearing man, not one with revenge in his heart."

His cheeks reddened as he pushed his face close to hers. "If you don't want to marry me, fine, but *he* won't have you either. I'll see him burn in hell before I let him come near you."

What had happened to the gentle, soft-spoken youth she had fallen in love with? Who was this man who stood before her with rage burning in his eyes and thoughts of murder tainting his heart? It was as if her entire future crumbled before her and there was nothing she could do to stop it. Emilie held her stance and clenched her fists. "Don't even suggest it." She stared hard at him. "I won't stand for it."

Ada rose and ran her hands up and down Robert's arms to calm him.

Emilie had never spoken so harshly to him, and it pleased her that he stood unmoving, thoughtful as if overcome. Had she gotten through to him? Had he truly heard and understood her?

Robert drew back, stretched out his arm, and pointed his finger at her. "He wants you! And I'll see him die for it!"

Emilie unleashed her own anger. "What harm have I done that you should kill a man on my behalf?"

"You!" Robert shouted. "I've begged and begged you to go to the priest with me and do as your mother described for us to get married. That would put a stop to all this nonsense. And you refuse! So do not dare tell me not to take matters into my own hands. I refuse to sit back and do nothing while this bastard destroys our lives." He turned his back to her and paced.

Emilie knew he meant every word. It was written on his face, in the coldness of his words. But Robert was no match for the powerful Seigneur Richard who had the ability to collect men and weapons like a bee gathers pollen. If something should happen to Robert, she would be at fault. Dare she risk losing him and his love? She studied him again. Pain, anger, frustration was reflected in his eyes. Her heart softened, for she loved him devoutly. Only she could prevent him from acting rashly. Only she could keep him safe. If she must sacrifice her convictions in order to save his life, then she would do so. Hadn't they suffered enough already? Emilie swallowed. "All right. I'll go to the priest with you tomorrow. I'll go now, if you like. Only, you must promise not to seek revenge."

"Do *you* promise?" He stopped pacing and studied her, his eyes hopeful, his voice hesitant.

A sudden quiet fell over them. Her words seemed to ease Robert's anger and it encouraged her. "*Oui*, I promise," Emilie said, her tone softer.

"Thank goodness!" Ada fell back into her chair fanning herself and exchanged a knowing look with Robert.

A sense of dissatisfaction overcame Emilie at the realization that Robert and her mother had manipulated her into consenting. Yet, if she had not agreed to go to the priest with him, she had no doubt Robert would have taken matters into his own hands and acted recklessly. "And in return, promise me you won't make any trouble."

"You're certain? You won't change your mind later?"

"Right or wrong, I gave you my promise and I won't withdraw it." She stood with her arms crossed. "I still do not feel right about it. God forbid that something should go awry when we go to the priest."

"Everything will go well. Why do you predict misfortune? God knows we did nothing wrong. Don't you know by now how much I love you? I can't bear to lose you, especially to a fiend like Seigneur Richard."

"Oh, Robert. There is no risk of that. You are the only man I want. Promise me that you won't do anything against Seigneur Richard."

He pursed his lips and hesitated before responding. "I promise. You have my word."

Emilie hesitated. "But I'm still angry at you for the way you forced my consent."

"Nevertheless, you've given me your word." He smiled and touched her cheek. "And for that, I'm grateful. You can't blame me for fighting for what is mine. I can't stand by and allow Seigneur Richard to destroy us."

"No, I cannot blame you," Emilie acquiesced. She understood why he felt this way, but it was still wrong. Yet, they had reached an accord, and although it wasn't fully to her liking, she had accepted her end of the bargain.

"I should go," Robert said. "I need to finalize the plans for tomorrow when we go to the priest, and it's late."

Emilie walked him to the door.

He lifted her chin in his hand. "*Bonne nuit, mon amour.*"

Emilie removed his hand and brought it to her lips. "*Bonne nuit.*" All the while, her gaze never left his. She didn't like the cold vengeance she saw burning within his eyes.

19

Still seething after Père Marc-Mathieu's departure, Seigneur Richard paced the length of his spacious salon, the heels of his red leather shoes clicking against the wooden floor. With his hand, he slid the silk kerchief around his neck back and forth in irritation. Portraits of his ancestors graced every wall. He stopped before the figure of one of his relatives, a military man who'd served with King Louis XIV, not only the bane of his enemies, but of his own soldiers too. In uniform, he stared at Seigneur Richard with a grim expression, as if he deemed him unworthy. His short hair stood erect from his forehead. Sharp whiskers covered his cheeks and hooked chin. His right hand pressed his side and the left grasped the hilt of his sword.

Seigneur Richard swung around. On the opposite wall hung the portrait of another forefather, a magistrate, the scourge of litigants. Donned in a black sable-lined robe with a white collar, the man sat in a tall chair upholstered with crimson velvet. Affluent and hostile-looking, he seemed to stare at Seigneur Richard with suspicion.

To his right hung the painting of a matron, the terror of her maids. Her sardonic smile accused him of weakness.

To his left, an abbot, the nightmare of his friars, glared at him with disdain.

All these tyrannical ancestors inflicted much terror while alive. Their likenesses on canvas inspired fear whenever he looked upon them. In the presence of these formidable relatives, shame and rage washed over Seigneur Richard. A lowly Jesuit priest had accused and insulted him in his own home. Now he could find no peace. The man had sullied his honour, shaken his confidence, and he must find a way to restore his self-esteem.

Hands clasped behind his back, he paced the room. Plan after plan of revenge against the Jesuit came to mind, but he dismissed each one as inadequate. The few prophetic words uttered by the priest haunted him. The man had almost laid a curse on him. A fireball of ire raged in his gut and tension squeezed his chest. His breathing came fast, his heart raced. The urge to restore his dignity burned inside him. He needed to clear his head.

Frustrated, he called out for a servant who hurried into the room. “Apologize to my guests. Tell them I’ve been detained by urgent business.”

The servant left to do as bid, but soon returned. “All the men give you their compliments and have taken their leave.”

“My cousin, Pierre, too?” Seigneur Richard stopped pacing.

“*Oui,* he left with the other gentlemen.”

Seigneur Richard knew he should have asked his cousin to stay and cursed his lack of foresight. “Have my horse saddled. Summon two of my men to ride with me and bring me my coat and hat.”

Head held high, he left his manor-house and rode straight into the centre of the settlement, surrounded by his entourage of men armed with muskets. In the dusk, villagers and *habitants* greeted him as he went. He acknowledged no one. Their reverence pleased him and confirmed that his status remained untarnished. Their homage restored his confidence.

The annoying image of the priest continued to creep into his thoughts. In an attempt to banish them, Seigneur Richard entered a house from which emanated the unmistakable sounds of a celebration. Every head turned in his direction and the guests stopped talking. The host nervously rushed forward to shake his hand and invite him in. The guests treated him with cordiality in the manner reserved for those who are feared. His self-importance soared.

He returned home later that night. His cousin, Pierre had returned and now awaited him. Together they sat down for a late night meal. They spoke of trivial matters until the servants cleared the table and left the room.

"I think it's safe to say you lost our wager. When will you pay me?" Pierre pushed back his chair and crossed the room to a small table upon which rested a decanter of brandy. He poured some of the amber liquid into two silver goblets before returning to the table.

"Not so fast. There is still time."

"Why don't you admit you lost? You'll have to pay up sooner or later. Years will pass before she will-"

Seigneur Richard raised his hand to stop him. "The results of our wager have yet to be realized."

Pierre shook his head as he swirled his brandy. "You may want to stall for time, but I believe I've already won. In fact, I'm ready to lay another wager."

"What is it?"

"I wager that the priest has converted you."

Richard belted out a laugh. "I think you need to curtail your drink this evening. The spirits have gone to your head."

"Converted indeed, cousin, and I, for my part, am delighted.

What a sight! To see you penitent with downcast eyes! And what a triumph for the Jesuit priest! How proudly he must have returned to his convent. You aren't the typical kind of fish they catch every day. They'll use you as an example and brag about you near and far. I can already hear them. *'In a small colony in New France, there lived a dissolute gentleman, a sinful womanizer, who set his eyes upon an innocent beauty-*"

"Enough!" Seigneur Richard dismissed, half amused and half annoyed. "If you wish to double our original wager, I am happy to do so."

"Indeed! Perhaps, then, you are the one who has converted the Jesuit?"

"Don't speak to me about that man. And as for our bet, you'll soon learn the outcome."

Pierre raised his eyebrows and leaned forward in his chair. "What are you scheming now?"

"Patience, Pierre. All will be revealed at the end of the year, and not a day sooner." Seigneur Richard refused to answer any more questions and changed the topic of conversation. For now, it was best to keep his plans to himself.

20

Seigneur Richard awoke before dawn feeling confident and self-assured. Much of his anxiety over the half-muttered curse of the Jesuit priest had vanished. Only a deep indignation remained, more intense because of the weakness he'd shown in light of the man's tirade. His triumphant ride through the settlement, with the many respectful greetings and the generous reception at the *fête,* helped restore his shaken spirit.

His thoughts wandered to Emilie. He first noticed her on May Day at the maypole obligation when the *habitants* appeared at his front door for the celebration. Ever since, he had been unable to sweep her from his thoughts. He conjured a vision of her in his mind. During the salvo of blank musketry and the planting of the pole, she had stood with her mother and the miller at the back of the crowd. Later, she laughed and danced, cheeks ablush and dark eyes gleaming while the women gaudily embellished the pole, a fir-tree with branches cut and bark peeled to within a few feet of the top. The young men and maidens danced round it, while he looked on, his eyes never wavering from her beauty. Later, when he invited the whole gathering to refreshments indoors, he tried to speak to her, but the miller never left her side. When the merry company departed, he watched her walk away, arm-in-arm with him. The echo of more musket-shots came back through the valleys as they strode out of his sight. At that moment, he knew he had to have her for himself. Her soul had touched his and he knew with certainty that she was destined solely for him.

He dressed with haste and went downstairs. After he bid one of the servants to summon Thomas, he sat at the prepared table where an omelette and a hearty slice of ham were laid out, and began to eat.

Only Thomas could help him - Thomas, the head of his crew of men, the one man to whom he assigned his boldest, most dangerous tasks. Richard trusted him more than he trusted anyone else in his employ. Guilty of murder, Thomas had sought the seigneur's protection to escape persecution. Richard took him into service and sheltered him from the long arm of the law. In return, the man demonstrated his loyalty by engaging in anything required of him. The acquisition of Thomas had been significant for Richard. Besides being the most courageous of his men, Thomas was proof that he could outsmart the law and that aggrandized his own power in the eyes of the people.

Thomas entered the room and stood before him, tall and

lanky, his face neutral with an unwavering gaze from his piercing green eyes. An ugly scar across his throat showed above the collar of his shirt. Thomas never spoke of it, but it was obvious to Seigneur Richard the mark was the result of some failed attempt on his life.

"I have a job for you," Seigneur Richard steepled his fingers as he sat behind his ornate mahogany desk, "one that will prove your worth."

"Never let it be said that Thomas shrank from the command of his protector."

"There is a young woman by the name of Emilie Basseaux."

"I've seen her before."

"I want her brought to my house before tomorrow. Take as many men as you need, use them in whatever way you think best, but don't fail. Above all, no harm must come to the girl."

"I may need to give her a little fright so that she won't make too much noise. It cannot be avoided."

Seigneur Richard pondered the suggestion then unsteepled his fingers. "A little fear is inevitable. Nevertheless, don't harm even one hair on her head. Treat her with the greatest respect. Do you understand me?"

"I can't pluck a flower from its stalk without touching it a little. However, I'll do no more than is necessary. On this, you have my word."

"Make sure you don't harm her." Seigneur Richard repeated and leaned forward. "How will you manage it?"

Thomas thought a moment. "It's fortunate that her house is at the far end of the village. The men and I will need a place to conceal ourselves. There's that uninhabited building in the middle of the fields not far from where she lives. It was severely damaged by fire a few weeks ago; and no one has come forward to restore it, so it's abandoned. The villagers are a superstitious lot, and it's safe to assume they would never go near there at night. We can hide there without fear of discovery."

"Then what?"

Thomas relayed the rest of his plan and together they devised a way to end the entire situation without a trace of suspicion pointed in their direction. The plan was brilliant. It imposed silence upon Ada and would fill the miller with such fear that it would keep him from seeking recourse from the law. Thomas rose and turned to leave.

"Wait," Seigneur Richard called out. "If this rash fool of a miller should try to fight you, it would not bother me if you gave him something to remember me by. You know, so that he understands to keep his mouth shut. But, don't provoke him. Do you understand?"

"Leave everything to me." With a tilt of his head, Thomas left.

21

The sun had barely risen when Emilie opened the door for Robert. While Robert and Ada discussed the wedding plans, Emilie served the porridge that simmered over the embers.

As they ate, they reviewed the layout of the rectory, predicted potential problems, and planned solutions for any obstacles they might encounter. Emilie listened to it all without speaking a word, but when Robert and her mother looked at her for agreement, she lowered her spoon and promised to do her part. Her mother gave her a look of approval and Robert sighed with relief.

"Are you going to see Père Marc-Mathieu like he asked you to do last night?" Ada inquired of Robert.

"No. If I do, he'll anticipate something. If he questions me, I might reveal our plans by mistake. I prefer not to take the chance. Besides, I have to stay here to arrange things. Better to send someone else."

"My nephew, Fabien, could go," Ada suggested.

"He's a good choice." Robert rose and grabbed his hat. "I have a few arrangements to make, but I'll be back soon."

After Robert left, Emilie followed her mother across the lane. At Emilie's knock on the door of the whitewashed cottage, her Aunt Felice answered.

"Emilie, Ada, *bon jour*," she said with a smile as she stepped back from the doorway and wiped her hands with a cloth.

From her earliest childhood, Emilie had always loved her father's kind-hearted sister. She looked with appreciation at the tall, solidly built woman of ample bosom and an unfortunate growth of hair on her upper lip. Her blue eyes sparkled with energy above round, ruddy cheeks.

"Can Fabien come and help me for the entire day?" Ada asked. "I have some tasks for him."

"Bien sûr." Aunt Felice turned her head toward the kitchen. "Fabien, *vien ici*! Her voice rumbled within the silence of her small house.

Fabien bounded through a door and came to stand beside his mother.

Emilie smiled. Tall for his age of ten, he bore the same joyful disposition as his mother; he was a hard-working, obedient child and Emilie loved him for it. She smiled and ruffled his hair, eager to display her fondness. "Want to spend the day with us? We have a task for you to do, in exchange for some fresh bread."

After an initial brief scowl, it pleased her to see the sprightly lad nod.

"Mind your aunt and cousin," Aunt Felice cautioned.

"I will, *Maman*," he smiled as he followed Emilie and her mother to their kitchen.

Emilie ladled porridge into a bowl and set it before him. "Eat now. I have to finish my morning chores. By the time I finish, I'll have a treat for you." She kissed him on the head and left the room, confident he had the ability to undertake the task. Then they wouldn't have to follow through with the devious plan to trick Père Jean into marrying them. In fact, she would do everything for it to be so.

22

"Now, for the errand I want you to run," Ada said when Fabien finished eating. "I want you to go to the Jesuit convent and ask to speak to Père Marc-Mathieu. He will give you a message for us."

Fabien wiped his mouth with a napkin, his lips pressed together in a bit of a sulk. "Which one is Père Marc-Mathieu?"

"He's the one with the short white beard; the one they call the Saint."

"I know him," Fabien replied. "He speaks kindly to children and sometimes gives us pictures of saints."

"That's him. And if he asks you to wait, do not wander away. And be sure you don't run off and play with other boys on the way there.

"I won't, *ma tante.*"

"Good, be prudent and when you return, these two sweet rolls are for you."

"Why not give them to me now?"

From experience, Ada knew if she did, he'd never complete the task. "No, attend to the errand then you may have them. I might even give you one or two more."

A knock sounded on the door. Thinking Robert might have forgotten something, Ada flung open the door.

A thin tall beggar wearing a grey ragged coat patched at the sleeves, stood at the threshold. His narrowed green eyes gazed at her. She shuddered at the sight of the nasty scar, which spanned the length of his neck below his Adam's apple.

"Please, have you anything for a destitute man?" His eyes darted about, as if he searched for something.

"Wait one moment." Ada didn't know whether it was his shifting eyes or morose expression, but something about him disturbed her. In fact, his presence intimidated her, and she had never felt that way about anyone before.

Eager to be rid of him, she left him at the door and went to the hearth where several loaves of bread rested on a shelf. She grabbed one and turned back around. The man had now entered the room and stood beside the table watching Fabien. She should have closed the door to keep him out.

At first, Ada intended to give him only a chunk of the bread, but now, anxious to see the last of him, she handed him the entire loaf. He dropped the bread into the leather pouch at his waist with indifference.

Much to her dismay, he didn't leave. Instead, he studied every corner of the room. "Do you live here alone?"

Aghast at his bold impudence, Ada contrived a response. "No, I live here with my husband and five sons."

His brows furrowed as he looked at Fabien. "And what is your name?"

Before Fabien could answer, Ada interjected. "His name is F- Nicholas. His name is Nicholas."

"What a nice looking boy." The man reached out to tussle the lad's hair.

Fabien dodged out of his reach.

"You have a good abundance of bread, *Madame*. It seems the drought has not affected you as it has many others in the village."

Thanks to Robert's generosity, she and the other women of the settlement had baked for the wedding celebrations. With all that had transpired, she hadn't had the chance to share the excess with her neighbors yet. She formulated another lie. "The food is not ours. It is for my cousin who lives in a village a day's ride from here. A distant relative of mine has died and I am waiting for someone to arrive any moment to take the food to the family." She crossed her arms over her chest. "Now, if you don't mind, I have much to do. Good day to you."

The stranger took one more look around, and then boldly, he went to the far end of the room to the doorway that led to the bedrooms and glanced about.

"Where are you going?" Ada grabbed a broom and prepared to swat him with it. He hurried to the door.

"*Pardon Madame*," he said with submission and humility that clashed with the fierce features of his face. With a tip of his hat, he departed.

"And don't come back." Ada stood in the doorway and stared at his back as he walked from her sight. Her chest heaved with anger. There was something more to his appearance, an ulterior motive perhaps. But what?

She closed the door and heaved a sigh of relief that he was gone. For now, she had other things to think about, so she tried to put the man out of her mind.

Now that the man had gone, she deemed it safe, and Ada pecked a kiss on Fabien's cheek, and sent him on his way to the Jesuit house.

23

Emilie re-entered the kitchen through the back door. As she set down her basket filled with washed pots, her mother told her about the mysterious beggar.

"He can't be a local man; otherwise you would have recognized him by that scar. I wonder who he could be." Emilie said.

Later, a short, fair-haired man knocked on their door to ask directions to the settlement of Yamachiche. Then, Emilie noticed another man walk back and forth, slackening his pace each time he passed in front of their home. Once, he even had the gall to peek through their window. Emilie closed the shutters and locked the front door leaving their small cottage in cool darkness.

By midday, the alarming appearances of strangers ceased. Emilie crossed the little yard to the street, looked around, and returned inside. "Thank goodness there's nobody outside," she said to her mother.

Haunted by an undefined disquietude, Emilie's courage at the approaching confrontation with the priest ebbed. She glanced over at her mother who had grown quiet. Emilie tried, but could not shake her growing unease. Something was underfoot, but what it was, she didn't know.

24

From a lower-storey window of Seigneur Richard's manor house, Etienne peered through a gap in the curtains and watched the group of men return.

He had worked for Seigneur Richard for over twenty years and knew almost everything that went on beneath this roof. He kept his eyes on Thomas and two other men who entered the dining room and closed the door behind them. Sheltered by the darkness in the hallway, Etienne listened at the door. If any of the other servants discovered him, he could easily explain his presence. It was common to find Seigneur Richard's private secretary nearby.

The men had described a small house and spoke of a mother and daughter who lived there. Etienne tried to make sense of all the ambiguous inferences. Soon, he realized they were plotting something. At length, he gained a clear understanding of their plans. They were going to abduct a young woman and it was near the time they would act. Already, a small group of Seigneur Richard's men had left the house to conceal themselves in the burned-out building he had heard them describe.

Etienne knew he played a dangerous game by spying on his employer, but gut instinct told him he must do what was right and fulfill the promise he made to Père Marc-Mathieu the night before. For years, he had watched in silence as Seigneur Richard plotted his works of evil, and he had grown weary of it. Of late, it bothered his conscience and kept him from sleep many a night.

Whatever the reason for the confrontation between his master and the priest, he sensed the priest was in the right and he must do what he could to prevent any wrongdoing. Under the pretence of going to visit his sick sister, he hurried to the Jesuit convent to tell the priest all that he had learned.

25

Thomas sent one or two men at a time to the burned-out house so they would not draw attention to themselves. Before he left to go there himself, he instructed the last two men to bring a small horse-drawn cart with them. When all the men had gathered at the charred hovel, Thomas dispatched three men to the small inn. He ordered one to stand at the door, watch the movements in the street, and make a note of when all the settlers retired. He ordered the other two men to remain inside, gaming and drinking, as if enjoying themselves, while watching for anything unusual. Thomas waited with the others in ambush.

26

The sun hung low in the sky when Emilie opened the door to Robert and invited him inside.

"Denis and Gervaise are waiting outside," Robert said. "First, we're going to sup at the inn then we'll be back to fetch you when all is ready."

Emilie stood still, the knot in her stomach uncomfortable. She had hoped Fabien would have returned with word or aid from Père Marc-Mathieu by now. She swallowed back her disappointment.

"Come, Emilie, have courage."

She sighed. "*Oui*, I have plenty of that. It has been an unusual day." She told him about the strange men and their lingering visits throughout the day. "What could it mean?" Emilie gripped the sides of her gown.

Robert shook his head. "I don't know, but we can't let it stop us. The sooner we marry, the sooner you will be safe." He reached out and took hold of her elbow.

Emilie's legs froze and she could not move. All was set, but she couldn't put her mind at ease. The way they were to marry still grated her sensibilities. A bad feeling gripped her.

He studied her face to understand her hesitation. "You haven't changed your mind, have you?

He looked so confident, so determined, and in the brilliance of his eyes, she could see how much he loved and wanted her. Emilie shook her head and sighed. "I gave you my promise to go through with it, but it doesn't mean I have to like it. In my heart, I still believe it is wrong."

He took her hand and planted a kiss on the back of it before he left. "And it is because of your virtue that I love you so much. You will see it is the right thing to do. I'll be back soon, and then we will be husband and wife. All of this will be behind us."

She prayed he was right, but she could not stop the fluttering in her stomach or the niggling warnings that crept into her thoughts.

27

Denis and Gervaise followed Robert to the inn, but they found the doorway blocked by a man who leaned with his back against one of the jambs. Arms folded across his chest, he occupied half its width. The man's small, griffin-like eyes shifted back and forth.

When Robert tried to enter, the man refused to move. Determined to avoid trouble, Robert said nothing. Instead, he turned sideways, and grazing the other doorpost, pushed his way through. Denis and Gervaise squeezed past in the same way.

Once inside, Robert studied two men who sat at a table. They played cards and alternately poured ale from a large flagon placed between them. Like the man at the door, they, too, eyed them from head to foot before glancing first at his companion then to the man in the doorway, who returned a slight nod in their direction.

Suspicious, Robert looked at Denis and Gervaise to see if they had noticed the exchange, but their hungry faces indicated nothing beyond a good appetite.

The proprietor approached with a coarse tablecloth under his arm, a flagon of ale in one hand, and three tankards in the other. He placed them at a vacant table nearby.

Robert leaned toward him. "Do you know those men?"

"Men from the countryside." The innkeeper shrugged and spread the tablecloth.

"Is that all you know about them?" Robert stared hard at his host.

"That's all I know about them." He shook his head as he smoothed the cloth with both his hands. "In this business, one never pries into the affairs of others. All I care about is whether my customers will pay me. Who they are, or who they are not, is not my concern. But, come now! I'll bring you a plate of tourtière, the likes of which you've never tasted."

Before Robert could utter another word, the proprietor plopped the flagon on the table, then turned and headed to the kitchen.

28

As the proprietor withdrew the tourtière from the oven, the man who had blocked the doorway of the inn came up behind him.

"Who are those three men?" he asked in a low voice.

"Men of the village." The proprietor gave him an annoyed look for standing too close.

The man refused to move and met his stare.

The proprietor huffed and reached around the man to grab three plates.

"Perhaps you didn't understand me the first time." The man's tone grew sharper as he took a step closer. "Who are they?"

"One is called Robert; the miller of Pointe-du-Lac. The other is a *habitant* by the name of Denis. The third man is a simpleton who eats whatever I set before him. Now, if you don't mind, I'm busy." The proprietor cut the tourtière and plated three portions. He passed between the stove and his interrogator and carried the dishes into the next room.

29

The moment the proprietor returned, Robert accosted him. “How do you know they are from the countryside if you don't know who they are or whether they are honest?

The proprietor placed the three dishes on the table before them. “I know men by their actions. Those who drink ale without complaining about it; those who throw their money on the counter without prating; those who don't quarrel with other customers; those who go outside to throw a punch so that I'm not drawn into their brawl.” He gave Robert a softer look. “Concentrate on filling your bellies with this magnificent tourtière instead.” Then he retreated into the kitchen.

But Robert could not enjoy his food. The three men and their strange behaviour made him uneasy and he wanted to leave. He hurried through his meal with the hope his companions would do the same.

“I'm happy to see you getting married,” exclaimed Gervaise, his voice far too loud in the nearly vacant room.

Robert threw him a savage look.

“Hold your tongue, *stupide*,” hissed Denis as he gave his brother a sharp jab with his elbow.

Gervaise's face reddened and he stared at his food as he shoved a large forkful into his mouth. The conversation between them lagged until the end of the meal.

Robert drank no ale and controlled the amount Denis and Gervaise consumed. He wanted them sober for what was to come. When they finished eating, Robert paid the bill and they rose from the table. From the moment they had entered the inn, the strange men had watched their every move, and he didn't like it one bit.

Robert and his friends left the inn. Around them, the world

buzzed with activity. Women arrived home from the fields, their infants in slings on their backs and elder children in tow. Men bore their spades and hoes on their shoulders. Fur traders led horses packed with pelts. Doors opened and bright gleams of light sparkled from the fires cooking the evening meal. In the street, villagers greeted each other and remarked sadly about the scarcity of the harvest and the poverty of the times.

As they made their way to Emilie and Ada's cottage, Robert glanced behind him. Two of the men from the inn followed them. He stopped with fists doubled and turned around to confront them.

The men halted and spoke in suppressed voices to each other.

Robert stared hard at the strangers until they turned and walked away. He and his friends then continued on their way in the increasing darkness. By the time they arrived at the cottage, night had fully fallen.

30

Anxiety continued to plague Emilie as she mindlessly washed a pot. Her mother sat at the table staring into the fire. Fabien had not returned from the Jesuit house. Where could he be? Could something have happened to him? He had left during daylight hours, but now it was dark, and he was a boy of ten. She rose to peer out of the window, but saw no sign of him.

With each passing moment, Emilie grew more anxious until fear flourished like weeds within her. Apprehension had become a formidable obstacle, her imagination wild with visions of their plan going awry. She regretted the promises she had made to Robert the night before.

A knock sounded at the door. Apprehension raced through her. In that instant, she would have suffered torture rather than proceed with her nuptials. She swallowed and swung the door open, praying it would be Fabien.

Grim faced, it was Robert who regarded her. "It's time to go."

Emilie opened her mouth to speak, but she had neither the heart nor the time to stall. With one arm linked with her mother's and the other with Robert's, they joined Denis and Gervaise who waited and set off. It would have been faster to follow the main lane, but instead, they chose the longer route because fewer people used it. After cutting through narrow pathways that ran between gardens and fields, they arrived at the parish rectory and parted company. Emilie hid with Robert behind a corner of the house. Her mother stayed with them, but stood a little more in the forefront so she might run out to meet Rose. Denis and Gervaise strode forward and rapped three times on the door.

"Who's there?" Rose called out after she threw open the window.

"It's me, Denis, with my brother, Gervaise. We've come to speak with Père Jean."

"At this hour?" Rose scolded then began to shut the window. "Come back tomorrow."

"I can't return tomorrow. I've scraped together the money to settle that little debt you know about." Denis reached into his pocket and pulled out a leather pouch that jingled when he shook it. "But if I can't pay it tonight, never mind. I have more urgent need of the money. I'll come back when I've collected the amount again."

"Wait! I'll go and tell Père Jean," she frowned. "Why did you come at such a late hour?"

"If you want to arrange another time, I've no objection, but I'm here now, and if the good priest doesn't want to see me, I'll go."

"No, wait one moment. I'll be back with the answer shortly."

Rose slammed the window shut.

Ada turned to face Emilie. "Have courage," she whispered. "Soon you'll be married and it will all be over."

Emilie's throat was so dry, her body so tense, she could not respond. She fought off a desire to flee as she watched her mother hasten into the darkness and join Denis and Gervaise at the door.

31

Rose found Père Jean in his second-storey study reading a book by candlelight. "Forgive me for disturbing you, Père Jean, but Denis is here with his brother to see you."

"Now? At this hour!" Père Jean glanced up with a scowl. "Didn't you tell him that I am ill?"

Rose rested both hands on her hips. "*Oui*, I did, but he waits at the door and insists on paying his debt."

"*Ah, bien*. Send him up."

She left the room, shaking her head. The man could be infuriating at times. What would he do without her to take care of his affairs? She shuffled down the stairs, but when she returned to the front door, the two men were no longer there. "Denis, are you there?" she called out.

The two brothers stepped forward from behind the door. To her surprise, Ada Basseaux now stood with them.

"Good evening, Rose," Ada greeted her with a smile.

"Ada! I'm surprised to see you. Where have you come from at this late hour?"

"I'm returning from the settlement at Baie-Jolie. I was delayed there because of a matter that concerns you."

"Me?" Rose's brows drew together. "About what?"

Ada shook her head and directed her eyes at Denis and Gervaise.

Rose understood Ada didn't want to speak in front of them. Whatever Ada wanted to tell her must be important, a secret of some sort, and Rose loved rumours. It brought respite to her dreary life. She smiled at the two brothers. "Go on inside. I'll be with you soon."

Ada waited for the men to enter the house then stepped closer and whispered in Rose's ear. "A gossiping woman, who knows nothing about you, is saying that you didn't marry Gilbert Coderre or Serge Langevin because they wouldn't have you! I insisted that it was *you* who refused *them*."

Rose's mouth fell open. She pulled away and glared at Ada. "Who is the false-tongued woman who dares say such a thing?"

Ada raised both her hands and shook her head. "I don't want to make trouble."

"I have to know because it's a lie."

"Well, if I had known all the facts, I might have been able to shut her up."

"It's a complete falsehood." Rose heard some whispering behind her. She turned to where Denis and his brother still waited in the entrance hall. "Go upstairs. Père Jean awaits you in his den." She shooed them away with a flap of her arms.

Denis shrugged and retreated into the darkness of the entry.

Satisfied, Rose turned back to Ada.

"Let's go where we can speak in private." Ada motioned for Rose to follow her to a small field beyond the two cottages at the end of the lane. When they could no longer see the rectory, Ada experienced a sudden, loud coughing spell.

Rose pounded Ada on the back until it subsided and waited for her to recover enough to tell her about the lies that unknown woman was spreading.

32

That was the signal! Every muscle in Emilie's body tightened the moment she heard her mother's coughs. Apprehension seized her, but Robert pulled her along the perimeter of the rectory until they reached the front door. He nudged it open and let her enter first.

Inside the dimly lit entrance hall, Denis and Gervaise waited for them at the bottom of the stairs. All was quiet. Robert led the way up the stairs, taking care to step on the ends of each tread to avoid unnecessary creaks. When they reached the upper landing, a gentle light escaped from beneath one of the doors. The brothers advanced to the door while Emilie waited with Robert out of sight.

"May God bless you, Père Jean," Denis called out as he rapped on the door.

"Enter!" replied Père Jean.

Emilie gripped Robert's hand and watched Denis push the door open wide enough for him and Gervaise to enter. As predetermined, he left it ajar for her and Robert to listen for their cue to enter.

Lamplight from within shone on Emilie. She held her breath, fearful of discovery. Oh, how she wished she were anywhere but here, but she had given her word to Robert. Sweat dampened her hands and clothes. Her heart beating faster, she clutched Robert's arm and waited.

From where she stood, she could see and hear everything. Père Jean, dressed in his soutane, sat in an old armchair near a window. He removed his spectacles and laid them on the book on his lap. A large writing table scattered with a candle-lantern and a tray with ink and quill rested against the wall opposite the window. Beside it a long embroidered runner covered the top of a large wooden cabinet. Candlelight cast dancing shadows across the brocade curtains.

"I apologize for coming to see you so late," Denis said.

Père Jean folded his hands across his chest. "Most certainly it is late, and in more ways than one. Did you not know that I am ill and not receiving visitors?" He glared at Denis who remained expressionless and silent. "The debt you owe me should have been repaid long ago."

"I'm sorry, but times have been hard."

The priest glanced up at Gervaise and turned to Denis. "Why have you brought your brother?"

"Only for company, Père." Denis patted his brother on the back.

"Very well."

Denis drew a leather pouch from his pocket and handed it to Père Jean. "Here is all the money I owe you."

Père Jean donned his spectacles, opened the pouch, and withdrew a handful of coins. He gasped and looked up.

"All in golden English guineas – not the worthless French money cards that have been circulating," Denis said.

Père Jean counted each coin, rubbing every one between thumb and forefinger.

"Now, please return my wife's necklace to me."

"*Oui*, of course." Père Jean removed a key from on top of the cupboard and opened one of the doors wide enough to withdraw a small leather pouch from which he lifted out the necklace. "This is the one, correct?"

Denis nodded. "Now, please record the transaction."

Père Jean's eyebrows rose. "You don't trust me?"

"Of course I trust you. But as my name is written in your black book on the debtor's side, I must now ask you to make note that the debt is paid."

The priest muttered as he pulled out the top drawer of his

desk and fumbled about until he removed a black book and some papers, which he dropped onto the desktop. He reached for his goose feather quill, dipped it into the ink, and scratched a quick notation in the book. On another piece of paper, he wrote out a receipt.

Cold sweat dampened Emilie's brow as she saw Denis and Gervaise place themselves in front of the desk, thus concealing the door from Père Jean's view. Then she heard their signal, two shuffles, and two taps of their feet on the wooden floorboards. Robert gave Emilie's hand a fortifying squeeze then led her into the den. Every instinct she possessed screamed for her to turn back and flee, but her sense of honor held her taut. She would never break a promise and held her breath as they stopped behind Denis and Gervaise.

His head down, Père Jean finished writing and read over the receipt without once raising his eyes. He took off his spectacles, blew on the ink to dry it, and handed the paper to Denis. "Are you content now?"

The moment Denis took it in his right hand; both he and Gervaise stepped aside. With Robert by her side, Emilie now stood face-to-face with Père Jean.

"In the presence of these witnesses, this is my wife." Robert spoke in a loud, clear voice, enunciating the latter part of his statement.

Père Jean's brows puckered in confusion. Then his mouth dropped open and his face twisted with alarm. The puzzled look on his face warped into one of rage.

Heart racing, Emilie opened her mouth, but before she could utter her part, Père Jean rose to his feet. With a sweep of his arm he sent candle-lantern, book, pens, and inkstand flying off the desk. He yanked the cloth from the top of the cupboard, sprang around the writing desk, and advanced towards Emilie.

"And this is Robert-" Emilie began, her voice shrill, wavering with alarm.

Père Jean threw the cloth over her head to shut her up.

"Rose!" The priest bellowed like a wounded bull. "Rose! Treachery! Help!"

In her panic, the more Emilie struggled to get the cloth off her head, the more she became tangled in it. She felt another pair of hands grapple with the cloth and Robert managed to yank it off. Père Jean darted past her and fled into the dark corridor. Emilie heard a door slam and the click of a lock. The candle in the upturned lantern on the floor burned out just as Robert ran into the corridor and began to kick the door behind which the priest had barricaded himself. "Open this door, Père Jean!"

From behind came the muffled shouts of Père Jean bellowing for help.

At a loss as to what to do, Emilie ran onto the hallway, too. "Let's go, Robert, please." She should have trusted her instincts and never come. Now it was too late. Oh, what had they done?

33

Père Jean flung open the window of the guest bedroom and shouted for help. Moonlight cast long dark shadows from the church, across the lane, to the house where the captain of the parish militia threw open a window and stuck his head out. "What's the matter?"

"Yves, help me! There are people in my house!" Père Jean yelled.

"I'm coming!" replied the captain who drew in his head and slammed the window shut.

A few moments later, Père Jean watched as Yves bounded from his house wearing only an untied banyan that flapped over his loose shirt and breeches and darted inside the church.

Within moments, the frantic tolling of the church bells cut the silent night. Père Jean crossed himself and whispered a prayer. It took him a few moments to understand what was happening. He had heard of that old canon law being used upon unsuspecting priests. Thank goodness he had his wits about him and had stopped them before it was too late. His life would have been over if he hadn't stopped Emilie from completing her utterance. Now all of Pointe-du-Lac would come to his aid.

34

Thomas set his plan in motion and donned the same ragged clothes he had worn earlier in the day. After grabbing a lantern and a small tinderbox, he and his men walked down the street to the women's cottage. His heart raced with anticipation as it always did before one of his missions. Confident in his well-thought out plan, he looked forward to a successful conclusion and perhaps receiving a bonus of some sort from Seigneur Richard. In fact, he'd insist upon it.

Once there, Thomas ordered his men to wait outside while he went in alone to explore. He peered over the hedge into the yard. The dark house seemed deserted. Beckoning his men forward, he swung open the gate, and gestured for them to hide behind a large maple tree. He knocked on the front door and waited. When nobody answered, he tried to turn the handle, but it was locked. Pulling his knife from the sheaf hidden at his waist, he picked, yanked, and pried until he heard it snap. The door creaked open. Not a sound came from within. With a raised arm, he gestured for his men to come forward, and then tucked his knife back into its sheath, concealing it with the flap of his coat.

Thomas stepped into the same room he had reconnoitered earlier, lit his lantern, and trod stealthily to the rear of the house. All was quiet. A floorboard beneath him creaked. He paused, cursing. Nothing happened. When he deemed it safe, he continued along the hallway. He had broken into homes many times before, and as a result, he tread softly, like a cougar stalking its prey. Several years ago, he remembered breaking into another home, but it had ended badly when the man of the house woke up unexpectedly and Thomas was forced to kill him. This time, with two lone women as his targets, he anticipated no problems.

In the kitchen, a door at the rear led him into a narrow hallway with two doors opposite to each other. He put his ear against the door to his right and listened. No snoring or breathing came from within. Raising the candle-lantern, with his elbow, Thomas nudged the door open a little wider. The room was in complete darkness. Inside stood a neatly made bed and a dresser. He shrugged and crept to the other door, listening. This room was empty too. A ripple of anger coursed through him. Where were the women? The men searched the entire house, prying into the corners of every room.

One of the men Thomas had left outside to stand guard burst into the house. "Get out! Someone is coming!"

35

Fabien hurried to his aunt's cottage. He had spent the better part of the day waiting for Père Marc-Mathieu, who deliberated with another priest behind closed doors. While he waited in the hallway outside, an elderly man was permitted entry before him. Before the door closed, he heard Père Marc-Mathieu address the man as Etienne, but Fabien did not know who Etienne was or where he came from. The two remained in the room a long time and Fabien continued to wait, the promise of his aunt's sweet-rolls ever present in his mind. Finally, Père

Marc-Mathieu came out and instructed him to go to Emilie and Ada and bring them to the Jesuit house with all haste. Fabien didn't understand why, but he knew it must be somehow connected with Etienne. He ran most of the way from the convent in the dark heeding the urgency he sensed from the priest.

When he arrived, he found his aunt's house in complete darkness. He ran past the hedges to the front door. The lock was broken and the door stood ajar. Beads of sweat formed on his lip and forehead. Something was wrong, but he did not know what. Cautiously, he stepped inside. "*Tante*?" he called out. "Emilie?"

Rough hands grabbed both of his arms. "Shut up or you'll die," a raspy voice growled.

Fabien uttered a shrill gasp. All his life he feared the terrors of the dark - unseen hands reaching out and grabbing him. Now those nightmares became a stark reality. Terror possessed him. The hands pressed a cold metal blade against his neck. He trembled like a leaf and bit his lip to keep from crying out again. Suddenly, the toll of church bells cleaved the air. The villain lessened his hold and Fabien stomped the man's foot. The rogue released his hold. Panic-stricken, Fabien fled the house towards the pealing bells.

36

Thomas cursed as he darted out of the house. What had happened? How had his mission gone awry? His plans never failed. If he found the person who had foiled his plans, he would kill him with his bare hands. In his haste as he ran down the dark lane. His foot landed on a rock, twisted, and he tripped, falling forward hard. Pain burned through his ankle as he tried to stand. His men came from behind, surrounded him, and swept him along as they dashed into the night, the tolling of the bells adding urgency to their flight.

37

In the dark field, Rose listened to what Ada told her, but she struggled to believe it. How could a woman she didn't know, from a settlement she had never been to, spread such malicious lies about her? It made no sense. Doubt crept into her thoughts. Was Ada lying, and if so, why would she do such a thing?

Rose grew weary of the conversation because Ada repeated the same facts over and over. The woman could add no new information no matter how many questions she asked of her. Rose decided she'd had enough. "Oh, no." She slapped her forehead with her hand. "I left the front door of the rectory wide open. And Gervaise and his brother are still waiting. I must get back to the rectory."

Ada gave her an odd, almost reluctant look, but followed. She seemed distracted and walked annoyingly slow. Suddenly, the church bells tolled, frenetic and urgent against the stillness of the night. "Mercy! What has happened?"

As she was about to dash back to the rectory, Ada grabbed her gown and yanked her back. "Wait!"

Rose struggled to free herself. "Let me go. It could be Père Jean who is ringing the bell."

"Wait." Ada seized Rose by the arm.

The pealing continued and Rose knew something was amiss. "Let me go!"

Rose shoved Ada away and ran to the rectory. As she put her hand on the door latch, it swung open. Inside stood Denis, Gervaise, Robert, and a white-faced Emilie.

"What are you doing here? What's happened?" Rose shrieked at them.

They rushed past her without a word of explanation.

Something had happened; she knew it. Rose rushed inside and scrambled up the stairs.

38

Heart in her throat, Emilie fled behind Robert to where her mother paced, chewing on a fingernail. “There you both are! How did it go? Why are the bells ringing?”

“There's no time for explanations. Hurry, we have to get home.” Robert tightened his grip on her arm, grabbed Ada with the other, and ran, dragging them both behind him.

Someone raced towards them in the darkness calling her name. Fabien could scarcely draw a breath when he stopped in front of them. “You have to come with me. Père Marc-Mathieu says you must go to him.”

“What's wrong?” Emilie struggled to catch her breath.

“There are bad men in your house,” Fabien's chest heaved. “I saw them. They tried to kill me. Père Marc-Mathieu said they want to kill you too.” He looked at Robert. “Especially you, Robert. Hurry, we must go now.”

Robert's features twisted and his mouth drooped open. “We'd better do as he says.” The fear in his voice matched her own.

The bells continued to toll frenetically; a sinister, evil sound instead of the harmonic ringing Emilie imagined after her wedding. Even worse, now that they had failed in their attempt, each ring seemed to scream out their deceit; their shameful attempt to trick a priest into marrying them. Guilt ridden, she sprinted away with Robert and her mother. They turned onto the first path they came to then ran through the freshly ploughed fields.

39

Yves continued to tug the bell rope until a group of men had gathered in the lane in front of the church. “Hurry, there's trouble at Père Jean's house.”

He led the men along the path to the rectory's front door. It was shut and bolted. All seemed quiet. He stepped back and looked up. The window shutters were also closed. He could neither see any light nor hear any sounds from within, so he cupped his hands and shouted. “Père Jean!”

One of the window shutters upstairs swung open. Père Jean and his housekeeper both stuck their heads out and peered down.

“What has happened?” he called out to them. “Are you in any danger?”

“We are fine, the trouble has passed. There's nobody here. Thank you, everyone. Please, go home now. I apologize for having woken you.” Père Jean made the sign of the cross over them in blessing.

“But what happened?” Yves frowned and ran his hands through his hair in frustration. “You shouted for help. Who was here and what did they want?”

“Some people were bothering me, but they've gone now. Please, go home. The danger is passed. I thank you for your kindness.” The priest drew back and slammed shut the window.

Yves watched with dismay as the crowd dispersed. Just then, a man burst through the crowd. Yves recognized him as a man who lived in the house next to Ada and Emilie Basseaux.

“I saw a group of armed men at Ada Basseaux's house. They surrounded a poor beggar who lay on the ground. The poor man limped as they dragged him down the street. I think they’re going to kill him.”

"How many men were there?" Yves asked.

The man shrugged. "It was dark. Seven or eight perhaps."

Yves pointed at an elderly man. "Ring the bells again. Tell anyone else who arrives to meet me at the Basseaux house. The rest of you, follow me."

When they arrived at Ada and Emilie's cottage, Yves found the door wide open and the lock broken. He and several men searched the house, but the invaders were long gone. There was no sign of a beggar anywhere. Even worse, neither Ada nor Emilie were there. He walked out of the cottage shaking his head. "There's no one inside."

The crowd of men emitted a collective gasp of outrage.

"Where are the women? We have to find the bastards who took them!" one said.

"This is a heinous crime, a disgrace to the village!" shouted another.

"What kind of person would do this to a poor beggar and two defenseless women?" cried someone else.

Men raised their fists in anger and exchanged fearful looks with each other.

"Ada and Emilie are safe in another house," came a shout from the back of the crowd. "There is no sign of the marauders and there is nothing to worry about. All is well. Everybody can go home now."

Yves scanned the faces of the men before him, but he couldn't identify the man who had spoken. But it had an instant effect and everyone walked away. "Come back. Don't assume anything. We must make further inquiries." It was too late. Not one man remained.

40

Fabien led the way as Robert half-dragged Emilie and her mother along. Occasionally, Emilie glanced behind her to see if anyone followed them, but the path remained deserted. The feverish ringing of the bell enhanced her fears. The sound pursued them – accusatory and increasingly ominous with each step.

Just as they reached a deserted field, the ringing ceased. But the silence disturbed her as much as the ringing had. Robert stopped and allowed them to catch their breath.

Emilie glanced at her mother who panted, hunched, hands on her knees to recover her breath. She looked first at Robert then at Fabien. "What happened?"

Emilie let Robert explain their failed attempt with Père Jean.

"*Mon Dieu*, what misfortune. I'm so sorry it failed."

Emilie faced her cousin. "And you, Fabien?"

Fabien repeated Père Marc-Mathieu's urgent request and described the horrific attack against him in their home.

Emilie took her cousin in her arms. "I would never forgive myself if something happened to you. Père Marc-Mathieu was right to send for us. He knows we're in grave danger."

Robert exchanged a fearful glance with her. He placed his hands on Fabien's shoulders. "You have been our guardian angel this night. I'm sorry you suffered such danger on our account."

"My mother must be worried about me. I must get home," Fabien said.

"Alone?" Emilie gasped. "*Non*, it is too dangerous. We'll walk back with you."

Robert stopped her. "We can't go back."

"I'll stay off the main roads," Fabien assured them. "Please don't worry."

"It's best for the lad to go home," Robert said. "They're after us, not him. They accosted him because he interrupted their ambush in the house."

Ada hesitated, embraced Fabien, and kissed him on the forehead. "Perhaps it is best for you to go home alone. I'll bring you an entire batch of sweet-rolls when I return home." She smiled at him and stroked his cheek.

Robert dropped a handful of coins in Fabien's palm. "Tell no one about the message you brought us from Père Marc-Mathieu and tell no one where we went. Take care as you go."

Fabien nodded.

Emilie hugged and kissed him. "Be careful."

Fabien turned and walked away.

"Come, we have to go," Robert urged with a wave of his hand.

Worry creased Ada's forehead. "My house! I wish to know what happened to it, or if anything is missing."

Robert shook his head. "There's nothing we can do about it now, but I'm sure someone will care for it."

"Aunt Felice will check on it as soon as Fabien returns home." Emilie retreated into her thoughts as they walked through the night. Why did someone want to kill them? Was Seigneur Richard the cause of all this? If only she could have convinced Robert and her mother to wait for Père Marc-Mathieu's response, things might have gone differently and they would not be in danger. So many questions without answers, but Emilie was certain Père Marc-Mathieu knew something.

Before long, they saw the light of the Jesuit convent with its attached chapel and surrounding farm.

Robert advanced to the chapel door and pushed it open. When she stepped inside, Emilie looked about. Moonlight fell upon the anxious face and silvery beard of Père Marc-Mathieu who sat in a chair near the entrance.

"God be praised!" He rose and waved at them to enter.

Père Nicholas stood beside him with a frown.

"Père Nicholas volunteered to keep vigil with me. He was kind enough to keep the doors open in order to receive you at this late hour."

After her mother stepped inside, Père Marc-Mathieu shut the door behind them.

"This is most irregular." Père Nicholas glanced at Emilie then her mother. He wrung his hands and shook his head. "To have women at night in our chapel. Our rules forbid it!"

"If we were dealing with a robber, you would make no such argument," scolded Père Marc-Mathieu. "This poor child is an innocent escaping from the jaws of a wolf. She and her mother and betrothed may well be in grave danger. It is our duty to help them, no matter the time. You must trust me."

Emilie looked away in discomfort while her mother glared at Père Nicholas with a face like stone.

Père Marc-Mathieu led them into the nave and invited them to sit on a wooden bench near the front. He lit the candles on either side of the altar.

In the dim light of the tiny chapel, Emilie studied her surroundings. A narrow aisle separated ten rows of wooden pews on either side of the tiny church. Wooden plaques depicting the Stations of the Cross hung evenly spaced around the perimeter walls. More importantly, a sense of peace enveloped Emilie, and she was grateful for the respite.

Père Marc-Mathieu glanced at Emilie. "You look tired. Fatigue casts dark shadows beneath your eyes. No bride-to-be should have to endure such anxiety."

At the sympathetic words, a lump formed in Emilie's throat. And guilt too, over their failed attempt to marry. She felt soiled standing before this good, honest man.

"Praise God, you've made it here safely," Père Marc-Mathieu

said. "I'm glad you came so fast after Fabien brought you my message. You are in grave danger and Pointe-du-Lac is no longer safe for you. Seigneur Richard plans to abduct you." He turned to give Robert a pointed look. "Do not indulge in rancor. Rest assured there will come a day when you will think yourselves happy that this has happened."

Emilie peered at Robert, who did not say a word about the night's events and avoided eye contact with Père Marc-Mathieu. Remorse consumed her as she retreated into silence. Now she could add lying to her sins. She should have put a stop to all this when she had the chance, and because she hadn't, now all their lives were in chaos.

"Soon, I hope, you can return to your homes, but in the meantime, I have found sanctuary for each of you." Père Marc-Mathieu looked at Emilie and Ada. "You must go to Québec to the *Séminaire des Missions-Étrangères*. It is a boarding school that prepares young men for the priesthood. Give this letter to Père Arnaud, the abbot, who will take you both to the women's convent."

He turned to Robert. "And you, Robert, must be kept safe from your own anger as well as that of others. Carry this letter to Frère Gregoire of the Récollet Franciscans. Their monastery is a common-looking house on an obscure street. They allocate one room for a chapel and divide the rest into dormitories or cells. You can stay in one of them in the care of the abbot, who will protect you like a father. He will direct you and find you work, until you can return to Pointe-du-Lac again and live peaceably. Be forewarned, it will be an austere sanctuary. The friars rely on alms and are not allowed to touch money. If they are short of victuals, they go forth and beg. They preach atonement and conversion, and their principal occupation is prayer, meditation, and penance. Their doors are always open to the poor, and the friars share whatever they have with them.

There is no safer place for you. Now, give me the keys to your houses. I promise to care for them."

Emilie frowned and glanced at Robert. The Franciscans were known for their strictness. Could he bear such austerity? But the plan had merit, because the monastery would put Robert beyond anyone's reach and would give him precious time to sort through all the trouble they now found themselves in.

"*Bon,*" Père Marc-Mathieu said with relief. "You must stay off the main roads. From here, go to the small dock on the shore of Lac Saint Pierre. A boat will await you. Say 'boat'. Someone will ask 'For whom'. You must reply 'Pointe-du-Lac'. The boat will carry you east along the Saint Lawrence River to Trois-Riviere. There you will find a carriage that will take you straight to your destinations in Québec." He held out his hand.

Robert tossed Père Marc-Mathieu the keys to the seigneurial mill. Ada heaved a sigh of relief when she delivered hers, but Emilie shot her a look to keep her from saying anything. She knew her mother was worried because of the broken lock and the rogues who had been inside the house. Thankfully, her mother didn't argue.

"Before you go, let us pray together." Père Marc-Mathieu led them to the altar and they knelt.

"Lord, please keep Robert, Emilie, and Ada safe. We also pray for Seigneur Richard, the unhappy person who brought us to this state."

Robert raised his head and stared at the priest, a look of disbelief on his face.

Père Marc-Mathieu ignored him and continued his intense prayers. "Have mercy on him. Touch his heart and reconcile him to You." He made the sign of the cross and rose in haste. "Come, you have no time to lose. May God protect and defend you."

"Thank you, *mon* Père," Emilie whispered as she took hold of the priest's hands and kissed them.

"My heart tells me we shall meet again." Père Marc-Mathieu retired hastily.

Emilie followed Robert and her mother out the door. Père Nicholas bade them farewell with a nod of his head as he slammed shut and locked the door after them with haste.

The moonlight cast a gentle glow as they hiked to the dock on the lake. A man stood waiting next to a rowboat tied to the dock. After the exchange of passwords, the waterman rowed them eastward.

Emilie inhaled the night air. Not a breath of wind stirred. The river lay bright and smooth, and almost motionless except for the gentle undulation of the moonbeams gleaming on the ripples made by their boat. Only the sound of the waves splashing against the pebbly shore and the distant slap of water against the piles of rock lining the shores disturbed the quiet night.

Emilie gazed upon the hills, illuminated by the pale light of the moon, which allowed her to distinguish the cottages and cabins that lined the shore. Somewhere to the west lay her home, now at the mercy of Seigneur Richard, the savage who caused all this turmoil, forever altering their lives. Her dreams for a life filled with love were forever dashed. Nothing would ever be the same. And even though she and Robert loved each other, happiness and marriage existed somewhere far beyond their reach. Emilie shivered in the cool night air. She leaned her elbow on the edge of the boat, laid her forehead on her arm, and feigned sleep, indulging in her need to silently weep.

41

In the morning, Yves dressed and hiked out to his field. He stuck his spade into the ground, kept his foot on the iron rest, and lowered his chin onto his hands, which gripped the tip of the handle. His thoughts swirled with the mysteries of the previous night. As the captain of militia for the parish, church law required that he do something. People had gone missing, brigands had assaulted beggars, and a house had been broken into. But how could he resolve anything when no one could tell him what had happened or why?

In the distance, two men on foot veered across the field toward him. As they drew near, he recognized them as Seigneur Richard's men. Yves straightened and gripped the handle of his shovel tighter.

"I heard you had some trouble, last night." The taller of the two stared hard at him.

"Anything you might know about?" Yves asked with suspicion.

The shorter man stepped forward, punched him in the gut, and elbowed him hard in the back.

Yves fell to his knees.

"Take care, captain, not to talk about anything that happened last night," the first man said.

The other man delivered a swift kick to his ribs.

Yves tumbled to the ground. A sharp pain in his side made it hard to breathe.

"And if you are asked questions, sometimes it's best not to tell the truth. You understand?"

The short man held a knife to Yves's throat. "*Oui*, and never gossip. It can be dangerous to one's health."

"And if I were you," continued the tall man, "I would discourage any gossip among the villagers, if you value your life."

The man with the knife grabbed his ear. "Just a little reminder so you won't forget what we told you today." With a quick flick of his wrist, he sliced off Yves's ear.

42

The scrape of the boat's keel against the pebbled shore roused Emilie. Melancholy gripped her. What had she done to deserve being forced from her home and future husband? She had caught the eye of an unscrupulous seigneur. Some believed beauty to be a blessing, but Emilie believed it was a curse, one that had ruined her entire future. All her life, she had been faithful, God-fearing daughter who guided herself by her virtue and morals according to the church. None of this misfortune was her fault, yet she suffered for it, and the thought angered her. For the first time in her life, she doubted her faith. She dried her tears in secret. Exhausted and spent of emotion, Emilie knew she must fight; she must face the future with courage, and somehow set things right.

Robert jumped out first and helped them alight. He extended the boatman his hand. "*Merci*."

"Think nothing of it. I was happy to help."

Robert pulled some coins from his pocket.

Before he could slip them into the boatman's palm, the man withdrew his hand. "Thank you, but I can't accept your money." He glanced at something behind Robert. "You should go, your carriage is waiting."

Robert looked up the short slope to the road. A man who stood beside a small one-horse carriage waved them over. Robert thanked the boatman again and escorted Emilie and Ada into the carriage. Once they were settled, the driver started the horse forward with a cluck of his tongue and a gentle stroke of the whip.

Fatigue weighed heavily on Emilie after their chaotic night and journey in the incommodious vehicle. For a moment, she envied Robert who closed his eyes and dozed. But she and her mother remained awake, each retreating into their own thoughts. Her mind raced with uncertainty. Every sound threatened - the hoot of an owl, the snort of the horse, the wind that whistled through the trees.

They reached the outskirts of Québec at dawn and wound their way through narrow streets lined with stone structures. At Robert's request, the driver turned into the stable yard of an inn so they could have a brief rest and a quick meal. Emilie's heavy heart knew they must soon part and continue to their separate destinations. Would they meet again soon? Père Marc-Mathieu reassured them they would be safe, but for how long?

Robert tried to pay this driver, too, for he was also to take the women to the convent, but like the boatman, he refused payment. Without a word the man placed his hands behind his back and retreated to tend his horse. Emilie marvelled at the long reaching goodness of Père Marc-Mathieu; the level of respect the people bore for him, the many kindnesses performed on his behalf. She trusted him and it reassured her somewhat. If he said they would be safe at the convent and monastery, then she knew he meant it.

The inn was small, but clean and virtually empty at this early hour of the day. They sat at a table in the farthest corner of the room near the hearth. No one spoke while they shared a frugal meal of cold beef with some crusty bread and cheese. A clutter of emotion, worry, and fatigue stripped them of words. Emilie's thoughts wandered to the wedding she and her mother had spent weeks planning and heaved a deep sigh. It seemed an eternity ago. Before her sat the man she loved, his dark brown eyes weary, yet brimming with love for her. His handsome face bore the strain of the past two days. Were it not for Seigneur Richard's interference, they would have been wed instead of seeking sanctuary like fugitives.

Her mother's awkward glances roved between her and

Robert, as if she wanted to say something, but instead, kept her silence. Far too soon, they finished the meal. Their driver approached, hat in hand, and cleared his throat. "The other carriage has arrived to take the gentleman to his destination."

Robert pushed away from the table, his expression pained. "Emilie, I hate to leave. I wish I could stay."

Emotion constricted her heart. "It pains me not to know how long we'll be apart."

They stood facing each other in silence as long moments passed.

His worried gaze roamed over her. "The longer we delay, the harder it will be." He spoke with regret.

"When we're in sanctuary, we can send word to each other," Ada added.

Emilie fought back her tears; determined Robert's last vision of her would be one of strength and courage- a memory that might ease his worry in the long days to come.

Robert took her in his arms and held her tight. He released her and pressed Ada's hand. "Take care of each other till we meet again," he said in a choked voice.

Tears blurred Emilie's last sight of him as he turned and walked from the room. When would she see him again, enjoy his laughter once more, walk with him among the maple trees? Forced into hiding, how would they survive the austerity of monastic life? Their separation represented a complete and utter loss of even the smallest freedoms. Emilie silently cursed Seigneur Richard, the monster who had turned their lives into bedlam, driving them from every comfort. Her despair mingled with the fear that her life would never be right again.

43

Cool morning rain transformed the roads to muck, slowing their carriage, but the driver soon conveyed Emilie and her mother to the gates of a walled complex near the colony's centre. Above the gates, a large plaque monogrammed with the black letters S.M.E. stood out against a stark white background. The driver alighted and pulled a bell rope set in the column to the right of the heavy wooden gate.

A tonsured friar in a brown cassock approached. After a brief exchange, the driver returned to the carriage and the friar swung open the gate for them to pass through. They rode into a cobblestone courtyard surrounded by the stone walls of the seminary. The friar asked them to wait for the abbot. Emilie and her mother descended from the carriage, stretched their weary legs, and breathed the fresh morning air.

In a few minutes, a tall slender man with a long grey beard and gentle eyes appeared. He was dressed in the same garb as the friar who had permitted them entry. "I am the abbot. What can I do for you, my children?" he asked in a deep, rich voice.

Ada removed the letter from her pocket and handed it to him.

He examined the envelope and looked up with a smile. "Ah, it is from Père Marc-Mathieu! I recognize the handwriting."

By the tone of his voice and the warm expression of his face, Emilie understood he uttered the name of an intimate friend. Relieved, she watched him unfold the note, and read. Periodically, he raised his eyes to study them with an expression of interest. When he finished, he stood for a while, deep in thought, his fingers running back and forth across the fold of the paper. "I am to bring you to the women's convent for refuge." He looked up at the rain. "It's a short walk from here.

I'll summon one of the brethren who will accompany us."

Within moments, he returned with a short, portly friar with a long nose and a milky eye that wandered and seeped tears. The abbot opened the gates and smiled before walking past them down the street. The friar studied them with his wandering eye and gestured for them to follow.

"May I offer a word of caution?" the friar whispered to Emilie.

His eye made it hard to look at him, so she kept her gaze fixed straight ahead. Trepidation filled her and she swallowed. "I would be most grateful."

"At the convent, you will meet La Bonne Soeur. She has been charged with all the novitiates and guests. You must be wary of her." A crooked smile arose on the friar's lips.

It was obvious to Emilie that this man enjoyed a good rumour, so she said nothing and let him talk.

"She is a woman unlike any other, neither a teacher, nor a nun. Many rumours exist about her. They say she was the daughter of a wealthy nobleman, a second cousin to the King of France himself and came to New France as a *Filles de Roi.* The sisters took her in and she helps teach the young native children in the school there. Now a woman in her fifties, they say she is wise and well-respected. Even the abbess often defers to her. It is said that the loss of her son hardened her soul." He lowered his voice and slackened his pace. "Even though she is a married woman, she wears the habit of a novitiate to signify her desire to take the veil someday. Her husband, a vile dangerous man, also banished her son, to be raised anonymously. Although the boy would be a man now, no one, not even the seigneur knows what name he goes by or where he is. She has searched for him her entire life, but never found him."

A chill ran down Emilie's spine. How cruel for a woman to have suffered so.

Up ahead, the abbot waited for them in front of a set of thick wooden doors near a grey colored church with a white belfry. "You may return to the monastery, now," he instructed the friar. "Please have a message sent to Père Marc-Mathieu in Pointe-du-Lac advising him the women have arrived at their destination safely."

The friar bowed his tonsured head, cast Emilie a brief warning glance, and took his leave.

The abbot rapped the iron knocker in the centre of the door three times and waited. A small aperture in the door slid open and the wrinkled face of an old nun peered out at them. "Ah, good evening, Abbot," the nun said in a raspy voice.

"We are here to see the Abbess."

From behind the opening, the nun examined Emilie and her mother from head to toe. She blinked in acknowledgement, opened the door, and permitted them to enter. After taking their wet cloaks, she ushered them into a long narrow room adorned only with several wooden benches, tables, and several religious tapestries. "Please wait here in the entrance hall." She took the abbot through an arched doorway. Several minutes passed before the two returned.

"The abbess has agreed to give you shelter, but you must first see La Bonne Soeur who will assign you to your quarters," the abbot announced.

The nun led them through the same door and into a tight corridor beyond an arched doorway, which led into a cloister.

"When you speak to La Bonne Soeur, be humble and respectful. Her name is Emmanuelle but you must always refer to her as La Bonne Soeur. It is a name she insists upon. Reply frankly to her questions, and when you are not questioned, leave it to me to talk," the abbot instructed.

The nun pointed to the opposite side of the cloister and a door criss-crossed with iron bars. "She will speak to you from there."

Before long, a woman of no more than forty-five years of age in a simple brown gown appeared behind the bars. She entwined her delicate fingers in the interstices and surveyed them as they drew near. Although a great beauty, she seemed worn and hueless. Her pockmarked face revealed she had once survived small-pox. A stiff brown veil stretched over her head, fell on each side, and stood out a little way from her face. A glossy ebony curl escaped onto La Bonne Soeur's temple. Emilie thought it either betrayed her forgetfulness or showed contempt for the strict rules of dress in a convent.

As if plagued by some painful emotion, La Bonne Soeur frowned and wrinkled her forehead. Beneath jet-black eyebrows, she studied Emilie with piercing scrutiny before lowering her eyes. One moment, she solicited affection with a gentle look, yet the next, she appeared to emit a smothered hatred. Her pale cheeks were delicate, but seemed hollow because of her slender physique. A tinge of rose suffused her lips, which contrasted with the paleness of her skin, and like her eyes, their movements were sudden, quick, and full of expression and mystery. Her figure seemed to disappear beneath the stoop of her carriage.

The abbot bowed his head and placed his right hand on his chest. "I trust the abbess has advised you of our visit?"

The woman blinked her eyes in acknowledgement.

The abbot raised his hand towards Emilie. "This is the young woman whom we have been charged to protect. And this is her mother."

Emilie smiled reverently, as did Ada.

La Bonne Soeur gestured her satisfaction with a wave of her hand and turned to the abbot. "It is my good fortune to serve you, but please tell me a little more about the case so I may know what to do to help."

"Please," began Ada.

The abbot silenced her with a glance and focused on La Bonne Soeur. "She has been recommended to me by a Jesuit priest from Pointe-du-Lac. She has been compelled to leave her village to avoid great dangers. She seeks asylum to live where no one will dare molest her, even when-"

"What dangers?" La Bonne Soeur narrowed her eyes. "Be good enough to speak with clarity."

"As you wish." The abbot inhaled. "Dangers, which ought not to be mentioned within hearing distance of your pure ears."

A flash of vexation appeared then faded on La Bonne Soeur's face, but her cheeks retained a slight blush.

"It is enough for you to know that a powerful man persecuted this poor girl with vulgar flatteries, and when he failed, tried to take her by force. Therefore she has been obliged to flee her home."

La Bonne Soeur stared hard at Emilie. "The abbot is a man renowned for his honesty, but no one is better informed about this business than you are. It rests with you to say whether this man we speak of is an odious persecutor or not."

Emilie swallowed, sensing the woman's hostile doubt. Just as she was about to respond, her mother took a step forward.

"I can bear full testimony that my daughter hated this man, as the devil hates holy water. He is the archfiend himself. My poor daughter was betrothed to a young, God-fearing man of good reputation. And if our village priest had done what he ought to, and married them on the day chosen, well, we would not be here. Were it not for Père Marc-Mathieu, a friend of the good abbot-"

"Hold your tongue!" La Bonne Soeur gave Ada a haughty, angry look. "Parents are always too ready to answer for their children!"

Ada drew back, mortified, and cast Emilie a frustrated glare.

Père Arnaud encouraged Emilie with a nod of his head and a gentle smile.

"What my mother began to tell you is the truth. With my own free will I accepted my betrothed's proposal to marry." Her cheeks grew hot. "Forgive me, if I speak too boldly, but I don't wish you to think ill of my mother. If you grant us sanctuary, I assure you that no one will be more grateful or pray for you more earnestly than my mother and I."

"I believe you," said La Bonne Soeur, her tone only slightly softer. "I know all too well how badly these seigneurs behave. But I wish to speak with you in private." She gave the abbot a dismissive glance.

The abbot opened his mouth to say something, but La Bonne Soeur raised her hand and stopped him. "There is no need to thank me. I would not hesitate to ask for the assistance of the good fathers at the Seminaire, should I ever require it." A sardonic smile played across her lips. "Are we not brothers and sisters in Christ?"

Before he could answer, she focused her attention on the nun who had escorted them and crooked her finger to beckon her forward. "Please escort the mother to their rooms. Then return a little later for the young woman."

Ada gave Emilie a pointed look of caution before she followed the nun from the room.

"I'm grateful for your help," the abbot said.

La Bonne Soeur's expression lapsed into neutrality. "You may leave the girl with me now, abbot. I shall see to her."

The abbot's face reddened. "As you wish. May God be with you." He gave Emilie a heartening look before leaving.

La Bonne Soeur leaned closer to the bars to study Emilie.

Emilie yearned to look away from the intense scrutiny, but forced herself to hold the woman's gaze.

La Bonne Soeur hurled her first question. "Is this man evil, deformed? Is that why you fear him?

The strangeness of the question caught Emilie off-guard. Where would this conversation lead? Uncertainty coursed through her. La Bonne Soeur seemed to enjoy the art of intimidation. Emilie had witnessed it against the abbot and her mother. She stood a little taller, refusing to allow this woman to affect her. If she was to live in peace here in the convent, then she must stand courageously before her. "No, he is very handsome."

"If you had not agreed to marry your betrothed, don't you think your reaction to this seigneur might be considered irrational and absurd? After all, you said he is a man of means who could provide well for you."

"My fears are well-founded. His evil ways are known throughout Pointe-du-Lac. I would never sacrifice my future happiness for material comforts, nor would I consider the suit of a man who sins because he does not fear God. Père Marc-Mathieu knows how dangerous he can be, and that is why he urged us to flee."

"Do you love your betrothed?" A wry grin raised one side of her mouth.

"With all my heart."

"Does he treat you well?"

"With utmost kindness."

"And you are still a virgin?" A look of amusement graced La Bonne Soeur's visage.

Emilie's cheeks burned and her mouth fell open. She clenched her fists, her nails pressing into her palms. "I have been taught that a convent is a place of refuge, even for fallen women. My status as a virgin should not matter to anyone but me, my future husband, and God."

La Bonne Soeur's eyes widened.

"But I am far from being a fallen woman," Emilie continued

stoically and not without some irritation at the round of questions posed to her. "*Oui,* I am a virgin and intend to remain so until the day I marry."

A glint of respect shone from La Bonne Soeur's eyes. "And your betrothed, he showed patience and respect in this regard and helped keep you chaste?" Her look became scornful.

Emilie inhaled a deep breath to gather her patience. This line of questioning made no sense, but she had little choice but to play the game. What would happen to them if she destroyed their chances of receiving sanctuary here? She nodded.

"Hm, he must be truly a saint, a rare man indeed."

Emilie ground her teeth, biting back a retort at the woman's sarcasm as her anger surfaced. She had been pushed to the edge by the events of the past two days.

A smile curved La Bonne Soeur's lips and she stood less rigid. "I admire a woman with fire in her soul. You responded to all my questions, and even though some of your answers lacked confidence, you maintained poise. You have been given asylum, but I doubt you will maintain anonymity for too long. Especially when a vexed seigneur is determined to find you. I know all too well the cruelty of such men." Her face twisted with hatred then softened as her gaze flitted back to Emilie. "No man will harm you here. That is my promise. Someone will come to take you to your room. It adjoins the cloister; I dare say you'll find it pleasant enough. Your service to the convent is expected." She turned dismissively and walked away.

44

In the middle of the night, certain that everyone in the convent slept, she crept from her cell. Anticipation drummed a fast cadence in her heart. Her steps light, she descended the stairs to the ground floor and entered the cloister. A half moon shed a dim light. Her hand trembled as she clutched her mantle tight to ward off the chill air. Careful to avoid making any sound, she crossed beneath the archways to the kitchen. She traversed the room, exited into a small herb garden, and crept past the fragrant herbs to the stone wall surrounding the convent. After unlocking a small iron gate, she stepped into freedom and inhaled a deep breath. Already excitement mounted within her.

Her heart raced in expectation. She was on her way to him, dressed for play in a silk chemise, naked beneath it. With each step, she relished the almost liquid feel of the sleek garment flowing across her awakened skin as she edged along the wall.

When she looked up, a gentle light burned in the second-storey window of the gatehouse that loomed next to the front entrance of the convent. The familiar churning within herself returned, as it always did before these encounters. Anxiety, buried deep during daytime hours, bubbled to the surface in anticipation of release.

At the gatehouse door, she made four sharp knocks- their signal. He would not answer. It was not part of the game. She placed her hand on the latch, lifted it, and pushed open the door, cringing at the long creak emitted from its rusty hinges. An air of mustiness filled her nostrils as she endured the sound of another loud rasp when she closed the door behind her.

From the pocket of her mantle, she removed an indigo mask and slipped it over her face. He demanded it. Twenty stairs to the top. She ascended slowly, thumping each foot to enhance his anticipation. At her gentle push, the door at the top opened.

He awaited her in a chair by the hearth.

She lowered her eyes in submission.

He appeared agitated tonight, which caused the tension within her to rise. He knew how she liked their game to go, but he always decided how things were to play out. It was never up to her; she was not worthy enough.

"How fare you this evening, Gaston?" she asked, her tone docile.

"You are late, and you know what that means, Soeur." His tone overflowed with malice.

"Please, Gaston. You must not address me thus," she begged. "You know how you must call me, don't you? You promised." The title mattered. It offered a glimmer of light in the darkness of her life.

"*Mais oui*. La Bonne Soeur." He spit the title from his mouth as if it tasted bad.

"I am grateful to you." She deliberately spoke in a soft voice.

He placed one finger beneath her chin and raised her face to meet his eyes. "Are you ready for our game to begin, La Bonne Soeur?"

The mask she wore blocked her peripheral vision. She could not glance away from the odium reflected in his eyes. "*Oui*, Gaston." Her voice shook in anticipation, so that her answer was nearly inaudible. "*S'il vous plait*," she added, lest she anger him.

"It is much too stuffy in here," he decided aloud, and with a sweep of his hand opened wide the dark, heavy curtains over the solitary window. "There, that's much better."

He swung around to study her. His eyes raked her from head to toe and back again. "Come closer," he commanded, his voice low, yet, ominous like the purr of a tiger as he circled her, his hand trailing along her hips as he went. "Your clothes, take them off. I want to see you fully." Gaston stopped in front of her and kept his voice low, sensuous.

She began, awkwardly at first, to remove her mantle until she stood before him in her delicate chemise.

Glancing nervously at the uncovered window, then back at him, she hesitated.

He arched his eyebrows to remind her of the command she

must obey.

"But, the window," she whispered. "Someone might see me."

"Little is required of you except obedience. You know that," he reminded her. "I can abandon you at anytime, and you must remember that if I do so, it will be forever."

Her shoulders slumped in acceptance as she slid first one shoulder then the next from her garment. It fell in a pool at her feet. She stepped over it. Defenseless, she stood naked before his cold gaze, bare to anyone who may be in the street below who might glance up. Fear of discovery enhanced her guilt, prolonged her unease.

He raked a fingernail down her neck to the depth of her cleavage, leaving a red welt in its wake. Then, taking her nipples between his fingers, he squeezed.

Ecstatic pain drove a shiver along her spine. Almost immediately, heat rushed to her womanhood and moisture dampened her thighs. Again, she sinned, its tentacles of temptation drawing her further into its black depths. She must be punished now- she desired it. God demanded it. She closed her eyes to better savour the sensation- her ragged breathing the only sound in the room other than the occasional crackle and snap of the logs on the fire.

He took her face in his hands and raised it to look at him, capturing her eyes with his. She hated the loathing with which he stared at her, as if he could pierce her soul and discover its secrets. He kissed her, pressing his mouth hard against hers, twining his fingers in her ebony hair, pulling her body to his, searching, tasting, and leaving her breathless when he let her go.

When he caressed her breasts, her chest rose and fell, her breath quickening. Her heartbeat accelerated and her skin moistened. Why must sin bring such pleasure? Why must pleasure be paid for in the currency of pain? Why did pain bring more pleasure? Her passion was a maelstrom that her broken bruised body would never escape. Her life was a sacrifice on the altar of pain at the hands of this cruel, heartless, satanic man. Yet she lived for these moments, to be battered and touched thus.

He forced her to kneel on the wooden floor in front of him, his rough hands on his shoulders shoving her down.

He turned his back to her and walked away, casting off his shirt, hose, and braies. With excruciating slowness, he meticulously folded each garment. Finished, he turned his head to glance back at her, his eyes narrowing for a moment as a wry grin arose on his lips. He reached for a black bag, which lay across the foot of the bed then turned around to face her.

She let out a small gasp at the extent of his arousal.

The fire in his gaze fell onto her naked form. From the black bag came the scent of lilac as he removed a candle, a small rope, and a leather whip. Sweat broke upon her brow when he lit the candle in the hearth.

She shivered with anticipation at the implements.

When he returned to her, he tied her wrists together behind her back. “Don't move,” he growled.

Longing burned within her as her body shook.

She knew her mask would not be adequate. The moment he blindfolded her, disorientation engulfed her. She never knew what was to come. He would make her guess, make her feel exposed, keep her afraid that someone would look up to the window and see her bare, bound, vulnerable, humiliated.

He strode loudly around her so that she could hear each footstep. Goosebumps of fretfulness spotted her arms. Her knees hurt from kneeling on the hard floor. A sudden sharp pain jabbed her nipple as his fingers clamped tightly around it. The sting was immediate, exquisite, and she could not prevent the moan of ecstasy that escaped her lips as he squeezed and pinched it with all his might. She needed this as much as the air she breathed and forced her body to remain rigid, to endure instead of fleeing such pain, for it brought him pleasure, and brought her pleasure too. She must not disappoint him, for if she did, he would stop.

Oh, how she deserved to suffer. Rotting always began from within, and only she knew how spoiled her black soul was because of her sins. The men in her life abhorred her, from her tyrannical father who forced her into a loveless marriage, to the abusive husband she fled from in France, and the seigneur who wed her when she arrived in Québec as a *Filles de Roi*. His enraged face when he discovered her bigamy was etched in her mind; an image she could never banish. She had nearly died from the blow of his fists. She endured each strike without fighting back for she had earned every blow, and hoped they would wash away her guilt. Afterwards, with a ruthlessness beyond her imagination, he forsook their infant son, banishing him from his sight, tossing a mother and child away like flotsam. No one knew what became of the child. Lost forever, like her innocence and her soul. Now, the memory of that beating resurrected itself in her thoughts. She longed for the physical pain that brought respite against the agony in her soul, her black sins. A whimper of urgency escaped her lips.

He breathed in her ear and stroked her hair. "La Bonne Soeur," he hissed with sarcasm. "My distaste for you knows no bounds. Perhaps I should leave you like this and let the nuns find you. No woman is safe with me, but if you obey my every word, you might come to no harm and perhaps live to enjoy more evenings as my pathetic plaything. Or then again, I might choose to end your miserable life then discard your body like shit. What do you think about that?"

His words brought a shudder of fear. She said nothing and waited transfixed for something to follow. It came swiftly.

Sudden heat seared her other breast. She sucked in a breath as the candle flame moved between her sinful breasts. He held it beneath one nipple, briefly, enough for her to feel its torturous agony and smell her singeing flesh. Then he moved the candle to burn the other. Next, hot wax spilled onto her tortured nipples, hot enough to elicit a low moan. Would he go too far this time? Drop by drop, the wax fell against her seared skin, burning away her sin. The aroma of lilac permeated her nostrils more intensely now. Scorching heat from the errant candle forced another moan from her lips. Still, the pain and the ecstasy were not enough. Perhaps he would kill her this time and end her tortured life. She would not be sad if she died in his cruel hands tonight.

"Is it good?" he asked.

"*Oui*, Gaston," she said, barely able to speak.

"I'm so glad. Do you know how much I like to hear you whimper?" He gripped the sides of her head – his grip firm as if to crush her skull.

She could smell the scent of stale sweat, his maleness that rolled off him.

"Now, you know what you must do." He grabbed handfuls of hair and yanked her head forward.

Obediently, her lips parted and her tongue stroked his erect flesh.

She heard him groan with pleasure and he pressed her face harder between his thighs, shoving himself into her throat.

Her heart sang for she could tell from his grunts that she pleased him. A rush of fire came to life within her and she let out a long, delirious moan. Nipples and breasts, raw with agony, she worked eagerly at her task, praying the agony of her flesh would cleanse her of sin.

He raised the whip and thrashed her back, the sound startling, and the pain spurring her desire to satisfy his lust and to atone for the horrors etched onto her lustful heart. God had laid this punishment before her. She must submit body and soul to this abasement and recoil in horror at the exquisite pleasure she found in such pain, such degradation. Woman must suffer pain to atone for her sin in the Garden. Lust, pain, love, pleasure, guilt, it was all the same. God willed it.

"Aaaahhh," she groaned, as a surge of debased, inhuman hurt and delight atoned her wickedness. A scourge of punishment to sear the wretchedness of her sinful heart. She buried her face deeper into his groin, nearly choking as she swallowed him into her depths, demanding the next strike of his lash to scar her wicked flesh.

45

Seigneur Richard paced the length of his bedroom. Now and then he stopped to move aside the brocade curtains and peer out the window. He had waited for Emilie's arrival all night, but dawn came and went. To abduct a young woman was a bold endeavour, the chances for success low, the risks high. He ran his fingers through his hair. Where were they? Could something have gone wrong? No, he must keep his faith and trust in Thomas' plans.

From the moment he first saw her, Emilie Basseaux haunted his every thought and infiltrated every dream. He pondered how she would look in the morning with her chestnut hair tousled after a night of lovemaking, or her pretty smile from across the table when she looked at him with her fathomless brown eyes as they shared a meal together; the look of joy on her face with a babe suckling at her breast. His obsession for her seemed endless. It mattered naught that she was of a lower rank. In this new world, women were a scarcity and the lines drawn by society were often overlooked. She was his and he would allow no other man to possess her.

Why had she caught his fancy so? Because she had spurned him? Because she preferred a poor miller to a wealthy and powerful man like him? He failed to fathom why, for his wealth and rank made it easy to attract women. Except for Emilie who remained aloof; a gem beyond his reach. Emilie. He savoured her name, conjuring her vision in his mind. He would have her, of that he had no doubt. He was seigneur of Pointe-du-Lac. His authority gave him absolute control. Nothing could prevent him from acquiring his prize – nothing!

No one who might suspect him of taking the girl would be stupid enough to come to his home looking for her. That rash fool of a miller, Robert Lanzille, wouldn't dare try. Neither would the priest or the mother. If they did, he would make them regret it. And he couldn't wait to see the look on his cousin Pierre's face when he realized he had lost the wager and would be forced to pay up.

Envisioning the flatteries and promises he would make to Emilie to gain her confidence and acquire control over her, soothed his doubts, and nourished his passion. At first, she might be terrified to find herself alone with him, but she would get used to him. She was the ideal woman to marry; beautiful, virtuous, soft-spoken, biddable, and he was a wealthy man. A woman could overlook much when it meant living in luxury.

From outdoors came the crunch of footsteps against gravel and he went back to the window and looked out. Thomas and the men had returned, but he didn't see the girl with them. He clenched his jaw and left the room to greet them. Thomas had a lot of explaining to do.

46

Thomas tossed his beggar's clothes into a corner of the ground-floor entrance. As he turned to climb the stairs to render his account, Seigneur Richard descended with a scowl.

"Well? Where is she, you boaster? You failed. Leave it to me, you said." His narrowed eyes glinted with ire.

Thomas met the stare without expression despite the anger that raged inside him. For years he had served this man loyally, without question, in exchange for protection from the law after he had murdered a priest at the behest of a voyageur who had found him in bed with his wife.

Lately, however, he had become frustrated at Seigneur Richard's demands and superior attitude. The man commanded him as if he were a beast of burden. Tight with his money, the pompous seigneur rarely paid Thomas adequately for the risks he was forced to take. Seigneur Richard was nothing more than a spoiled nobleman, used to getting his way, snubbing those of lower rank. One day, Thomas would find a way to free himself of him. Time would erase the memory of his crime. Until then, he must endure. He returned the Seigneur's look without wavering. "It's unfair to be greeted with reproaches after having laboured so faithfully, and doing one's duty at the risk of one's life."

Seigneur Richard's countenance relaxed a little. He gestured for Thomas to follow him into the parlour and invited him to sit in one of two chairs set before a desk. "What happened?"

In a neutral voice, Thomas recounted the details of the stymied undertaking.

Seigneur Richard listened without interruption. Then he leaned back in his chair, steepled his fingertips together, and gave him a look as if to judge the veracity of the explanation.

"You are not to blame. It sounds like they were forewarned, but by who? No one outside this house knew what we had planned. If there's a spy under this roof, I'll find out, and he'll wish he had never been born."

"I suspected the same." Thomas rubbed his chin. "If it's true, and we discover who betrayed us, let me deal with him for having caused me all this trouble." He paused. "Maybe there's a reason this happened, which we haven't yet discovered."

"Do you think someone recognized you?"

Thomas shook his head. "No, I was careful and the ragged beggar's clothes I wore provided ample cover. Afterward, I sent two men to visit the parish captain of the militia to ensure he filed no report of the matter. We left him with a permanent reminder of our warning." Thomas made a slicing motion at his ear. "Trust me when I say he's too scared to pose a problem."

Seigneur Richard nodded. "Have two men watch the girl's house and get rid of anyone who comes nosing about. In the meantime, take some men and roam about Pointe-du-Lac for any rumours. I want to know exactly who knows what."

"I'll find out, don't worry." Thomas paused to rub his sleep-deprived eyes. "Someone's going to pay for all this trouble." And in his mind came the thought that he would also make Seigneur Richard pay too.

47

Seigneur Richard rode to Pierre's house on the opposite side of the settlement.

"Come to pay up on our wager already?" Pierre asked with a smug look.

Seigneur Richard dismounted and tossed the reins to a stable lad who scurried out of the barn at his approach. "I'll pay the wager, if I have to, but that isn't why I've come. I need to speak with you. I told you nothing before, because, well, I confess, I thought to surprise you with my victory this morning. But, I should let you know what happened."

Pierre frowned. "Come inside, you can tell me everything over the morning meal."

Seigneur Richard followed him into the dining room where servants set another plate. The smell of bread and pork sausages wafted in from the nearby kitchen. Because of the drought, it had become difficult to acquire flour, but some seigneurs hoarded it, so he was not surprised Pierre had an ample supply.

Pierre waited for the servants to leave the room, then leaned forward across the table. "Tell me what's bothering you."

Seigneur Richard heaved a sigh before he relayed his plan to abduct Emilie and all that had gone awry.

"I'm convinced the Jesuit priest is involved somehow." Pierre toyed with the knife beside his plate. "I always believed him to be a hypocrite. They call him 'The Saint', yet I've never liked him, and I don't trust him. You should have told me earlier about your argument with him."

"Well, I've told you now," Seigneur Richard glowered.

Pierre shook his head. "I can't believe you allowed him to speak to you in such a manner then leave. It's not like you to pass up an opportunity for a little revenge."

"What? And have me earn the wrath of the clergy?"

"I'll help you get rid of Père Marc-Mathieu. He'll soon learn he can't speak to seigneurs of our rank disrespectfully."

"Don't make matters worse."

"Trust me for once, cousin."

"What do you intend to do, Pierre?"

"I don't know yet, but rest assured he won't bother you anymore. Don't forget, our uncle is part of the Sovereign Council and owns the largest seigneury near Sillery. I'll solicit his help when I see him next week. He has influence with the

Church."

Breakfast was announced and served.

Seigneur Richard waited for the servants to leave. "There's no proof of my involvement in this. And even if there were, I'm not worried. The captain has been warned, at the risk of his life, to make no report about anything that occurred last night. So, I'm confident nothing will come of it."

"Even if the parish captain of the militia dares make a report, it will have to go to Antoine Rivet, and that obstinate, addled magistrate, knows his duty is to you. He'll bury any documentation."

"It's a wonder Rivet feels loyal to me at all, what with you contradicting and laughing at him all the time."

Pierre gave him a look of admonishment. "I think you're afraid."

"No, all I'm saying is we must be careful."

Pierre reached for another piece of bread, broke off a chunk, and popped it into his mouth. "That's true. This is a serious matter." He chewed as he spoke. "I'll visit the magistrate in person and forewarn him to ignore anything that comes his way."

"And if he disagrees?"

Pierre grinned. "I'll remind him of the far-reaching arms of our beloved uncle who holds the biggest seigneury in all of New France, a close friend of the Governor and a member of the Sovereign Council appointed by the King. One word from our uncle, and Rivet would lose everything. That will shut him up. Just like it will shut up the Jesuit priest."

Seigneur Richard heaved a sigh. "Good, that will be one less thing to worry about."

Pierre nodded and gave him a smug look. "You'll be safe from repercussion. Power feels good, does it not?"

48

"Well, what did you and your spies learn?" Seigneur Richard stared at Thomas and tapped his fingertips on the writing table. It was midday already and Thomas looked tired. The man hadn't slept all night, but there was plenty of time for rest once this matter was settled. After his discussion with Pierre, he experienced a surge of confidence. If he planned things carefully, nothing could stop him from acquiring Emilie, not even the law.

Thomas heaved a sigh. "The disappearance of three people has stirred up a whirlwind of talk. Père Jean's housekeeper, Rose, was assailed with questions from the villagers about what occurred there last night. It's a good thing for us she's not one to keep her mouth shut because I learned that Emilie, Robert and two other men got past her somehow and accosted the priest. That's why we found the girl's house empty. They were with the priest attempting to trick him into marrying them."

Seigneur Richard opened his mouth to say something, but Thomas raised his hand to stop him. "Don't worry. Their attempt failed miserably. The priest shouted for the captain of the parish militia who tolled the church bells to summon help. The bride and groom fled before they could finish speaking their vows."

"Who were the two men who accompanied the bride and groom?

"A friend of Robert's by the name of Denis and his mindless brother, Gervaise. Denis told his wife everything and her mouth is flapping like a flag in the wind."

Seigneur Richard rolled his eyes and shook his head. "Never trust a woman to keep her mouth shut."

"Then there's the boy we caught in the house. His parents

are afraid because he was used in an undertaking against you, so they're keeping him shut up inside the house. Another thing we don't have to worry about." Thomas inhaled a deep breath. "But it's our invasion of the girl's home that is causing the worst speculation. I can understand why, too. It's a serious event, but nobody knows anything about it. Your name is being whispered, but it is all conjecture and dissonance. Much is being said about our men who watched the street and the inn. Thank goodness the innkeeper is a man who hates gossip and knows how to keep his lips sealed."

"Can anyone identify you?"

"As you know, I was disguised as a beggar. Some believe I was a poor soul who came to aid the women. Others think I was a vagrant or an imposter who came by night to steal or ravage the women. Certain people believe I was murdered because I was about to arouse the village. There are so many rumors, no one will ever learn the truth. We are safe in that regard too."

Seigneur Richard breathed a sigh of relief and leaned forward in his chair. "Where are Robert and Emilie now?

"They fled with the mother to Trois-Riviere. After that, no one knows."

"Fled together! Find them. Until then, I can have no peace. Go to Trois-Riviere immediately. I'll pay you four *ecus* and promise you my protection." He slammed his fist on the table. "And that villainous priest!" The words burst hoarsely from Seigneur Richard's throat, half-smothered between his teeth. He puckered his face in response to the brutal passion mounting inside him. "He interfered somehow and he shall answer for it, Thomas."

49

Later that day, Thomas returned to speak to Seigneur Richard. "They are in Québec. The girl and her mother were brought to the women's convent, and Robert is with the Récollets Franciscans."

Malicious satisfaction arose in Seigneur Richard. Hope that he might accomplish his wicked designs seeped back into his thoughts. He withdrew a leather money pouch from the top drawer of his writing table and tossed it to Thomas. "Excellent work. There's sixteen *ecus* in there; the four I promised you earlier to go to Trois-Rivere, and twelve more to go to Québec and fetch Emilie."

Thomas shook his head as though about to refuse. "You want me to go?"

Seigneur Richard frowned. "Didn't I make myself clear?"

"You should send someone else."

Seigneur Richard narrowed his eyes. "Why?"

"I have always been grateful for your protection, but I doubt you would risk my life unnecessarily."

Seigneur Richard frowned. "What do you mean?

"There is more than one price on my head. Here in Pointe-du-Lac I am under your protection. Magistrate Rivet is your friend and he ignores my presence. I live quietly here, but I am too well known in Québec. Anyone who turns me in, alive or dead, would receive fifty gold *louis*."

Seigneur Richard shook his head as though he didn't believe it. "You're afraid!"

"*Non,* you know I've proven my courage to you many times."

"So, prove it again."

Thomas stared at his hands. Silence fell upon them like a pall. He looked into his master's eye. Hatred burned in his soul.

"Forget what I said. I'll go."

"I didn't say you should go alone. Take some of the men with you and go with a good heart. Don't worry about the fifty *louis* reward. I'm not unknown in Québec and a servant of mine would not be treated badly there." He studied Thomas's red eyes. "Get some sleep first. I expect you to have your wits about you. You can set out early in the morning." The man was more than loyal, with cunning and brains, and there was no one he trusted more to complete the job. He leaned back in his chair and watched Thomas leave.

Seigneur Richard strode to look out the window. Of everyone he knew, Thomas alone could bring the girl to him. It was only a matter of time. He needed to find a way to keep Robert from her, and the surest way to accomplish that was through shrewd use of the law.

He decided to speak to Antoine Rivet. With so many obscure laws, Antoine was certain to find one to suit his purposes; some quarrel to pick, some charge to lay against Robert Lanzille. Seigneur Richard grinned. How easy it would be to put a price on the miller's head.

50

Robert's impatience flared. The rain had stopped, but it had left mud and deep ruts in the road, which made progress slow. The driver of his carriage lost his way in the maze of streets. Robert spotted a well-dressed man hurrying through the deluge and asked for directions to the Récollets monastery.

"It is not far from here. That narrow street leads to the monastery and you cannot mistake it." The man lifted his collar and tilted his hat against the cold, and continued on his way.

They followed the man's directions until the monastery came into view, but the road that led to it became narrower and grew muddier.

"I can walk from here." Robert thanked the driver and offered him payment, but like the others, the man refused. With a nod of his head, the driver turned the carriage around and headed in the opposite direction.

Robert huddled beneath his coat and as he maneuvered around the puddles, noticed a loaf of bread laying on a patch of grass. Someone must have dropped it. How unusual to find it scattered in such a haphazard manner. More loaves lay scattered up ahead. In disbelief, he picked one up. It was fresh, round, and of a quality few could afford. It must have recently been dropped because it was not sodden from the damp. Why would someone have discarded it like refuse? His stomach rumbled with hunger and he stared at the bread. It tantalized, and despite the pang of guilt that possessed him, he decided to pick it up. Besides, if the owner came forward, he'd gladly pay for it. He stuffed a loaf into each pocket on the inside of his coat, took a bite out of the third, and proceeded on his way, more uncertain than ever.

A man and woman with a young boy walked towards him. Flour dusted their faces and tattered clothes. The woman held up the hem of her gown to form a makeshift container. Within it she carried loose flour, which overflowed and sprinkled over the ground. Although her legs were exposed to the knees, she tottered on despite the unwieldy burden she carried. A small sack of flour hung from a rope around her waist while the man and boy each carried a sack on their back. The boy staggered under the weight of his burden. A scatter of flour escaped from a small hole at every stumble and waver of his balance. Weighed down by a basket of bread, which hung from his arm, the lad lagged behind. When he ran to catch up, the basket tipped and two loaves fell out.

"Don't you dare allow another loaf to fall," the mother

snarled.

"I don't *allow* them to fall. I can't help it," he whined.

"It's a good thing my hands are occupied," she snapped. Still gripping her hem, she shook her fist at him. This caused a fresh cloud of flour to shoot into the air.

"Pick them up or somebody will do it for us," the man growled. "We've been hungry for a long time."

More people now filled the street. A man stopped the woman. "Where did you get the flour and bread?"

"Back there," she replied with a gesture.

Desperation and hunger clouded every face Robert encountered. Where had they gained access to bread and flour in this shortage?

Down the street stood the church and Récollets monastery. Robert tucked the remaining half loaf of bread into his coat and went straight to the door. He pulled out his letter, held it ready in his hand, and yanked on the bell rope. In mere moments, a small aperture in the door slid open and the weathered face of the porter appeared behind the grate. "Who is here?"

"I bring an important letter to Frère Bonaventure from Père Marc-Mathieu of Pointe-du-Lac."

"Give it me." The porter stuck his gnarled hand through the grate.

"No, I must deliver it to him in person."

"He's not here."

"May I come in and wait for him?"

"You may wait in the church. At present, you cannot be admitted into the monastery." The porter slammed the wicket shut.

Robert stood irresolute. He took a few steps towards the door of the church, but changed his mind. Instead, he returned to the road and stood with his arms crossed to watch the growing crowd. He took out the half-eaten loaf of bread, chewed a piece, and made his way into the multitude.

Amid a steady increase of people, Robert wandered the streets. At every turn, ravenous, hollow-eyed folk with hungry children in tow fled with sacks of flour slung over shoulders or bread loaves tucked beneath arms. Others, empty-handed, rushed in the opposite direction for their share of the spoils. An air of rebelliousness lingered. Robert had never seen anything like this before. The people were rioting.

Two years of food scarcity and drought had caused immense suffering. It seemed things were as dire here as in Pointe-du-Lac. Circumstances always worsened in the spring when provisions were at their lowest and ships bearing seeds and products had yet to arrive in port. Seigneurs owned exclusive milling privilege, with *habitants* bound by title deed to bring their grist to his mill and surrender one-fourteenth of their grain.

Seigneurial mills like the one he operated were not efficient either. Crude, awkward, poorly built affairs; they did little more than crack the wheat into coarse meal, which hardly passed as flour. Robert often complained the product was unfit for consumption. His own banal mill was fitted with clumsy wind-wheels, somewhat after the Dutch fashion. The weather often failed them, however, and the *habitants* would hold their grist for days, waiting for a wind to turn the wheels.

As the people grew hungrier, Robert heard rumours of many who starved to death rather than beg or admit to being poor, for the French were a proud lot. The English fared a little better, but not by much. They sustained themselves longer on potatoes, whereas the French considered them distasteful and unfit for human consumption.

All around him, the passion of the crowd increased. Some, like Robert, stood watching the desperation in every face. He listened to snippets of conversation as people rushed past. Hope for the forthcoming year dwindled. Land remained uncultivated and deserted by the *habitants*, who instead of working to provide sustenance for them and others were forced to forage for food.

Robert listened to the enraged crowd around him. He caught snippets of conversation about overflowing granaries and immense quantities of grain secretly dispatched to France. People raced past him, but where to?

It was mid-morning and Robert noticed a delivery boy step out of a nearby bake-house with a basket loaded with bread. A man snatched the basket from him. "Let me see!" The boy tried to protest, but the words died on his lips when a small crowd surrounded him. He slackened his arms to disengage himself from the straps.

"Give us the basket!" the crowd chanted. Many hands seized it and pulled it to the ground.

"We want bread!" A man grabbed a loaf and tore a huge chunk from it with his mouth.

Frenzied hands pillaged the basket until all the bread disappeared. Those who got none, raced off, shouting, "To the bake-houses!"

The crowd swept Robert along to the bake-house where the baker questioned the visibly upset lad. They turned, gaped at the swarm of people heading in their direction, and dashed into the shop, bolting the door behind them. The crazed mob rushed the door, pounding and shouting for the baker to open.

"Stop," Robert called out in an effort to calm the frenzy. "This is not the way!" The dissonance that surrounded him drowned his pleas. To see such naked wrath made him wish he could do something to help.

The militia arrived; a troop of twenty men armed with muskets running down the street. He hoped they could calm the tumult before someone got hurt, but he held out little hope.

What good could so few men do against such a multitude? Much to Robert's amazement, the throng gave way as the militiamen pushed their way to the front of the shop.

The captain faced the mob. "Friends," he yelled, his arms raised high to quiet the people. "Go home. We don't want anyone harmed. No good will come of rioting." He moved forward to drive the people away.

"Move back," the militiamen snarled as they followed his lead and threw themselves into the mass of people, pushing them back with the butt of their weapons. The people protested as they retreated, pressing against those behind them. The people at the rear continued to shove their way forward. Screams of those trapped in the middle resounded as the throng crushed them from both sides.

"Make room! Give way!" the captain bellowed with alarm. Robert heard him as he turned to the nearest of his men and said, "Don't hurt anyone, but circle the shop to protect it."

The baker peered out from an upper story window then disappeared. Some attempted to breach the line of militiamen, but were threatened with the muskets.

"Go home," the captain called out. "Rioting is a hanging offence!"

"Bread! Open!" the horde screeched savagely.

"You'll have bread, but this is not the way," the captain called out. Someone hurled a large rock, which struck him in the forehead, and he fell, slumped over his gun. His men pulled his body behind them.

The people brandished stones, sticks, and iron bars at the bake-house. The baker and shop-boys appeared at all the upper windows, armed with bricks and stones likely ripped from a hearth. "Leave us alone!"

The crowd responded with shouts and gestures.

The baker and his boys hurled their rocks and bricks.

Screams cleaved the air as the rocks struck their mark and people fell. One blood-curdling scream came from the centre of the throng of people. "You killed him," a woman shrieked. Fury increased the crowd's wrath and they surged forward and broke through the line of militiamen.

Robert watched in horror as the door of the bake-house gave way and the crowd poured inside like a torrent of water. The too few militiamen, volunteers who were poorly trained, were overwhelmed. People fell and were trampled. Looters emerged with clay jars, money, flour, bread, and even pieces of the counter. Several women and children scurried forward to gather loaves or sacks of flour that were accidentally dropped, while others ran with balls of dough in their grasp. People pushed and fought in a mist of white flour that arose in clouds and cascaded upon everyone and everything.

Trapped, Robert pushed his way out of the crowd. Once free, he noticed two militiamen pointing at various people. One held an inkpot and the other dipped his quill and made notes in a brown book. The one with the inkwell stared at him. He leaned over and said something to his partner who glared at Robert through narrowed eyes before scribbling a notation.

A rioter leaped onto a nearby wall. "The Intendent keeps bread from us. He is to blame for the high costs and lines his pocket on the backs of our labour and sweat."

Robert could not deny the man's words. The Intendent administrated the financial affairs and economics in all of New France.

"Seigneurs are the real thieves," shouted another.

"*Oui*, but the Intendent is at the head of them," replied the man on the wall. "He oversees the distribution of grain and corn."

Robert lost track of time and looked up at the dark sky. He should make his way back to the monastery. A cold breeze blew over the thinning crowd. Structures, defaced with stones and bricks, existed at every turn- broken windows and destroyed doors everywhere. People ran past him hauling bins, tubs, the pole of a kneading instrument, a bench, a basket, a journal, a book or other items belonging to a bake-house. Strange how everyone ran in the same direction, likely to some fixed place.

Curious, Robert wound his way back to the monastery. He came to a bonfire in the middle of a street fueled with the accoutrements of the plundered bake-houses. Around it, people danced and clapped their hands, the sound mingling with the roar of a thousand shouts of triumph. Smoke and flames blazed as bystanders shouted, "Death to those who starve us! Away with hunger!"

Robert shook his head. The destruction of sieves and kneading-troughs and the pillaging of bake-houses was not the wisest way to ensure a steady supply of bread in the future, but this would never enter the minds of starving, fired-up people.

Rumours circulated that another bake-house had come under siege. The crowd broke up and rushed away in a frenzied gaggle to the next unfortunate target. The torrent dragged Robert along. He desperately wanted to get to the monastery, but his conscience would not let him. Perhaps there was something he could do to prevent some of the rioting or the destruction of the next bake-house. At the risk of broken bones or worse, he chose not to mingle in the thickest part of the crowd, but kept himself at a distance. His stomach rumbled with hunger. He removed the second loaf from his coat, and, biting off a mouthful, followed the clamorous multitude to the bake-house.

When he arrived, instead of the crowd he expected to find already at work, he saw only a few irresolute men and women hovering some distance from the shop, which was fastened up and protected by armed militiamen at the windows. Most of the crowd turned back and paused; some continued onward in random directions, while others remained behind. An ill-omened voice arose from the midst of the crowd. "The house of the Intendent is close by. Let's go!" The crowd moved with unanimous fury, hauling Robert along with it.

51

The Intendent of New France, Jean Bochart de Champigny sat alone in the dining room at the head of a long table, digesting a meager dinner of venison stew and a chunk of coarse bread. He paused when an urgent pounding sounded on the front door. One of his servants answered and he heard an excited exchange before his valet rushed into the dining room. "*Mon* Seigneur, an angry crowd is headed here to accost you. You are in grave danger."

"What for?"

"They are hungry and there is no bread."

He rose to the window. A mob rushed into sight, weaving towards his house. The servants locked the doors and windows.

"Go out through the back door," he ordered his valet. "Hurry to Chateau Saint-Louis. Tell the Governor we need help! Tell him to send troops."

Outside, the howls of the horde increased as they hurled stones. The sound resounded through every corner of the house.

The valet paled and hesitated.

"Go now! And make haste!" the Intendent shouted.

The valet turned and fled.

The shouts of the crowd grew louder, angrier. "We want the Intendent, dead or alive!"

"Face us, you tyrant!"

"You are starving us!"

He wandered from room to room, breathless with terror, imploring his servants to stand firm until they found a way to escape. But, how, and where? He took the stairs two at a time to the garret, and there, through an aperture between the ceiling and floor, looked out onto the street. Hundreds of people blocked the road in both directions. He prayed for the tumult to abate. Instead, the uproar became more savage; the blows against his door more frequent. His heart sank.

52

Carried along by the crowd, Robert found himself an unwilling participant. He wanted justice too, but when the crowd shouted for the Intendent's blood and threatened to kill him, he recoiled with abhorrence, for he could never abet murder.

Robert stood near the front door of the Intendent's manor house while the vicious throng assailed it. They hammered at the lock to break it open. Others pounded on the door with stakes, chisels, or hammers. Some, with sharp stones, blunted knives, broken pieces of iron, nails, and even their fingernails, defaced walls to loosen the bricks and form a breach. Those too far away to reach shouted encouragement from behind.

By the time the militia arrived, the house was surrounded. The troop halted at one end of the street, unable to get any closer.

The mass of people grew still.

“Everyone go home,” the militia leader shouted.

The throng replied with a deep and prolonged grumble; but no one moved.

The leader hesitated, as if unsure what to do next, outnumbered by the mass of rioters.

The crowd taunted the soldiers with mocks and jeers.

At the house, the battering against the door and walls

continued. Among them was an old, half-starved man, who rolled his sunken, fiery eyes, and composed his wrinkled face into a smile of diabolical complacency. He raised a hammer, rope, and four large nails above his hoary head. "I'll nail the bastard to the posts of my own door, alive as he is. He'll die a slow death!"

"For shame!" Robert scolded, horrified at the bloodlust.

Others looked askance at the old man, disturbed by his words.

This encouraged Robert. "You would murder the Intendent? It is not up to us to issue justice. We must follow proper protocols and make our complaints lawfully."

"You dog! Traitor to New France!" the old man shouted, his face purple with rage. "You must be a servant of the Intendent. Get him!"

Robert tried to turn back around as the crowd surged toward him. Some who supported him, encircled him and shouted back. He'd had enough. He had been a fool to think he could exert any influence over people in the clutches of such madness. All he wanted now was to leave this tumult behind him and get to the monastery. He struggled to elbow his way out.

"The Governor has arrived!" someone shouted.

Curses and shouts of praise burst from the crowd. Everyone turned their heads to watch the Governor's carriage approach.

"He has come to take the Intendent prisoner for the lack of justice dealt to us!" someone bellowed.

Perhaps there could be a peaceful solution to this riot, Robert thought. He decided to do all he could to help the Governor and sought to catch a glimpse of him, but it was no easy matter. The carriage proceeded a little way into the crowd, but could go no further because of the sheer volume of people in its path. Somehow, Robert managed to elbow his way to it.

The Governor, Louis-Hector de Callière, peered out one

window then the other. He wore a long white wig and had a long, narrow face with high cheekbones and eyes that darted about assessing the situation. Robert had heard much about him. The year before, he had negotiated a peace treaty between the Iroquois and a number of western tribes allied with the French. Some people believed him to be inflexible and high-handed, but Callière was respected for his leadership during the wars with the English and the Iroquois. Surely, he could appease this crowd.

Robert saw him mouth words, but he could not hear what he said because of the jeers of the roaring people. The Governor waved warmly and gestured for them to let him pass.

The crowd parted a little, but not enough.

"Make room, if you please," the Governor called out.

"Long live the Governor! We will have justice," the crowd chanted.

"*Oui*, I promise." The Governor placed his hand on his heart. "A little room please. I am here to deal with the Intendent." He leaned forward and called out to his driver. "Go on, if you can."

The coachman gave the multitude a smile of gracious condescension, and with ineffable politeness, waved his whip to the right and left. "Be good enough to make a little room."

Robert put aside every thought of leaving and tried to encourage the crowd to step back. Others followed his lead until a path opened and the carriage moved forward. The Governor stuck his head out the window again and lavished the crowd with his gratitude. He caught Robert's gaze and acknowledged him with more than one smile.

Delighted, Robert smiled back, certain the Governor would remember him well.

The carriage advanced slowly. The distance to the Intendent's house was a stone's throw; but it seemed infinite. The crowd surrounded the carriage, their voices a storm, shrill and discordant.

Robert and several others begged and threatened until they guided the carriage to the Intendent's house. The coachman jumped off, let down the carriage steps, and the Governor stepped out. The crowd craned their necks to catch a glimpse of the highest-ranking official of New France. Their curiosity produced a long span of silence.

The Governor stood for a moment, glanced around, and saluted the people with a bow.

Robert placed himself in the Governor's path and kept the crowd away with his shoulders as the man followed him to the door. The hinges were almost wrenched out of the pillars. The doorposts were in pieces, crushed and forced. Through a large hole in the door, a piece of chain was visible, twisted, bent, and almost broken in two.

"Open for the Governor," Robert shouted into the aperture.

From inside the house, someone yanked off the chain and partially opened the broken door wide enough for a man to slip through.

"Quick," huffed the Governor. "Let me in." He turned to Robert. "Keep the people back; don't let them follow me!" He turned and squeezed his body through the narrow opening, closing the door as best as he could while others braced it with bars.

Outside, Robert and a few other men laboured with shoulders, arms, and cries, to keep the space clear.

The crowd fell silent as they waited.

Before long, the door opened. The Governor led the way, followed by the Intendent, who crept along behind his deliverer. "Keep your mouth shut and I'll get you out of this mess," the Governor said to the Intendent.

Robert heard the comment and realized the Governor didn't care what happened to the Intendent as long as this riot ended without bloodshed. He and the others, who had kept the space clear, now raised their hands and hats to shield the Intendent from the perilous gaze of the populace long enough for him to enter and hide himself within the carriage.

The Governor followed the Intendent in and shut the door. As soon as the Governor seated himself, Robert overheard him warn the Intendent to keep concealed in the corner, and not show himself. At that moment, Robert understood there would be no justice. The Governor protected the Intendent, nothing more.

As the carriage pulled away, the Governor stuck his head out the window and took one last long and extensive look at Robert before the carriage disappeared from view.

53

After the Governor's carriage rolled away unimpeded by the crowd, Robert looked about. Twilight spread its somberness over the streets and weary people shuffled home. For a while, he walked among the dispersing crowd then turned into a less congested street. Hungry, he looked for an inn, knowing it was too late to go to the monastery.

Robert walked on and paused near a group of men huddled together discussing something. He listened and when he heard them plot to riot the next day, he could not resist joining them. "Food scarcity isn't the only inequity. We must voice our concerns until all our grievances are resolved. Some seigneurs are tyrants who make our lives miserable and believe they are always right. The more tyrannical their actions, the higher they esteem themselves. I say there are far too many of them. Why suffer feudalism in this new world? The English don't suffer such tyrannical overlords. They grant land freely, without encumbrances, so why should we, the French?"

"*Oui*, there are far too many seigneurs," agreed one man.

Robert rested his hands on his hips. "And the laws never apply to them. Try to seek justice like I did and you will come away unsatisfied. It's enough to make honest men turn desperate. Yes, the seigneurs also desire good and just laws, but when they break those laws, nothing is done because they are in league with each other. We must seek an audience with the Governor tomorrow and tell him how things stand."

The men looked at him with blank faces, pondering his words.

"Let me explain: there is a law authorized by the Governor and Intendent which applied perfectly to my situation. It should have given me justice, but the magistrate refused to apply the law against the seigneur who aggrieves me. The Governor ought to order all magistrates to indict anyone responsible for iniquities. If the punishment is imprisonment according to the law, they should go to jail, no matter who they are or what their rank is. Don't you agree?" Robert asked.

After some applause, although the majority nodded in agreement, others walked away shaking their heads. Those who remained agreed to meet the next day in front of the church for further discussions.

"Now, who can direct me to an inn where I can eat and lodge for the night?" Robert asked.

"I am at your service." A middle-aged man who stood aloof listening to his harangue, stepped forward. "I'll take you to one and introduce you to the proprietor."

Robert smiled. "Is it far?"

"Not far." The man's left eyebrow raised a fraction.

Robert shook his new acquaintance's hand and set off with him. "My thanks for your assistance."

"No thanks necessary," the man said as he shouldered his way through the crowd and waited for Robert to catch up.

"Where do you hail from?"

"Pointe-du-Lac. I used to operate the mill there."

They strolled casually side-by-side now.

"From your speech it seems you've been badly treated," the man commented.

Robert's mood soured. "I spoke carefully to avoid making my private affairs public, but one day my problems will become known, then-" Robert stopped. Across the street, a sign that read The Full Moon swayed in the breeze above a shabby door. "Here's an inn. This one will do just fine."

The man nudged his elbow. "No, not this one. The one I told you about is only a little further on."

Robert shook his head. "I don't need anything elaborate. Simple fare and a straw mattress are enough for me. Please, come inside with me and allow me to buy you a drink."

A flicker of frustration flashed across the man's face then faded. "I accept."

Inside, two large candle chandeliers suspended from hooks in a ceiling beam illuminated the long narrow room. A scurvy looking lot of men lounged on benches along both sides of one long table. Judging by the ragged look of these denizens, Robert surmised they seemed passionately devoted to the avoidance of work. Some played cards or cast dice amid tables laden with flagons and tankards, dishes and cups. Many had toppled over making the table wet. The clamour in the room was near deafening. A smell of unwashed bodies, ale, and onions wafted through the air.

A serving boy hastened back and forth carrying dishes and cups or chessboards and dice. The innkeeper, a sunken-cheeked man with red hair and a neatly trimmed auburn beard, sat alone at a table near the fireplace occupied in tallying sums from a stack of papers. Periodically, he lifted his gaze to scrutinize what was happening. When he noticed them, he rose and advanced towards them, his face a mask set in a perpetual frown. "What can I do for you?"

"A good flask of ale and something to eat." Robert took a seat at one end of the table and his companion sat across from him. It felt good to sit after having walked for so long. Almost immediately, his thoughts wandered to Emilie, Ada, and the table he had shared with them. The memory forced a sigh and he shook his head to drive away the thoughts.

The proprietor returned with a flagon and two pewter tankards and banged them down in front of them. Robert poured and slid a cup towards his new friend. "To moisten your lips," he said as he filled his own cup, emptied it in one draught, and looked up at the proprietor. "What can you bring us to eat?"

"Cassoulet. That's all I have."

Robert puckered his face at the thought of eating his least favourite dish, but hunger overrode taste and he nodded to accept.

The proprietor stopped the boy. "Bring out two dishes of food to these men." He eyed Robert. "And, don't expect any bread. There is none."

"Ah, but I have my own," Robert said. From his pocket, he removed the third and last loaf.

Everyone in the room turned to look, and for a few brief moments, no one spoke. From across the table, his companion scowled.

"Bread at a low price!" a man with a short goatee shouted as he raised his right fist into the air. Robert noticed he was missing several fingers.

"Not at a low price," laughed Robert. "I got it for free."

His companion tensed.

"Even better," shouted a man whose shirt and vest was stained with mud.

"But I didn't steal it," Robert announced. "I found it on the ground."

"Yeah and my wife's tits don't sag to her waist!" an old toothless man slurred.

The room broke out in raucous guffaws.

Robert ignored the remarks. "If I find who owns it, I'll pay for it." He studied his companion's icy expression.

A corpulent man with the purple bulbous nose of one who loves to drink rose to his feet. "A toast to this honest man!"

All raised their tankards, ale sloshing and spilling, before they drank the contents and refilled their cups.

Robert frowned and glanced at his associate. "They think I'm joking; but I'm not. You'll find no one more honest than me." He turned the loaf over in his hand and offered it to him. "It's a little crushed, but there were plenty others where I found this one."

The man shook his head refusing the offer, so Robert devoured three or four mouthfuls and swallowed another tankard of ale. "I've never had such a parched throat."

His new friend gestured to the proprietor. "Prepare a good bed for this fellow. He needs lodgings tonight."

The proprietor stared his nose at Robert. "You want a bed for the night?"

His tongue relaxed by the influence of the ale, Robert nodded. "*Oui*, but only for one night, and only if the sheets are clean."

The innkeeper's face colored as he lumbered off to his table and grabbed his inkstand, paper, and quill. He returned, stepped over the bench, and slid beside Robert.

"What's all this for?" Robert said as he took another swig of ale and stared at the paper. "That's not what I meant by a clean sheet."

The proprietor leaned forward and dipped the quill into the

ink. “What is your full name and where do you live?”

Robert puckered his brows. “What has that to do with providing me a bed?”

“It's the law.” The proprietor exchanged a strange look with Robert's companion. “We are obliged to account for everyone who sleeps beneath our roof: name and address, what business they came to conduct, if he is armed, and how long he intends to stay.”

Robert swallowed the dregs in his tankard. “Ah! The law! If laws favouring good people are worth nothing, then those working against them are worth even less. I know all too well of a law's importance.” The tension of the past few days began to melt away.

“I'm serious.” The proprietor flashed a stern look at the man with Robert. He rose, returned to his table, brought over another sheet of paper, and slammed it down in front of Robert. “Here is a copy of the law. Read it for yourself.”

“I see!” Robert raised his refilled cup and emptied it again. He pointed at the sheet. “I'm delighted to see it. I even recognize the signatures.” He shoved it back to the innkeeper. “I'll tell you what – when you can show me a paper that decrees that an honest man may marry an honest girl, I'll tell you my name. Besides, I have good reasons for not telling you. If a villain wants to know my whereabouts to do me an ill turn, will that paper protect me? No! So I won't tell anyone anything.”

Silent, the proprietor stared hard at Robert's cohort who seemed unmoved by the argument.

Robert swallowed more ale. “Take all these bothersome papers of yours away and bring me another flagon of ale instead; this one is cracked.” Robert went to tap it with his knuckles but missed. He tried again and grinned when his second attempt succeeded. “See, it even sounds cracked.”

By now, Robert's actions had attracted the attention of the

crowd and a general murmur of agreement arose.

The innkeeper shrugged and raised his brows at Robert's colleague.

"That man makes good sense," said a drunk who raised his tankard to Robert.

"Those papers are filled with nothing more than tricks and impositions." Robert raised his own cup. "What we need are real laws." His words sounded slurred, but he felt good and confident.

Robert's mate cast a look of reproval at the proprietor and waved him away. "Let him be for now."

The innkeeper shrugged. "As long as you see that I've done my duty." He scowled, retrieved his writing utensils then grabbed the empty flagon and shoved it at a serving boy.

"Bring s'more ale," Robert said, his words seemed to run into each other.

"More of the same," the proprietor said with a curt voice as he glowered at the lad before returning to his seat at the hearth.

Robert gave his new friend a nod. "I understand how good people can support each other." He waved his hand. "Isn't it admirable for our rulers to use quill, ink, and paper to intrude on our privacy. They have a mighty passion for wielding the pen!"

"Wanna know why?" asked the winner of a card game.

"Let me hear it," said Robert.

The man rose unsteadily to his feet, his tankard in both hands. He was the ugliest man Robert had ever seen, with frog-like eyes and a pointed chin. "The seigneurs eat so many geese, and have so many quills, they are obliged to use them."

Everyone chortled except the poor man who just lost the game.

A man with one eye that meandered about at random pointed a shaky hand at Robert. "This man speaks eloquently.

You'd be wise to listen to him." He fell backwards off his chair, drunk.

This brought another resounding laugh.

Robert recalled his elegant proposal to Emilie and how carefree and giddy with love he and Emilie had been after she accepted it. His loss angered him anew. "But the lawmakers wield the pens and believe the words they write don't apply to them. But any words someone like me utters, are recorded on paper to be made use of later. They also have another trick for those who can't write but are of good wit." Robert tapped his forehead with a forefinger. "As soon as they realize that we understand, they throw in a little Latin to confuse us and prevent us from defending ourselves. We must do away with such practices! Today everything was done without pen, ink and paper. Tomorrow, if people govern themselves properly, we can achieve even more without harming anyone."

His companion leaned forward across the table. "If I ruled New France, I would find a way to make things right."

Robert focused his eyes on him. "How?"

"I would ensure everyone had enough bread; the poor as well as the rich. First, I would set a moderate price everyone could afford. Then I would distribute bread according to the number of mouths to feed. I'd give a note to every family, listing the number of persons in their household, to be presented to bake-houses. For example, my note would say, "Ambroise Fuselle, by trade a blacksmith, with a wife and four children, who reside in Québec." The note allows me enough bread at a set cost. Your note would say" he paused and peered at Robert with narrowed eyes. "What is your name?"

"Robert Lanzille."

"Ah, *oui*, Robert Lanzille," the man repeated. "Have you a wife and children?"

"I ought to have a wife and children, but no, not yet."

"So you are single! Then you would receive a smaller portion."

"But what if I marry?"

The man rose from his seat. "The note would be changed and the amount increased. As I said, the amount of bread would list the number of people to be fed."

Robert struck the table with his hand. "It makes sense. Then why don't they make it law?"

"How should I know," Ambroise shrugged. "It's time to bid you good night. I must be off. My wife and children have been waiting for me long enough."

"One more drink." Robert filled his friend's cup; and rising, seized him by the shirt to force him to sit again. "Otherwise you insult me."

Ambroise disengaged himself with a sudden tug. "I bid you a good night," he said curtly and walked away.

Robert called him back, but failed to persuade him to return. He sank back into his seat. Eyeing the cup, he had just filled, and seeing the boy passing the table, he grabbed his arm and pointed to the tankard. "See, I offered this to that gentleman. Full to the brim, fit for a friend. But he wouldn't have it." Robert spoke with a slow and grave enunciation. "People have odd ideas. I mustn't let it go to waste." Robert took it and emptied it in one long draw then wiped his mouth with his sleeve.

"I understand," said the boy, going away.

"You understand, do you?" Robert shook his head as the room spun. He was unaccustomed to such excesses. The ale he had swallowed to cool his parched throat, one cup after another, had gone to his head. Both ale and words flowed between Robert's lips without measure or reason until he knew he had gone beyond his ability to govern himself. He indulged his desire to talk to those around him, but his ability to connect sentences failed. Thoughts clouded his mind and vanished.

Words he yearned to speak became inapplicable as he struggled to form a sentence. Perplexed, he sought recourse in more ale then looked around for the proprietor. "What kind of innkeeper is he?" he shouted to no one in particular. "Where did he go? I can't abide the way he tried to trick me into giving him my name and business and residence. Innkeepers ought to help us, not work against us."

Everyone laughed.

"Don't laugh, I am a little too far gone, I know, but my reasons are justified. Besides, who keeps him in business? Us! I don't see any lawmakers in here wetting their lips."

"They only drink water," laughed one man.

"To keep their heads clear," called out another.

"Yeah, so they can tell their lies lucidly."

The room erupted in laughter.

"I'll wager the good Governor has never come here to drink a toast or spend a pretty coin. And that dog of a villain, Seigneur Rich – I'd better hold my tongue. The only good men I know are the Governor and Père Marc-" He stopped himself again. "There are so few good men in the world. The old are worse than the young, and the young worse than the old. Bread; *mais oui*, I found some loaves, but I gave some away too. Long live justice." Robert belched, rested his chin on his chest and remained like that for several moments. When the room stopped spinning, he heaved a sigh and looked around the area.

Nearby, a man scowled. "Look at him."

All heads turned in Robert's direction and the unruly, drunken mass laughed. Robert could no longer concentrate on what they said, but he knew they taunted him, and provoked him with foolish and unmannerly questions.

"He's so drunk, I'll bet he won't know the difference between piss and ale." While everyone laughed at the comment, the young man who made it grabbed Robert's tankard and held it in front of his groin as he feigned pissing into it.

Robert blundered a reply. He muttered incoherent words to them, yet managed not to mention any names, especially that of Emilie. He could not bear it if they made fun of her too. He rested his head on the table and shut his eyes to stop the spinning.

54

"That's enough! Leave him alone," the proprietor shouted.

Robert raised his head from the tabletop, wet with spilled ale. He tried to say something, but the room swirled at an alarming speed, and he squinted to bring the room into focus.

The proprietor yanked the tankard from his grip. "You've had enough. It's time for you to go to bed and get some sleep. I'll take you to your room now."

Robert knew he was drunk, but could not trust the innkeeper because of the man's earlier attempt to prod information from him. The words 'bed' and 'sleep' sparked some lucidity and Robert placed his open hands on the table and tried twice to stand, unsuccessfully. Undaunted, he sighed and tried once more, but staggered and nearly fell. The innkeeper caught him and steadied him, then guided him to the stairs. Patrons raised their tankards and shouted as he stumbled past. He turned his head to look back at them. If it wasn't for the proprietor's taut grip on his arm, he would have fallen. All he could manage was a quick wave of his free arm.

The innkeeper shoved him up the narrow wooden staircase and into a small room. A solitary candle-lantern shed dim light into the musty smelling room.

The moment Robert saw the neatly made bed, he looked at his host with gratitude. On unsteady legs, he reached out to pat the man on the shoulder, but missed. He made a second attempt, but the innkeeper grabbed his hand and pushed it away.

"You've been kind," Robert stammered. "But you tried to trick me into giving you my name."

The innkeeper scowled. "I didn't do it to vex you or to pry into your affairs, you fool. What would you have me do? Disobey the law? I'd be the first to be punished. So do me this favour and tell me your name so we can both go to bed with a clear mind."

"Ah, why don't you leave me be," Robert rebuked with a wave of his arm.

The innkeeper's face reddened and he shoved his finger into Robert's chest. "Shut your mouth, simpleton. You've given me enough trouble for one night. Go to bed."

Robert's anger burst. "You're in league with them, aren't you? Wait, I'll settle it." He stood and headed to the open door. "Friends," he shouted down the stairs. "The innkeeper is one of them."

"Stop! I only said it as a joke!" The man yanked him back into the room. "It was a joke. You understand? Don't make any more trouble for me."

"Ah, a joke you say. Now you are making sense." Robert flopped onto the bed and tried to lift his foot to remove his shoes, but failed.

"Undress yourself and be quick." The innkeeper helped him pull off his coat then checked the pockets. His search was successful and he removed a handful of coins. He looked at Robert. "You're an honest man, aren't you?"

"An honest man," Robert slurred as he endeavored to unbutton the top of his shirt.

"*Bon*, let's settle our account tonight then, shall we? I may not be here in the morning when you awake."

"That's fair," muttered Robert. "I may be a fool, but I pay my own way."

"It's all here," the innkeeper said as he pocketed what was owed and left the rest. "Consider your account settled."

Robert fumbled with a stubborn button. Frustrated he looked up at his host. "Lend me a hand, will you?" Robert yawned.

Exhausted, Robert let the man slip off his shoes and stockings then flopped onto his back in his breeches and shirt. The last thing he remembered was the innkeeper tossing a quilt over him.

55

The innkeeper held the candle-lantern near the face of his sleeping guest and studied his features. "*Cretin!*" he whispered. "You're nothing but a fool who has brought more trouble on yourself than you know." Shaking his head, he left the room and took great care to lock the drunken sot in the room.

He walked to the far end of the hall and opened the door to the bedroom of his private apartment where his wife slept soundly. A few annoying snores reverberated from her throat which became a cough when he nudged her awake. "I need you to go downstairs and watch over the tavern for me. I have to go out."

"At this hour?" She sat up with a grimace and rubbed her eyes.

"Yes, thanks to one of our drunken lodgers. The fool came in with the Provost of the Maréchaussées and didn't even know it. When I asked him for his information according to the law, he refused. He's now sleeping it off in the room at the far end of the hall. I've locked him in, so he won't be giving us any more trouble. Now I have to go to the office of the Maréchaussées and report him for refusing to give his information, otherwise, I'll be the one in trouble with the law."

"You can't report him in the morning?"

"No, it has to be tonight. If he's wanted by them, and he leaves, they will hold me responsible. I prefer not to chance it. Best to keep on the good side of the authorities. With all the trouble today, who knows what the man was involved in." He sat on the bed and watched his wife get dressed. "Take care and keep your eyes on everyone and everything. There's been too much trouble on the streets today."

"Oh, for goodness sake," she muttered as she laced her bodice over her unfortunately inadequate breasts. "I'm not a child. I know what to do."

"Well, make sure they pay and if they say anything about the Intendent, the Governor, or the Captain of Militia, pretend not to hear and tend to another patron instead. I'll return as soon as I can."

He went with her into the kitchen, and looked out into the tavern. More than half of the patrons had left. Only a few lagged behind to finish the slag in their flagons. He reached for his hat and cloak from a peg behind the door. Putting them on, he checked that the short thick stick he carried for protection was still secreted in his pocket, repeated his instructions to his wife, and stepped out into the cool night.

Small groups of people and soldier patrols still roamed about, but unlike earlier in the day, all was peaceful now. Walking briskly with his head down, it did not take long for him to arrive at the office of the Maréchaussées

Inside, on the main floor of the three-storey structure, magistrates, soldiers, and officers of the Maréchaussées were occupied in a variety of activities. Some penned their reports. Others sat around tables discussing the day's events and strategizing for tomorrow. He overheard snippets of conversations – more guards to protect the Intendent's house, certain streets were to be barricaded with timber or carts.

The innkeeper removed his tricorne and looked around for Ambroise Fuselle. He spotted him at a table occupied in writing. Brushing past several people, he made his way to him and cleared his throat. "Pardon, Monsieur Fuselle."

Ambroise looked up. "What can I do for you?" He sat back and laid his quill on the desk next to the blue baton decorated with the gold fleurs-de-lis of his office. The Provost now wore a blue velvet bandolier embroidered with the fleur-de-lis, which identified him as the leader of the Maréchaussées.

"About that man you brought to my inn earlier; I came to tell you that I tried to learn his name, but he would not give it."

"You've done your duty in coming here to tell me, but I already know who he is."

"You do? How?"

A sardonic smile arose on the Provost's face. "We have our methods." He leaned back in his chair and peered up at the landlord beneath furrowed brows. "But you haven't told me everything."

The innkeeper blinked twice then frowned. "What more could there be to tell?"

"I know he carried stolen bread, likely plundered."

"A man arrives at my inn with one loaf of bread in his pocket and I'm supposed to know where he got it? I've never seen the man before in my life. I'm only an innkeeper, not a soothsayer."

"You can't deny that this patron of yours had the temerity to utter injurious words against our laws, and made improper and shameful jokes about the Intendent."

The innkeeper turned his hat round and round in his hands. "It was you who brought him into my inn."

The Provost narrowed his eyes. "Nevertheless, while in your inn, in your presence, he uttered inflammatory speeches, unadvised words, and seditious propositions." Ambroise rolled the quill between his fingertips and stared hard at him.

"How can you blame me for what drunken patrons utter? I have no more control over them than you have over the weather. It was all I could do to keep things from getting out of hand in my tavern after the day's events. I'd better return and hope my inn is still standing." He put his hat on his head and turned around to leave.

"And this customer of yours, what is he doing now?"

The innkeeper stopped and turned back around.

"He has gone to bed."

"Good. Take care not to let him get away."

"I locked him in his room."

"I'll send someone to fetch him in the morning. He faces serious charges. I'll hold you responsible if he gets away. Now go home." The Provost picked up his quill and looked down at the papers before him in dismissal.

56

"Robert Lanzille. Wake up."

Two rough shakes and the voice at the foot of the bed roused Robert from a deep slumber. He groaned. His head pounded as if someone had hammered spikes into it, and with great difficulty, he opened his eyes. A stern-faced man with greying hair and a black coat peered at him from the foot of the bed. Two men stood on either side of his pillow. Groggy from sleep and last night's drunkenness, Robert lay bewildered. He must be dreaming and rubbed his eyes so as to awake from the nightmare.

"Get up and come with us," demanded the man in the black coat.

Robert's head ached so bad, he doubted he could lift it. His mouth tasted like a handful of rotten leeks. Worse, his bladder felt as if it were about to explode if he didn't find the chamber pot soon. But the powerful realization this was no dream propelled him into alertness and he sat up in bed. “What is this about? How do you know my name?”

“No talking. Get up,” said one of the men who grabbed him by the arm. Robert noticed he was missing both upper front teeth. The other man, who loomed above him with wind-reddened face, merely scowled. All three men wore the traditional blue velvet bandoliers with fleurs-de-lis that marked officers of the Maréchaussées.

Robert yanked back his arm and glared at the man in black. “I demand to know what this is all about!”

“I am Lieutenant Gerard of the Maréchaussées and these are my men.”

“Shall we carry him off in his shirt and breeches?” the toothless Maréchaussée officer asked.

The lieutenant eyed Robert with impatience. “They will do it if you don't get up now and come with us.”

“What for?” demanded Robert.

“The Provost himself will tell you that.”

“I've done nothing; and I'm astonished-”

“So much the better for you. If that's true, you will be released and can go about your own business.”

Robert sat up. “Let me go now. I've not contravened any laws.”

“Shall we carry him?” the toothless Maréchaussée grumbled.

The lieutenant narrowed his eyes. “Get dressed, Lanzille.”

“I ask you again, how do you know my name?”

The lieutenant nodded to his men. “Get him up.”

The two men hoisted Robert to his feet, but he shoved their hands away. “Don't touch me! I'll dress myself.”

“Then do so and be quick about it,” said the lieutenant, his brows furrowed.

"I'm getting up," replied Robert as he rose from bed and searched for the chamber pot, which he found tucked beneath it. He turned his back to the men, relieved himself, and gathered his clothes, which were scattered over the bed and floor. "Since you unjustly put this affront upon me, I should like to be conducted to the Governor. I know him; he's a gentleman, and is under some obligation to me."

"*Mais oui*, you shall be conducted to him directly," replied the man in black with a wry grin. "In fact, he has already prepared a meal and comfortable accommodations in your honor."

The two men broke out in laughter.

The lieutenant silenced them with a stern look.

While dressing, Robert tried to think of a reason for these men to accost him like this. The law requiring disclosure of one's personal information must be the cause of this disagreeable occurrence. Still, how had this man learned his name? Robert had over-imbibed last night, but what could have happened for lawmen to take him into custody? Especially after all his efforts to instill peace and reason during the turmoil of yesterday's riot. He glanced out the window and observed the increasing bustle in the street. He looked at the lieutenant who had crossed his arms and tapped his foot impatiently.

Robert stalled to find a way out of this trouble. "If this is because I refused to give the innkeeper my name last night; I was a little muddled. The innkeeper plied me with treacherous ale and it affected any words I may have spoken. If this is all, I am now ready to cooperate. Besides, you know my name already. Who told it to you?"

"It's good to see you have some sense," said the lieutenant. "It's the best way to get yourself out of this difficulty. And I'm sure that when I take you in, and you tell your story to the magistrate, you will be dismissed and set at liberty. But I cannot release you, as I should like to do."

"Will we pass by a church or monastery?" Robert asked hoping to convince them to let him stop and find the abbot he had come here to seek.

The lieutenant shrugged. "I do not know for certain. The sooner we get there, the sooner you will be set at liberty," the lieutenant replied.

Shouts resounded from the street below. He glanced out the window and saw a group of citizens, who, upon being urged by a patrol of soldiers to disperse, snarled back at them.

Robert now stood dressed except for his coat, which he held in one hand and searched his pockets with the other.

The lieutenant opened the door. "Let's go."

Robert frowned as he checked all his pockets. "I had some money and a letter in my pocket."

"I've got it. It will be restored to you when the formalities are executed," the lieutenant said. "Let's be off."

Robert shook his head. "No. I want my money and my letter. I'll give an account of all my doings, but I want my items returned to me first."

The lieutenant gave him an assessing look then withdrew the coins and letter from his inner pocket and handed them to him.

Robert tucked them into his own pocket and took up his hat.

The lieutenant beckoned his men to lead the way downstairs with Robert jammed between them. When they reached the main floor, Robert glanced about for the innkeeper, but the officers seized his hands and secured his wrists with a small-knotted cord that had two straight pegs tied to either end. The cord encircled his wrist; the pieces of wood were held by one of his captors who tightened it to demonstrate control. Pain shot through Robert's hand, not only because of the tightness, but because of the many knots that dug into his flesh.

Robert struggled. "What is the meaning of this!"

The lieutenant nodded at the officer and he released a bit of pressure. "A mere formality, nothing more. Brave this well and it will all soon pass. And, since you're cooperative, I'll give you another piece of advice. Walk without making eye contact with anyone. Bring no notice upon yourself and things will go much easier for you." He turned to his men. "Take care you don't hurt him. As we walk, let it appear as if we are four men out for a stroll. I want no trouble." With a pleasant smile, he faced Robert again. "Do as I tell you and all will be well. Now let's be off."

The moment they stepped onto the street, Robert looked about. Three men approached from the opposite direction, deep in conversation. As they drew closer, Robert overheard them mention a bake-house, concealed flour, and justice. He coughed and enlarged his eyes to attract their attention. It worked and they stopped to stare at him.

Upon the two groups meeting, others gathered around until a small crowd formed.

"Have a care, lest it go worse for you," the lieutenant warned Robert through the side of his mouth.

The two officers exchanged a wary look and twisted Robert's manacles tighter in warning.

"Aaahh!" Robert groaned.

More bystanders gathered and they now encircled them. Some carried sticks, others stood with arms crossed.

"Make way. He is a thief caught in the act of stealing and eating bread yesterday!" the lieutenant shouted. "Step back!"

Robert seized the moment. "They are carrying me off because I shouted out for justice yesterday. I've done nothing! Help me!"

A murmur of approbation arose. It was followed by more explicit cries in his favour. All three Maréchaussées officers commanded, then asked, then begged the crowd to let them pass, but the ever-increasing mob only trampled and pushed forward to reach Robert. Their angry shouts escalated with their outrage.

"Let him go!"

"Hunger is no crime!"

Sensing the danger, the two officers released Robert's manacles, turned and tried to run off, but some of the crowd chased after them.

Alone, the lieutenant paled and crouched as if to slip away, but the storm of people gathered against him. Like a straw frozen in ice, he found himself trapped. He came face to face with a man who scowled at him.

"You ugly raven!" growled the man, spittle flying from his mouth.

"Raven! Raven!" the crowd resounded. Pushes enhanced their cries as they pressed towards him, swallowing him in the vortex of their rage.

The lieutenant fell to the ground in a blur of massive punches and kicks pummeled him into utter stillness.

Aghast, Robert watched, frozen at the sight of such rampant madness. Helpless to stop them, his chest exploding with alarm, Robert seized the opportunity and fled lest he be blamed.

57

Heart pounding, Robert darted into the crowd and raced down the street. When he deemed it safe, he slackened his pace and forced himself to walk casually to avoid attracting attention.

He had no choice; he must leave here and soon. Now that the authorities knew his name, they might blame him for causing the assault on the lieutenant, and could trace him. Had the mob killed the man? Robert doubted anyone could survive such an attack. He couldn't return to Pointe-du-Lac because that would be the first place authorities would search. As to receiving sanctuary in the monastery, Père Marc-Mathieu had recommended, he would be trapped there, and he doubted it could protect him from his pursuers. His only option was to go where nobody knew him. Far better to be a bird in the woods than a bird in a cage.

He fought the panic growing within him. A smart man thought at a time like this, a stupid man ran until the authorities caught him. The only safe place he could think of was with his friend Bastien in the settlement of Saint-Anne-de-Beaupre, but first he had to find his way there. He had no idea which road to take and needed to ask someone for directions. After escaping the angry mob, the Maréchaussées officers would be searching for him. Rumours of his flight might already be circulating and he must be careful who he asked.

A generously proportioned man with a double chin and corpulent belly stood in the doorway of his shop with hands behind his back, repeatedly rising on his toes and lowering himself on his heels. Robert decided to avoid him because he looked too idle and might pose more questions than replies.

A man walked towards him with a deep frown, eyes on the ground, and who scarcely seemed to know where he was going. Not him either, Robert decided.

A stout boy leaned against a tree. He looked intelligent enough, but his sardonic grin made him appear maliciously inclined and he might delight in sending him off in the wrong direction.

At last, he spied a middle-aged man who approached as if he had some pressing business to attend to. This one might be trustworthy enough to give him a direct answer. "Pardon," Robert asked. "Will you be good enough to tell me which road will take me to Saint-Anne-de-Beaupre?"

"To Saint-Anne-de-Beaupre? It is a good two-day walk from here. There is no direct road, but it's east up the Saint Lawrence River."

"*Merci*, and which road will lead me out of town?"

"Turn left along this street and go back to the church." The man scrutinized him.

"*Merci*," Robert said with a quick wave.

The man gave him one last discerning look then continued on his way.

The directions took him past the monastery of the Récollets he was supposed to go for sanctuary. The doors, windows, and gates had been boarded up against the rioting. A heap of cinders and extinguished combustibles, the relics of a bonfire from the riot of the day before. Next to it, soldiers guarded a bake-house left barely standing. His head lowered, Robert proceeded past them as quickly as possible. How he wished he could knock at the convent and hand Père Marc-Mathieu's letter to whoever answered the door. But no one would answer now. A pang of regret seized him. He should have listened to the friar who had answered the door and told him to wait in the church. Too late now.

The street leading out of town was not far beyond the monastery, but soldiers patrolled it on either side. Robert hesitated and glanced back and forth before hurrying past. Better to be a bird of the woods, as long as I can. He thought of Emilie, too, but with all that had happened to him, he could not trust anyone to get a note or message to her. It would have to wait until he deemed it safe.

He glanced up the street. More soldiers ahead. Surely they weren't monitoring every street leading out of Québec? He watched them for a while, but they stopped only those who entered, not those leaving it. He set off again and slackened his pace. Heart pounding and eyes to the ground, Robert ambled past the soldiers without notice.

Eager to put as much distance between himself and the town, he lengthened his stride. From time to time he glanced behind him, occasionally rubbing one or the other of his wrists, which were still a little numb and marked with a red line from the pressure of the rope manacles. His thoughts rambled with a mixture of disquietude and vengeance. He tried to recall what he had said and done the night before to have brought all this trouble upon himself. How had the authorities discovered his name? His suspicions fell on the man who had escorted him to the inn and with whom he had spoken frankly. The man had drawn him into conversation, his behavior aloof, his questions probing. Robert's suspicions changed to near certainty – he had revealed himself to someone with authority. He remembered talking to someone after the man left, but to whom? His memory remained blank. He had not been himself yesterday evening. Now, all he knew was that his life teetered on chaos and he didn't know how to restore it to order again.

After walking some distance, he realized he needed to ensure he was on the right road. Before long he noticed a *habitant* farmer ploughing his field and stopped to ask him.

"You're on the wrong road," the man said as he pointed to an area at the end of his field. "The main road is over there."

Robert thanked him and headed in that direction. He must have inadvertently taken a different road out of town. Once he reached the road, he snuck into the woods that ran parallel along its course to keep out of sight.

He walked a jagged course trying to keep abreast of the road. When it wasn't in sight, he relied on his own judgment and allowed himself to be guided by the fields and meadows he traversed. But he soon became confused and feared he had lost his way.

He knew he had to ask for directions again.

In the distance, he came upon a solitary cottage outside a tiny settlement of no more than ten houses. Fatigued, he knocked.

"Who is it?" a woman's voice called out from within.

"A weary traveler who will pay for some food and refreshment."

An old woman partially opened the door, her distaff and spindle pointed at him like weapons. "Open your coat and prove to me you have no weapons," she said, her eyes narrowing to small slits.

Robert did as he was told, even spinning around to show he had nothing to hide.

Satisfied, she opened the door fully. The small cottage consisted of a neatly made bed in the corner, a large hearth, and a tall cupboard. She invited him to sit at the table in the centre of the space and offered him some cheese, chicken stew, and ale. He accepted the food, but excused himself from taking any ale, sickened by the sight of it after the troubles of the night before. Instead, she brought him water.

"Where do you come from?" she asked.

"A small settlement west of Québec," Robert responded, careful to reveal as little information as possible.

"Then you must have travelled through Québec. I heard there was trouble there yesterday. The people are rioting and raiding bake-houses. Is it true?"

Robert raised the tankard to his lips and drank to give himself time to think before responding. The water was cool and fresh and it eased the burning dryness in his throat. With a sigh of satisfaction, he placed his tankard on the table. "I heard the same rumours, but don't know for certain, because I passed around it and never entered it."

"Where are you going?" Her eyes narrowed again.

"I have to go to many places," Robert said, "but I'd like to stop a while and visit my aunt who lives in a small settlement on the road just before Saint-Anne-de-Beaupre. What do they call that settlement?" There must be one there, thought Robert.

"Château-Richer, you mean," replied the old woman.

"*Oui*, Château-Richer." Much relieved, Robert repeated the name of the settlement to imprint it in his memory. "Is it far?"

"I don't know exactly. If one of my sons were here, he could tell you for certain. He travels there regularly."

"And do you think I can get there without taking the main road? The dust of the road makes me quite ill." He hated lying, especially to someone who was treating him kindly.

"I think you can."

Robert rose, paid the woman for his scanty meal, thanking her heartily. He set off following the road to the right, careful not to wander from it more than necessary. With the name of the settlement echoing in his mind, he proceeded from farm to farm, until, about an hour before sunset, he arrived at Chateau-Richer.

He entered an inn and took a seat at the end of the table nearest the door, the usual place for those who wanted to make a hasty exit. He ordered a small measure of ale and a bowl of stew. The additional miles he walked and the lateness of the day overcame his temporary, but fanatical, hatred of the beverage. "But I must ask you to be quick," Robert said to the innkeeper. "I'm obliged to be on my way again as soon as I've finished." He couldn't spend the night for fear the innkeeper might ask him his name and where he came from.

The landlord nodded and promised to return with the ale.

Robert studied the other patrons who lounged at the other end discussing the riot. One detached himself from the others and took the seat opposite to him. "Have you come from Québec?" the man asked. "Have you any information about what happened there?"

"Me?" asked Robert, feigning surprise to gain time to think.

"*Oui*, you, if you don't mind answering the question."

Robert shook his head. "Québec, from what they say, is not a good place to go at present."

The man's blue eyes widened. "The uproar continues then?"

"I'm not sure," Robert said.

"You're not from there?"

"I come from Boischatel," Robert lied. Strictly speaking, it wasn't exactly a lie because he had passed through there.

"And at Boischatel, you didn't hear anything?"

Robert shook his head. "Only that there was a rebellion against bake-houses." He had spoken the words with such finality, the man rose and returned to his companions at the other end of the table.

The innkeeper arrived and set out his meal.

"How far is it from here to Beaupre?" Robert asked him. He knew that Beaupre was past his destination and by asking this question, he could discern how much longer before he arrived at Saint-Anne-de-Beaupre.

"Why do you ask?"

"I am merely curious."

"It is about eleven miles, more or less."

"Eleven miles! I didn't know that."

"Do you intend to arrive there tonight?" The innkeeper scrutinized him.

"I had hoped to."

The man shook his head.

This silenced Robert and prevented him from asking any other questions. He pulled his plate closer and picked up his wooden spoon.

"*Bon appétit*," the innkeeper said before turning his attention to the other patrons.

A plague on these innkeepers, Robert thought. The more of

them I encounter, the worse they are. He ate heartily while he listened to their conversation, trying to appear aloof so he could learn as much as possible.

"This time, the people of Québec wanted to make their needs clear," a lanky man dressed in black said. "We'll have to wait until tomorrow to learn anything more."

"I'm sorry I didn't go to Québec this morning," said a second man with a long beard and a big belly.

"If you decide to go tomorrow, I'll go with you," said a third man, his large moustache twitching with every word he spoke.

"What I want to know," said the first, "is whether the people of Québec will fight for us too? No one ever considers the poor *habitants*."

From outside came the sound of hooves, which come to a stop. One man craned his neck to peer outside the window. "It's that merchant from Québec."

A large man with a long brown beard swept into the room. After dusting his tricorne against his thigh, he took a seat at the far end of the table nearest to a window where he could eye his cart. All the men surrounded him.

"What is the news from Québec?" someone asked.

"Ah, you've heard."

"We know little," replied the mustachioed man.

"There is both good and bad news," the merchant said.

The innkeeper approached, took his order, then hurried into the kitchen to see to the food.

"What have you heard?" the merchant asked the circle of men as he leaned back in his chair and stretched out his legs.

"Not much," one man said.

The innkeeper returned with the ale.

"Let me wet my lips first." The merchant raised his tankard in his right hand, and after settling his beard with his left, drank it all. "Ah, that was good." He set down his tankard and watched as the landlord refilled it. "Today was as rough as yesterday, perhaps even worse. I can scarcely believe I'm here to tell you about it because I was busy protecting my shop from damage during the rioting."

Robert kept his eyes downcast as he finished the last few mouthfuls of his stew.

"Today, the rebels accosted a group of Maréchaussées officers who had arrested some poor fellow."

"What happened?"

"They were overwhelmed. Two of the officers managed to run off, but the lieutenant was severely beaten by the mob. They say he is near death." At their collected gasps, he took a long swallow of his drink. "Afterwards, several men were taken into custody. Four of them are to be hung. One man was seen escaping and they're looking everywhere for him."

The food inside Robert's mouth suddenly tasted like sawdust.

"But will they really hang them?"

"Undoubtedly, and quickly too, especially if the lieutenant dies," the merchant replied as he wiped his beard with a napkin.

Robert put down his spoon as a shudder of cold fear ran through him. He forced himself to remain calm and fought the urge to flee. How could they blame him for what happened?

"They don't exactly know where he came from, who sent him, or what kind of man he was, but he was definitely one of the instigators. The officers, who had him in manacles, found a letter of conspiracy on him and were leading him away to prison. But the rebels arrived in great numbers and after the lieutenant was beaten, he escaped. He may have fled the town or he may still be concealed in Québec."

Robert's meal tasted like poison. They were indeed blaming him for the lieutenant's assault. His mouth went dry and could not swallow. He needed to leave this inn as soon as possible, but the fear of attracting suspicion prevailed. It kept him rooted to his seat, his limbs numb. He decided to wait for the merchant to stop talking about him and would leave when their discussion switched to another topic.

The landlord, who'd been listening, glanced at him.

Robert seized the opportunity and raised his hand to call him over. He settled his account without dispute, though his purse was quite depleted. Without delay, he went straight out the door, taking care not to take the same road that had brought him here.

He set off in the opposite direction to where he was going, all the while fighting the urge to break into a panicked run.

58

Robert walked steadily away, desperate to put as much distance as possible between him and the men at the inn. Who knew how many soldiers or officers of the Maréchaussées now pursued him, or what orders had been forwarded to settlements to watch for him? He tried to calm himself. After all, his name wasn't written on his forehead, but then, stories of fugitives recognized by their particular gait or by their suspicious nature raced through his mind and increased his alarm.

The further he travelled away from Château-Richer the more the increasing darkness heightened his sense of vulnerability. Fearful of discovery, he struggled to make his way through the heavy woods, instead of walking on the road that lay somewhere to his right. A cool breeze rustled the leaves on the trees. A half moon in a pure black sky shed an eerie light, barely adequate to help him navigate through the trees and bushes. Insects feasted on his skin, but he dared not slap them away lest he make noise.

He heard the sound of a hideous bird, a crow, as it flapped

its wings and flew off startled into the night air. Robert felt like a solitary deer chased by a pack of starving wolves as he hurried onward, his heart pounding in his chest. His breath lapsed on him and he broke out in a heavy sweat. The cold air felt like ice upon his moist skin. He began to despair.

On the road up ahead, he heard the quick bark of a dog. He froze, holding his breath as he heard the clop of horses hooves draw near. He broke out into another cold sweat. Three horses walked by, a fur trader atop one, an Indian and a pile of furs on the others. He heard a whistle then the footfalls of a dog that ran to his master's call. Fear held him still lest the dog discover him. Soon, the group disappeared out of sight. Robert was going to die in this place. He could barely pull any air into his lungs. Although it was unlikely the fur trader would pose a threat to his anonymity, he could not take the risk.

That innkeeper said eleven miles. Never had that distance felt longer. Full darkness fell and Robert's fatigue increased with each step. He reached a winding lane that weaved to the left, and pursued it. His mind churned with thoughts of the injustices that had befallen him. In Québec, his efforts had been to quell the rebellion, not incite it. Yet, somehow, it had been misinterpreted and now they wanted to hang him. And, what of the letter of conspiracy it was said he carried? He had only one letter, its contents an introduction, which would enable him to seek sanctuary in a convent. To think he had endangered his life to help save the Intendent, a man he never knew or saw before. Bile rose in his mouth at the thought of the load of woe Seigneur Richard had thrust upon him.

With every step Robert took, he suffered the grind of weary bone on weary bone. It wore him down as he pushed on through the night. *I'm a failure as a man. I cannot even protect myself much less my beloved and her aged mother.*

A twig snapped. A marauder? A bear? He stopped and

listened hard trying to attune his hearing into the dark bushes that lined the road. His heart pounded in his chest. The cold seeped into his bare hands but he dared not move. After a long while, when he decided he must move or freeze to death on the spot, he crept forward rejecting the fiends and ogres that turned out to be tree trunks and bushes when viewed from a different angle. The half moon broke through the clouds and the monsters retreated for now. Would he reach the village, or would they find his lifeless body curled up in the road at first light? He did not know which way to wager nor did he know whether to cry or move on. In the end, he did both.

Solitude, a piercing cold breeze, and painful fatigue tortured him. He had no provisions with him and his clothes were woefully inadequate. And what rendered everything doubly irksome was his vulnerability, with no weapon or means to defend himself against man or beast.

He encountered only a single light in the window of a *habitant* farmhouse in the distance. He didn't dare knock and ask for shelter lest he be taken for a rogue or for fear of being asked who he was, or where he came from or where he travelled to. Every so often he paused and listened, but heard no sounds except for the mournful howl of wolves or owls in the distance, which made his heart skip a beat.

On he walked, through maple groves, the stakes, and buckets of the spring maple harvest long gone. Bushes assumed strange forms. The shadows cast from the tops of trees alarmed him. Agitated by the breeze, they quivered, illuminated by the pale moonlight. The rustle of withered leaves he trampled echoed loudly in his ear. His limbs seemed scarcely able to support him. The cold night breeze blew icy and sharp against his forehead and throat, piercing through his clothes to his skin. He shivered uncontrollably, the chill blast penetrating to his bones, extinguishing the last remains of his vigour. Weariness and fear of being out in the blackness of night almost overwhelmed him. He almost lost his self-control, but summoned up his courage, and with great effort, held his fears in abeyance.

In the distance he heard the reassuring roar of the Saint Lawrence River, then saw a small group of homes with the steeple of a church standing tall and proud between them. Safety. Saint-Anne-de-Beaupre. The sight of it in the distance was like the welcome of a long-time friend. His weariness almost disappeared and his blood circulated warmly through all his veins. His confidence increased. The gloominess and oppression of his mind vanished.

At last he reached the edge of a steep decline and, peering through some bushes, he surveyed the broad landscape scattered with small houses and the glittering river beyond. It was the dead of night and everyone would be asleep. Should he clamber up into a tree to await dawn, braving the chill night-breeze and frosty air in his inadequate garments? He could pace the night away, but even that would have be an inadequate defence against the severe temperature. Besides, his legs were numb and sore from having walked such a great distance in so short a time.

He glanced about and spotted a small shack nestled in a maple grove nearby. Its walls were a crude collection of logs and wooden planks, but it presented a solution to his dilemma. He made his way to it and pushed open its unlocked tumbledown door. A small hearth took up one entire wall. A large table swallowed the remaining space with the exception of a hammock suspended in the corner. He walked to the hearth where a large copper cauldron for boiling maple sap hung suspended from a cross pole at its centre. To the right, atop a neat stack of logs, was a tinderbox. He started a fire then searched for food. Nothing. His hunger would have to wait. He stretched his weary frame on the hammock and closed his eyes.

Exhausted as he was, and warmed by the fire, sleep did not come easily. The mocking faces of those he had encountered over the past several days tormented him – the merchant, the Intendent, the rioting crowds in the street, Père Jean, the innkeeper – all reminded him of his misfortune, of his impossible life, of sudden flight, of all that he had lost. The memories knifed him with their keen edge.

Only three images presented themselves to his mind, divested of bitter recollection, clear of all suspicion, pleasing in every aspect- Père Marc-Mathieu, Emilie, and Ada. Yet, the consolation he felt in contemplating them brought no tranquility. In picturing the good Jesuit priest, Robert felt more keenly than ever the disgrace of his faults, his shameful intemperance, and his neglect of the kind priest's paternal advice. Then there was Emilie. Envisioning her brought to mind the extent of his loss. Neither did he forget poor Ada who loved him as a son and accepted him as her only daughter's husband. Filled with grief he considered the trouble he had brought to them. Ada and Emilie were now almost homeless, uncertain of the future, and reaping sorrows and troubles instead of the joy and comfort he had dreamt of giving them.

If Seigneur Richard had not interfered, by now he and Emilie would have been married for five days. Instead, he slept upon a hammock in a forlorn sugar shack far from home.

Harassed by such thoughts, Robert despaired of obtaining any sleep. He longed for morning and measured the slow progress of the hours.

At the first sign of dawn, Robert rose, stretched his limbs, and opened the door of the sugar shack. He looked warily about. With no one visible, he searched for the path he had followed the preceding evening and set off in that direction.

The morning sky was spectacular and held the promise of a

beautiful day. Remnants of the pale, rayless moon remained visible on the horizon suspended in a spacious field of azure. A tinge of morning grey softened into a primrose hue. A few irregular clouds streaked across the sky like vibrant flames. Robert hoped its beauty heralded a change to his fortunes. He walked rapidly, eager to reach the safety of his destination in spite of his sore, tired limbs.

His appetite sharpened with every step. He reached into his pocket and withdrew his money, counting it in his palm. Enough to purchase a small meal. He clutched it, grateful for its existence.

On the road in front of him, two native women and a man approached. One was elderly. The other was much younger with an infant at her breast. The babe, after vainly endeavouring to satisfy its hunger, cried bitterly. The man's face and limbs still held the remnants of his former robustness, but now he appeared broken and almost destroyed by long poverty. All three were as pale and emaciated as death. They stretched out their hands to Robert, but none of them spoke. By law, begging was forbidden. Another law put in place by those in authority that hurt only the most vulnerable. Robert glanced about. No one else appeared nearby or on the road. He thrust his hand into his pocket, removed the last of his money, and placed it in the palm of the woman with the baby. The woman stared at the treasure in her palm. "*Yontonwe*," she muttered with astonishment.

"*Ti-jiawen,*" the man said in his native tongue. His voice was strong, but lacked emotion.

The old woman gave him a toothless grin that quickly faded.

The three continued on their way.

This sole act energized him. Everything seemed to brighten. Famine and poverty must end soon, for there would be a harvest in the fall. He trusted in his own abilities to work and he knew his friend would help him too. Robert also had a little store of money at home, which he could send for. With all this to aid him, at the worst, he could live economically until he could buy and furnish a small cottage and bring Emilie and Ada to live with him in Saint-Anne-de-Beaupre.

His heart lighter, he reached the outskirts of Sainte-Anne-de-Beaupre. Great hope filled him, for this was a town known for its miracles. The small chapel in the centre of the settlement housed a marvellous statue of Ste. Anne. His friend often spoke of it. During the construction of the shrine, one of the builders who suffered from a pain in his limbs was cured of all his ailments after placing three stones upon the shrine's foundation. This was followed by other testimonies of healed people. Hence, both the shrine and the settlement had grown in popularity. Many pilgrims came to the shrine hoping to receive a miracle. As a result, his good friend Bastien earned a healthy living operating the only mercantile which purchased and sold goods from newly arrived ships in port. Robert hoped good fortune would bless him too.

He spotted Bastien's house, a two-storey structure with the mercantile shop on the main floor and living quarters above. He pushed open the door and entered.

Shelves lined every wall, filled with muskets, furs, bolts of cloth, pottery and myriad other household items. His friend stood behind the long wooden counter that ran along the entire right side of the shop. His face broke out in a confused smile, which turned into a grin. “Robert! What a surprise. It's good to see you,” Bastien said as he raced out from behind the counter and patted him on the shoulders. “I'm glad you've come. I've invited you so often, what brings you here now?” He stepped back and studied Robert with a frown. “You look exhausted. What's happened?”

The robust face of his jolly friend made Robert feel safe,

secure, for here was someone he could trust. "Much has brought me here." Exacerbated by his fatigue, Robert relayed his mournful story with much emotion.

Bastien listened without interruption. "Times are hard here too, but the seigneur who rules here is a good man. I'm sure you'll find work." He patted Robert's shoulder. "Are you hungry?"

"Yes, I had a little money, but I gave it away to a trio of beggars. They needed it more than I did."

"Never mind," said Bastien. "I have plenty. Pluck up some heart. Things can only get better."

"I've a trifling sum hidden at home and can send for it." But, not for a while, he thought. Not until this trouble passed and it was safe.

"*Eh, bon,* and in the meantime, allow me to help you. God has given me much and who better to help than my best friend?"

"I knew I could count on you." Robert pressed his friend's shoulder. Bastien led him to a table in the corner and pulled out a chair for him.

"So, they've had trouble in Québec. I'm not surprised. They're all a little mad. There are many rumours; but I'd prefer to hear your version. Here, surrounded by the wilderness, we are more prudent, for when we lack flour for bread, we eat meat. Tomorrow I'll take you to the seigneur. I've mentioned you to him. He's a kind-hearted man. After he hears your story, he'll find a way to help you. Besides, he knows how to value good workmen; for the shortage of food must come to an end, and business will go on."

The burden that weighed on Robert's mind lifted. In its wake came relief and the promise of better things. It was all he could do to stop himself from weeping in relief.

59

Magistrate Antoine Rivet sat behind the ever-growing pile of documents on his desk and stared up at the Maréchaussée officer who stood before him officiously.

Lieutenant Gerard handed him a dispatch.

Antoine broke the seal, and after he read the document, looked back up at him. "This doesn't make any sense. Robert Lanzille inciting a riot? I know this man and it seems out of character. Are you certain?"

"I assure you, we are more than certain. You are ordered by the Provost of Québec to ascertain whether the fugitive, Robert Lanzille, has returned to Pointe-du-Lac. You are to make a complete search of his residence. If found, he must be turned over to me to be conducted to prison in the ville of Québec."

Antoine studied the dispatch again. He could not dispute its authenticity. Incredulous that the same young man who had sought his help a few days ago had descended into such disgrace, Antoine knew he had no choice but to comply with the order. This must be what that pompous sot, Pierre Robillard, must have been blathering about when he visited a day ago. Robillard had warned him to do nothing to aid the case of Robert Lanzille.

Antoine knew he could not risk the ire of Seigneur Richard or Seigneur Pierre because their uncle was a member of the Sovereign Council, appointed by the king to make and enforce laws. His position as magistrate depended on it and he must do everything to ensure compliance. "I'll take you there myself. But first, we'll have to summon the captain of militia of that particular parish, a man by the name of Yves Dupuis. He is in charge."

After reaching for his hat and coat, he led the way outside to where two other officers of the Maréchaussées waited with their horses. When the groom brought around his own horse, the group set off.

60

At the sound of hoof beats, Yves peered out his front window. A linen binding encircled his head to protect the open wound of his severed ear. The pain of the last few days had been excruciating. When he recognized Antoine Rivet and the blue neck scarves of the *Maréchaussées,* he stepped out his front door.

Antoine Rivet reined his horse to a sudden stop and dismounted. "What happened to you?" he asked, his eyes wide.

"I had some trouble, but it's over now." Yves glanced behind Rivet to the mounted men. "Why are all of you here?"

Lieutenant Gerard tipped back his hat. "We have an order to search for and arrest Robert Lanzille."

"And as captain of the militia for the parish," Antoine added, "your presence is required."

"Robert Lanzille? What has he done?" Yves tensed, his suspicion aroused. He knew Robert was somehow connected with the disappearance of Emilie and Ada, but he did not know how or why. Yves had taken to heart the threat of the men who had sliced off his ear, and he wanted no part of this.

"He is wanted for inciting a riot in Québec," the leader of the *Maréchaussées* said.

Yves raised his palm to them. "I have been ill and cannot help you." He pointed to the cottage with the whitewashed shutters across the road. "Go to the home of my assistant who has assumed my duties temporarily." Without waiting for further comment, Yves turned his back to the men and re-entered his house, closing the door behind him.

From the window, he watched the retinue of officials cross the road.

The officers ordered the assistant to help them, and rode to the mill where Robert lived. The mill's door was locked and no one answered. They kicked open the door and entered, turning every item asunder. But when they came out, Robert was not with them.

61

By the time Père Marc-Mathieu heard about the search party for Robert Lanzille, they had long departed. He hurried into the village and learned they questioned everyone they encountered as to Robert's whereabouts, habits, and his life in general. The entire settlement was in an uproar- Robert's reputation in tatters.

It shocked Père Marc-Mathieu when he heard that Robert had escaped custody during a disturbance in Québec and had not been seen since. Some settlers whispered he had committed some heinous crime. What it was, no one knew, but none believed him capable of such a thing, for everyone knew Robert was an honest, respectable young man.

Père Marc-Mathieu suspected this search by officials might have been contrived by Seigneur Richard to ruin Robert, his unfortunate rival. Yet, no matter what the discussion entailed, Père Marc-Mathieu believed in Robert's innocence. Determined to find out what happened, he knew he would do everything he could to help the young man.

He hurried back to the Jesuit house and penned a letter to Père Bonaventure of the Récollets in Québec to ascertain if Robert had arrived there safely. He entreated his colleague to keep Robert's presence there a strict secret. Then he sent Père Nicholas to Québec to inform Emilie and Ada.

62

At the Ursuline convent, Emilie and Ada embroidered in the calefactory, a small intimate room with large windows to let the sun in, and heated by a large hearth that ran the entire span of one wall. From time to time, Emilie glanced at the tapestries of saints hanging on two walls. And sometimes she looked at the statue of the Virgin Mary nestled in a curved niche beside the door. The quiet industriousness of the few nuns in the room, who read, embroidered, or prepared lessons for their native students, soothed Emilie.

Everyone in the convent had heard of the rioting. By virtue of her position, the portress saw or received the news first then imparted it to the rest of the convent's inhabitants, including Emilie and her mother. So when the portress hurried into the calefactory, Emilie glanced up with anticipation to hear the latest report.

"Seven men have been imprisoned, but four are condemned to hang." The portress made the sign of the cross. "A fifth man, from Pointe-du-Lac, managed to escape." The portress stared at Emilie and Ada. "That is your settlement, is it not? He is a miller by the name of Lanzille. Do you know him?"

Emilie's embroidery fell from her hands onto her lap. Robert? In trouble? It could not be true. Iciness formed in her stomach as she glanced at her mother.

Ada's face paled, but she managed to maintain a calm expression. "In a tiny village, everybody knows everybody, so, *oui*, we are acquainted with him. He is a peaceful, charitable young man. I find it impossible to believe him capable of any wrongdoing. Do you know for certain that he was involved in the trouble and that he escaped?"

Emilie held her breath and clasped her hands on her lap to

keep them from trembling. Fear squeezed her chest as she broke out in a cold sweat. There must be a mistake.

The portress shrugged. “How should I know? I am repeating what I heard. Everyone says he has escaped, but where to, no one can say. If the authorities catch your charitable young man again, well-”

Before she could finish her sentence, a nun entered the room, gave the portress an annoyed look, and announced a visitor at the gate. Having been scolded for abandoning her post, and with nothing more to say, the portress rushed out of the room to attend to the visitor.

Emilie could not believe what she'd heard. “How could this be, *Maman*?” she whispered.

Ada frowned. “I don't believe it,” she said through tight lips and took hold of Emilie's hand. “Something's not right, but rest assured, I'll find out what I can.”

Emilie nodded and swallowed the alarm jamming her throat. She picked up her embroidery hoop and tried to resume her needlework. Overcome, Emilie sat in stony silence, too disconcerted to carry on a simple conversation. For as long as she had known him, Robert had only ever demonstrated a gentle spirit and a kind heart. He was peace-loving and detested violence of any kind. On many occasions, she had witnessed him give his share of grain from the mill to a poor family in need. She could not believe he would become embroiled in any trouble, especially not a riot.

Before long, the portress returned and approached them. “A Jesuit Father has arrived and wishes to speak to you both. He awaits you in the entrance hall.”

Emilie's spirits soared. Who could it be other than Père Marc-Mathieu? She knew he would not abandon them. He might know the truth about what happened, but more importantly, he would know how to help them. Much to her surprise, however, it was not Père Marc-Mathieu who greeted them, but Père Nicholas. Brows pressed together in concern, he stepped close to them. "Père Marc-Mathieu sent me here to speak to you," he said in a low voice.

"What news have you, *mon* Père?" Emilie asked.

To her profound disappointment he relayed the same information the portress had. Hope perished with every word he spoke.

"Officials searched the mill," he added in a low tone. "Thankfully, Robert wasn't there, but they continue to search for him. Père Marc-Mathieu ascertained that he never arrived at the Récollet monastery either, but he wants me to reassure you that he is doing all he can to help Robert and beseeches you to have patience and put your trust in God. Père Marc-Mathieu will not fail to bring you all the news he can gather. I hope to return soon."

Although his words helped soothe Emilie's frantic heart, she stifled the tears that threatened. Yet, she clung to a glimmer of hope with all her heart.

"I'll return next Thursday. Hopefully, I'll bring good news."

Her words embroiled with emotion, Emilie nodded.

63

Night brought Emilie no peace. Unable to sleep, she sat up in bed and glanced at Ada whose light snores resonated in a steady cadence. Emilie rose, donned a robe, and reached for the prayer book on the nightstand between their beds. Perhaps the peaceful chapel would ease her worries. She walked through the upper corridor, past the dormitories of the student boarders, and descended the stairs to the main level and the chapel. She placed her hand on the door and pushed it open. A waft of cool air breezed over her.

The sound of a woman weeping haunted the eerie silence within. The chapel lay in darkness except for a few burning candles set on a small table at the foot of a statue of the Virgin Mary. Face down and prone on the stone floor in front of the altar lay a woman, her body heaving with anguished sobs. She wore the black habit and white veil of a novice.

Unsure what to do, Emilie hesitated, stunned. As if the woman sensed her presence, the weeping stopped. The novice raised herself to her knees and looked back at Emilie who stood like a statue at the doors. Their eyes locked. In the dim light, Emilie could not be sure, but it looked like Emmanuelle.

"You! What are you doing here!" Emmanuelle's voice echoed in the arched nave.

"I couldn't sleep so I came to pray." Uncertain, Emilie did not move.

La Bonne Soeur averted her face and wiped her eyes with the sleeve of her habit. She gathered herself to her feet, and with her head bowed, moved toward Emilie, and reached past her for the door handle.

Impulsively, Emilie laid her hand on Emmanuelle's arm. "Please, may I help?"

La Bonne Soeur raised her head. Pain glimmered in her red and swollen eyes. "You? *Une petite bébé*?" Her face puckered with misgiving.

"I may be young, but I know how to keep a confidence. If all I can do is listen, well, that's worth something isn't it?"

Emmanuelle removed Emilie's hand from her arm and gripped it until it hurt. "You must forget you saw me like this."

"Of course, I will never speak of it."

Awkwardly, Emmanuelle pulled her hand away and her expression softened. She studied Emilie's face then swung open the door and swept past her.

64

Three days later, Emile encountered Emmanuelle under different circumstances. La Bonne Soeur sat on a bench in the cloister, absorbed by a book that lay open on her lap. Her lips moved in prayer and brilliant sunlight shone on her serene face like a halo.

Ever since the incident in the chapel, Emilie had been unable to strike the vision of the tormented woman from her mind. She had longed to help her, but felt helpless as to what to do. Emmanuelle had given her refuge, had promised to protect her. And if La Bonne Soeur refused to accept her aid, the least she could do was offer the poor woman her friendship. She owed it to her.

Emilie gathered her courage and approached. “May I sit with you, Soeur?”

La Bonne Soeur's eyes sprang open and her cheeks reddened when she saw Emilie. Although a frown replaced the look of calm on her face, she acquiesced with a slight nod.

“May I ask what you are reading?” Emilie asked.

“The Madonna in Sorrow, a prayer from the 15th century.”

“May I read it?”

Emmanuelle passed the book to her.

“O Virgin Mother; to Thee do I come, before thee I kneel, sinful and sorrowful. Despise not my petition, but in Thy clemency, hear and answer me.”

The words hung in the air for some fleeting seconds.

“But this is a prayer of penance,” Emilie said.

“Things are not always what they seem.”

“No, I suppose not.” Emilie's thoughts turned to the truth of those words as they pertained to her own problems. “Enclosed within these walls, there is so much peace and safety. How sad that the troubles of the outside continue to plague us within."

La Bonne Soeur's head tilted and she raised her eyebrows. "Well spoken for one as young as you."

"It is the truth. You already know the troubles that brought me here." Emilie paused, her hands on either side of her on the bench seat. The conversation stalled and she decided to change tactic. "What made you wish to become a novice?"

A long pause ensued and Emilie sensed Emmanuelle somehow at war with herself. Much to her surprise, the older woman's eyes became reflective. She heaved a long sigh and cleared her throat.

"I came to New France as a *Filles de Roi,* filled with trepidation, but eager for a new life. It was not long before a wealthy seigneur chose me for his wife. We married and I bore him a son. The child came early, but he was strong and survived." Her voice wavered with emotion. She swallowed before continuing. "Then the fates turned against me. My husband beat me and cast me from his home without my son. Somehow, I found my way here. The sisters accepted me and nursed me until I recovered. I have been here ever since, a married woman unable to take the veil. I wear the clothes of a novice because one day I hope to become a nun. For now I am trapped – neither wife nor nun."

"What could have caused him to treat you so terribly?"

"You are young, innocent. It is not for you to know the reasons." Emmanuelle's curt tone cut with force.

"And your son?"

Emmanuelle swallowed and shook her head. Pain etched her face. "I do not know what became of him." Her eyes welled. "My husband sent him away, but I do not know where or with whom. I have searched for him ever since. He would be grown now, a young man. The only means I have to identify him is by the birthmark in the shape of a horse's head on his right hip."

Her voice faded and it seemed as if her thoughts wandered to a time and place long in the past.

The sun disappeared behind a bulbous cloud and a breeze wafted over them.

Too shocked to speak, Emilie was at a loss at what to say. She contemplated her own troubles, which paled in comparison. All her life, she had known the loving arms of a kind mother and the indulgence of a generous, wise father who was taken from them much too soon. She could not fathom such horrors. Agony burned deep in this poor woman's soul. Now Emilie understood her strange behaviour. How could one face each new day burdened with the pain of the past? Emilie's heart opened to her. Now that Emmanuelle had shared her deepest secrets, the desire to befriend her burgeoned. Tentatively, Emilie touched the woman's sleeve. "There is nothing that can replace all you have lost, but I wish there was something I could do."

"There is nothing you can do. Nothing anyone can do."

"No, I suppose not, but I can offer you my friendship."

Emmanuelle gave her a cold look. "There are better friends to be found than me." She clutched her book, rose from the bench, and without casting a glance at Emilie, glided away.

65

A whirlwind of emotion churned through Emmanuelle as she walked away from the cloister. If she aided this young woman, she might erase some of her guilt over the loss of her only son. She had caused the destruction to his young life. Not a day passed that she didn't pray that he was safe, well cared for, even loved. By helping Emilie, could she expiate her own sins? Alternatively, was Emilie a minion of Satan sent to torment her? If so, how would she discern the difference?

The abbess had once told her that God often whispered to errants. However, her sins were many and of the worst kind. God would never whisper to her. Atonement was a gift beyond her reach. Or was it? Could that whisper of God have come in the form of a *jeune fille* asking for aid in a fight against a corrupt Seigneur? Must she demonstrate to God that she can help the defenseless before He granted her the balm of reparation she so desperately sought? Perhaps she had suffered too much for herself, and now she must suffer for others if her sins were to be forgiven. In the end, would she lose herself? Or would helping Emilie only bring more pain, more guilt, and more brokenness?

Emmanuelle fought to stifle the anger that burned inside her. What had possessed her to tell the girl the partial tale of her sordid past? Her own foolishness frustrated her. She was the elder, old enough to be the girl's mother, a benefactress, the one whose duty was to protect and care for her, yet Emilie seemed to have taken on the role of nurturer. And she knew little about her. At every encounter, Emilie demonstrated the utmost respect towards her. Although her mysteriousness sometimes displeased her, all was forgotten at the knowledge she was helping Emilie escape a terrible fate by another ruthless seigneur. Seigneurs – the thread that bound them together.

Emilie touched something deep inside her, a long-buried mothering instinct. Her heart ached so much for her lost son. Emilie was good, but she was evil and dirty. Yet, the young woman provided the balm, which helped ease some of her torment. If she was careful, perhaps she could help the girl without soiling her in the process. This was her chance to do something right. For that reason alone, Emmanuelle would do everything she could to protect Emilie. To befriend the young woman did not seem like such a bad idea after all. In fact, she longed for it.

66

The following Thursday, Père Nicholas returned to the Ursuline convent to speak to Emilie and Ada. "Père Marc-Mathieu wishes you to know that the rumours about Robert are true. He was arrested for inciting a riot, but escaped."

Emilie's hand flew to her mouth. She could not believe it. This was not the Robert she knew. She reached for her mother's hand and braced herself to ask the question for which she feared the answers. "Does anyone know where he is?"

Père Nicholas shook his head. "Please do not let this distress you."

Emilie inhaled a deep breath. "I am fine, *mon* Père. Please tell me all."

He glanced at her mother, who nodded for him to continue.

"Père Marc-Mathieu sent a letter to Frère Bonaventure of the Récollets asking if Robert had arrived. Unfortunately, the good friar confirmed that he had seen neither Robert nor the letter."

"Where could Robert have gone? When we parted ways, he was on his way there." Emilie's voice quivered. "What happened? How did things go so terribly wrong?"

"No one knows. Frère Bonaventure did reveal, however, that a stranger had been to the Jesuit convent in search of Robert, but after not finding him there, the man left and hasn't returned since."

67

Père Nicholas did not return the following Thursday. Emilie had waited anxiously with Ada the entire day until night fell and the portress locked the front gates and retired to bed.

Far too distracted, Emilie had avoided Emmanuelle, fearful

she would be unable to disguise her worries beneath the Soeur's discerning gaze. Besides, Emilie could not concentrate, let alone maintain a decent conversation. Only in the privacy of the small room she shared with her mother, could she release the tumult of worry she had carried so stoically since morning.

"I've been thinking, Emilie. What would you say if I were to return to Pointe-du-Lac?"

"To do what?" Emilie raised herself up on her elbow.

"To find out for ourselves what is happening."

Emilie's first instinct was to reject the idea. She didn't want to be separated from her mother, but her need for more information and her sense of security in the convent conquered her unwillingness.

"Emilie?" Ada asked. "What do you think?"

"Yes, you should go."

"Good. I think it's for the best. One of the sisters said she could arrange transport by way of a merchant and his wife who travel regularly from here to Trois-Riviere then on to Pointe-du-Lac."

Emilie chewed her lip and stared out of the window. "Can we wait one more week? Perhaps Père Nicholas will come next Thursday with good news."

"*Oui*, that will give me time to make arrangements. If Robert is found, then I won't have to return to Pointe-du-Lac at all."

68

The following Thursday, Père Nicholas did return to the convent, but with nothing new to report regarding Robert's whereabouts or welfare. Ada took her leave of Emmanuelle and Emilie. Amid tears and promises to send news soon, she departed.

69

Seigneur Richard shoved open the creaky, broken-hinged door of the outhouse while still adjusting his knee breeches and stepped out. When he glanced up he nearly collided with Thomas who waited, arms akimbo, his face furrowed by a tense scowl.

"*Tabernac*, man, it seems I can't even enjoy the privacy of my *bécosse* without interruption. I swear you are like a cat creeping upon its prey," Seigneur Richard complained.

"I need to talk to you," Thomas said without altering his expression.

"So, talk."

Thomas glanced about. "In private."

"Don't know too many people who hang around an outhouse." Seigneur Richard tilted his head towards the house. "Come inside."

They entered through the back door into the kitchen and made their way to the main sitting room. A settee and two wing chairs rested on either side of a tiny round table topped with a candle-lantern. Seigneur Richard glanced back at Thomas. "Shut the door behind you."

Thomas shoved the door closed with his foot.

Seigneur Richard sat and invited Thomas to sit in the chair across from him. "What news have you from Québec?"

Thomas placed his tricorne on his lap. "The girl was granted sanctuary with the Ursulines in Québec."

"Sanctuary? Her mother too?"

Thomas nodded. "She is concealed there as if she were a nun herself, never setting foot outside, assisting with the services at the church, and doing her share of the work in the convent. A most unsatisfactory arrangement for you. I'm afraid it'll be impossible to gain access to her."

"And the miller?"

Thomas shrugged. "The authorities still seek him. He seems to have vanished and no one knows where he went."

Seigneur Richard ran his hands through his hair then slammed his fist on his thigh. "A convent. How in the blazes of hell am I to get at her there?"

"I studied the building at some length, but could find no way to breach its walls, either by force or fraud. The portress at the gate is shrewd and meddlesome, asking far too many questions for her own good. Unless you're a saint or the pope himself, she never lets anyone pass."

Seigneur Richard's muscles tensed and his pulse raced with rage. All his efforts so far had been for naught. The more the girl eluded him, the greater his need to possess her. He would make her his and no one would deny him. This was his seigneury and if he ordered a woman of lower class to spread her legs then so be it.

He rose and strode to the window. Things had gone from complicated to impossible and he had already spent far too much time on this matter. Time to end the ordeal. Besides, he despised the resignation in Thomas' attitude. It only made him angrier. "You think I should give up, Thomas?" he asked, his eyes not straying from the rich fields of his seigneury, his voice dripping with derision.

"It's not like you," replied Thomas.

"You're right, it's not like me to cut my losses and admit defeat. And I won't tolerate it in my men either." He swung around, leaned against the windowsill, and crossed his arms. "I could go to Québec myself to see if there is anything to be done." He punctuated his words with a direct glower at Thomas.

Thomas glared back at him. A muscle twitched in his jaw.

"You think I missed something?"

"I suppose not." Seigneur Richard dismissed the thought and pressed his lips tight. He had struck out to win the girl and failed miserably. Out-witted by a miller, a young girl, a middle-aged dimwitted woman, and a black-robed Jesuit priest! If he were to give up the chase for the girl now, he'd never dare to hold up his head among his peers and subordinates again. Incessant and bitter remembrances of his failure would always trouble him. And he hated failure. He would never give up.

"There is one man who might be able to help you," Thomas offered, one eyebrow raised.

"Who?"

"Seigneur Claude Prudhomme." Thomas said.

"Prudhomme?" Seigneur Richard tested the name as he returned to his chair by the hearth.

Thomas's eyes glimmered with malice. "*Oui.* If anyone has the cunning to breach the convent, it is he. In fact, there are rumors he already has."

Seigneur Richard stroked his chin. Seigneur Claude Prudhomme; the one man he knew whose reach was more powerful than his own was. His vast lands bordered his. "Prudhomme is part man, part devil."

"*Oui*, but he takes on the most difficult, most hopeless of challenges," Thomas added.

"To seek this man's help brings its own dangers. He has been known to kill a man for looking at him askance. If I seek his help, I would be indebted to him. And the price he might demand could be more than I can pay."

Thomas crossed his arms across his chest. "The way I see it, he might be your only option."

True, Seigneur Richard thought. It was either that or risk humiliation and failure. He rubbed his chin with his thumb and fingers and nodded. "I'll go pay the man a visit tomorrow.

You're coming with me."

70

Seigneur Pierre Robillard arrived in Québec and went straight to his uncle, Count Georges Le Barroy, who lived in a wide two-story home on a vast tract of land near the outskirts of the town. They sat facing each other in a set of chairs on either side of an unlit hearth. Two large open windows allowed a pleasant breeze to flow through the room.

After paying all due ceremony to his uncle, and delivering his Cousin Richard's compliments, Pierre addressed his sire's brother with a look of seriousness. "I have a matter to discuss with you. Although I am betraying Richard's confidence, it is my duty to tell you about it. Unless you interfere, the situation may become serious and produce negative consequences."

Georges heaved a sigh. "One of Richard's usual scrapes, I suppose?"

"This time the fault is not Richard's, but his spirit is roused; and, as I said, no one but you can resolve his dilemma."

"Well, let me hear it." Georges leaned back in his chair, his fingertips pressed together over his corpulent belly.

"There is a Jesuit priest in Pointe-du-Lac who bears a grudge against Richard, and matters have escalated between them."

Georges puckered his face. "I've told you both more than once to stay away from the clergy unless it is absolutely unavoidable!"

"But Uncle, Richard would have let him alone, had it been possible. It is the *priest* who has gone out of his way to provoke *Richard*."

"What the devil has this priest to do with either one of my nephews?" Georges straightened in his chair and leaned forward.

"Well, the priest is well known as a restless spirit, one who takes pride in stirring up matters. He has taken a girl of Pointe-du-Lac under his protection, whom he regards with *great* affection." He paused and looked pointedly back at his uncle. "And I don't know what else."

"Affection? What sort of affection?" His uncle leaned forward, eyebrows raised.

"A jealous sort of affection."

"Ah, I see," Georges said, leaning back again. "This priest believes that Richard has taken a fancy to 'his' young woman."

"Taken a fancy is the least of it. You know Richard. When he wants something, he will stop at nothing to get it. And now you see why this situation needs an advocate like you to intervene."

Georges nodded. "I think I'm beginning to understand."

"Richard had an enchanting encounter with this girl when he met her on the road and has since fallen for her charms. Richard is a young man, not a priest. But this is not what I came to see you about. The real problem lies in the fact that the priest has begun to talk of Richard disrespectfully, as if he were a low-born *habitant* or coarse fur trader, and has tried to instigate the entire village against him."

Georges cupped his right fist in his left hand. "And his fellow priests? What do they do to stop their brother's shameful behaviour?"

"They don't do anything to rein the priest in. They know him to be a hotheaded fool and are used to his rants. The Jesuit priests in Pointe-du-Lac all bear a great respect to Richard and don't want to do anything to incite his displeasure. Besides, this priest has such a good reputation among the villagers that they call him a saint."

"A saint who bears a secret affection for a young girl?" Georges shook his head and pinched the bridge of his nose. "I assume this priest doesn't know that Richard is my nephew?"

"Oh, he does, he knows full well how high you stand in the level of government. It is exactly what encourages him."

Georges's eyes narrowed. "What do you mean?"

"He goes to great lengths to disguise it, but he delights in vexing Richard because he is your nephew. He scoffs at the nobility and politicians, at their lack of power compared to that of the Church."

"He does, does he? What is this priest's name?" Georges said, cheeks red.

"Père Marc-Mathieu of the Jesuit House of Pointe-du-Lac."

His uncle rose, crossed to the small writing table near the window. He reached for his quill and dipped it in ink. With an incensed flourish, he inscribed the name on a blank sheet of paper.

"This priest has always had such a disposition," continued Pierre, encouraged by his uncle's growing ire. "His former life is well known. He was born into a wealthy family with enough money to rival the nobles who lived in his region of France. Enraged at his failure to make them all yield to him, he killed a young nobleman, and turned to priesthood to escape the gallows."

"Despicable!" exclaimed the Count, panting and puffing with an important air as he returned to his place by the hearth.

"Lately, he is more enraged than ever, because he has failed in something, which he was eager about. The girl." Pierre leaned forward. "And from this, you will understand what sort of man he is. Secretly, he desires this young girl whom he considers his protégée; at least until he learned of the young man, another of his young protégées, who wants this same girl, and plans to marry her."

"She must be quite a beauty to have three men vying for her attentions."

"That she is, *mon cher oncle*. This young man is someone

you may already know of. He is the miller in Pointe-du-Lac. I think the Sovereign Council has had some recent dealings with him."

"Who is he?"

"His name is Robert Lanzille."

"Robert Lanzille!" exclaimed the Count. "He is most definitely being sought. Apparently he possesses some sort of letter, which caused quite a bit of trouble. Why did Richard not tell me of all this sooner? Why did he let things go so far without seeking my direction and help?"

"I will be candid with you. On the one hand, knowing how busy you are and how many issues you face each day, he felt duty bound not to give you any additional trouble."

As if to agree, his uncle drew a long breath, and put his hand to his forehead, intimating the fatigue he underwent because of the duties and responsibilities of his rank.

"Besides, he is so vexed, so angry, so annoyed at the insults made against him by this priest, that he is determined to seek justice by his own means rather than to obtain it prudently through you. I tried to help resolve the situation, but since matters seem to have taken a wrong course, I thought it my duty to inform you of everything. You are, after all, head of our family."

"You should have mentioned this to me sooner."

"True, but I hoped the problem would have disappeared, or that the troublesome priest would come to his senses or been transferred from that convent, as is often the case among the clergy. Then it all would have ended quietly."

"Now it falls to me to settle it."

"That's what I believe, Uncle. You, with your discretion and authority, will know how to keep this situation from escalating, and at the same time secure Richard's honour. You have many means at your disposal that I'm not even aware of. I do know, however, that the previous Bishop had a great deal of respect for this priest. But Québec has a new Bishop now and if perceived that the best course of action would be to give the priest a change of scenery, all it would take would be a few words from you to this new Bishop."

"Leave all the arrangements to me," said the Count.

"Oh, *bien sûr*!" Pierre could not prevent the grin that broke free. "I do not mean to direct you, but the regard I have for the reputation of our family bade me to inform you." He paused. "And I'm afraid I've been guilty of another error. I fear I might have wrongfully portrayed Richard to you. I would have no peace if I were the cause of making you think that Richard had no confidence in you, or would refuse to speak to you himself. Believe me, Uncle, it is merely that he didn't wish to bother you. And I felt compelled to make sure you knew everything before things got beyond our control."

"Oh, I know. You two have been close since boyhood. You would never bring harm to one another if it could be helped. The both of you will always be friends, even though I often have to extricate you from one scrape or another." Georges heaved a profound sigh and shook his head. "Together, you and Richard give me twice as many problems to deal with than all other affairs of state."

Pierre did not wish to hear about his uncle's political troubles. "Well, I thank you, Uncle, and I know Richard will too." Pierre rose. "I don't wish to take up any more of your time."

"Very well. Be prudent," the Count said.

Pierre grinned. That was his uncle's usual form of dismissal to him. "We most definitely will."

71

Mon cher cousin, Richard,

Uncle Georges and I send you our most cordial salutations. Negotiations between us progressed better than expected. You can be assured of the assistance you require to resolve the matter we discussed. In fact, the results will be evident even before I arrive home.

This, cousin, should bring you great comfort. You must proceed with your original plan to acquire the prize with post haste. Should you fail to do so at this stage, or decide to withdraw, then you shall suffer intolerable ridicule from me when I return. And I shall then seek the compensation owed to me at this failure. When I return, I look forward to sharing a glass of wine at your fine table where we can celebrate a most satisfactory victory and settle the wager between us.

Your cousin,
Pierre Robillard

72

To solve his nephew's problem, Count Georges de Barroy knew he must speak to the Bishop whom he had not yet met. Bishop Nicholas de Laval had been in New France only a few weeks. The best way to meet the man was to host a supper in his honour. Georges wasted no time in sending out the invitations. To guarantee the Bishop's attendance, Georges invited the highest-ranking men of New France including the Governor and the Intendent.

The elaborate dinner consisted of split pea soup, roast duck, roast moose, and cassoulet. After partaking of two deserts, a maple sugar pie, and apple cranberry galettes, Georges invited the Bishop into his private den under the guise of reviewing his collection of books.

"Quite impressive, I must say," the Bishop said. "You have a personal favourite of mine, the *Collection of Traditional Tales* by Charles Perrault."

Georges offered the Bishop a cognac and invited him to sit near the window beside a glass-enclosed bookcase. He raised his cup. "Here's to our good friendship," he toasted and studied the Bishop with a discerning eye. The man was of slim build with a narrow face. A round bulb tipped his long thin nose, which drooped over his top lip. Clean-shaven except for a thin moustache and a tiny clump of beard between lip and chin, he was neither ugly nor handsome. A kind intelligence sparkled in his eyes.

The Bishop raised his glass and sipped the cognac. "Ah, a fine cognac indeed."

"I import only the best from the Charente region of France," Georges said with a smile.

A brief silence befell them.

"I thought I might speak with your Reverence on a matter of mutual interest, which would be best to settle between ourselves," Georges said with caution.

"Most certainly," the Bishop encouraged.

"I will speak candidly about something, and I have no doubt you will agree with me. In the Jesuit House near Pointe-du-Lac there is a certain priest by the name of Père Marc-Mathieu."

The Bishop bowed assent. "I have heard of him. In fact, his name was put before me to consider as abbot of his own convent."

"Your Excellency would be wise to allow me to tell you what I know of him first. I don't know him personally; I am acquainted with several Jesuit priests, zealous, prudent, humble men, who are worth their weight in gold. But in every family, there is always one individual who may be a little troublesome. And this is Père Marc-Mathieu. I know by several occurrences that he is a person who is inclined to disputes, who is not always prudent, and who I dare say, gave your predecessor some anxiety."

"I heard no such reports. In fact, only the highest praise has been given regarding Père Marc-Mathieu."

"*Mais oui*, I have heard much the same," said Georges. "I am not surprised to hear that your Excellency entertains such a high opinion of Père Marc-Mathieu. Some say he is an exemplary priest and is held in much esteem. However, as a sincere friend to you, I must tell you what I know. And even if you are already acquainted with it, I think it my duty to caution you about possible consequences."

A puzzled look came over the Bishop. "Please go ahead. Tell me."

"Père Marc-Mathieu has taken a fugitive under his protection whom you may have heard mentioned. This man escaped in disgrace from the hands of justice after inciting the recent riots in Québec. His name is Robert Lanzille.

"I am unfamiliar with the name. But, it is a priest's duty to seek those who have gone astray and recall them to goodness."

"Yes, but contact with such offenders is a dangerous thing- a delicate affair." Georges puffed out his cheeks and blew the air out. "I thought it best to bring this to your attention because this may not reflect well upon you, Excellency."

"I am obliged to you for this information, but I am confident that Père Marc-Mathieu has had no intervention with the person you mention other than to try and set him right again."

Georges leaned forward and lowered his voice. "I presume you know what kind of a man the priest was as a layman and about the life he led in his youth?"

"It is one of the glories of priesthood that a man becomes a different person when he assumes the habit. This is so in Père Marc-Mathieu's case."

"I would gladly believe it, Excellency. Wolves may change their skins, but never their nature." Georges paused. "Besides, I have proof."

"If you know for certain that this priest has been guilty of any fault, and we are all liable to err, you must inform me of it. I am his superior and it is my duty to correct and reprove."

"Very well, I will tell you." Georges took a long sip of brandy. "In addition to the unpleasing circumstance of the favour this Père displays towards Robert Lanzille, there is one other grievous thing, which may settle any doubts you may have at once. Père Marc-Mathieu has begun a quarrel with my nephew, Seigneur Richard Tonnacour."

"Indeed! I am sorry to hear it, very sorry indeed!"

"My nephew is young, hot tempered, and is not accustomed to being provoked."

"I shall make every inquiry on the subject. We are all human and liable to err, and if Père Marc-Mathieu has failed, then something must be done."

"I caution you, Excellency, that this matter must be settled quietly and remain secret between us. Too much meddling will only make matters worse. These disputes frequently originate from a small incident and become more serious as they proceed. My nephew is young, and the priest, from what I hear, even though he is older, has all the spirit and inclinations of a young man. It is up to us who are empowered to remedy their errors. Fortunately there is time. The matter has caused no great stir yet. There is plenty of time to remove the straw from the flame. Your Excellency, without doubt, knows where to post this priest so he can avoid falling under any suspicion. By placing him at a distance, we shall kill two birds with one stone. All will be settled and no harm will be done."

The Bishop took a long sip of his brandy, leaned back in his chair, and studied Georges with a critical eye.

Georges met his gaze without wavering, even though the Bishop made him a little nervous. He could tell the Bishop was no fool.

"I understand what you are implying," said the Bishop. "I must take this under serious consideration."

"If it is not quickly resolved, I foresee a mountain of woes. Without undue haste, it will not remain a secret for much longer, and if that happens, it is not only my nephew who will be affected."

"I understand."

"I'm much relieved, Excellency. It is important that the Jesuits continue to build upon their good name and remain free from strife and live in harmony with those who they serve."

"Certainly," said the Bishop. "There are many places for Père Marc-Mathieu to continue his good work. But if I act too swiftly it might look like a punishment; one that is issued without having ascertained all the details."

"I speak of no punishment, Excellency. I merely suggest a prudent arrangement to prevent any future troubles."

"I am aware of that, but as you have related the circumstances, it is possible that rumours of this matter may already be circulating. There are mischief-makers who take a mad delight in seeing the nobility and clergy in discord. Everybody has his dignity to maintain; and I also, as Bishop, have an express duty to make a fair and justified decision. Your noble nephew, if he is as high-spirited as you describe, might take it as a satisfaction offered to him, and may boast of his triumph."

"Surely you jest. My nephew is a gentleman of rank and wealth, but he will do what I tell him to do. I give you my word that he knows nothing of our discussion this evening. We do not need to tell anyone of what we have decided here this night." He heaved a deep sigh. "As to gossip, what do you suppose can be said? After all, the departure of a priest to preach somewhere else is not unusual. So you see, we need not worry ourselves about any gossip."

"At any rate, it would be wise to take precautions by having your nephew prove his friendship and deference, not for our sakes as individuals, but out of respect for the habit. A sizeable donation to the church, in land or money will suffice."

"Certainly, this is fair, but there is no need. I know the Jesuits are always well treated by my nephew. He does so from inclination; it is the disposition of our family; and besides, he knows it pleases me."

The Bishop stared at him, his jaw twitching.

Georges raised his fist to his mouth and coughed. "In this instance, however, a good donation is only right. Leave me to settle it, Excellency. I will make a cautious suggestion in this regard to my nephew, lest he come to suspect what has passed between us. And in return, I would be satisfied if you could find some post for the priest at a good distance from here."

"I have received a request for an additional Jesuit father at the convent at La Prairie de la Madelaine."

Georges nodded and smiled. "That sounds reasonable indeed."

"Since the thing must be done, it had better be done at once." The Bishop rose.

"*Oui*, Excellency. Better today than tomorrow." Georges rose. "And if I can do anything for the Jesuits, my friends, I shall be only too happy to assist."

"I have heard of your many kindnesses," replied the Bishop as he followed Georges to the door.

"We have extinguished a spark," said Georges, "one that might have become a dangerous flame. I am pleased to know that a few words spoken between good friends has settled this unfortunate matter."

Georges opened the door and invited the Bishop to pass first. They returned to mingle with the rest of the company.

73

Père Marc-Mathieu had just finished milking the cow when Père Nicholas hurried through the paddock towards him. "A Jesuit priest has arrived from Québec. The father superior wishes to see you in his office."

"Me? I wonder why?" Père Marc-Mathieu handed the bucket of milk to Père Nicholas and wiped his hands on the apron he wore over his habit.

"I don't know, but it seems important."

Père Marc-Mathieu hurried to the rear of the house, scooped some water from the rain barrel into a bucket and washed then dried his hands. He entered through the back door, made his way to the father superior's office, and knocked. At the father superior's invitation, he entered. Inside, a man in the black robe of the Jesuits sat in one of two empty chairs opposite the father superior's desk. Both men rose to greet him.

"This is Père Philippe Sabourin from Québec," introduced the father superior.

Père Philippe was a stern faced man of middling years, short and stocky, with bulging eyes and greying hair in a balding crown. After exchanging greetings, the father superior invited Père Marc-Mathieu to sit.

"Père Philippe has delivered a dispatch to me from Bishop Laval in Québec. It contains directions to transfer you to La Prairie de la Madelaine."

Père Marc-Mathieu's mouth fell open. "Transfer? I don't understand. Does it explain why?"

The father superior held up the document. "It doesn't say, but you are to leave today. It also requires you to relinquish any involvement you may have in Pointe-du-Lac and not to correspond with anyone here. Père Philippe is to accompany you to your new post." The father superior handed him the document.

Père Marc-Mathieu read it. It contained no more information than what the father superior had already told him. He looked first at the father superior then Père Philippe. "Did the Bishop at least give a verbal explanation?"

The man shook his head. "It is not for us to question why. This is the command of Bishop Laval and it must be obeyed without question."

Thoughts of Robert, Emilie, and Ada rushed into his mind. To abandon them in their hour of need. What would they do without his help? And after all the promises and reassurances he had given them. But he reproached himself for want of faith, and for having supposed that he was necessary in anything. He bowed his head in obedience and left the room to gather his belongings.

It took mere minutes to collect his meager possessions, which consisted of two additional black robes, several pairs of braies, and his breviary and sermons. He tossed them into a thick sack and slung it over his shoulders, twisting it to rest comfortably over his back. With a heavy step, he descended the stairs. The father superior, Père Philippe, his trusted friend Père Nicholas, and the other members of his order waited for him at the front door. After a few words of advice, a blessing from the father superior, and hearty embraces from his fellow brethren, he took leave of the convent. The route they were ordered to take did not even allow him to pass through Pointe-du-Lac one final time.

74

One day after Seigneur Richard received Pierre's letter, Thomas brought him the news that Père Marc-Mathieu had been sent away from the Jesuit house. A surge of excitement raced through him. Any doubts disappeared. He was now more than ready to risk everything rather than give up now. It was time to pay Seigneur Claude Prudhomme a visit and make a plan to acquire the girl once and for all.

75

Ada's journey home to Pointe-du-Lac with the kind merchant and his wife passed without incident. They spent the first night at a comfortable and clean inn, and after setting off before sunrise, they arrived in Pointe-du-Lac the next day before noon. Ada alighted on the road in front of the convent and thanked the couple, assuring them she would enjoy the walk home from there. She waved to them as they rode away and watched the cart make its way into settlement. Ada turned down the long path that led to the Jesuit convent and farm. At the front door, she pulled the rope for the bell on the porch.

Père Nicholas answered. His eyes widened the moment he saw her. "Madame Basseaux! I wasn't expecting you."

"I came to see Père Marc-Mathieu. Is he here?"

"Why no, he's not."

"Will he be back soon?"

"Soon!" answered the priest, shrugging his shoulders. "Only God knows that answer."

Ada frowned. "What does that mean? Where has he gone?"

"To the Jesuit seigneury at La Prairie de la Madeleine."

"La Prairie?"

Père Nicholas nodded. "*Oui*, La Prairie. It is a settlement at the confluence of the Saint-Jacques River and the Saint Lawrence River. The Jesuits have owned the seigneury there since Anno Domini 1647."

"Is it far?"

"*Mais oui*," replied the priest, waving his extended hand in the air to signify a great distance.

"But why?"

"Because the Bishop ordered it."

"But why, when he was doing so much good here?"

He shook his head. "If our superiors were obliged to render a reason for all the orders they give, where would be our obedience, my good woman?"

"But Emilie and I will be lost without him. This will be our ruin."

"Unfortunately, this is the life of a Jesuit priest. They probably needed a good priest at La Prairie."

"There are many good priests. Why him?"

"Good priests are everywhere, to be sure, but sometimes they want a particular priest for a specific purpose. The abbot there would have written to the Bishop requesting an additional priest, likely to meet a need within their order, and the Bishop decided Père Marc-Mathieu was the right man to send."

Ada tried to overcome her rising panic. "When did he go?"

"The day before yesterday."

"Oh, if only I had done as I first wished, and come a few days sooner! And you don't know when he will return? Can't you guess at all?"

"My good woman! Nobody knows, except the Bishop, if even he does. When one of our Jesuit priests is called to a particular duty, one can never foresee when it will end. We Jesuits are needed everywhere and there are so few of us. We have convents in all four quarters of the globe. Rest assured, Père

Marc-Mathieu will be a great success at La Prairie among the Iroquois."

"He was like a father to us!" Ada's voice trembled with disappointment. "What are we going to do now? His leaving will be our undoing."

"Please try not to worry. Père Marc-Mathieu was an admirable man; but we have other priests, full of charity and ability, who can assist you. You have me, or I will have Père Jean-Paul or Père Henri come to your aid. We are all men of good worth."

"Oh, *non*," Ada exclaimed. "Père Marc-Mathieu knew our affairs and had made preparations to help us. No one else will be able to understand."

"Then you must have patience."

Ada's disappointment weighed as heavy as a rock on her back. "Please forgive me for troubling you."

"I am sorry, but if you decide to confide in any of us here, well, we are willing to help in any way we can."

"I know and I am grateful for that. Good-bye *mon* Père," Ada said as she turned and made her way back to the path toward her home. Now she knew how a blind woman who had lost her cane felt.

76

Accompanied by Thomas, Seigneur Richard set off on horseback for the manor house of Seigneur Claude Prudhomme. The warm sunny day made their short journey pleasant and comfortable. As they rode, Richard retreated into his thoughts, which wandered to the man he was about to visit.

"You've grown quiet. Second thoughts?" asked Thomas. "There's still time to change your mind."

Seigneur Richard shook his head. "*Non*, you know me better

than that. Once I make up my mind, it's as solid as a brick wall. I'm merely trying to recall everything I know about Prudhomme. It's best to be prepared." He hated having to seek outside help, especially to acquire a woman, but things had gotten away from him somehow and he needed to regain control. If the rumours about Prudhomme were true, then he must be guarded and not allow him any advantage.

"Nobody knows much about Prudhomme." Thomas tilted his tricorne back, exposing his forehead. "He's known for his acts of revenge and outrageous impulses, but I doubt anyone knows the extent of all that he's committed. In his case, which rumours are true and which are false is akin to trying to sort the fly shit from the pepper."

This made them both laugh.

"I do know he amassed considerable wealth before coming to New France and gaining his vast seigneury," Thomas offered.

"He wouldn't have been able to buy it all if he wasn't wealthy." Seigneur Richard changed the reins from one hand to another. "But he's a bit of a recluse, I hear."

"*Oui* and he's been known to shelter an outlaw or two," Thomas added. "At a price of course. And the price is not always monetary. He often extracts payment in the form of a boon or two."

"Terms are always negotiable."

"Not with Prudhomme. If I were you, I would pay him with money so he won't have anything to hold over your head."

"Others might fear him, but not me."

Thomas chuckled. "True, people are more scared of him than you, and with good reason. Prudhomme acquired his power and wealth by committing the dirtiest of deeds. His secret alliances often result in murder. Are you certain you want to get involved with him?"

Seigneur Richard adjusted himself in the saddle. "It's the

only way I can think of to get the girl out of the damn convent."

Both men fell silent.

Thomas rubbed his chin. "I wish you luck. It is unfortunate that you have no other option than to owe Prudhomme a favour."

They rode through a valley lined with *habitant* farms on both sides.

"When we arrive, keep alert," Thomas warned. "Servants who were once in trouble of some sort run his household. By offering them protection, they serve him loyally. Take care how you speak of him too. He has supporters who wouldn't hesitate to inform him of every word."

Whenever Richard had encountered Prudhomme, he had been magnanimous, offering his assistance, should it be needed. Well, he needed it now. Before long he spotted Prudhomme's lone manor house on a high hill in the distance on the north shore of the Saint Lawrence River. Made of stone, the two-story structure loomed above a grouping of a dozen or smaller timber and stone houses with strips of farmland behind each. Much grander than his own seigneurial estate, Richard buried the surge of envy that arose inside of him and kicked his horse into a canter. Thomas followed him up the lane.

77

On the occasion of his sixtieth birthday Seigneur Claude Prudhomme peered out the attic window of his home to the fabulous vista below. Built on a cliff over a rich and narrow valley, his manor house presided regally over *habitant* farms as far as the eye could see; land and people whose livelihoods depended on the whims of his munificence.

The attic was his most private domain and he allowed no one to enter, not even for cleaning. Neatly placed against the walls, two locked chests and three trunks contained his darkest secrets; documents that could destroy lives and a stache of deadly weapons including knives, daggers, swords, and muskets. A metal box inside a locked drawer in his desk contained enough money for him to start a new life should circumstances require it.

The garret was his refuge; where he came to think and plot, or sometimes to escape the pressures of his responsibilities. Like an eagle perched in its nest, Prudhomme had a clear view of his lands from this lofty elevation. No visitor could approach in surprise, for he observed them long before they arrived at his door. In years past many with vengeance in their hearts or murder on their minds had tried to get at him, but the musket fire of his *habitant* men thwarted them ere they could come within a stone's throw.

He watched with interest at the two mounted men who rode up the lane to his house. From this distance he could not discern their identities, but his men would soon greet them, and if they deemed it safe, they would be permitted into the house. Whatever the reason for their visit, he suspected they wanted something from him. But was he in a generous enough mood to entertain their request? He didn't know. In anticipation, he left the attic and went downstairs to wait.

78

Thomas waited outside with the horses while a burly man with a red bulbous nose and bulging biceps showed Seigneur Richard into a handsome hall ceiled with oak. Prudhomme stood in front of the stone chimney, his back to the door. Before the servant could announce his arrival, he swung around to face him.

"Ah, Tonnacour, to what do I owe the pleasure of your visit?"

Prudhomme advanced to the table in the centre of the room and gestured for Richard to sit.

Richard scrutinized Prudhomme from head to foot. It had been more than a year since he had last seen him, but during that time, the man's appearance had coarsened. Prudhomme peered back at him from behind a wrinkled face. Tall, sun burnt, and with a receding hairline of grey hair, the man carried his age well. His carriage and movements, the cutting sarcasm of his facial features, and the deep fire that sparkled in his eye, indicated vigor of body and mind, which would have been remarkable even in a young man.

"I came to solicit your help on a certain matter."

"Please, have a seat." Prudhomme looked at the servant who waited by the door and dismissed him with a brusque nod of his head. When the door clicked shut, he leaned forward. "I'm listening."

"I find myself in a difficult situation which my honour will not allow me to abandon," Richard began.

A spark of interest flashed in Prudhomme's eyes and he leaned closer.

Choosing his words carefully, Richard relayed his problem. The moment he mentioned Père Marc-Mathieu's name, however, Prudhomme's eyes narrowed.

"I know that name; one I find quite odious. That priest is an open enemy to men of our ilk. He defames seigneurs of New France merely because we are wealthy and because he preaches we don't do enough for the people who serve us. I'm sure you are as weary of it as I am."

Eager to build upon this understanding between them, Richard nodded. "I am interested in a certain young woman from Pointe-du-Lac. This priest has placed her beyond my reach at the Ursuline convent in Québec. I am told she is now the protégée of a woman known only as La Bonne Soeur."

The moment he spoke the name, Prudhomme's face reddened and his eyes flashed with malevolence. He pounded his fist on the table. "I've heard all that I need to hear. You did well in coming to me. You have my word that I'll see to this matter on your behalf and get the girl out of there. For now, go home and I'll send word when I know more." He swung open the door and swept from the room.

Stunned, Richard hesitated, unsure of what he'd said that spurred such an agitated reaction. As he turned to leave, the well-muscled man re-appeared in the doorway. "Come with me. I'm to escort you back down the hill."

79

Prudhomme watched Richard and his companion ride away. He paced the length of his attic, vexed at having reacted so impulsively and making a promise he had no heart for. But at the mention of La Bonne Soeur, he had nearly lost his mind with rage.

Jaw clenched, he removed a key tucked behind a loose wallboard and unlocked the centre drawer of his desk. On the top lay a palm-sized portrait in a scratched gilded frame of a woman and child. A beautiful woman. Emmanuelle. A *Fille du Roi*. The woman he had married and loved with his entire heart and soul. A lying bitch and the son she had tried to pass off as his. Even now it was too painful to speak her name. To celebrate the birth of their son, he had commissioned this small painting from a local artist. He slid his finger across her face then over the image of the infant in her arms. But their love had been fleeting; their happiness had dissipated as quickly as a water droplet upon parched dirt. Emmanuelle wounded him, his pride. He had given her his heart and she had destroyed their love, leaving him as an empty shell with a hollow heart, incapable of love. No other person had harmed him so deeply or altered him so indelibly. And for that, he hated her.

The destruction of their lives happened not long after the birth of the boy. He had encountered a man in a tavern searching for a woman who fit her description. That conversation revealed a dark secret, one that had changed everything. Emmanuelle was married; her husband alive and well in France who sought her whereabouts. Aghast, he wisely said nothing to the man.

When he confronted Emmanuelle, she tried to deny it, but the information was far too accurate. After a heated argument, her face awash in a flood of tears, he had goaded the truth from her lying lips. Because of her deception, and the fact the child she swore was his had come early, he believed the child was not his. Blind with rage, he beat her to within a hair's breadth of her life and cast her from his home.

The next day, upon hearing the cries of the baby Emmanuelle had tried to pass off as his son, he ordered a servant to get the child out of his sight. Later, he learned the servant had brought the baby to a childless *habitant* couple who raised him. Eager to wipe away all memory of Emmanuelle and son, he didn't care enough to ask their names.

His sources were everywhere and he learned that Emmanuelle had survived the beating. The Ursuline sisters had taken her in. He gripped the portrait. She must have lied to them too, because she had become a novitiate. A married woman, a bigamist no less, cannot take the vows of the veil. He kept this information to himself, for knowledge was power and one day it might become useful.

He planted one of his most loyal men, Gaston, to live in the gatehouse next to the Ursuline convent. Through Gaston, he controlled Emmanuelle and knew her every movement.

He cast aside his thoughts. Some things were better

forgotten. Seigneur Claude returned the portrait back to its spot, slammed the drawer shut, and locked it again, returning the key to its hiding place.

These memories of Emmanuelle re-ignited his internal pain. For months, he had grown conscious of the passing of time, wearying of the depraved life he had led. Lately, each time he committed a new evil, these feelings accumulated in his memory and became nearly intolerable. The future seemed distant, uncertain, bleak, and it embittered him. To grow old! To die! Then what? His mortality confronted him now like the devil himself.

When facing an enemy, the threat of death had always inspired him with impetuous courage, but now, in the solemn stillness of night, it brought him horror and alarm. With every passing moment, his life was growing shorter. When he was young, violence, revenge, and murder excited him. Now an indistinct but terrible dread haunted him. All his wrongdoings had pushed him into a strange solitude; a mad hole of blackness he could not claw out of.

Shoving these thoughts aside, he watched Richard Tonnacour ride out of sight. He battled against the temptation to change his mind, to break his word, but if he did, he would sink low in the eyes of the man and others. That, he could not risk.

He descended to the main floor and gathered three of his most daring men – the ones he trusted most to administer his atrocities. "Take some horses and a carriage, one unmarked by crests, and go to Québec. You are to inform Gaston he's to get a young woman named Emilie out of the convent and bring her to me." He gave them a severe look. "Immediately. Unharmed."

80

In the upper story of the gatehouse, Emmanuelle kept her eyes lowered to the floor, hands clasped behind her back, and spine straight. Her hair flowed down her naked body. She heard footsteps outside the door; heavy footsteps that made a dull thud on the wooden floor boards. She shuddered as the door creaked open.

In a low, dull tone, he said, "Close your eyes."

A chill ran through her at the coldness in his voice. The footsteps grew lighter as he entered the room and came to stand behind her.

"Do not turn around and do not open your eyes or you will be punished," he said. His hand caressed her outer thigh. "Kneel."

Emmanuelle sunk to her knees and waited.

The rustle of cloth told her he was undressing.

"Open for me." He pushed her torso forward.

She lowered her head to the floor, parted her thighs and raised her buttocks, exposing herself fully to him.

From behind, his hand caressed her cheek, her neck, her breast and flicked the nipple.

She moaned softly when two of his fingers rolled her nipple about. A deeper, longer moan escaped her lips when he pinched and twisted it hard.

"Perfect," the whisper of his breath passed her ears.

Fingers grasped her hair and tugged her upward to pull her to her feet. She kept her eyes closed, half in fear of punishment, half in fear that she would wake from the pleasure of this erotic dream. He slid his hand between her thighs, brushing them delicately against her womanhood. A long, thin finger slipped inside her.

She whimpered with pleasure and tried to extend her thighs further apart. Another of his fingers pressed her nub of pleasure as his lips touched her ear. Her eyes fluttered, but didn't open, for that would displease him. Instead, she fought to maintain her composure.

"Lay on the bed, your derrière toward me," he whispered into her ear.

She crawled onto the bed and knelt with her head resting on her forearms in front of her.

He trailed his hand over her bottom. She moaned in anticipation. His finger twirled and rubbed against her raw pearl, tantalizing her, heating her desire. She panted, yearning for more, desperate for him to fill her.

He continued to inspect her with his fingers, feeling every crevice with the constant movement of both his hands.

She leaned her head back and moaned, her hips arching towards his finger for more, to get him inside her.

He stopped. "*Non*, you must sit still. I will let you know what I want to do and when I want to do it."

Motionless, she waited. He resumed his ministrations, teasing her until she could stand it no more.

"You do not have my permission to release, if you do, you will regret it." He grabbed her breast and kneaded it with one hand. Suddenly, he jammed a finger deep inside her.

Emmanuelle groaned, long and low, and shivered. She contracted her muscles around his finger as he plunged it in and out, soon adding another finger. She struggled to hold still and had to fight to control the urge to rock in rhythm.

He slipped a third finger inside.

She couldn't hold back anymore and thrust her body back against him.

He came to a halt. "You want more, La Bonne Soeur?" He spoke her name with scorn.

But, Emmanuelle ignored it and nodded.

"You must do something for me first."

Emmanuelle swallowed, unsure of what he would demand.

He waited, the utter silence in the room uncomfortable.

"I'm waiting for your answer." He ran his finger against her small nodule of pleasure.

A shard of bliss forced a shudder from her. The heat of her arousal demanded resolution. "Please... please yes!"

He expelled a prideful laugh and slipped a finger back inside of her. "But you do not yet know what it is I want." He replaced all three fingers and started to work them in and out again while he stroked her pearl with the other hand.

She screamed out in ecstasy.

"You want me inside you, don't you?" he asked in a sultry voice that made her drive herself onto his fingers more.

"*Oui*, please, I want you inside me," she moaned.

He stopped. "First you must bring me the girl named Emilie." He resumed his ministrations.

Now Emmanuelle stopped cold.

He grabbed her by the hair and held her still as he rubbed his erection ever so delicately against her entrance.

She softened, her desire renewing itself, her body desperate for fulfillment.

He stopped again. "Say, yes, La Bonne Soeur, you must say yes, for if you don't, these secret trysts of ours shall be no more."

He let go of her hair and she turned around to face him, her eyes wide open.

His face came within a hair's breadth of hers, twisted with malice. "It would not go well for you if your love of pleasure and pain should be made public, now would it?"

When she did not respond, he swung his arm back and slapped her face hard with all his might.

She recoiled from the strike, but he bent and took a nipple

in his mouth and sucked on it hard as his fingers found their way back into her moistness. He moved from one nipple to the other and continued the same sweet torture.

As she drifted again into the abyss of pleasure, he took her pebble in his mouth and sucked hard. Burning sensuality surged through her. Delirious with pleasure, the welcoming abyss drew near.

He stopped and struck her again. At once, his mouth renewed its assault on her womanhood. This time, she could no longer contain her moans of pleasure, and her body thrashed with ecstasy. Her pleasure intensified. On the verge of release, he stopped and raised his hand once more.

Guilt was her inflexible tyrant. Her body screamed for release; her need for him so great, so powerful, she truly believed she could not live without him and their little games of pleasure. "*Oui,*" she cried out. "I will do it," Emmanuelle screamed out in rapture as he drove himself mercilessly into her.

81

Emmanuelle could not drive away the vision of a shepherd coaxing a lamb to slaughter when she invited Emilie into her private apartment the next day. Her heart laden with guilt, she forced a smile. "I want you to do me a great service; one that nobody but you can do. It is an important task. I will explain it fully when you return. I must speak in person to Père Marc-Mathieu who brought you here to me; but no one must know I have sent for him. I have come up with a plan to solve all your problems, but I need the Jesuit priest to help us. Only you can convince him to come to me."

With each word, another unatoneable sin accrued upon her soiled spirit. Hell drew nearer each day. Soon it would swallow her. No amount of penance, pain, or humiliation could ease her torment at harming this innocent soul. She had promised to protect her, yet it would be by her own hand the girl would suffer. And suffer she would. Her instincts howled with warning that it was a man behind Gaston's demand, likely the seigneur Emilie was so desperate to flee. Emmanuelle despised herself. Yet she could not find the inner strength to refuse Gaston's demands. She lacked the forbearance to walk a path of goodness. Torment was her soul mate, now and forever.

"But to go back to the place where I faced danger? To be near the man who ruined my life? You ask too much of me."

"I shall see to it nothing happens to you." And in her heart, she recognized herself as a most despicable liar, unparalleled by anyone she had ever encountered. Self-loathing slithered over her flesh. Somehow, she held herself taut, expressionless, disguising all signs of the turmoil that burned inside of her and chipped away at her spirit. "You will be transported by private carriage to the Jesuit convent outside of Pointe-du-Lac."

"And my mother? If she returns and does not find me, she will be most distressed."

"Do not worry in that regard. I shall inform your mother of my request. I know she will understand. If you don't encounter her during this errand, she will wait here for your return."

"Without an escort, by solitary roads? I'm not certain." Emilie twisted her finger round and round a loose thread that hung over the side of her small sewing box.

"Your reluctance surprises me, Emilie. These are frivolous worries. You shall be in broad daylight on a road you have travelled many times before. Nothing can go astray. I cannot believe you hesitate to accept this errand."

While Emilie listened, she kept her eyes on her sewing box.

Emmanuelle swallowed, summoning the gall necessary to convince her young charge. "I have known you for such a short time, but in that time, you have become my greatest confidante. And you know that there is nothing I would not do for you in your hour of need, do you not?"

Emilie's shoulders drooped. At length she looked up. "But what shall I say to the portress, who has never seen me go out, and will therefore be sure to ask where I am going?"

"Try to get out without her seeing you; and if you can't manage it, tell her you are going to church to offer up some prayers."

Emilie twisted in her chair. "To tell a falsehood?" She shook her head.

Emmanuelle sighed. Oh, to be so pure, so innocent that one tiny falsehood could bring such hesitation. She brushed away the thought and kept her mind focused on the task. She must not waver. She must convince Emilie or she would lose all. If Gaston followed through with his threats, then what would become of her? Emmanuelle scowled and crossed her arms.

Emilie blushed. "Very well; I owe you so much. I will go."

82

With a leather pouch that contained a change a clothing, a few coins, and her rosary, Emilie stepped into the courtyard of the Ursuline convent. Grey clouds covered the sky and a cool summer breeze drifted over her. She hesitated and glanced about uneasily. Although she had agreed to go on this errand for Soeur Emmanuelle, who she trusted, she could not shake off the sense of disquiet that hung over her. Inhaling a fortifying breath, she crossed to the front gate. Thankfully, the portress was not at her post. Emilie lifted the latch and swung open the gate. As she prepared to pass through, she heard her name called.

"Emilie, wait!"

Emilie turned in the direction of the voice.

Emmanuelle stood in an upper story window. The breeze billowed her white veil. Her hands clutched and twisted the rosary, which hung from the leather girdle at her waist. She opened her mouth as if to say something, but closed it again.

"*Oui*, Soeur?" A jolt of hope that she might call her back fluttered in her belly.

La Bonne Soeur looked down at her, shoulders hunched, and standing unnaturally still. "Do everything as I have told you and return quickly," she called weakly, her tone resigned.

Before Emilie could utter a response, Emmanuelle backed away from the window and disappeared from sight.

Emilie clutched the gate for a moment and looked out at the world beyond. Fist pressed to her lips, she straightened, and then stepped beyond the walls to the road outside. Behind her, the forgotten portal swayed against the breeze.

She walked, eyes to the ground, following the road that led to the outskirts of Québec. In accordance with Emmanuelle's directions, she arrived at a juncture and took the road on the left. It rested between two high banks of earth bordered with trees, which spread their branches over it like a vaulted roof. The sound of her own heartbeat roared in her ears. She had never walked alone like this and quickened her steps as she progressed along the vacant lane.

Ahead, she noticed a carriage stopped with its driver in front and two men standing about as if they waited for someone.

Emilie approached warily. One of the two men stepped towards her. "Pardon, mademoiselle, can you tell us which is the way to Trois-Riviere?" His voice was courteous, but his round face held no warmth.

"You're going in the wrong direction." Emilie's instincts warned something was amiss. The hair on the back of her neck rose and her skin prickled. "It lies to the west." She turned to point behind her.

Coarse hands came from behind and seized her around the waist, hoisting her off the ground. Emilie screamed. The ruffian flung her into the carriage. A third man, concealed inside, shoved a handkerchief into her mouth to stifle her cries. Panicked, she struggled for breath as she fought for her life.

The two men on the road thrust themselves into the carriage, slammed shut the door, and the driver clucked to the horses, setting off at a good clip. In the matter of a few seconds, Emilie's world had been shattered.

Terror rumbled through her body. Her pulse hammered in her chest and she gasped for every breath. With every shred of strength, she writhed to escape the men who held her down. Desperate, she thrust her body towards the door; but the rugged arms of her captors kept her pinned. Though she attempted to scream, the handkerchief in her mouth smothered her cries.

"Be still; don't be afraid," growled one of the men.

"We don't wish to harm you," said the other.

Their harsh voices resounded like cannons in the confines of the small carriage. After moments of futile struggle, her arms sank by her side and her head fell backwards. She half opened her eyelids and she fixed them on the horrible faces hovering over her as one monstrous image. All warmth drained from her body and she broke out in a cold sweat. Her consciousness blurred. Then she swooned into the blackness that swallowed her.

83

"She's dead," said the burly armed man.

"She's not dead, imbecile." Gaston removed the handkerchief, tucked it into his pocket, and leaned closer to study her. "It's only a swoon. It takes more than this to send someone into the next world. Grab your muskets from under the seat and keep them ready."

The two men reached for the weapons and lay them across their laps.

"Not in your hands! Behind your backs. If she sees firearms, it will be enough to make her swoon outright. When she recovers, don't frighten her, and keep your filthy hands off her. Leave her to me."

The two men exchanged a wily grin and nudged each other. "We've heard of your special way with women."

Gaston scowled at them. "Wipe those smirks off your ugly faces. I mean only to talk to her. The seigneur doesn't like his goods damaged."

84

Emilie stirred from unconsciousness and opened her eyes. A sudden remembrance of the attack flooded her memory and she lunged for the door. One of the men yanked her back. She uttered a cry, but Gaston pulled the handkerchief from his pocket and held it up again.

"Come," he warned in the gentlest of tones. "Be silent. It will go better for you. We don't want to do you any harm; but if you don't hold your tongue, we'll force you to keep quiet."

Panic arose in her. "Let me go! Who are you?"

Not one of the men answered.

"Where are you taking me? Please, let me go!"

"Don't be afraid." The man with the handkerchief studied her with his cold eyes. "If we wanted to harm you, we could have murdered you a hundred times already. So be quiet and cooperate."

Emilie forced back her fear and looked Gaston in the eye.

"Please, I beg you, let me go. I don't know you. I promise not to say anything about this. Why have you taken me?"

"Because we have been ordered to do so."

"Who ordered this?"

"Shut up!" Gaston scolded with a stern look. "Don't ask any more questions."

Emilie tried again to throw herself at the door, but he shoved her back.

"If you let me go now, all will be well. I'll not cause you any trouble. I forgive you sincerely. If any of you have a daughter, a wife, a mother, think what they would suffer in my place. Let me go. I'll find my way home and no one need know anything. Please, I'm begging you."

"We cannot."

"You cannot! Why can't you?"

"Save your breath. No amount of begging will help you."

Overcome with distress, Emilie sank back into the corner, crossed her arms, and reluctantly acquiesced.

85

From the main floor salon, Seigneur Claude Prudhomme watched the entrance to his manor house with solicitude. How odd that he, who had disposed of so many lives with an untroubled heart, who in so many undertakings had not cared about the suffering he inflicted on anybody, should now recoil at the abduction of this young woman.

The carriage came into view, its pace unhurried. His heart beat rapidly as regret swallowed him. He should have refused to help Richard Tonnacour. Something about this didn't seem right, but he couldn't place his finger on why or what it was. He trusted his instincts and decided to heed them. It was not too late to free himself from this obligation.

Weariness settled into his bones. Although he had lived a life of murder and revenge, he could not tolerate such a life any longer. In the sunset of his years, he found himself craving tranquility. For as long as he could remember, people had always sought something from him; and he had always acted willingly, albeit for a hefty price. But, no more. He'd had enough. There was no one in his life that cared for him. If he were to die tomorrow, he would die alone, without mourners and immediately forgotten.

Why was Richard Tonnacour so interested in this particular woman that he would go to such lengths and take such risks to acquire her? More importantly, why should he help him quench his nefarious desires? Richard Tonnacour was spoiled, impulsive, and infantile to deal with. This abduction might entangle him in a situation he could not control. Could he tolerate more complications in his life? The answer struck him hard. No, he could not. He was too tired, too old, and too disinterested. It was time to stop all the mayhem that had dogged him his entire life. And he would start with this girl.

He called for his housekeeper. She had been married to one of his men who had lost his life after a dangerous mission. The swift vengeance Claude had dealt to the murderers seemed to console the widow. From that day forward, she rarely set foot outside his seigniorial lands. He did not confine her to any particular service. Among his crowd of ruffians, one or another always found something for her to do, to which she never complained. Sometimes she would have clothes to repair, sometimes a meal to provide in haste for one of the men newly returned from a mission, and sometimes she exercised her medical skill in dressing a wound. She was used to the demands, reproaches, and insults of his men seasoned with jokes and rude speeches. She often returned their jibes or compliments with colourful speech of her own.

"You see that carriage there?" Seigneur Prudhomme asked when she entered the room and came to stand near him.

She approached the window, protruded her sharp chin, and stared out the window at the approaching carriage. "I see it."

"I want you to meet it. Inside there is a young woman. You are to share your room with her. If she asks you any questions, don't answer them."

"Oh?" Her brows drew together.

"Try to comfort her."

Her face puckered with confusion. "What do you mean? What should I say?"

"How should I know? Surely, at your age you know to deal with other women. Have you never been afraid? Don't you know any comforting words? Be kind to her. That's all I ask." He waved her away with both arms. "Hurry, get on with it."

When she left, he stood at the window, his eyes fixed on the carriage, which had drawn closer. He studied the sun as it dipped into the horizon. The fleecy clouds assumed a fiery tinge, and like his own life, faded into darkness. Drawing back, he slammed the window shut and bellowed as he kicked a chair and knocked it to the ground.

86

Dusk had darkened the sky when the carriage came to a stop in front of a large manor house.

An unattractive woman, old enough to be her mother, swung open the door, and peered inside with a forced smile. "Come with me."

"Who are you?" Emilie asked.

"I'm the housekeeper and I'm to see to your needs." With a stern look and cold eyes, the woman beckoned her to step out.

Emilie hesitated.

"Let's go." The man with the handkerchief gave her a severe look.

Emilie glanced about in search of escape. When he leaned menacingly towards her, she stepped out the carriage.

"Where are you taking me?" Emilie asked the woman as she followed her to the front door.

"To see someone who will make sure you're well cared for," the woman said. "Don't be afraid. He wanted me to comfort you." She gripped Emilie's arm, a little too hard. "You'll tell him, won't you, that I tried to comfort you?"

"Let go of me!" Emilie's anger surfaced. The woman smelled of perspiration and she tried to pull away from her. "Who is he and what does he want? Tell me where I am!"

The woman turned away and continued toward the front door.

"Please," Emilie pleaded. "You're a woman. Surely, you can understand. Help me."

The housekeeper pursed her lips while she stepped aside and waited for Emilie to enter the house.

87

Seigneur Claude watched the exchange from the salon. He waited impatiently for one of the servants to bring Gaston to him. The moment Gaston entered, Seigneur Claude turned and faced him. "Well? How did it go?"

"Everything went as planned," Gaston replied. "The girl showed up alone and on time. She screamed once, but nobody heard. The coachman was ready, the horses swift. It was very easy, but..."

"But what?" Claude's suspicions surfaced.

"But, to tell you the truth, it would have been easier had I not heard her speak or seen her face."

"What do you mean? Surely you're not becoming soft."

Gaston scratched his head. "*Non*, but I feel compassion for her."

Seigneur Claude laughed. "Compassion! What do you know of compassion?"

Gaston's face coloured and he stared at his feet. "I never understood it until I laid eyes on her. Compassion is worse than fear – once it grabs you, you are no longer a man."

Seigneur Claude crossed the room and sat in one of two chairs near the hearth. "What did she do to elicit such compassion in a man like you?"

Gaston shrugged. "It was her valour in the face of danger. Her pallor revealed her fear, but she never shed a tear, and during the entire time in the carriage, she was not afraid to look me in the eye. She has courage and pride. She is quite a woman."

Seigneur Claude rubbed his brow. None of this made sense. The deeper he became involved in this sordid mess, the more he wanted no part of it. He had promised Richard Tonnacour he would get the girl for him, but in this, he had erred. He should have made inquiries, learned more about what drove the man to make such an outlandish request. "You've come through for me once again, Gaston. A room has been prepared for you here. Get some rest. In the morning, I may have something more to ask of you."

"And if not?"

"Then you may return to your duties at the gatehouse."

"You haven't asked about Emmanuelle."

Seigneur Claude inhaled deeply. "No, I didn't."

Gaston hesitated, and when Seigneur Claude remained silent, he left the room.

88

Seigneur Claude crossed one leg over the other and fixed his gaze on a spot on the wooden floor. The first rays of moonlight entered through the window. The girl must be an angel to have warmed the heart of someone like Gaston. In the morning, he'd rid himself of her. And Tonnacour had better not return.

Gaston, compassionate? He shook his head. What had this woman done to melt that man's heart? He decided to see for himself, ascended the stairs to his housekeeper's room, and knocked on the door.

The bolt grated in the staples and the door flung open. The housekeeper's eyes widened. Before she could utter a word, he brushed past her and entered. By the light of a lantern, which stood on a three-legged table, he discovered the girl sitting on the floor in the corner farthest from the entrance. His anger rose instantly. "This is how you treat her? Like a bag of rags on the floor?"

The housekeeper wrung her hands. "She chose to sit there. I have done my best to encourage and comfort her, as you asked me to. She can tell you so herself, but she will not mind anything I say. When I offered her a nightdress, she refused and kept her on clothes on. When I invited her to sit on the bed, she chose the floor." The housekeeper shrugged. "I don't understand it."

"Do not speak about me as if I weren't here," Emilie interjected.

Seigneur Claude turned his gaze on her and approached. "Please get up. You have nothing to fear from me."

She straightened and remained motionless, her gaze never wavering.

What beauty, what courage. Seigneur Claude offered her his

hand. "Please, you'll be more comfortable in a chair or on the bed. I will do you no harm. In fact, I can help you."

She said nothing and continued her stare.

"Get up!" he thundered, irritated at having twice commanded in vain.

Her stare never faltered and her face took on a serene quality. "Here I am, kill me if you will."

He hesitated, unsure and cleared his throat. "Kill you? I've already told you I would not harm you," he softened his tone, marvelling at her beautiful but stoic features. Her chestnut hair, dishevelled from her ordeal, framed the depths of her almond shaped eyes that glistened with courage.

"Please," said the housekeeper who rushed to her side and tried to raise her to her feet. "If he tells you he will do you no harm, then you can trust him."

The girl brushed her hands away. "Trust is something that is earned. I am accosted by three thugs, thrown into a carriage, and transported to a strange place. And you want me to trust you?" She rose to her feet and her gaze never wavered. "What have I done to deserve this?"

Seigneur Claude frowned. "They treated you badly? If they did, you must tell me."

"Treated me badly! Of course, they treated me badly. They seized me by treachery, by force! Why? Where am I? In the name of God, let me go."

"God! Those who've lost, can't defend themselves and call God, as if He could reach down and help them." His voice boomed with frustration in the confines of the small room.

It drew no reaction from her. "God pardons many sins for one deed of mercy," she said.

He ran his fingers through his hair and paced across the room. Why did she unnerve him so?

"Let me go. Your men brought me here by force, but you can

bid them to take me to my mother in Pointe-du-Lac. She is a widow, alone in the world except for me."

He stopped and stared at her, shocked, but enchanted. While she spoke, her features became almost angelic. Warmth tinged the skin over her cream coloured cheeks. Her mussed hair cascaded over her shoulders in shimmering waves. And even though she stood before him in the poorest gown of homespun drugget he had ever seen, she held herself like a queen. The thought of Tonnacour despoiling her made him shudder. How could he deliver her to a pig like him?

"It's not too late. God pardons many sins for one single act of mercy!" She paused and swallowed.

If she were the daughter of one of his enemies, he might have enjoyed her sufferings, but at her pleas, his heart constricted with shame, and, he thought with disbelief, compassion.

Her expression grew more animated the longer he hesitated."It will cost you nothing to let me go."

"You don't know that," he said with gentleness. "Have I done you any harm? Have I threatened you in any way?"

Her gaze roamed over him and her shoulders drooped. "*Non*, I suppose you speak the truth. If you wanted to hurt me, you would have done so already." Her expression brightened. "Set me free."

"In the morning."

Her features sunk. "Set me free now."

"In the morning, I'll come see you then." He offered her his hand again. When she placed her hand in his, warmth settled over him. He helped her rise. "Come, take a little rest. You must want something to eat. I'll have something sent up. He released her hand with reluctance.

It was not like him to show such kindness. What was it about her that made him want to protect her? How could he have such fatherly feelings? As he turned to go, he faced the housekeeper. “Persuade her to eat something then help her into bed. Keep her spirits up. Make sure that she has no cause to complain about you.” He made for the door.

As he started for the door, Emilie sprang up and ran to detain him. “Please, promise you'll let me go.”

But, he turned away and left.

89

The housekeeper closed the door and locked it with a key on a chain, which she hung around her neck.

Tears of disappointment blurred Emilie's vision, but she willed them away when the housekeeper faced her. “Who is he?” Emilie asked.

“It is not for me to say.” The housekeeper studied her through narrowed eyes. “You're a proud one, aren't you? You'll have to wait for him to tell you.” Without explanation, her face grew gentle. “Come, cheer up. Do not ask me questions that I cannot answer. Pluck up your heart,” she said in a softer, more humane tone. “You cannot imagine how many people have longed to hear him speak as kindly to them as he has spoken to you! Be cheerful, eat something, and afterwards, you can sleep.”

Perhaps the woman was right. Emilie sat down on the edge of the bed.

The housekeeper raised her brows. “You will leave just a little corner for me, tonight, won't you?” She spoke with suppressed rancour.

“Oh, the bed, you mean?” Emilie did not trust this woman, whose insincerity contradicted her words. Yet she felt safer in her presence because of the man's instructions. “You'll stay with me, won't you?”

“I'll stay with you.” The woman sat in an old armchair. She

glanced at the bed with a vexed look and mumbled something unintelligible.

Soon there came a knock at the door. Emilie rose to her feet, her hands twisting the front of her gown. With everything so unfamiliar, she feared every sound.

"It's the cook bringing something to eat." The housekeeper stood and unlocked the door. A chubby woman with wisps of hoary hair escaping the sides of a coif of plain linen entered the room and studied Emilie with interest.

The housekeeper took the basket from the cook and waved her hand to dismiss her. Then she locked the door, and set the basket on the small table in the corner of the room. She lifted the lid and pulled out the items one at a time, announcing each one. A delicious aroma filled the room. "*Jambon* in galantine, a pot herb pie, barley bread, and anise comfits. Come and eat. It's a tempting repast prepared just for you. There is even some wine."

Although she had not eaten since before her capture, Emilie could barely eat. She remained on the bed.

"Why won't you eat?" sniffed the housekeeper. "Please come to your senses and do as you are bid." So saying, the woman ripped off a chunk of bread and stuffed it into her mouth as she pulled plates and cutlery from the basket. After glancing at Emilie, she applied herself greedily to the food and drink.

When she finished eating, she rose and bent over Emilie. "Come now, eat something."

"No, I'm not hungry," Emilie replied. Exhausted, she needed rest more than food. She pushed herself to her feet and stepped towards the door.

The housekeeper sprang in front of her, stretched out her hand to the lock. She seized the handle, shook it, rattled the bolt, and made it grate against the staple that received and secured it. Her eyes narrowed. "Do you see? It is locked. And I have the only key." With her hand, she fingered the chain around her neck, lifted the key from its place between her ample breasts, and waved it about. "Are you happy now?" She tucked the key back beneath the top of her gown.

"No, I'm not happy. I'll never be happy in this place." Emilie returned to her place on the corner of the floor.

"Sleep in the bed. Why do you crouch like that in a corner like a dog? I've never seen anybody foolish enough to refuse such comforts as these."

"Leave me alone," Emilie said wearily. She must not allow herself to trust this woman who was no friend to her.

"As you wish." The housekeeper lifted the covers of the bed and slipped beneath them. She pushed herself to the edge. "I'll leave you plenty of room. I've asked you often enough. The rest is up to you." She turned her back to Emilie and before long, light snores escaped her lips.

Emilie sat motionless against the corner, her knees drawn close to her breasts, her hands resting on her knees, her face buried in her hands. The horrors of the day played in her mind whenever she closed her eyes. She dwelt on the hopeless reality of her circumstances. She struggled to find a solution, a means of escape, but the seclusion of this manor house and the fact that she could never seize the key from the housekeeper without awakening her made her realize the futility of any attempt. Overcome with exhaustion, she relaxed her hold on her benumbed limbs and stretched out. She lay in this position for quite some time, fighting her fatigue, hovering somewhere between sleep and wakefulness.

Almost asleep, her eyes opened and Emilie regained her scattered senses. She listened to the slow, deep breathing of her companion. The wick of the lamp cast a faint light. It glimmered then died. Her dire predicament returned to mind. This was her prison. For how long? More importantly, why?

Was this the handiwork of Seigneur Richard? She could think of no other possibility. Would she never escape him? The terror of a future submitting to him burned in her thoughts. The hopelessness of her situation struck her hard. Was death her only escape? All she could do was pray, and pray she would. And in that thought shone a single ray of comfort. She removed the rosary from her leather pouch and prayed. As the words fell from her trembling lips, an indefinite faith took hold of her heart.

A new thought took root in her mind. Her prayers might be more readily heard if she were to offer something in exchange. She tried to recall what she prized. Her heart could feel no emotion other than fear or conceive any desire except deliverance. It came to her and she resolved to make the sacrifice.

Emilie clasped her hands, the beads of her rosary interlaced between her fingers. “Please God. Help me! Bring me out of this danger; bring me safely to my mother. And if you grant me this, I will dedicate my life to You.”

After uttering these words, she bowed her head and placed the rosary around her neck. The act was a token of her consecration, a safeguard, and her armour for the new warfare she now faced. She leaned back against the wall. An incredible peace and tranquility came to life in her spirit. The morrow promised deliverance. Her senses, wearied by her struggles, gave way to these soothing thoughts. By daybreak, Emilie sank into a profound and unbroken sleep.

90

Claude Prudhomme tried in vain to sleep. Emilie's image remained vividly in his mind. Her words resounded clearly. What had possessed him to go see her? It had been a mistake.

Gaston had been right about compassion – after experiencing it, one was no longer a man. Many had begged for their lives before him. Neither entreaties nor lamentations had ever succeeded in deterring him from what had to be done. But these remembrances, instead of inspiring him to complete his task, or dispelling his feelings of compassion, caused him consternation. There was still time, the girl's life was in his hands. He could ask for forgiveness. From a woman, no less? If seeking forgiveness could ease the torment that had possessed him of late, he would do it.

What had happened to the old Seigneur Claude Prudhomme? Had old age weakened him? He rolled over and fussed with the covers. The damn bed wasn't soft enough and there were too many blankets.

Something had changed. Things that once slaked his desire, no longer charmed him. He stared ahead to a bleak life, devoid of all interest, deprived of all will, divested of every action, and only laden with insupportable recollections of deeds best forgotten. He thought of enemies, but no hatred stirred his spirit. Tomorrow, he must liberate his unfortunate captive. Could one act of kindness atone for a life of cruelty? No, but a single act of kindness might unburden a heart too heavy with sin and guilt. It would be nice to know that one person might mourn him when he died.

However, what of his promise to Seigneur Richard? What had induced him to inflict so much suffering without incentive on a poor unknown girl for the sole purpose of rendering a service to this debauched man? Out of old habit perhaps? Now he found himself examining his whole life. Backwards from year to year, from engagement to engagement, from act of bloodshed to act of bloodshed, from crime to crime; each one stood before his conscience-stricken soul. He owned them all and their weight had moulded him into the despicable man he had become. How he loathed himself.

He sat up in bed and reached for the pistol tucked beneath his pillow. Moonlight shed a gentle light in the room. He stared at the cold metal weapon in his hand. How easy it would be to end his torment. He gripped the handle and raised it to his temple.

To pull the trigger would be a simple thing, a mere moment in time, and then the torment would end. A vision of his disfigured corpse, lying motionless, slithered into his mind. The silent night presented death in a frightful aspect – the confusion of the manor's servants in the morning; everything turned upside-down; and he lying dead, powerless, voiceless. His enemies would rejoice. Emmanuelle would rejoice.

Was there a Heaven? What about Hell? Surely that is where he would end up. Already he could feel the hands of imps tugging him into a black abyss. This single thought thrust him into black despair, from which death afforded no escape.

The pistol dropped from his hand. He lay with his fingers twined in his hair. His teeth chattered. Every limb trembled. The Devil's hand was upon his heart. How long before the beast squeezed the life from him?

Her pleas flooded his thoughts. *God pardons many sins for one deed of mercy*! Those words reverberated in his mind. They became a lifeline. A glimmer of hope came into being. Her face appeared to him, angelic, dispensing mercy, and consolation. He had the power to change things.

He waited for dawn, for the moment to come when he could liberate her. Richard Tonnacour be damned!

91

Bishop de Laval's visit to Pointe-du-Lac gave Claude a glimmer of hope. Perhaps the Bishop would hear his confession. A cleric of his high rank was likely wiser, more seasoned, and better prepared to deal with a black-hearted sinner like him. His past weighed like an anvil upon his shoulders, smothering and pressing down on him without reprieve. His shame and torment drove him with the desperation of a drowning man fighting for air.

He dressed in haste and donned a light, military-style coat to boost his floundering confidence. The pistol lay on the bed where he had dropped it last night. It taunted him- an ominous reminder of his desperation. He reached for it as if it were poison. A man of his ilk could not walk the streets without fear of reprisal. He secured the weapon to one side of his belt, hating the weight of it. Should a drowning man weigh himself down with such things? After slinging his *fusil boucanier*, his favourite musket, across his shoulders, he lifted his tricorne from the hook behind his door and walked across the hall to the housekeeper's room. He rapped on the door. "It's me," he called out, careful to avoid using his name.

When the housekeeper swung open the door, his gaze swept the room, and then he spotted the young woman. She lay motionless in the corner. "Why is she on the floor?" He gave the housekeeper a pointed glare. To see her huddled, so forlorn, offended him. Guilt was a knife twisting in his gut.

The housekeeper glanced back and forth between him and her charge then retreated a step. "I did all I could, but she wouldn't eat and she refused to sleep on the bed."

He rubbed his chin and studied the girl. She slept with her head nestled in the crook of her arm. Her long chestnut brown hair cascaded over her arm and back. A ray of sunlight beamed through a crack in the closed window shutter and illuminated her face. In sleep, her face had a perfection reserved only for angels; a face a sinner like himself should not even look upon, much less touch. He sighed. Why must this vision of beauty afflict him now? Was this a preview of God's punishment? Would he spend eternity in the presence of perfection contemplating how far he had fallen short? "Let her sleep. When she wakes, the cook will prepare anything she wants. Tell her that I've gone out for a while. When I return, I'll see to her release."

The housekeeper's mouth dropped open.

"*Ferme ta bouche*! It's wide enough for a swarm of bees to enter."

The housekeeper paled and bowed her head in submission.

He went downstairs and repeated his instructions to the cook. As he stepped from the back door, he spoke to two of his men who sat in chairs in the sunshine oiling their pistols. "Keep an eye on the house. Lock the front and back doors. No one is to come out or go in. And I mean no one."

"*Oui*," the men acknowledged. One tucked his pistol in his belt and lumbered off to the front of the house to do as bid.

After waiting for a groom to saddle his horse, Claude mounted and rode briskly toward Pointe-du-Lac.

Along the way, people greeted him with a nod or wave before bowing too low. They whispered and exchanged suspicious looks. Not one person looked him in the eye, smiled, or exchanged a pleasantry. Why hadn't he noticed before? There was a time when he didn't care. Now it stung like salt in a fresh wound.

When he reached the settlement, he found a crowd assembled outside the church with its tall narrow bell tower and attached rectory. Parishioners stood about talking in small groups, but fell quiet at his approach. He heard his name whispered as they cleared a path for him. He halted his horse before a well-dressed man. "Can you tell me where I can find the Bishop?"

"He's inside the church with the parish priest," the man

replied. "There's to be a mass soon."

"I thank you." He tipped his hat and dismounted. After tying his horse to a fencepost, he entered the church, the onlooker's gazes burning into his back as he went. In the cool dimness, three priests stood near an open door on the right side of the nave at the rear of the church.

Claude slid his *fusil boucanier* from his shoulders and leaned it against the wall below a window. Hat in hand, he approached them. "Can someone tell me where to find the Bishop? I must speak to him."

A Jesuit priest raised his eyes with uneasy curiosity and hesitated. "I am Père Nicholas. I do not know whether his Excellency is available, but I will check. Please wait here." He cast a look at his colleagues then turned and left the room.

Claude wiped his sweaty hands against his breeches and waited in the awkward silence.

92

Père Jean Civitelle sat across the table from Bishop de Laval, an open breviary between them. He was in the midst of explaining his plans for the special mass and subsequent dinner in honour of his superior's visit. Père Jean wanted to make a good impression and planned carefully for these events. Judging by the Bishop's nods and smiles, he knew he had pleased him.

Both men looked up as Père Nicholas entered.

"Excuse me Excellency, but there is a man here to see you - a very unusual visitor indeed!"

"Who is he?" asked Bishop Laval.

"His name is Seigneur Claude Prudhomme." Père Nicholas emphasized each syllable of the name. "He waits outside and demands to speak to you."

"Seigneur Claude Prudhomme?" Père Jean blanched and

made the sign of the cross.

The Bishop frowned at him, shut the breviary, and sat back in his chair, a neutral expression on his face. "Show him in."

"But Excellency," stammered Père Jean. "You must be made aware that this seigneur is dangerous. He is a most notorious outlaw-"

The Bishop raised his hand and stopped him. "It pleases me to have such a man seek an audience with me."

"But it is my duty to warn you, so that you are prepared."

"What has this man done that I need to be prepared in order to speak with him?" The Bishop raised one eyebrow.

"He is a murderer, a desperate character who is aligned with the most violent criminals; unscrupulous men who-"

Bishop de Laval cast Père Jean an admonishing look. "The Lord would never hesitate to receive such a man; he would have sought him out."

Père Jean felt the heat rise in his cheeks and stared at his hands.

The Bishop turned to Père Nicholas. "Admit the man; we have kept him waiting long enough."

93

Seigneur Claude followed Père Nicholas into the room. Coldness took root inside of him, the manifestation of his disgrace.

Bishop de Laval, dressed in the magnificent purple robes of his office, advanced toward him. He bore a serene look, tall and confident, and greeted him with a firm handshake. Behind the Bishop stood Père Jean Civitelle. When the Bishop dismissed the two priests, they practically ran from the room.

Claude broke out in a sweat, his stomach somersaulting. An inexplicable compulsion had brought him here, but suddenly, he found himself at a loss for words. He had come to alleviate his inner torment, yet now he was ashamed at arriving like a wretched penitent to confess his guilt.

The Bishop looked at him thoughtfully. Kindness flickered from his solemn eyes. Grey locks revealed he was a man of about sixty years, yet his body seemed neither bowed nor wasted by age. Beneath his calm demeanour, Claude sensed inward peace. Envy arose inside him. He would trade all his wealth for such tranquility.

The Bishop raised an eyebrow. "You look troubled," he said in a gentle voice, "but I am happy you came to me. I blame myself that you had to do so."

"Blame yourself? I don't understand." Claude could never remember a time when a man willingly took the blame for something beyond his control.

The Bishop gave a solitary nod of his head. "I can tell that you are burdened. Your visit today is a reminder, a reproof to me for not having come to you first."

"But how could you know of me? We have never met. How were you to know I existed?" Claude swallowed, his mouth suddenly dry. "Do you know who I am? Did they not tell you my name, warn you about me?"

"You are exactly the person whom it is my duty to seek out and pray for."

Astonished, Claude did not know how to respond.

The Bishop placed an arm around his shoulder. "Well? You have some good news to tell me, so why do you keep me waiting?"

"Good news, Bishop?" Claude swallowed the lump that formed in his throat. "I have allowed Satan to possess my heart. What good news can you expect from a damned soul like mine?"

"That God has touched your heart and you are changed."

"I do not deserve God's attention. If I could see Him! If I could hear Him! Where is this God? Perhaps then I could quench this guilt that sears like the fires of Hell inside me."

"He is in your heart driving out the Devil as we speak, disturbing your tranquility. This is how you experience him, how He draws you to Him. He is presenting you with hope for salvation. Your soul is not forfeit; God is telling you it is not too late. And you shall have salvation as soon as you acknowledge Him."

"You say it is God who torments me?" He pondered the thought. Such a thing never occurred to him before. "I am beyond redemption, an unworthy wretch." Claude despised the despair he heard in his own words. His voice cracked, ready to burst like a dam from the weight of guilt.

The Bishop's face remained calm. "God will make you a token of His power and goodness."

Claude shuddered with shame as the fearsome tiger of remorse gnawed at his heart.

"You recognize your wretchedness, your deplorable heart. However, when you condemn your past sins and agree with your accuser, God will invigorate you with love, hope, and repentance. He sees all, loves all, and forgives all when He finds a contrite heart!" While these words fell from the Bishop's lips, his face, his expression, his whole manner, radiated sincerity.

With each word, something inside of Claude changed. Agony yielded to warmer, less painful, emotions. His eyes, unaccustomed to weeping since infancy, now filled with tears. He covered his face with his hands and sobbed.

The Bishop raised his hands and eyes to heaven. "Praise be to God for such a glorious miracle." He reached out for Claude's hand.

"No!" Claude recoiled. "Keep away from me. Do not defile yourself by touching filth like me. You don't know the horrors I have committed."

The Bishop grasped his hand with affectionate strength. "It doesn't matter. If God forgives you, how can I not follow his example? You can repair those wrongs against your enemies."

"There is too much to atone for! A lifetime of evils." Claude shook his head, his arms raised to ward off the Bishop's attention. What a fool he had been to think he could find redemption. A lifetime of murder, rape, and thievery stood between him and redemption. "I should go, Excellency. There is a crowd of people outside waiting for you who are more worthy. Many came long distance. You should not waste your time with the likes of me."

"My flock outside rests securely in God's hands. A good shepherd finds the one who is lost." The Bishop threw his arm round Claude's shoulder.

Claude resisted and attempted to pull away in his personal darkness, but a single ray of God's light made him yield. Overcome by the Bishop's vehement affection, he hesitated. Layer by layer, the light overcame his resistance banishing the darkness until he fell into the Bishop's embrace and buried his face in the man's shoulder, his burning tears darkening the Bishop's majestic cassock.

He wept until bereft of all emotion. Then, slowly, he disengaged himself, dried his cheeks with his sleeve, and raised his face to heaven. "God is, indeed, great! I understand what I am; my sins are present before me and I shudder at the thought of all that I have done. Yet I feel more joy than I have ever known in my horrible life!"

"God seats you on his right at the table of the blessed and walks beside you as you enter into a new life. There is much you will have to undo, much to repair, much to mourn over, but all things are doable through Him."

"There is much I can do nothing about, but there is one

small thing I can rectify."

The Bishop listened while Claude told him about Emilie's abduction and the frenzy of emotion that her pleas had unleashed within him.

"Then you must lose no time!" The Bishop seemed breathless with eagerness. "This is an example of God's forgiveness! He urges you to protect the person you intended to ruin. May God bless you! Do you know where your unhappy protégée comes from?"

"She is from here."

The Bishop went to a little table and rang a bell. Père Jean and Père Nicholas both re-entered. Claude bore their looks of abhorrence and faced them without flinching. He deserved their scorn.

Père Jean turned an inquiring gaze on the Bishop.

"I have good news to share and a joyful boon to ask of you," the Bishop said. "One of your parishioners, whom you have lamented as lost, Emilie Basseaux, is found. She is at the house of my good friend, Seigneur Claude here."

Worry broke across Père Jean's nervous face. His chin dipped to his chest and he fixed his eyes on the ground.

"As Emilie's parish priest, there is no one I trust more than you to protect the girl. Go with Seigneur Claude and bring the girl home. Do you know of a trustworthy woman who lives nearby who can accompany you?" the Bishop asked. "I suspect the company of a woman will put our charge at ease."

"What is her name?"

"She is Madame Juliette Tremblay, the wife of Gilles Tremblay, a tailor. They are good, hard-working people."

"Doesn't the young woman have any relatives?" the Bishop asked.

"She has only a mother," Père Jean babbled. "Ada Basseaux, the widow of a fur trader."

The Bishop heaved a sigh. "Well, is the mother home?"

"Yes, she is, Excellency," Père Nicholas jumped in.

"It will be a great consolation for Emilie to see her mother after such a traumatic ordeal."

"But she has recently returned from Québec, Excellency," Père Nicholas added. "She is likely worried about her daughter. It might be prudent to prepare her first."

"I concur." The Bishop smiled at Père Nicholas with approval. "Please take my horse and carriage and fetch Madame Tremblay. As soon as she arrives, Père Jean and Seigneur Claude can escort her to Emilie. Then bring Madame Basseaux to me and I will explain things to her and prepare her for her reunion with her daughter."

"Would it not be best for me to fetch the mother, Excellency?" Père Jean interjected, his face puckered. "After all, she is my parishioner."

Claude knew how to read a man, and this priest was not only worried, he was afraid. He had heard talk about his lack of strength before, and now he witnessed it first-hand. All his life, he had despised weak men, stepping on minions as if they were repellent insects. Claude stopped himself. He must not allow such thoughts to intrude. Instead, he needed to be tolerant of weakness.

The Bishop paused, rubbed his chin, and then gave Père Jean a pointed look. "I think it's best for you to wait here with me."

"But Excellency, it is best for me to prepare Ada. She is a sensitive woman who is worried about her daughter. I know her well and how to best break the news to her." Père Jean glanced awkwardly at Père Nicholas. "Someone else might do her more harm than good."

Père Nicholas frowned at his colleague.

"Père Nicholas is just as capable," the Bishop interjected, folding his arms across his chest.

"As you wish, Excellency," Père Jean muttered weakly.

"Time is of the essence. The girl has suffered enough."

Père Jean's shoulders slumped. His fingers clasped and unclasped the sides of his soutane.

"Is something wrong, Père Jean?" The Bishop's gaze narrowed.

Père Jean shook his head.

"Good," the Bishop said. He turned to Claude. "Don't think that I shall be content with only this visit. You will return, *n'est pas*?"

"Will I return?" Claude said, his heart lightened by hope. "Should you refuse me, I would obstinately remain outside your door like a beggar. We must speak again so my soul can heal."

The Bishop took his hand and pressed it. "Good. Do Père Jean and me the honour of dining with us this evening. In fact, I shall expect you. For now, however, I must see to the people outside." He turned around and swept from the room.

94

Père Jean's heart pounded. What if the Bishop learned of his refusal to marry Emilie and Robert? His mind raced to find a way out of this predicament.

Alone with Seigneur Claude, he studied the wretch from the corner of his eye. What should he say? That he was glad for him? Glad for what? That having once been a vile sinner, he now resolved to become a man of honour? He doubted a man could change so suddenly. Could this conversion be a ruse? These pestilent seigneurs dispelled any hope of tranquility in his life.

Père Jean dreaded having to travel with him. What ill luck! He re-opened the breviary and feigned reading to avoid conversation. Thankfully, Seigneur Claude stood lost in thought at the window. The awkwardness in the room brought sweat to his brow.

It seemed to take forever, but finally Père Nicholas returned to announce that Madame Tremblay waited in the carriage outside.

Seigneur Claude turned away from the window, but upon reaching the door, paused and waited for Père Jean. Père Jean had scarcely set foot out the door, when he shrivelled with alarm at the sight of Seigneur Claude who grabbed a musket leaning against the wall, and with military precision, swung it over his shoulder.

Père Jean broke out in a cold sweat. What would Prudhomme do with the weapon? Was it possible that Emile and Robert had managed to get married and now Prudhomme was sent to kill him? After all, the man murdered anyone who stood in his way. But, he shook the thought off because of the Bishop's involvement. He prayed for this ordeal to be over and avoided any untoward movement that might arouse Prudhomme's attention.

After they stepped outside, Seigneur Claude untied a horse at the side of the building and mounted. Madame Tremblay waved at him from inside the awaiting carriage. He waved back with a forced smile.

The groom held the reins of a saddled horse. "This one's for you, Père Jean."

Père Jean stopped. He had assumed he would ride in the carriage with Madame Tremblay. He had never ridden a horse before. Wiping his hands on the side of his cassock, he approached the groom as Seigneur Claude tipped back his hat and looked at him with seeming amusement.

"I pray this beast is a quiet one. To tell the truth, I am a poor horseman."

"She is a sturdy, but calm mare," replied the groom with a

half-grin.

"I hope so." Père Jean stood with one foot in the stirrup and the other on the ground. "You're sure it isn't vicious?"

The groom gave the mare a pat on the neck. "Go with an easy mind; this mare's as gentle as a lamb."

Père Jean grasped the saddle, and with the groom's undignified shove to his posterior, he mounted. The mare remained still, and he released a breath when he found himself safely seated on the creature's back.

To his right, the driver of the carriage gave a slap of the reins and a click of the tongue. They started their slow procession through the settlement.

When they reached open country, Père Jean realized he had not spoken a word to his companion. Thankfully, Seigneur Claude seemed absorbed in thought. Père Jean allowed his own thoughts to drift and reflected on how troublesome people were, always meddling with his life. They dragged him unwillingly into their affairs when all he wanted was a meat pie and a tankard of ale at the end of his day. He blamed Seigneur Richard for this trouble. The man was rich, young, and powerful, but sick with too much authority and prosperity, and he troubled others. Seigneur Richard had chosen to molest poor Emilie, a most absurd, vile, insane business, and he had played a small part under duress. Surely, God and the Bishop would forgive him his one sin of omission?

What of Seigneur Claude? After tormenting the world for years with his wickedness, now he tried to restore it with his conversion. How had the madness of these two men so embroiled him in their wicked webs- one who sought to violate an innocent woman and the other who commits murder but now repents and disturbs his peace? Why could the man not repent in Québec instead?

What of the Bishop who believed every word this

prevaricator uttered? He even called him his friend. Worse yet, he sent him, a poor parish priest, to accompany this fiend without any security. At least he should have had a few stout men to protect him. A holy Bishop ought to value his priests. To think that it was his lot to accompany this evil spider of a man to his own web! How was Emilie involved? Obviously, Seigneur Richard had designs upon her, but how did she fall into Claude Prudhomme's clutches? What was the connection? Père Jean found it best to overlook the affairs of others, but when forced to risk his own skin, he had a right to know. How he hated all this chaos that had befallen him.

And Emilie. Heaven knows what she has suffered. Although he pitied her, she was the catalyst to his ruination.

Père Jean wished he could peer into Seigneur Claude's withered heart and understand all that had happened. One moment the man behaved like Satan, the next like the Pope himself. Oh, poor me. He fretted and prayed for Heaven to look after him. After all, he had not gotten into this mess through any fault of his own.

95

As Claude rode along, the words of the Bishop echoed in his mind, renewing him. His vigour returned. He looked forward to a life of purpose and would make amends where he could, and beg forgiveness where he could not. Hope radiated throughout his core and elevated his spirit at the idea of mercy, pardon, and love; but sank again beneath the insurmountable weight of sins committed. He reviewed recent deeds of iniquity he might repair; those he could arrest immediately. He considered remedies - how to disentangle the numerous knots of his life and what to do with all his accomplices. But it became all too overwhelming. Best to focus on one thing at a time. To free the girl would be the easiest deed to rectify. God knew how much she had suffered at his hands. Even as he burned to liberate her, the knowledge that he had caused her suffering unsettled him.

Arriving at a fork in the road, the carriage driver looked back at him for direction. Claude pointed to the left and gestured for the drive to make haste. He must shed himself of this burden. Until he restored Emilie to her mother, there could be no peace. Perhaps there would never be.

96

When they arrived at the manor house, Père Jean brought his horse to a halt. He stretched his aching back and shifted in the saddle to ease the numbness.

Seigneur Claude dismounted and handed the reins to a waiting groom. He walked to the carriage, opened the door, and helped Madame Tremblay descend. "I'm grateful for your help," he said with a smile. "I'll take you to the young woman now. Please help her understand that she is free and among friends."

Madame Tremblay adjusted her reticule in the crook of her arm. "Rest assured, I shall do my best."

"I can ask nothing more." Seigneur Claude bowed gallantly..

"And you, Père Jean," he said as he lent him his arm to help him dismount. "I apologize for the trouble you have endured on my account. You are bearing it for God who I am sure will reward you bountifully."

The words heartened him, and Père Jean drew a long breath and accepted the hand so courteously offered. He slid from the saddle with as much confidence as he could muster. Seigneur Claude handed the reins to the driver and bid him to wait. Taking a key from his pocket, he opened the front door. He admitted them inside. They advanced to the stairs and ascended in silence.

97

When Emilie first awoke, she struggled to rid herself of the nightmares that had haunted her in the night. Fatigue clouded her thoughts.

"So you are awake. You look terrible. You should have slept in the bed." The housekeeper's scolding words carried a touch of smugness. In the process of making the bed, she whipped a bed sheet into the air and let it drape over the mattress. "I said it often enough last night."

Emilie sat up and rubbed the sleep from her eyes.

"You must eat something," the woman urged as she came to stand in front of her, fists on her hips. "Otherwise, when he returns, he'll be angry with me!" She held out her hand to help Emilie rise.

Emilie ignored the hand, rose, and straightened her gown. Annoyance already simmered within her. The sudden realization that she didn't like this woman didn't help matters. "The only thing I want is to go home. The seigneur promised me. He said it would happen in the morning. Well, it's morning now, so where is he?"

"He's gone out, but he said he'd be back soon. He said you will have all that you wished."

"Truly?" Emilie's spirits brightened.

The sound of footsteps resounded in the corridor followed by a gentle tap on the door.

"Who is there?" asked the housekeeper.

"I've returned. Open the door."

Emilie's heart raced at the sound of the seigneur's voice.

The housekeeper unlocked the door and drew back the latch.

Her captor stood in the doorway and permitted a woman,

visibly with child, to enter before him. Much to her surprise, Père Jean also followed them into the room.

"Don't be long," the seigneur said, rolling his hat round in his hands. "I'll await you outside." He crooked his finger at the housekeeper and together they left. Only the sound of their footsteps descending the stairs broke the silence.

"Père Jean?" Confusion clouded Emilie's mind. "What are you doing here?" Was he here to punish her for having tried to trick him into marrying her and Robert? A month had already passed since that dreadful night. Had it really been that long? Emilie searched his face for answers, but he returned a nervous look. He opened his mouth to say something, but closed it and looked away instead.

Being held against her will was intolerable and the sudden appearance of her priest and this strange woman caused her additional alarm. What did Père Jean's presence here mean? Why did he keep averting his eyes from her?

The woman softened her gaze. She was well dressed in a simple blue sack gown neatly trimmed with crisp cream coloured lace. A few strands of her swept-up golden hair escaped from her straw bonnet. She looked to be about thirty years old and her cheeks glowed with the bloom of motherhood. She took both of Emilie's hands into hers. "Oh, my poor girl! You are to come with us."

Emilie pulled back her hands. "Who are you?" Her eyes darted to Père Jean who met her gaze with nervous compassion.

"We are here to take you home," Père Jean said.

As if she had suddenly regained all her strength, Emilie stared with disbelief, first at Père Jean then at the woman. "My prayers were answered," she uttered, her hand to her mouth. A flutter of utter joy somersaulted in the pit of her stomach.

The woman smiled. "I am Juliette Tremblay and I've come to accompany you back to your mother." She rested a hand on her swollen belly.

"You will take me away from here?" Emilie lowered her voice. "He promised it would be so, but I dared not hope he meant it."

Père Jean edged further into the room. "*Mais oui*. He arranged it all and waits for us outside. Let us go at once. We mustn't keep him waiting." He turned at a sound behind him. "Ah, here he is now."

The seigneur re-entered the room.

Emilie took a step closer to the woman and faced her captor with a steady gaze.

He swallowed then glanced away. A long pause ensued before he raised his eyes to hers. "Emilie, can you find it in your heart to forgive me?"

Juliette took hold of her hand. "See, it's true. He's come to set you free."

"Come, we can go immediately," urged Père Jean, already in the corridor.

Emilie studied the man who stood before her with his head bent low, his posture slumped. Pain etched his face and he appeared beaten down. Her anger and fear dissolved. In its place came a mixture of pity and empathy, but most of all gratitude for heeding her pleas to him the night before. "I'm grateful for your change of heart, Monsieur! May God bless you."

The tension left his face and he brightened a little. "And the same to you for your kind words." His Adam's apple bobbed, just the way she remembered her father's once had. He seemed vulnerable now, not as intimidating. Her heart warmed to him. Without another word, he spun round and led the way out of the room.

Outside, the seigneur opened the carriage door, and with a polite nod, offered his hand to help her and Madame Tremblay step inside. His touch was gentle and his face bore a smile of humility. When she gave him a sincere smile of her own, she detected a slight blush in his cheeks.

The seigneur took the reins of two horses from the driver's hand, helped Père Jean mount, and then rose up into his own saddle.

Madame Tremblay drew the curtains over the windows and took Emilie's hands into hers. "You've been through a terrible ordeal, but it will soon be over, *ma cherie*, and you'll be home."

"With my mother," Emilie said wistfully as she leaned her head back against the seat. To be safe with her mother once more brought much needed comfort. "But I don't understand why you are here."

"The Bishop sent word to me through a Jesuit priest named Père Nicholas. He wanted me to accompany you, to reassure you and make you feel safe."

"The Bishop? Père Nicholas? But how did they know I was here?"

Juliette rested her hand against her back and stretched. "Because this seigneur came to speak to the Bishop." She lowered her voice. "He repented of his sins and wished to change his life; and he told the Bishop that he had caused a poor innocent woman to be seized at the instigation of another seigneur. But I don't know who that other seigneur could be."

Emilie inhaled a sharp breath. In her heart, she had suspected Seigneur Richard. Now she knew. Was there no end to the lengths he would go? Emilie glanced away from Madame Tremblay's searching glare, keeping her thoughts to herself.

"Well, regardless, the Bishop thought my presence would make you more comfortable. I could not refuse."

Emilie reached over and took her hand. "I am grateful for your kindness, especially so because you are expecting a child and this cannot have been a comfortable journey."

Juliette removed a fan from her reticule and flapped it back and forth.

"Are you feeling ill?" Emilie asked.

"It's only a touch of nausea, normal for someone in my condition. It will soon pass."

Emilie studied her face. She did look a little pale.

"All will be for the best, you'll see. Miracles happen when least expected," Madame Tremblay smiled.

"It truly is a miracle," Emilie whispered as she looked out the carriage window. A man clearing a heavily timbered plot of land, paused from his tedious work to wipe his brow and watch them pass. Beyond the tree line, she caught a glimpse of the Saint Lawrence Seaway, the sails of ships and boats upon its waters visible against the horizon. Soon she would be with her mother, but would they be safe? God had heard her desperate prayers and the vow she made. Already, her troubles faded, confirmation that her promise to enter religious life in exchange for rescue was the path she must follow.

"You must forgive the seigneur and be thankful that God has saved him. Pray for him too. You'll be rewarded for it, your heart lightened."

"I know," Emilie said. "It won't be easy, but I will try."

"And your parish priest, Père Jean, the Bishop thought it best to send him with us, too." She leaned forward and lowered her voice once more. "To tell you the truth, he's been of little use. I hear he is a poor-spirited man. He seems as frightened as a chicken in a sack."

Emilie inhaled a deep breath, reminding herself that although she liked Madame Tremblay, she didn't know this woman and it was best not to say too much. Rather, she decided to change the course of their conversation. "And this seigneur who had me abducted and who now has become good; what is his name?"

"You've never heard of Seigneur Claude Prudhomme?"

"Seigneur Prudhomme?" Of course, Emilie had heard of him, but whenever someone spoke his name, it was in a frightened whisper. At the thought of having been in the clutches of a murderous rogue and now finding herself under his protection, her fears came flooding back. She recalled his face each time he had spoken to her. The first time it had been haughty, the next agitated, and the last time so humbled, it left her feeling confused.

"Many will be relieved to learn he has changed. To think of how many people feared him; and now he's become a saint! We're seeing the fruits of this divine change. Who knows why?"

Emilie sensed Juliette wanted to learn the details of her plight, but for whatever reason, refrained from asking outright. Yet, she comforted her and seemed concerned.

"Are you certain you are not ill?" Emilie asked.

"I cannot deny I'm fatigued." Juliette arched her back. "The carriage ride has been long and uncomfortable." She looked out the window and turned back to Emilie. "We aren't far from my home. How long has it been since you've eaten?"

"I don't remember. Not for some time." Emilie had been too upset throughout her ordeal, but now that it was over, her stomach growled.

"Poor thing! You must want something to strengthen you? *Bien*, let's end our journey and stop for something to eat at my house. Take heart, for it's not far now." She stuck her head out the window and called out to Seigneur Claude. "My home is nearby. I am feeling a little unwell and Emilie is feeling fatigued. Would you mind if we stopped here? You and Père Jean could continue on and have Emilie's mother come to my home."

"I am concerned for you both," Seigneur Claude said, his brows furrowed.

"We are both fine, but tired," assured Juliette. "A little rest will do us both good. I promise Emilie is in the best of hands."

"It shall be as you wish," Seigneur Claude said.

Emilie sank languidly in her seat. Soon, she would be with her mother. Much relieved, she retreated into her own thoughts. Thankfully, Juliette did the same.

98

While Père Jean found the return home less bothersome, he did not enjoy it. He hated travelling by horseback. By the time his initial fears subsided, other worries haunted his imagination. The carriage driver, at Seigneur Prudhomme's insistence, drove the carriage at a rapid pace forcing them to follow with corresponding speed. Unfamiliar with horses, he had to grip the pommel to keep his balance. He did not dare request a slower pace.

They rode along a large wide lane on the edge of a steep bank. Instead of riding in the middle, his horse walked on the brink and no matter how hard he yanked on the reins to steer the beast to the opposite side, the stubborn mare refused to budge. He muttered a curse. Even the horse seemed inclined to invite danger. Vexed by fear, he suffered in silence. Why had it become his lot to be thrown into this situation?

They reached the foot of the descent and the valley fell behind them. Soon he would be home. Père Jean breathed easier and with a calmer mind, proceeded to contemplate other dangers. What would that villain Seigneur Richard think of his role in keeping Emilie away from him? Surely, he would be angry. He had already sent two demons to meet him on the road and threaten him with death should Emilie and Robert's wedding take place. What if Emilie told the Bishop of her plight? The Bishop might order him to marry the couple. Seigneur Richard would most certainly follow through with his threat to kill him. Venom flowed from that rogue's veins. Who knows what that man would do? Oh, when would all this trouble end? Blame would likely fall upon his shoulders. How cruel, when after so many inconveniences and so much agitation, without deserving it, that he should have to bear the punishment. What could the Bishop do to protect him, after having dragged him into this? Could he stop these wretched seigneurs from harming him? No, the Bishop had so many responsibilities, how could he attend to them all? He doubted that these seigneurs, both with a taste for evil, would ever change their ways. Rot lived inside them like a canker.

If Seigneur Richard confronted him, he would tell him that he rescued Emilie at the command of his superior, not of his own will. After all, it was the truth. But then it might appear as if he aided these reprehensible seigneurs. Oh, sacred Heaven! What should he do?

What if the Bishop should feel the need to know everything and he was forced to give an account of that wedding business! This was all that was needed to add to his troubles.

Père Jean caught himself. He was allowing his worries to flood like a river. He forced himself to stop thinking about what could happen and focus on the here and now. He carried enough burdens without these additional problems. For the present, he decided that his best recourse was to shut himself up in the rectory due to illness. As long as the Bishop remained in Pointe-du-Lac, Seigneur Richard would not make a stir. But afterwards?

Soon their retinue turned into a long rutted drive, which led to a two-storey timber home. A row of tidy bushes separated the home from a large garden at the side. A long field spread out behind the house as far as the eye could see. What were they doing here?

Alarmed, Père Jean remained mounted while Seigneur

Claude helped the women out of the carriage. "Why are we stopping?"

"Didn't Seigneur Prudhomme tell you? I was feeling a little fatigued, so I thought it best that Emilie and I stay the night at my home."

"Yes, I think it's for the best." Seigneur Claude looked up at the sun. "It's late afternoon already. Besides, I can have Emilie's mother brought here."

"Won't you both come inside for some refreshment?" Juliette glanced first at Seigneur Claude then at Père Jean.

"I thank you for your generous offer, but we should continue on to Pointe-du-Lac. The Bishop and Emilie's mother will be anxious for word of her safety. Besides, the good Bishop awaits us for dinner."

Père Jean breathed a sigh of relief. Nothing would happen to him if the Bishop expected them.

After bidding the women adieu, they set off on the remainder of their journey. Père Jean did his best to avoid riding beside Seigneur Claude by lagging behind him and his men or riding to the side.

When they arrived at the church, Père Jean dismounted and approached Seigneur Claude. "Please make an apology for me to the Bishop, but I am still recovering from an illness and cannot dine with him this evening. I am fatigued from the journey and do not feel well. Assure the Bishop that a few days rest is all I need to restore myself."

Before Seigneur Claude could respond, Père Jean turned about and hurried away.

99

Juliette invited Emilie to sit at a table in the centre of her kitchen. The large room was immaculate. Shelves on the wall near the window displayed neatly stacked plates and porringers between which rested a cloth-lined basket with the handles of cutlery evident over its edges. A long counter ran the length of a lace-curtained window. Beneath it, rows of jarred provisions sat in perfect alignment. The whitewashed walls contrasted with the dark color of the clean wooden floors.

Emilie watched Juliette place kindling in the hearth and light a fire. Upon the crane hung a large vessel in which floated a good-sized capon and some vegetables. When the broth came to a boil, she poured it into a porringer already furnished with sops of bread, and offered it to Emilie.

The soup proved to be delicious and revitalized Emilie with every spoonful.

"We have been blessed," Juliette said as she watched Emilie eat. "There are many who have no bread or millet. We, thank Heaven, are not so badly off. With my husband's business and a little plot of ground, we can live well. Do eat with a good appetite." She then turned away to prepare dinner for the rest of her family.

Juliette showed Emilie to a bedroom where she could refresh herself and gave her a change of clothes. Refreshed, Emilie stood before a small mirror on a dresser, shocked at her unruly appearance. Her hair hung loose and dishevelled around a pale face. Shadows lolled beneath her lustreless eyes. Her fatigued body screamed for rest. Soon - when safe with her mother again. Then she could rest. Home brought memories of Robert and the pang of loss surfaced. She poured some water from a pitcher into a ewer, dampened a cloth, and washed before brushing her dishevelled tresses and fastening them into one long braid.

Her fingers caressed the cross of her rosary. Lifting it up, she examined it. It reminded her of her vow. A sense of desperation came over her. A tumultuous burst of regret formed in her mind. What had she done in promising her life away? Fear returned. Her anguish, her despair, her fervent prayers, and the emotion with which she had made her promise tumbled about in her thoughts. Now, after having been granted her wish, to repent of it seemed sacrilegious. If she reneged, her unfaithfulness would bring additional misfortune.

She renounced her momentary regret. Instead, Emilie lifted the rosary from her neck and held it in her trembling hand. She spoke again the vow she had made.

Dear God, help me! Deliver me from this danger; bring me safely to my mother, and if you grant me this, I vow to renounce my betrothed so that I may belong only to Thee! Give me the strength to fulfill my promise and spare me from any regrets that may sway my resolve.

Her separation from Robert, which had brought her so much pain, now seemed a blessing. But she needed to tell Robert it was over between them. How to convince him it was the right thing to do?

Emilie struggled to dispel the regret that refused to leave her heart.

At the sound of joyous cries on the path outside of the house, Emilie left the room wearily, like a wounded soldier after a brutal battle.

Two little girls and a young boy bounded into the kitchen. They stopped to cast an inquisitive glance at Emilie then ran to their mother, attempting to relate the wonderful things they had witnessed on their walk home from church.

"Who is she?" asked the smallest girl, a pretty child with chestnut coloured hair that cascaded over her shoulders in two long braids.

Juliette smiled indulgently at her brood. "Hush, be quiet."

The master of the house entered, his step sedate, his expression cordial. Although not much taller than his wife, he was broad-shouldered with a handsome face. Plenty of lines around his eyes revealed him to be a man prone to a cheerful disposition. He kissed Juliette on the cheek then smiled at Emile. "Welcome to our home."

"I am pleased to meet you, and grateful for your help," Emilie responded, instantly at ease.

He removed his hat and hung it on a hook against the wall, revealing a crown in the early stages of baldness. "I was present when Père Nicholas came to ask my wife to accompany you here. I not only gave my approval, but would also have added my persuasion, had it been necessary. And as soon as the pomp and joyful concourse of the Bishop's mass ended, I rushed home eager to learn that all went well and that you are now safe."

"She most certainly is!" said Juliette.

Emilie felt herself blush.

"Welcome to our home and I am glad you're safe." Sidling up to his wife, who took the pot off the hook over the fire, he whispered in a voice loud enough for Emilie to hear, "Did everything go well?"

"Very well. I'll tell you afterwards." Juliette carried the pot to the counter, removed the capon, and began to cut it up. "Please sit. Dinner is ready."

As the family sat to eat, Monsieur Tremblay spoke with Emilie about the solemn mass, despite interruptions by the children. "To see such a good man like the Bishop at the altar blessing us was truly a sight," he said.

"And he had a big gold thing on his head," said the little girl.

He smiled at her then raised a forefinger to his lips to hush her. "The Bishop is a learned man and spoke in a way that everyone understood."

"Even I understood, Papa," said the eldest girl.

Monsieur Tremblay grinned. "What did you understand?"

"I understood that he was preaching the Gospel."

He sat a little straighter. "Without ever mentioning the name of Seigneur Claude Prudhomme and his miraculous conversion from evil to goodness, everyone knew who the Bishop alluded to. The Bishop stood with tears in his eyes. Then everyone present began to weep, too."

"But why were they all crying in that way, like children, Papa?" burst forth the boy.

"*Mon fils,* there are many hard hearts in this world. And though there is hardship and toil, the Bishop made us understand that we ought to be thankful for what we have. We must do whatever we can, work industriously, help one another, then be content, for it is not a disgrace to suffer and be poor. The true disgrace is to commit evil. And these are true words by the Bishop because everyone knows he lives like a poor man himself and takes the bread out of his own mouth to give to the hungry. Ah! It gives one great satisfaction to hear such a man preach, not like the others who want you to do what they say, not what they do. Then he told us that those who have more than they need ought to share it with those who suffer."

As if checked by some thought, he hesitated. Then he filled a platter from the dishes on the table, and adding a loaf of bread, he wrapped it into a large cloth. He held it by the four corners and handed it to his eldest daughter. "Here, take this." He placed a small flask of wine into her other hand. "Go to the widow Marie. Give her these things and tell her to enjoy them with her children. But do it kindly so that it doesn't seem like charity. And don't say anything to anyone you might meet."

The girl turned to leave.

"And take care you break nothing."

"I won't, Papa," she said with a smile as she left.

Emilie's eyes glistened. The conversation comforted her more than any sermon. It erased the ache from her own sorrows and filled her with strength. Even the thought of the tremendous sacrifice she would soon make, though still bitter, brought her joy. Her hands trembled with a mixture of joy and excitement. Yesterday, she despaired of any happiness and of seeing her mother again. Reunite me with my mother, she had prayed. Now it was about to come true, reinforcing her conviction to keep her promise.

100

Ada watched Père Nicholas walk away from her home. She had listened with shock when he told her of Emilie's abduction and was confused as to how it all happened. She believed Emilie would be safe at the convent. When she questioned him, Père Nicholas admitted he did not know many of the details. She wanted to know how it happened.

After a long wait, the carriage arrived to fetch her. As she passed the church, she noticed Père Jean rush into the rectory. "Driver, stop!" she called out.

She stepped out of the carriage. "Père Jean!"

His shoulders slumped as he swung around to face her. His face was pale and his mouth slack.

Ada rushed toward him. "Do know anything about what happened to Emilie? Have you seen her? Is she well?"

Père Jean tucked his hands into opposite sleeves. "*Oui*, she is fine and awaits you." He glanced away. "If you don't mind, I'm feeling a little ill today and need to retire."

Ada rolled her eyes. "Maybe I should speak to the Bishop. Père Nicholas said it was the Bishop himself who brought her to safety."

He tensed and grabbed her arm. "If you speak with the Bishop, keep your wits about you and make certain you don't tell him too much."

Ada narrowed her eyes and squinted at him. "What have I to

be careful about?"

Père Jean took a step back and wrung his hands. "It would be wise not to say anything about Emilie's failed wedding. He knows nothing about it."

Ada raised her hand to cut him short. "I make you no promises. When I return with Emilie, if the Bishop asks to see us, I will go. If he asks me anything, I will answer with the truth." Unable to look at him one second more, she turned, and without another glance, re-entered the carriage, determined, more than ever, to get at the truth.

101

Emilie sprang from her chair the moment she heard the crunch of gravel and the clomp of horse's hooves outside. She swung open the door and flung herself into her mother's outstretched arms.

"Oh, my poor baby," Ada said as she patted Emilie's back. "Let me look at you." Ada pulled back and scrutinized Emilie from head to toe. "Are you well?"

Tears blurred Emilie's sight as she nodded. It was hard to believe she was safe and in the comfort of her mother's company once more.

Madame Tremblay came out of the house with a grand smile on her face. "You must be Emilie's mother. I am Juliette Tremblay."

"Ada Basseaux. I'm grateful to you for your help."

"It was nothing, my utter pleasure. Please come inside."

Madame Tremblay offered them something to eat and drink which Ada graciously refused, then discreetly left them alone.

"Tell me all that happened," Ada said as she reached over and took Emilie's hand in hers.

Emilie drew in a deep breath and recited everything that had transpired.

Ada listened, caressing Emilie's cheek or taking hold of her hand as she spoke.

When Emilie described the carriage and the men who had accosted her, her mother gasped with alarm. "Seigneur Richard must be behind this," she said through nearly clenched teeth, her face red. "Who else could do such a thing? The black villain! That infernal firebrand! His hour will come, then he, too, will feel the pain of injustice."

"No, Mother; no! Do not wish for such things. It will only bring more misfortune. We should pray that God will touch his heart in the same way he has touched Seigneur Claude's heart; a man who was far worse than Seigneur Richard."

Ada grazed Emilie's cheek with the back of her hand. "You're right, but you can't blame me for being angry at all that has befallen you. You should have been married by now with perhaps my grandchild in your belly."

Emilie smiled and marvelled at her mother. Always kind, always generous, forever protecting her and making her feel safe. She continued telling her all that she knew, but when she came to the part about the vow she had made, she hesitated. If she took the vows of the veil, what would happen to her mother? She might be angry with her for making such a reckless vow and might make her feel guilty for abandoning her betrothed.

Emilie's greatest fear in telling her mother lay in the fact she might confide in someone to gain their counsel and thus make her vow known. Emilie shrank back in shame, but something warned her to keep the vow a secret, at least until she could speak about it to Père Marc-Mathieu. "Have you heard from Père Marc-Mathieu?"

Ada shook her head. "He's gone."

"Gone where?" The first waves of alarm ran through her.

"He's been sent away to duties in La Prairie de la Madelaine."

"And Robert?" Emilie dared ask.

"I suspect he's in Sainte-Anne-de-Beaupre with his friend that he speaks so often about, but no one knows for certain, and up to now, he has sent no news of himself."

Emilie became lightheaded. What could have happened to him?

102

The moment Seigneur Claude entered the church, Bishop Laval gave him a hearty smile and rose to greet him. "Welcome back. Did all go well with Emilie's return?"

"Most definitely, Excellency. She is safe at the Tremblay house awaiting her mother's arrival."

"God be praised." The Bishop smiled. "Come and sit, you can tell me all about it during dinner." He led him into a room off the nave. Groups of priests stood around a long table set for dinner. The moment they entered, the priests stopped talking.

The Bishop took his place at the head of the table and gestured for Claude to take the seat to his right. He noticed how Claude walked with a lighter step and seemed much more relaxed.

An uncomfortable silence lingered in the room. Looks of shock existed on the priests' faces, for that seat belonged to the highest-ranking cleric. "We are waiting for Père Jean to arrive then dinner will be served," Bishop Laval said.

"Père Jean asked me to pass on his apologies, but he has taken ill. I think it was the fatigue from our journey."

The Bishop frowned. "I'm sorry to hear that. I have decided to visit the Tremblay home in the morning to speak to Emilie and her mother myself. As they are his parishioners, I had hoped Père Jean would accompany me."

"I do not think that will be possible. He looked quite pale when last I saw him."

"I pray that he is not afflicted with anything serious."

"He seemed a little *yellow* and feeble," Seigneur Claude said with emphasis on the word yellow. "I suspect a good night's sleep to rest his weary muscles will revive him. He seems to have a delicate constitution."

"Yellow? I will pray for his health and take Père Nicholas with me instead."

At bevy of servants entered the room to serve the meal. The two men dropped their conversation of Père Jean.

103

The next day, Ada stood mute with surprise, as did the Tremblay family, when Bishop de Laval arrived. Père Nicholas accompanied him. The Bishop placed his hand on Emilie's forehead and made the sign of the cross. "Poor girl. God has put you through a great trial; but He restored you to safety, and has made you the catalyst that changed a man. If there is something more I can do, you need only ask."

Ada straightened and edged forward. "It would be wonderful if all priests were as generous as you, helping people out of difficulties instead of creating problems for them." Her annoyance at Père Jean for having brought all this trouble upon them surfaced, and then intensified when she thought of how he had dared discourage her from talking to the Bishop. She had had enough of that coward.

"Please speak freely," encouraged the Bishop.

"If our parish priest had done his duty, things wouldn't have unfolded as they have."

The Bishop's face became serious. "I am listening."

Her mind raced and she suddenly regretted having spoken.

In order to relate the whole story, she would have to admit her part in encouraging Emilie and Robert to trick Père Jean into marrying them. Now, she had to say something. So, she inhaled a fortifying breath and told him about the intended marriage, Père Jean's refusal, and all the arguments the priest had made against performing it. She related how rogues had broken into their home and how they managed to escape. "If Père Jean had told us the truth from the start, and married Emilie and Robert like he should have, we would have moved away to some other settlement. Now look at all the troubles that have befallen us."

"Père Jean shall render me an account of this matter," the Bishop said sternly.

"Please, Excellency, no!" replied Ada. If he spoke to Père Jean, the priest would reveal their foiled attempt to trick him. "Don't scold him. What is done is done. Besides, it will do no good; it is his nature and if this were to happen again, he would do the same."

"But we have also done wrong," Emilie said.

Ada frowned to signal her to say nothing.

Emilie scowled back and faced the Bishop. "We also erred."

"What can you have done wrong, my poor girl?" asked the Bishop.

Emilie ignored her mother's protesting glances and told the Bishop of their attempt to marry in Père Jean's house. "We acted wrongfully and now we are suffering."

"Be of good courage," said the Bishop. "Those who have suffered have reason to rejoice and be hopeful. Where is your betrothed now?"

Pain clogged her throat. "He fell into some trouble and is now being sought by the law."

"Trouble? What sort of trouble?"

Ada stammered out what she knew of Robert's history.

"What is his name?"

"Robert Lanzille."

"I have heard talk about this youth." The Bishop frowned. "How is such a man betrothed to someone like you?"

"He is a good man," Emilie said in a firm voice.

"A generous, kind-hearted man," added Ada. "Anybody you ask will say so, even Père Jean. Who knows what happened in Québec? It takes little to turn someone into a rogue."

"Indeed." He gave them a reassuring look. "I'll make some inquiries and see what I can do." He turned to address the Tremblays. "There may still be a risk of danger. Are you able to keep Emilie and her mother for a few more days until I can ensure their safety?"

"We will take good care of them both, Excellency," Monsieur Tremblay said.

"It will be good to have some company," replied Juliette.

The Bishop nodded. "May God bless this house."

104

After prayers that evening, the Bishop stopped Père Nicholas on his way out of the church. "How can I compensate the tailor for any expenses he may incur by his hospitality to Emilie Basseaux and her mother?"

"In truth, Excellency, neither the profits of his business nor the produce from his small fields will be enough this year to allow him to be too liberal to others, but he is among those in the best circumstances and will care for them well. He is known for his generosity."

"*Bien*, but it is asking a lot in these difficult times."

"I can assure you, Excellency, under any circumstances, he would deem it an insult to be offered money in compensation."

"Surely he must be affected by people unable to pay him."

"You may judge yourself, my most illustrious Lord. Poor

people pay him from the surplus of the harvest. Unfortunately, last year there was no surplus."

The Bishop stroked his chin. "I will take all his debts upon myself. Please ask him for a list of all outstanding sums owing to him, and I will pay them all."

Père Nicholas raised his eyebrows. "A most generous offer, Excellency."

"So much the better. Are there many more people near destitute?."

Père Nicholas nodded. "One does what one can; but how can we supply everyone in times like these?"

"Tell the tailor to clothe them all at my expense, and pay him well for it."

105

When Claude Prudhomme rode into the small courtyard in front of his home, he remained mounted and bellowed out one of his thundering calls – a familiar signal all dependents within hearing distance immediately heeded.

Everyone from the manor house and fields who heard him hurried towards him with unease. After they'd assembled, Claude raised his hand and their whispers gradually ceased. "Friends, the path we have all been on is leading us to hell. I am not here to lay any blame, for I have been the worst. Nevertheless, God has called on me to change my life; and change it, I will. I would rather die than break another of His holy laws. I hereby revoke any heinous commands you may have received from me. No one in my service will break any laws. Anyone who disagrees must leave. I'll pay you what you are owed, but you cannot stay here unless you are willing and able to change your life. Those who reform themselves and decide to remain, will be treated well. You have the night to think it over. In the morning, I will ask you one-by-one for your reply. For now, you all may return to your posts."

An air of shocked silence hovered over the group. His eyes roamed over each face, but no one showed any emotion. They were accustomed to receiving his orders; commands from which there was never any appeal. Now that he announced he had changed, would they follow? He did not doubt his words were odious to some of them, but he had spoken from his heart and he knew they understood.

Many seemed confounded. He imagined some were thinking about where to find shelter and employment should they choose to leave, and questioning whether they could truly become honest men. Others, those most moved by his words, might feel inclined to change. No one, however, uttered a word.

When they dispersed, they moved off in various directions. He watched them by the dim evening light as they returned to their various posts.

Only then did he dismount, hand the reins to a waiting groom, and enter his house. Never had he been so burdened with urgent responsibilities, yet he was sleepy. The remorse, which had robbed him of sleep the night before, now spoke to him more sternly.

With these few words, he had overturned the orderliness of his home. He had shaken the fidelity of those who served him and had brought confusion and uncertainty into his household.

In his bedroom, he approached the bed. The memory of how he raised a pistol to his head and nearly pulled the trigger flashed in his mind. He had just freed an assortment of villains, thieves, and scoundrels that he knew too much about. What if they turned on him, afraid he would confess their crimes to the authorities? One of his former henchmen may come in and slit his throat. Life would come full circle. How ironic that he now experienced the same terror he used to inflict on others.

He experienced bitter contrition and a sense of hopelessness at ever finding a way to clear his conscience. Bothered, he laid in bed, but sleep eluded him.

106

Despite the fact the sun had been up for some time, Père Jean lay staring contemplatively at the ceiling above his bed. A small dish of *creton* made with ground pork and Rose's secret combination of spices sat beside a crust of bread and a tankard of water untouched on his bedside table. The upheaval in his life, caused by Seigneur Richard's threat, continued to worsen. He did not know how much more he could take. For the first time in his life, he thought about fleeing; in fact, at this point, he would embrace any form of escape.

The responsibilities of being a parish priest weighed heavily, like a boulder slung between his shoulders. It was a constant challenge to navigate the treacherous path between right and wrong. For a simple man who wanted nothing more than to lead an uncomplicated life, his choice of vocation kept that dream beyond his reach.

A knock on the door interrupted his thoughts. "Go away," he called out. "Can't you find something better to do with your time, Rose?"

The door swung open. Bishop de Laval stood like a regal apparition in his amethyst-colored soutane, a frown on his narrow face.

"Bishop!" Père Jean sprung out of bed and ran his hands over his unshaven face. "I was not expecting anyone, uh, I've been ill."

"I heard that you were ill and I would be remiss in my duties as your superior were I not to check on you." His eyes roamed over Père Jean.

Père Jean cringed beneath the scrutiny and adjusted his wrinkled soutane, the same one he had worn yesterday.

"Shall I summon a healer? I've heard much about the healing skills of one of the Jesuit priests nearby."

"No, no, I thank you, but I am certain a little rest is all I need" Père Jean added, tucking his hands behind his back. "May I offer you some refreshment?"

The Bishop glanced at the tray, but raised his hand to refuse. "Thank you, but I have recently eaten." He paused. "There is something I would like to speak to you about."

Père Jean swallowed.

"May we sit?" the Bishop asked after glancing at the two chairs set beside the window.

"Yes, please forgive my manners. I have not been sleeping well of late." Père Jean waited for the Bishop to sit then followed. He clasped his hands in his lap and waited.

"What do you know about the character and conduct of Robert Lanzille?" the Bishop asked.

Père Jean fought the tension that stiffened his body. "Only that he is an obstinate, hot-headed fellow."

"Yet others speak of him as generous beyond a fault; a man known to share his last grain with someone of lesser fortune."

"Well, yes, uh, aside from his rather passionate nature, he is a praiseworthy young man, which is why I cannot understand how he could have become embroiled in such trouble in Québec."

"And about the young woman?" continued the Bishop. "Do you think it is safe for her to return home?"

"For the present," Père Jean added with a sigh, "while your Excellency is near at hand. After that..." he shrugged.

"Perhaps it is best to place her in safety." The Bishop paused and narrowed his eyes. "Why didn't you perform their marriage?"

Père Jean's heart nearly stopped and his mouth fell open. "Uh, hmm, your most illustrious Excellency, ah, you will, doubtless, have heard of this affair. It has all been so intricate, that, to this day, even I am not clear about it. The young girl is here, after so many misfortunes, as if by a miracle; and the bridegroom, after having endured even more mishaps, is who knows where."

"That is not my question," replied the Bishop. "I asked you whether it is true that, before all these circumstances took place, you refused to celebrate the marriage, when you were requested to do so, on the appointed day. Why?"

"If you only knew the terrible threats I received." He paused and leaned back in his chair, hoping to insinuate that it would be indiscreet to speak any more about it.

"But it is I, your Bishop, who wishes to learn why you have not done your duty."

Père Jean shrank in his seat. "This situation has become so entangled, so hopeless, that I considered it useless to bring it to your attention. However, because I know you will not abandon me, I will tell you."

"Tell me," nodded the Bishop, his hands folded over his chest. "I wish to find you blameless."

Accosted in such a manner, Père Jean had no choice but to relate the doleful history. Instead of speaking Seigneur Richard's name, he named him only by title, a prudent act in the face of this confrontation.

"And you had no other motive?" asked the Bishop.

"Perhaps I have not sufficiently explained myself," Père Jean took a deep breath. "Under threat of death, I was clearly warned not to perform the marriage." He enunciated each word clearly.

"And does this appear to you a sufficient reason for omitting a duty?"

"I have always endeavoured to do my duty, even at great

inconvenience; but when one's life is threatened, one must do what one must do."

"And when you received Holy Orders, did you believe that your duties would be free from every obstacle, exempt from every danger? Or that where danger begins, there your duty would end?"

Père Jean shook his head.

"In fact, it is the contrary. You were sent forth as a sheep among wolves. Did you not realize that you would face oppressors who would find your work in the Church displeasing? That is why God instituted the holy unction, the imposition of hands, and the gift of the priesthood. He left it to us to teach this virtue, to advocate this doctrine. For shame! Where would the Church be if all brethren acted as cowardly as you did?"

Père Jean hung his head. He felt like prey in the talons of a hawk soaring to a miserable height. The Bishop waited for his reply. "Excellency, I am to blame. I don't know what to say. I had to deal with a powerful seigneur who refused to listen to reason. I don't see what was to be gained even if I had taken a stand. This Seigneur is impossible to reason with."

"Don't you know that suffering for the sake of righteousness is our victory? If you don't know this, what do you preach? What is the good news you announce to your flock? Who told you that you should conquer force with force? Surely, you will one day be asked whether you did what was required of you, even when your enemies tried to prevent you. How will you answer then?"

It appeared the Bishop cared more for the affections of two young people than for the life of a poor priest. Père Jean wanted the conversation to end, but the Bishop waited with the air of one who expects a reply, a confession, or an apology, anything but silence.

"I repeat, Excellency, that I am not to blame. One cannot give oneself courage."

"Then why did you undertake the priesthood, which binds you into continual warfare with the passions of the world? How is it you did not know that courage was necessary to fulfill your obligations? God will bestow it upon you if you ask Him. Do you think all the millions of martyrs naturally possessed courage? That they naturally held life in contempt? Martyrs-mothers, the elderly, even children? All possessed courage, because courage was necessary, and they relied upon God. Knowing your own weakness, and the duties of priesthood, have you not prepared yourself for the difficult circumstances in which you might be placed? After so many years in this parish, surely you must love those committed to your spiritual care? When you saw two of your flock threatened, and weakness of the flesh made you fearful, love should have made you fear for them. You should have done all in your power to avert the dangers that threatened them. What have you done for them?"

Père Jean knew not what to say. He opened and closed his mouth several times, words failing him altogether.

"You give me no answer!" resumed the Bishop. "Ah, if you had done what charity and duty required, you would have an answer! See what you have done? You have obeyed the voice of iniquity, unmindful of your duties against treachery. You have transgressed and kept silent. I ask you, now, whether you have not perhaps done more?"

Père Jean looked up sharply.

"You will tell me whether it is true that you lied to disguise your true motives for not wedding the couple." He paused and waited.

Ada the telltale must have told him, thought Père Jean. Anger rose to the surface. Try as he might, he could not respond.

"It is true, then, that you lied to these poor people to keep them in ignorance. It only remains for me to blush with shame at your actions!" He shook his head as if in disbelief. "You have deceived the weak and lied to the Church's children."

Père Jean allowed his distress to wash through him. That fiend, Seigneur Richard, had brought this misery upon him. All he had done was utter a small deception in order to save his life and now all this fuss and embarrassment. "I have done wrong, but what else could I have done in such extreme circumstances?"

The Bishop's face reddened. "You still ask this? Have I not explained it already? Must I tell you again? You should have loved, my son; loved and prayed. You should have united those whom the seigneur wished to put asunder. You should have granted these unhappy innocents the ministry they had a right to expect from you. Because you did not do any of that, you are now answerable for this mess! Did you not remember that you had a superior? Why didn't you consult me? I am bound to assist you in fulfilling the duties of your office."

The very advice of Rose, thought Père Jean. He could not erase the image of the two men who had accosted him on the path that day. Seigneur Richard was still alive and well, and one day would return to find him, eager for revenge, regardless of the Bishop's protection. This knowledge filled him with confusion and fear. After all, the Bishop carried neither musket, nor sword, nor men to fight on his behalf.

The Bishop leaned forward in his chair. "I could have protected you and those poor innocents. This evil man would have been rendered weak when he learned that I knew of his plots."

Exactly what Rose had said to him, thought Père Jean again.

"But you saw nothing but your own temporary danger. No wonder you were blind to any other solutions."

"You did not see the faces of those terrible men," stuttered Père Jean. "You did not hear their words. Your Excellency speaks well, but had you found yourself in my shoes, you might have reacted similarly." The moment he uttered the words, he bit his tongue in vexation. He had allowed himself to be carried away by petulance. Now he must face the storm. But, as he raised his eyes doubtfully, he was astonished to see the Bishop's face transform itself from the solemn air of authority and rebuke, to a sorrowful and pensive gravity.

"It's true. Such are the trials of our work." The Bishop stroked his chin. "If you are aware of my having failed in any part of my duty, tell me of it candidly, and help me to amend. Remonstrate freely with me on my weaknesses and my words will acquire more value in my mouth."

What kind of Bishop would open himself to such criticism? "Oh, Excellency, surely you jest. Everyone knows of your fortitude of mind and intrepid zeal." Too much so, Père Jean added in his heart.

"I did not ask you for praise. God knows my failings. I must find a way to help you understand that your conduct has been contrary to the faith you preach."

"All blame falls on me," Père Jean conceded. "But I suspect Ada did not tell you of how Emilie and Robert entered into my house to trick me into marrying them."

The Bishop lowered his chin and glared at him. "They did tell me. It is this that grieves me; that you attempt to excuse yourself by accusing others. Who forced them to resort to it? Would they have attempted it if the legitimate way had been open to them? Would they have surprised you if you had not concealed yourself feigning illness? If they provoked or offended you, then all the more reason to love them because they have suffered. It is you who needs to be pardoned."

Père Jean fell silent, for he had much to think about. He

experienced dissatisfaction with himself, a kind of pity for others, a mixture of compunction and shame. He would have accused himself bitterly, he would even have wept, but the threats of Seigneur Richard still lingered in his memory.

"Now we have a young couple who have had to flee their homes. We cannot predict the future, but from this day forward, you will do all that you can to keep them safe."

"I will not fail, Excellency, I assure you." Père Jean's sincerity came from his heart.

"I hoped to have a different conversation with you. We have both lived long and it pains me to reprimand you when I prefer to talk about the concerns of the people we serve. Perhaps I am too impatient and I allowed your initial hesitation to admit guilt to vex me?"

Père Jean hung his head and cracked his knuckles. In his mind, Père Jean cursed Ada for having told the Bishop. That vile woman never did know how to hold her tongue.

"You have much to contemplate, Père Jean," the Bishop continued. "I leave you to do just that." He rose, strode to the door, and looked back. Pity glimmered in his eyes.

Père Jean stared out the window. When he looked back, the Bishop had gone. He stood alone with his conscience.

107

For Emilie, the days with the tailor and his family passed peacefully. She kept herself busy by plying her needle and aiding the tailor by sewing hems on sleeves and breeches. Her mother travelled back and forth between their home and that of the Tremblay's. Their conversations were more melancholy, as well as more affectionate because of their impending separation. Emilie knew the Bishop needed to send her to a more secure dwelling, for the lamb could not dwell so near the wolf's den. When would all this separation end? Her future seemed bleak, inextricable.

Her mother tried to keep her spirits up. If nothing horrible happened to Robert, he would eventually send news of himself, and if he found employment elsewhere, he could live happily. Emilie listened to her mother's banter beneath a cloak of silence. She kept her vow a secret. Although she hated concealing it, shame kept her from speaking of it. She could not help it, but of late, she had given herself up to whatever destiny awaited.

"You've suffered so much, Emilie, and I know it doesn't seem possible that any good can come of this, but it will. The Bishop will find you a safe haven where you can pass the days until this trouble ends. All will be well, you'll see," her mother reassured.

Emilie was not so certain.

108

The following day, Bishop de Laval sent Père Nicholas to the Tremblay home. The friar came in a carriage to escort Emilie and her mother to the Bishop. Once again, Emilie braced herself to face an unknown future.

They alighted in front of the church and were brought to the Bishop who was talking with Père Jean. At their appearance, the Bishop gave a hearty smile. Père Jean's eyebrows drooped and his mouth slid into a glower. After an exchange of greetings, the Bishop drew a letter from his pocket, smiled, and handed it to Emilie.

"I am to go to the Hôpital Général of Québec?" she said glancing up after reading it.

"*Oui*, the superior there is a good woman by the name of Louise Soumande de Saint-Augustin of the Religious Hospitallers of Saint Joseph. Her past is similar to yours and she has agreed to help you on my behalf."

Emilie clutched her mother's hand. The moment to part had arrived. Unease possessed her, but she knew she had no choice. She must go where Seigneur Richard could not harm her. Although she had been happy at the Ursuline Convent, she had come to harm there and understood she could not return. Soeur Emmanuelle herself had put her in harm's way.

"I pray you accept all this uncertainty calmly. Trust that it will soon be over and that God will bring matters to an end according to His will." He paused and placed a hand on her forehead and blessed her. "My carriage will transport you there tomorrow." He blessed Ada and exited the room.

When they left the church, a crowd of friends surrounded them, offering a flurry of congratulations, sympathy, and inquiries with offers to guard their cottage that night. The warmth and good wishes of the settlers confounded Emilie. It warmed her heart and distracted her from her troubles. Never had entering her home felt so good.

109

To sleep in her own bed, to eat at her own table, and to spend a peaceful day with her mother brought Emilie a renewed sense of peace. She dreaded her imminent departure, preferring to remain in Pointe-du-Lac with her mother to await word from Robert. As she and her mother finished their morning meal of crepes drenched with maple syrup, someone rapped at their door. They exchanged a look of concern.

Ada rose, shifted the curtain aside, and peered outside. "It's Seigneur Prudhomme," she said, letting the curtain fall back. "He's alone." She removed her apron, tossed it onto the back of a chair, and tucked away some loose tresses. After straightening her gown, she swung open the door with a smile. "*Bonjour*,

Seigneur Prudhomme, what a surprise."

"I hope I am not disturbing you."

"Not at all, please, come in."

Claude's face broke into a smile the moment he entered and saw Emilie. He swept off his tricorne and bowed from the waist.

Emilie warmed at the unanticipated gesture of respect. He wore a silk waistcoat the color of sapphires. A fleur de lis border lined the collar and wrists of his white linen shirt. Tucked between his arm and waist, he held a wooden casket inlaid with mother of pearl.

"I, ah, came to bring you something," he stammered. He raised his eyebrows, lifted the casket, and gestured at the table. "It's quite heavy, may I?"

"*Mais oui*," Ada said as she whisked away the remnants of their morning meal.

Seigneur Claude placed the casket down and looked up at Emilie. "The past can never be altered, but there is much I can do to change the future."

Emilie glanced first at him then her mother, who nodded in encouragement.

Seigneur Claude gestured at the box. "This is for you. Go ahead, open it."

Emilie raised the latch and lifted the lid. A small hoard of gold coins glittered upon a red velvet interior. Her mouth fell open as she looked up at Seigneur Claude.

Ada clasped her hands to her chest, eyes wide.

"Gold Louis," he added. "Three hundred of them; a dowry for you or any other use you may have for it."

"Seigneur Prudhomme, this is far too generous." Emilie had never seen so much money before. His generosity astounded her. What did this mean? Questions raced through her mind, but the shock rendered her unable to ask them.

"You do us a great honor, Monsieur, and we are grateful to

accept it." Ada cast Emilie an admonishing look.

"It is a small offering to compensate for all the trouble I caused you, of which I regret. You must promise me that if ever, on any occasion, I can render you both any service, you must ask. I will not hesitate to provide whatever you need."

"May God reward you for this," whispered Emilie.

"It is reparation I seek, not reward. Of that, I am unworthy." Seigneur Claude seemed to shrink a little upon speaking the words as he turned to leave.

"Wait," Emilie called to him.

He turned slowly around.

Emilie rose on her toes and kissed him on both cheeks. When she pulled away, she noticed tears glistening in his eyes. Encouraged, she threw her arms around his neck and embraced him. When his arms pulled her tight against him, she could not restrain her own tears.

"If I were to have a daughter, I'd want her to be like you." Seigneur Claude's voice trembled with emotion.

Before Emilie could say another word, he turned on his heel and departed.

Ada rushed to the window and watched him leave. "He's gone," she announced as she scurried back to the table and let out a shriek of delight as she dipped her hand into the hoard, pulled out a palm-full of gold coins, and let them slip through her fingers. "I've never seen so many coins all together, and all ours." She took one out and bit it. "They are real."

"Of course they are real!" Emilie took hold of a coin and studied it. She had never seen a gold Louis before. Its weight and coolness felt good in her hand. The coins held the promise of a life of comfort, but sadly, it would not change her circumstances. She must still flee the reaches of Seigneur Richard and keep her vow to take the veil. She dropped the coin back into the pile.

Ada lowered the casket's lid and fastened the latch. "We have to hide this."

Emilie followed Ada into her bedroom and watched as she shoved the bed over and lifted a floorboard. She tucked the box into it, replaced the board, and pushed the bed back over their secret. They spent the remainder of the day in quiet contemplation. Emilie no longer worried about her mother and how she would fare when alone. The gold coins would see to her every need. As for herself, trepidation still roiled inside of her. Regret seeped into her thoughts. If only she could stay with her mother. A worry-free future filled with comfort tempted her. She doubted her resolve and felt more uncertain than ever. Troubled as she was, however, she still could not abandon her vow.

That night, sleep eluded Emilie. When sleep did come, it came in broken pieces, tossing her in a sea of apprehension and regret. She dreamt of Robert calling for her at the end of a long hallway. The more she ran toward him, the more distant he became, until she lost him altogether.

By the time morning came, fatigue and a heavy heart made it difficult to rise. She knew she must tell her mother about the vow, for this would be their last conversation for a long time.

In the kitchen, Ada greeted her with a brilliant smile. "I've never slept so well in my entire life. Our future is assured. There's so much we can do now."

"God bless Seigneur Claude." Emilie reached into the cupboard for two bowls. "Now you have enough to live comfortably. You have enough to help others too." She set the bowls on the table.

"I have nobody but you and Robert. I've always considered him my son, but now everything depends upon what has happened to him. Surely, our fortune will change. I would have been happy here in Pointe-du-Lac, but now, thanks to that villain, Seigneur Richard, the thought of staying here is out of the question. With you and Robert, I can be happy anywhere. When Robert finds a way of letting us know where he is and whether he is safe, I'll come to Québec and fetch you. Then we can start a new life wherever we want."

With every word, Emilie grew more dejected.

Ada stopped abruptly in the midst of her speech. "But what's the matter? Aren't you happy?"

"Oh, *Maman*!" Emilie threw her arms round her mother's neck.

"What is the matter?"

"I ought to have told you right away." Emilie raised her head and composed herself. "But I never had the heart."

"But tell me now."

"I can never marry Robert!"

"Why not?"

Emilie hung her head. Her heart beat fast as she disclosed her vow. "Please forgive me for not having told you sooner."

Ada flopped into a chair, speechless.

"Don't speak of this to anyone," Emilie implored. "All I ask is for you to help me fulfill my promise."

Ada shook her head and frowned. "I should be angry with you for not telling me, but to do so would seem as if I cursed Heaven itself."

"Please understand, *Maman*, I was trapped. I believed I was going to be killed. Desperate, I prayed for deliverance. To exchange my freedom for religious life seemed the right thing to do. And the next morning, my prayers were answered." Her voice faded as she studied her mother. "I cannot renege on my promise."

Ada shook her head. "No, you can't. Strange and terrible punishments follow the violation of a vow. But not to tell me of it at once!" Frustration tinged Ada's voice.

"I didn't have the heart. What use would it have been to upset you?"

"And what about Robert?" Ada wrung her hands.

"I must not think of him anymore. Fate pulled us apart. I hope he is safe and that he'll be happier without me."

"But things are different now," Ada replied. "All this gold is a remedy to our problems."

"We wouldn't have it if I hadn't passed such a horrible night and prayed." Emilie's voice became choked with sadness.

Ada remained silent.

"*Maman*, you must help me. Find Robert while I'm in sanctuary. Write to him. Tell him what happened to me, where I have been, all that has happened. Help him understand why I can't be his wife. Explain the vow to him; one I cannot break. Then write to me; let me know he is well. After that, let me never hear anything more about him. It hurts too much."

Ada rose to the window and looked out into the settlement.

"Please *Maman*, you must do this for me."

Ada swung back around and nodded. "I would do anything for you."

A weight seemed to rise off Emilie's shoulders even though her heart was breaking. "There's one thing more I have to ask of you," Emilie said. "If Robert had not the misfortune of knowing me, all this would never have happened to him. He's wandering lost somewhere in the wilds of this new world, a ruined man who has lost his savings and livelihood. Now that we have so much wealth, and you look upon Robert as a son, divide it between you. Find a safe bearer and send some to him. Heaven knows he'll need it."

Ada nodded. "Of course. Wealth makes life easier, but it won't make anyone rich. Richness is found in the arms of a loving family." She looked at Emilie expectantly, as if she was giving her one last chance to change her mind.

"And I hope he will be so blessed, one day." Emilie took her mother's hand. "Thank you."

"What will I do now; a solitary widow, without my only child?" Ada's eyes brimmed with tears.

"And I without you. But we'll see each other soon, I know it in my heart." Emilie sat on the ground, her head in Ada's lap. Her hair, caressed by her mother's loving hand; she waited for the Bishop's carriage that would soon part them.

110

Summer's warmth faded into the coolness of a brilliant autumn. That year, a bountiful harvest eased the strife in New France. Although the casket of gold made Ada's life nearly carefree, Emilie's absence blanketed her in endless melancholy. The days grew shorter and winter soon depleted the world of colour, casting an icy blue whiteness everywhere.

Ada remained concerned about Robert. Neither letter nor message reached her from him; and among all those whom she could ask from Point-du-Lac or Trois-Riviere or Québec, no one knew anything about him. Yet unusual rumours about him persisted. Some believed Robert perished crossing the Saint Lawrence River. Others were convinced he boarded a ship to France. Many swore he became a voyageur and now traded furs in unexplored territories. Ada did her utmost to discover which was the true account, but never succeeded. Each story proved unfounded. Nevertheless, she refused to stop searching. She had made a promise to Emilie; one she was determined to keep.

111
Winter 1703

In an isolated sugar shack, deep in the woods north of Saint-

Anne-de-Beaupre, Robert threw another log into the hearth and jabbed at it with a poker until the fire burned stronger. He set down the iron rod and blew into his hands to chase the cold from his fingertips. The heat from the hearth soothed his body as he stared into the flames. Pity it could not soothe his tormented spirit, he thought. A man could go mad isolated in the wilds like this. The notion burned in his mind, stirring the fury in his soul.

Not long ago, his life had been full of hope, brimming with possibilities. A future so rich with the promise of family and love that its loss pressed upon his heart like an anvil, suffocating him. Not a day passed that he did not conjure Emilie's beautiful image in his mind. He had been hours away from making her his wife when Seigneur Richard interfered. His entire destiny shifted then, all hope for a happy future lost in a cesspool of evil intent. The loss of the mill, his farm, the only home he had ever known, and his life savings paled in comparison to the loss of Emilie.

Robert turned away from the fire and crossed the space to the tiny window. A thick frosting of ice glazed it so he could no longer look out at the knee-high mantle of snow covering everything. His hair had grown long, unkempt. A thick beard and moustache now covered the lower half of his face.

He looked around at the sparse cabin dominated by a large hearth. A table and chairs rested beneath an undersized paned window. The only other adornment was a small cot covered with quilts and a large bear fur.

The split-log cabin and the land surrounding it belonged to Bastien, who kept Robert supplied with beans, salt pork, flour, and whatever else he thought to bring. More important than the food, was news, or lack thereof. Soon, the maple sap would begin its flow and there would be much to occupy his time. However, until then, he spent his days keeping Bastien's accounts or reading and keeping himself concealed from the world.

He longed to send news of himself to Emilie and receive word from her in exchange. But he could not, at least not until Bastien returned to tell him he'd found someone trustworthy enough to carry his letters without revealing his whereabouts to the authorities in exchange for the bounty on his head. It was not easy to find a man in whom confidence could be placed, particularly in New France where few had old acquaintances.

Robert had nothing but time on his hands, nothing to do but wait. With a sigh, he reached for the book, *Les Avantures de Jacques Sadeur* by Gabriel de Foigny. Perhaps reading about someone else's misadventures in the far off land of Australia would take his mind off his own woes.

112

Two days later, Bastien arrived with the news Robert had long awaited.

"A fur trader who owes me a substantial amount of money has offered to deliver correspondence in exchange for a reduction in his debt."

Robert's hopes soared, but crashed almost immediately. "What good is writing a letter when I don't know where everyone is?"

"Ah, but I found out where Père Marc-Mathieu is. He's moved to La Prairie de la Madelaine."

Robert let out a whistle. The mercantile was the centre of endless rumour, gossip, and the trade of information. "La Prairie de la Madelaine! When did he go there?"

Bastien shrugged. "All I know is that he is there now." He paused. "I'm sorry; I've heard no word about your bride and her mother."

"Keep asking, please."

"I will," Bastien nodded. "Write a letter to your bride. We'll enclose it in a letter to Père Marc-Mathieu to forward to her. I'll have the fur trader deliver it to him."

While he waited, Robert wrote one letter to Père Marc-Mathieu and another to Ada describing what had happened to him in Québec and how he was forced to flee. He assured them of his safety and took care to reveal only the most minimum of details, lest the letter should fall into the wrong hands. In Ada's letter, Robert wrote warm and impassioned inquiries about Emilie and ended it with his hopes and plans for the future.

Bastien took both letters and sent them off the next day.

Several months passed. The warmth of spring melted the snow and ice of a long winter. Sap flowed from the sugar and red maple trees surrounding the shack. Robert spent his days tapping a few trees and collecting their sap into buckets. He boiled the sap in a pot hung over the fire in the hearth. After it thickened, he strained the liquid, pouring the rich golden syrup into clay jars to later sell at the mercantile. The enterprise kept him occupied and helped break the monotony of his solitary existence.

In all this time, he had not received a reply. So he sent off a second letter, this time addressed to Père Nicholas in Pointe-du-Lac asking him to forward the sealed letter within to Ada Basseaux, should he know her whereabouts.

In the late spring, when the green of the world was fully in bloom, Bastien brought Robert a letter and a rather heavy leather money pouch. Puzzled, he untied the leather string and looked inside. A treasure of gold coins glimmered from within, more than he had seen in his entire life. He looked incredulously up at Bastien.

Bastien grinned back at him. "The Jesuit priest who delivered it, made me count each one to make sure it was all there. One hundred and fifty gold Louis! And it is all yours!"

"But I don't understand."

"The priest explained it to me. But the letter explains it clearly."

With trembling hands, Robert unsealed the letter and devoured each word like a starving man at a banquet.

Mon cher Robert,

May God continue to keep you safe. Although your letter did not reveal much, it sufficed to ease some of the worries that burden this old woman's heart. This is not an easy letter to write, but it must be done, for much has changed since we last laid eyes upon each other. It grieves me to tell you that some time after we parted, a devious plot by the unscrupulous seigneur at the heart of our problems resulted in the abduction of my poor Emilie. She was taken away from Québec and locked in a manor house owned by another more evil seigneur. Certain her fate was doomed, my daughter prayed desperately to God to release her from her dire circumstances, and in exchange, she vowed to enter religious life.

I am overjoyed to tell you that God heard Emilie's prayers and granted her wish. She is in safety now, but to keep her from further harm, I cannot reveal her whereabouts to you. God also touched the heart of her captor. In retribution for his terrible sin, he gifted Emilie and me with 300 gold Louis, enough to see to our care for the remainder of our lives. Emilie wished for me to share our good fortune with you, and you should find enclosed in the accompanying sack, no less than 150 coins for your use.

A vow made cannot be broken, especially one to God. Emilie has asked me to tell you she must take the veil and serve God for the remainder of her life. She prays for your understanding and for you to empty your heart of her. With all her heart, she asks you to forget her, forget us, and look to the future. We hope you will find yourself another good woman, marry her, and make a family and good life with her. I have loved you as a son, and it is because of this love, I pray you do not attempt to find Emilie. Let her go, for she now belongs to God. We both pray that happiness will grace your future life. May God Bless you and keep you,

Ada Basseaux

Robert trembled as he read the letter several times, struggling to comprehend. After crumpling the letter in his fist, he reached for his quill.

Chère Ada,

I am outraged at the horror of the vile act committed against my beloved Emilie, but I am grateful she is safe once more. The knowledge that the unscrupulous rogue will stop at nothing to steal my bride away from me only makes me even more convinced that we must wed. I love Emilie more than life itself and I refuse to release her from my heart and our betrothal. That, I swear, I will never do.

I have received the gold coins, an astounding amount, but I refuse to touch any of it. Instead, I'll preserve it for Emilie's dowry, for one day, I am determined to make her my wife. I know nothing of her vow, but God would never wish for Emilie to break a troth made so faithfully between us. With these golden coins, we have enough to keep house upon new lands.

I continue to face numerous difficulties, but it is a storm I am certain will pass. When that day comes, I will claim Emilie and sweep you both away to a new life, free from strife. Until then, I remain your loving future son.

113

Emilie stood motionless in a small cell located on the third storey of the recently built Hôpital Général of Québec. From the tiny window, she could see beyond the rooftops to the scaffold in the distance and the crowd that dispersed. Four bodies hung from ropes, their bodies still against the listless and grey winter day. It was a miracle Robert was not one of them. Two days prior, the men's names and crimes had been posted on every lamppost and corner; instigators of the riot against bake shops the papers said. She nearly collapsed with relief when she saw Robert's name was not on the list. She whispered a silent prayer to God in gratitude. A sense of loss possessed her and she fought against it.

Louise Soumande de Saint-Augustin of the Religious Hospitallers of Saint Joseph Hôpital Général of Québec looked on as the sister of the wardrobe helped Emilie dress in the black habit and white veil of a postulant. Black, the color of mourning. Emilie could not help but make such a comparison. Already the band of white linen across her forehead and the white linen coif fastened under her chin felt odd, making it awkward to turn her head. How could she live under such restriction? She had arrived several months ago, but was not ready to take this step until recently. Now, the impact of her decision hit her with full force.

At last, the sister of the wardrobe tied the black cincture around her waist, and after adjusting the rosary to hang over her left hip, she stepped back and assessed her handiwork.

"*Merci*, Soeur Marie," dismissed Abbess Louise.

The nun blinked in acknowledgement, gathered Emilie's discarded clothes, and swept from the room as silently as she entered.

"When a woman professes her desire to become a nun, it is not an easy journey." Abbess Louise said as she studied Emilie. "As a postulant, you must undergo a three month probationary period. At that time, if the desire to take the veil has taken root in your heart, you may become a novitiate and will train for four years, after which, God willing, you may take your vows, which are final. You will be required to dedicate three hours a day to regular devotions in addition to working with the sick and elderly." Her face softened. "It will not be easy, but for those who can endure, it is rewarding." She paused. "You must be certain. Are you, child?"

Emilie studied the face of the woman who was to undertake her training. Her small frame contrasted with the strength of her poise and outward show of confidence. Tiny wrinkles lined her eyes. A mole decorated her upper lip. Intelligence glimmered from her vibrant blue eyes. Her expressions were gentle, filled with sympathy and kindness. "I am certain, *ma mère*."

"Have you given up thinking of him?"

"I am trying," replied Emilie.

"Ah child, I know it is not easy for a young girl to forget a great love, even if he has turned to villainy."

"He has done nothing to give occasion for anything but good to be said of him. He is a man with a kind and gentle heart." Emilie defended him because she had known him since childhood. She would continue to defend him out of duty and her love of truth.

"There will be time to search your heart to ensure this is the correct decision for you. Your veil is a reminder of the vows you may one day make. As your footsteps become more certain and your mind more at ease with the newness of your surroundings, you will find life here much easier. Trust me in this." Her face gentled. "Take a few moments, and then you are expected in the kitchen where you will assist in preparing the evening meal." She turned on her heels and left the room, closing the door behind her.

Emilie studied her surroundings. The only adornment in the room was a small wooden cross hanging on the wall above a narrow bed. Tucked beneath the bed slats was a chamber pot. A wooden chest containing her personal possessions rested at its foot. A candlestick, prayer book, pitcher and ewer, rested on a rough-hewn bedside table. Beneath the window on a plank bench with rough-hewn legs, a tabletop brazier waited to shed gentle heat against the frigid air of fall and winter.

She reached into the chest and retrieved the latest letter from her mother. She read it once more. Robert was alive and safe. Her mother assured Emilie she told Robert about her vow. It was what she wanted to hear, yet she found no solace in it. An inexplicable sense of loss took hold of her. Robert's image remained imprinted on her mind. She tried to dispel it, but it refused to fade. She could not help letting her thoughts wander to a vision of a new life with Robert as her husband and her mother by her side. He crept into every remembrance of her past. Sadly, she tucked the letter back into the chest and closed the lid. Straightening, she inhaled a deep breath then left the cell determined to walk away from her old life forever.

114
Summer 1703

Emilie found her days aiding the sick in the hospital long, yet satisfying. To give to those in need, to offer a few drops of water to weakened mouths, or place compresses on fevered brows, or any of the myriad of small tasks she was assigned, humbled her.

Emilie knew she had much to learn, but the knowledge that her hands eased someone's discomfort or her words brought solace in the valiant moments before death, gave her a sense of fulfillment. She learned to lend a compassionate ear and share in the sorrows and joys of her patients. Her heart danced each time someone walked away healthy and plummeted every time she experienced a loss.

Summer would soon arrive. With the longer days, she enjoyed sitting on a bench near the hospital's front entrance after work. The crisp air cleared her mind while she rested her aching legs. Almost daily, she wrote letters to her mother, delivered by a merchant who travelled between Québec and Pointe-du-Lac. Other times she read or watched people pass by. Thoughts of what became of Robert always crept into her thoughts. The pain of her loss had faded somewhat, but she could never stop loving him. On this day, more tired than usual, she sat and enjoyed the golden sun as it began its descent into the horizon.

The lane bustled with sights and sounds. An ox-cart loaded with goods creaked by. A young woman, her cheeks ablush, strolled by with a handsome man by her side. Two Jesuit priests paused to discuss a point then continued on their way. Three young boys raced past laughing, a small white dog yipping at their heels. They nearly felled a young native woman who walked slowly with her head down. She staggered as she walked, almost as if every step sapped her energy. A cradleboard over her back hung from a strap cross her forehead and the bitter cries of the baby within it cleaved the air. Emilie sensed something wrong and rose to her feet.

The woman stopped, grabbed the strap on her brow, and swayed as she looked up at the hospital. Her eyes rolled back in her head and she fell to her knees then crashed forward onto her face. The infant's cries became hysterical.

Emilie swung around and yanked open the front door of the hospital. "Help, I need help," she yelled before rushing to the native woman's side. The smell of vomit and excrement emanated from the baby. She turned the woman onto her side and removed the strap to release the cradleboard, which she laid on the ground.

The red-faced infant continued its screams. Having freed the mother with deft movements, Emilie rolled her onto her back. The leather-beaded headband on the woman's forehead identified her as Iroquois. The exquisite beading looked like fine lacework. Emilie checked for a pulse. The woman's skin burned with fever, and her pulse was weak, but she was alive. Emilie ran her hand over the baby's face. A horrific fever raged in the infant too.

Three nuns and a priest rushed outside with a litter. Together, they lifted the woman onto it and carried her inside. Emilie followed with the child.

While the others tended to the mother, Emilie laid the cradleboard on a table and freed the infant from its restraints. Soiled, the child had vomited several times. Emilie worked frantically to remove its clothing and discovered it was a little girl.

After bathing her in a basin of tepid water, she wrapped her in a clean wool cloth. One of the sisters brought a small feeding cup filled with warm honeyed milk and Emilie retreated to a nearby chair to feed the infant. The baby swallowed several drops before she fell asleep, cradled in Emilie's arms. Little moans escaped from her tiny pink lips, her body a miniature inferno. Emilie cradled the vulnerable life in her arms.

Even when another nun came to relieve her, she refused to abandon the infant. Instead, she placed the sleeping baby in a crate lined with soft blankets and dozed in the chair beside it.

When she awoke an hour later, the baby's temperature had abated somewhat. Weak with relief, Emilie tried to feed the baby again. Yet when the infant opened her mouth, Emilie noticed small reddish spots on the inside of her mouth and tongue leading back to the throat. Alarmed, she cried out for one of the other nuns.

Soeur Marie, a thin, agile nun of middling years rushed into the room and peered into the baby's mouth. Her face paled and she made the sign of the cross as she took a step back. "*Mon Dieu*, it is the speckled death!" she cried.

115

Three days later, spots appeared on the baby's forehead, then spread to the whole face, the torso, and lastly to the limbs. The child's mother was also afflicted. Smallpox spread wildly throughout the hospital and all of Québec. Within days, feverish people flocked to the hospital seeking aid. Emilie worked hard, along with the sisters, to treat as many people as possible, barely taking enough time to eat and sleep herself.

Fear existed in Emilie's every thought, but she drew on the courage of the nuns who worked tirelessly with little thoughts for themselves. Never before had she seen such suffering, nor had she ever been surrounded by so many people dying. She worried about her mother, alone in Pointe-du-Lac and sent her a letter begging her to keep herself secluded and to avoid contact with others. And what of Robert? She prayed he would not be affected after all the misfortune that had befallen him.

An overpowering smell of sickness suffused each ward. Emilie knew she must avoid touching a sick person and must not inhale their breath, or touch their clothes or bed coverings. So she carried trays, replenished the supplies, or carried water and clean cloths to bedsides. But like the sisters she worked with, she could not deny the comfort the afflicted sought. She heeded none of these warnings and refused to think of herself. If she became afflicted, so be it. The demands made upon her were too great to ignore. So, she held a cup to sick lips or helped fluff a pillow, and even held a hand or two.

Emilie hurried to the bedside of a young boy who was no more than twelve years. He lay on his back, and though his eyes were open, they were glazed with fever. When she spoke to him in soothing tones, he showed no reaction. His cheeks glowed bright red and sweat streaked his forehead. Pustules covered his entire body, some of which were filled with clear liquid, while others had already become pus-filled. Emilie knew these poxes would heal and leave a permanent pit when the scab dropped off. He was one of the lucky ones and would survive. Those whose pustules filled with blood never survived. There was no cure and no remedy other than to keep those afflicted as comfortable as possible.

When Emilie took hold of his burning hand, he whimpered with discomfort, a feeble, delirious sound. She fought off a surge of concern. Would the sickness infiltrate her body? It was only a matter of time. Would death take her, too? She fought the urge to run from his bedside. Instead, she remained beside him, holding his hand, whispering tender words she knew he could not hear, but eased her own grief.

Emilie reached for a cool washcloth and dipped it in the small basin beside the bed. After wringing it, she placed the cloth on his forehead. His tension seemed to ease. Already, the cloth absorbed his body heat. She replenished the cloth with more water and mopped his brow and chest, all the while speaking to him soothingly.

For hours, she moved from bedside to bedside, easing the torment of the others who lay in beds and in cots. Every corridor was lined with the sick that emitted a cacophony of cries and groans, all pleading for relief.

Wracked with fatigue, Emilie stumbled about by rote, and only when someone took the cloth away from her and pulled her to her feet, did she allow herself to stop. She returned to her room and flopped on her bed. Every muscle in her body ached and a chill had grabbed hold of her. Fully clothed, she slid beneath the bedcovers, shivering. She succumbed to an exhausted sleep and remembered nothing until a persistent knocking on her door roused her. She tried to sit up, but her body shook and nausea coursed through her. "Enter," she rasped in a fever-ridden voice.

The door burst open and Sister Marie entered.

Emilie tried to search for the chamber pot, but the pain in her back and muscles prevented her from moving quickly enough. Before she could lift her head from the pillow, she vomited onto her clothes and bedcovers.

The worried look on Sister Marie's face confirmed Emilie's worst fears. The pox would soon ravage her body.

For three days and nights, Emilie's fever raged. By the fourth day, it abated and the first visible spots appeared in her mouth, tongue, palate, and throat. They enlarged and ruptured, releasing a horrible taste in her mouth. She knew the illness would travel through her body and afflict her with terrifying vengeance.

Within days, her fever returned and pustules consumed her entire body. In her delirium, she recalled little, only the occasional warmth of the broth someone spooned into her mouth or the coolness of a dampened cloth on her forehead. Darkness and light melted into a blur of non-existence. Time no longer held meaning. All she knew was sleep and occasional moments of awareness and discomfort as the pox consumed her flesh.

116

Slowly, Emilie drifted into consciousness. Extreme thirst rasped her throat and a burning itch scoured her flesh. She opened her mouth to speak, but her voice failed. All she could muster was a hoarse croak. In the darkness of the room, she heard the stirrings of someone near her bed. Almost immediately, gentle hands raised her head and placed a cup to her lips. Fresh, cool water filled her parched mouth and throat. Before she could drink her fill, however, the cup was removed.

"You've been sick with the pox, so you must drink slowly. I'll let you have more in a few moments."

It was a woman's voice, one she was familiar with, but from where? Fog clouded her thoughts. She heard movement- the rustle of garments, the rasp of a tinderbox opening, and then the strike of flint against fire steel. Against the gentle light of the candle lamp, a nun swung around.

Emmanuelle, her face neutral, stared at Emilie.

Memories of her ordeal at the hands of the abductors flooded Emilie's thoughts. Emmanuelle had played a part in it, of that she was certain.

Emmanuelle gave Emilie another drink of water and when sated, Emilie laid her head back on the pillow. Although weakened by the illness, questions raced through her head. "Am I going to die?"

La Bonne Soeur's expression softened. She sat in the small chair by the bed and placed her hand on Emilie's forehead. "Perhaps, if it is God's will, but you must fight to overcome this. I will do everything I can to prevent that from happening."

"Why do you care?" And there it was, the question that Emilie had longed to ask. It lay above them like a black pall.

"I feel responsible for what happened to you."

It fell short of an admission of guilt, but it invited further conversation. Emotion clogged Emilie's throat. "Why did you do it?"

The novitiate stared at her hands. When she looked up, her eyes were glazed with torment. "I've lost my soul to the devil and I don't know how to gain it back."

117

The pustules over Emilie's body bloated with pus, erupted, then scabbed over. During bouts of lucidity amid the delirium, Emilie prayed for God to spare her life. After nearly two weeks, her fever abated and it became clear she would survive the deadly epidemic that was killing people by the hundreds. Rendered weak by the illness, Emilie convalesced for almost a month as her strength returned. Despite the scars that would forever mark her once flawless complexion, Emilie felt healed enough to return to work without fear, for those who recovered could never be re-afflicted.

People afflicted with the pox crammed every room, spilling out into the corridors and the grounds outside. Half the sisters had fallen ill and there were not enough to tend the ever-growing mass of people flooding through the doors of the Hôpital Général. The Hotel Dieu, another hospital located in the upper colony of Québec, fared just as badly.

A survivor of the pox, Emmanuelle never strayed far from Emilie's side. Together they tended to those who suffered from the deadliest strain, which turned the skin black from bloody pustules that formed beneath the skin.

As they worked together, Emilie knew Emmanuelle watched over her. Although Emmanuelle never elaborated about her part in the abduction, Emilie sensed the deep sorrow and regret hidden beneath her guarded expression. Her demeanor towards Emilie was humble, contrite, and always sincere, but Emilie could not yet trust her.

The mortality from the epidemic was so great; the priests could scarcely keep up with the requiem masses and internments. One day ran into another as more and more people died in the streets or in their homes. Some died of starvation because, in many cases, entire families took sick at once and could not care for each other. The most destitute found their way to either one of the overcrowded hospitals, but many more languished alone.

No matter where she went, Emilie could hear the mournful laments or wild shrieks that resounded from every corner. Corpses multiplied in the streets and a great stench arose. In the hospital, people slept crammed and heaped together, twenty and thirty in each ward and lying on the floor in the corridors. Each breeze carried despair; every sunrise brought news of more afflictions; grief existed in every heart. Emilie worked tirelessly, without reprieve or thought except to respond to the dolorous cries of the sick and dying.

118

In Pointe-du-Lac, when Yves Dupuis, the parish's militiaman came down with the pox, fear possessed Père Jean. Within days, the disease spread to four more people, driving entire families behind closed doors in Pointe-du-Lac. Fearful of contagion, people ventured out only for the direst necessities.

Père Jean cancelled all masses. He knew he must flee if he wanted to save himself, but where would he go? He could not remain in Pointe-du-Lac, otherwise he would be forced to deal with the sick and dying. It was impossible to hire a conveyance, for everyone avoided contact of any kind. On foot, Père Jean could not manage any great distance, but what choice had he? He ran through the rectory, half out of his senses, following Rose who was busy collecting the most valuable household goods to hide them under floorboards or to bury behind the house in preparation of them leaving.

As he followed her into a spare bedroom, she pushed by him with her arms full, preoccupied. "I'm almost finished putting these things away, then we can leave."

Père Jean pursed his lips. The woman never failed to test his patience. Their lives were at stake and all she could do was fuss about dishes and silverware when they should have been long gone.

"Others are protecting themselves, and so am I, and you stand there useless, hindering my efforts. Do you think you're the only one trying to save yourself from the pox? You might lend me a hand instead of nattering." Rose shoved the bed over the floorboard, glared at him then spun on her heel, and left for another room.

Alone, he retreated to the window. A man and woman drove past in a horse-drawn wagon loaded with what looked like their entire household possessions. A young boy and girl dangled their legs over the rear of the cart. "Where are you going?" he called.

The man looked up. "To Ville Marie."

"Take me with you, please, I beg you."

The man, already burdened by the weight of so many possessions shook his head, snapped the reins, and urged the horses forward.

"The selfish sot!" Père Jean slammed the window shut. "There's no charity left in this world. Everyone thinks for themselves and no one cares for a priest anymore." He rushed out of the room in search of Rose and found her in his bedroom.

"Where's all your money?" she asked.

"What are you going to do with it?"

"Give it all to me. I'll bury most of it in the garden together with the silver and knives and forks. The rest, we'll need for our journey."

"But..."

She held out her hand. "Give it to me. There's no time to waste."

Père Jean went to a trunk, took out a money pouch, removed a handful of gold and silver coins, and then handed it to Rose.

"I'll bury it out back at the foot of the maple tree."

He watched her from the kitchen. When she returned, she filled a basket with cheese, biscuits, and apples and then covered it with a cloth.

"Surely you don't believe we can make it all the way to Ville Marie with that paltry amount of food? Why, it won't last more than a day or two at the most." Père Jean's gaze fell on the plentiful shelves of the open pantry.

She narrowed her eyes. "That's all I can carry on foot. We'll go westward. From there, who knows what will happen. Perhaps we can find someone to drive us the rest of the way."

Père Jean's hands shook as he reached for his hat and coat.

119

It had been weeks since Ada received a letter from Emilie and her worry grew with each passing day. When the pox struck in Pointe-du-Lac, she feared the worst. Nothing except illness would have kept Emilie from writing. Ada had survived smallpox as a child. The scars on her face had faded with time, and she was immune to it, but Emilie was not. Possessed with fear, Ada knew she must go to Québec and find Emilie. The trouble was, that because of fear of contagion, no one would transport her, no matter how much money she offered.

The words of Seigneur Claude reverberated in her mind – if she should ever need help, she must not be afraid to seek his aid. But, she had no idea where he lived. Only Père Jean knew the way to the secluded manor house. She sewed some money into the hem of her gown and buried the remainder underneath a rock behind the stable at the rear of her cottage. Then she set off for the rectory to convince Père Jean to take her there. As she was about to knock on the rectory door, it swung open, and she came face to face with Rose and Père Jean.

120

"What do you think, Rose?" Père Jean asked after he and Rose had listened to Ada's pleas and left her waiting outside for their answer.

"I say that we mustn't lose any time before we set off."

Père Jean paced, his alarm increasing. "To Prudhomme's home? Are you mad?"

"When we get there, we shall find ourselves in good hands. Seigneur Claude is a changed man. I've no doubt he'll receive us. You told me his house is isolated. That should keep us safe from the speckled death. Besides, our provisions wouldn't have lasted us until we arrived at Ville Marie."

Père Jean rubbed his sweaty palms against his soutane and looked at Rose. "You believe he's converted?"

"Why should you doubt it after all that is being said and after what you've seen? Ada's arrival here is a blessing. We should seize the opportunity." Rose grabbed the food basket, passed her arms through the straps, and lifted it onto her back. Just as she was about to open the door and give Ada their answer, Père Jean grabbed her arm.

"Wouldn't it be better if we found a man to come with us? Someone to guard and protect us? If we should meet any ruffians, what help could you and Ada give me?"

"Another waste of time!" Rose's red face puckered with disgust. "Grab your breviary and hat and let us be off."

Père Jean obeyed and Rose opened the door to Ada. "We'll be happy to escort you. Come inside and we'll go out the back way."

He led the women through the house and out through a

door that led into the churchyard. Rose locked it behind her and dropped the key between her breasts.

Père Jean cast one last glance at the church as he walked away. "It's the people's business to take care of it, for it's they who use it," he muttered. "If they've the least love for their church, they'll see to it; if not, then it will be their misfortune."

They took the road through the fields. Père Jean watched for anyone suspicious. Much to his relief, they encountered no one. People were either locked away in their homes or fleeing for places unknown. He grumbled as he walked, muttering about the Bishop, the Governor, and all who had failed to forewarn everyone of the spreading disease.

"Stop your prating," Rose hissed at him sotto voce. "There is nothing anyone can do when it comes to the pox."

"You're fleeing the pox?" Ada asked, her voice shrill with incredulity. "What of the sick and dying in Pointe-du-Lac? Who will administer the sacraments to them?"

"Well done, Rose!" growled Père Jean. "When will you learn to keep your mouth shut?"

Rose came to an abrupt halt and rested her hands on her hips. "How dare you scold me, when all I've ever done is help you."

Père Jean felt the heat rise from his neck to his face as he faced Ada. "I've been called to Ville Marie."

Rose rolled her eyes and looked away in disgust. Ada studied him through narrowed eyes. Then she shook her head and kept walking.

121

Ada retreated into her own thoughts as she walked. Her aversion for Père Jean was so strong, she could not bear to look at him. What kind of priest abandoned his duties to save himself? The same priest who would refuse to marry a loving couple on their wedding day! As they left the footpath through the fields and came to the main road, Ada recognized the land that surrounded the Tremblay's farm. In fact, she could already see the farmhouse in the distance.

"We must stop and check on Juliette and her family," Ada announced. It had been months since she had seen her. Juliette would have had her baby by now.

Père Jean came to an abrupt stop and shook his head, his mouth open ready to argue.

"Yes, let's rest a little," Rose said, glaring at the priest. "The basket is heavy. Besides, we should stop to eat."

Père Jean gave Rose a pointed look. "I don't think we should waste any time, we're not journeying for our amusement. Besides, the sooner we get to Seigneur Prudhomme's manor house, the sooner Ada can be reunited with Emilie."

Ada gave him an admonishing look. "I refuse to walk past this farm without checking on the welfare of these good people after all the help they gave me and my daughter." It pleased her to see Père Jean's cheeks redden. With that, she turned onto the rutted path that led to Juliette's home. When she knocked on the front door, no one answered. She knocked again and this time it was Monsieur Tremblay's voice she heard from inside. "Who goes there?"

"It is Ada Basseaux and Père Jean Civitelle with Rose Babbette, his housekeeper."

"Ada!" Monsieur Tremblay's voice was joyful. "Please forgive us but we cannot open the door to you for fear of the pox."

"Is everyone well?" Ada could not hide the alarm in her voice.

"Yes, we are all well, thanks be to God. We are merely protecting the children. Please understand and forgive us for our inhospitality."

"Of course we understand," Ada said as she made the sign of the cross. "And the baby?"

"The baby is well too, a strapping boy."

"How fare you and Emilie?" Juliette's voice called out from within.

Tears welled in Ada's eyes. "I'm not certain. I haven't heard from her for several weeks. She is in Québec, at the centre of the epidemic. I'm afraid something's happened to her." Having given voice to her fears, Ada burst into a flood of tears. Rose placed a consoling arm around her shoulders while Père Jean stared at the ground as he shuffled a pebble about with his foot.

"Are Père Jean and his companion going with you then?" asked the tailor.

"*Mais oui,* of course." Rose gave Père Jean a pointed look. "Aren't we, Père Jean?"

"We are escorting her to Seigneur Prudhomme's home," Père Jean called out.

Ada wiped her tears with her sleeves and eyed an outdoor table and chairs beneath an elm tree. "May we stop to rest a bit? Then we'll be on our way."

"Of course," called out the tailor. "We'll set out some food for you."

Père Jean frantically waved his hands to signal her to refuse.

Ada frowned at him, annoyed, but she understood. "We thank you, but we have our own food," Ada said. "We'll eat then be on our way."

"Pray for us as we will pray for you," Juliette's voice rang out.

Emotion choked Ada's throat and she could not respond.

After Père Jean made the sign of the cross over the front door, they sat in the shade beneath the tree, and ate their meal in silence.

122

Claude Prudhomme sat behind his desk in the garret, scanning the pages of the open ledger before him. He had given away food, money, and land, but much of his wealth remained. The knowledge that he had more to give away reassured him, yet he was not satisfied. No matter how much he gave away, peace alluded him. He must do more.

His life had changed over the last months. He had worked hard to atone for his wrongs, seeking solace, relieving the poor, and performing any good deed that came his way. Though he had laid down all his weapons, dismissed his bodyguards, and walked alone, he no longer feared encounters arising from his dark past. Should someone harm him, he would not defend his life, for he considered it just retribution for all his sins.

Claude knew that because of his former tyranny, many longed for revenge. However, most people admired him for changing and this guaranteed his safety. The man whom no one could humble had now humbled himself. Most people's rancour vanished in light of his new humility. Those he once offended were delighted he lamented his past deeds. Others greeted him with respect, in awe of his new beneficence.

His conversion added to his fame. Sources told him that magistrates publicly rejoiced at his altered demeanour; and it would have appeared incongruous to rise against him now because of the many generous reparations he had made. It would only incite the people's anger. Bishop Laval's intervention served as a sacred shield. Claude knew he had been a hated man, but now, he was revered by many and spared by all.

As for his enemies, they held him in contempt. The rogues he once employed in his household who could not tolerate the changes in him, had likely returned to their previous lives of villainy away from his reach. New servants worked contentedly for him.

In one corner of this garret, he glanced at his collection of weapons; his famous carabine, muskets, swords, pistols, huge knives, and poniards. Now, they lay on the ground or sat propped against the wall, untouched.

Yet, nothing brought him ease of spirit. One sin, greater than all the others ate away at him; that of his wife and son. He pulled open the drawer of his desk and reached for the portrait.

Emmanuelle. He ran his finger over her face. Through regular reports from Gaston, he knew she still suffered, just as he did. The contempt he once held her in had vanished. He, who committed more evil than anyone could imagine, realized he had judged her harshly. He had been wrong, very wrong. Murder, assault, robbery; those were his sins. Lying had been her only sin and it paled in comparison to his crimes.

Even worse was the fate of the boy, and his part in separating mother and child. He recalled her hysterical tears as she insisted he was the boy's father. At the time, he refused to believe it. Could she have been telling the truth? Had he given away his only son? The knowledge ate away at him like black rot. The realization that his soul could find no peace unless he righted his most heinous crime struck him like a bolt of lightning. If it took every bit of his wealth, he would atone for what he'd done by finding the boy and reuniting mother and son.

123

At first sight of Seigneur Prudhomme's home, Ada thought about Emilie. “To think that my poor baby once passed along this road and suffered so much. It changed her life forever.”

“Pray hold your tongue “ Père Jean scolded. “Don't say

anything to remind Seigneur Claude of his past. Who knows how he may react."

"But he's a changed man," argued Ada.

"That's what everyone thinks, but one cannot be certain," Père Jean said. "Say as little as possible and do not make him angry."

Ada cast him a stern look, exasperated at his fear. "Do you think I don't know how to be civil?"

"Civility means not speaking disagreeable things, particularly to a man like Prudhomme. Don't chatter mindlessly and be prudent. Weigh your words and let there be few of them, only when necessary. One is never wrong when one is silent."

Rose's cheeks flushed and her eyes flashed. "You are far worse, with your-"

"Hush! He's here." Père Jean removed his hat and made a profound bow as Prudhomme exited the house to meet them. "Seigneur Prudhomme, how nice to see you again."

"*Bien venu*!" Seigneur Claude smiled. "To what do I owe this most welcome visit?"

Before Ada could say a word, Père Jean stepped in front of her. "We apologize for intruding, but we've come under the most urgent of circumstances."

Rose nudged him and glowered, her arms akimbo.

A look of puzzlement crossed Père Jean's face before it brightened. "Ah, yes, let me introduce my housekeeper, Rose Babbette."

"It's a pleasure to meet you, Monsieur," Rose said cordially.

"The pleasure is all mine, Madame." Seigneur Claude tipped his head to her.

"I am a Mademoiselle, Monsieur," Rose said, her cheeks ablush, and her eyelashes aflutter.

Père Jean patted Ada on the back. "I've accompanied this good woman here in the hopes that you might transport her to the ville of Québec."

"I'm worried about Emilie." Ada gripped the side of her gown and puckered the cloth in her fist.

Prudhomme looked at the ground, ashamed, and then glanced back at her. "Emilie? Why? What has happened?"

"Oh, I'm so afraid. Emilie is in Québec where the pox is rampant. I haven't heard from her for several weeks. I've tried to find someone to take me there, but no one will take me. Everyone's afraid of the illness." She wrung her hands and swallowed. "Please help me."

Without hesitation, Seigneur Claude took Ada's hand in his. "Of course. I shall escort you there personally."

Ada noticed the glint of pain in his eyes.

"I too am looking for someone there," Seigneur Prudhomme added. "Come inside for now and I'll have everything prepared for our journey. We can leave at first light tomorrow."

Père Jean's eyes widened as his face grew pale. "Ah, well, perhaps it might be best for Rose and me to remain behind."

Seigneur Claude stared at Père Jean with confusion. "But I don't understand. I assumed you wished to go there too. I've heard that most of the clergy in Québec has fallen ill and there are not enough priests or friars to attend to the sick and dying."

"Of course Père Jean will accompany me the rest of the way," Ada interjected. "I've never known Père Jean to shirk a duty. Isn't that correct, mon Père?" She gave him a false smile.

A powerful coughing fit seized Père Jean and Rose pounded him hard on his back.

"Are you not well?" asked Seigneur Claude, his face craggy with concern.

"Oh, no, he is well. He is suffering from the exertion of the journey, that is all." Ada stared harshly at the priest.

Père Jean gripped his hands together. "Ah, the contagion, uh, if it spreads here, I'll be needed in Pointe-du-Lac."

Seigneur Claude pondered the fact then nodded. "I suppose that's true." He paused. "I'll find some people to send back into the village with you. They can assist if the illness spreads. I daresay you'll need their help." He extended his arm and invited them to pass before him. "*Bon,* but where are my manners? Come inside. There is much to do if we are to leave in the morning."

Père Jean's shoulders sagged as he ambled behind Rose and entered the manor house.

Triumphant, Ada smiled. A wave of satisfaction swept through her at the knowledge Père Jean would have to face his fears and do his duty.

124

The sun had barely risen over Québec when Seigneur Richard Tonnacour rose from his bed at the inn of *Le Gros Cochon;* a structure aptly named after its proprietor whose corpulence, flattened nose, and unnatural pale complexion complimented the title. More fatigued than usual, he dressed with care; donning a sober coloured coat and brushing his straight hair back from his forehead. Judging by his reflection in the cracked mirror hanging behind the door, it gave him a serious air. He must look respectable and avoid any semblance of a romantic tendency when he visited the Ursuline convent to inquire about Emilie.

Richard entered the corridor and walked past Thomas' room. No sound came from within. It came as no surprise; Thomas had retired with one of the local whores and likely still slept. On his way out of the inn, he grabbed some bread, and with walking stick in hand, sallied forth upon his expedition, walking leisurely beneath clear skies until he reached the convent gates. After brushing a few specks of dust from his coat, he settled his high collar, and pulled the weather-beaten bell chain with one steady yank. First, he must ascertain she was there and then he would formulate a plan to get her out.

Despite the lethargy that had plagued him since awakening, he felt no sense of nervousness. He was as deliberate in his movements and as calm in all respects as he had ever been in his entire life. He believed it was right for him to be here to claim his bride. Soon, she would become his wife. He would make sure of that. A half-humorous smile bent his even lips, but disappeared when he heard the slap and shuffle of slippers in the vaulted archway. An instant later, the small aperture in the gate slid open, and a nun with a wizened face gazed at him through narrowed eyes. She held her veil over her mouth, an obvious attempt to ward off any contagion.

"*Bon jour*," he said, tipping his hat. "I have come in search of a young woman who I heard was given temporary shelter here."

The nun's eyes roamed from his head to his feet and back again.

"It is most urgent that I speak with her. I am a solicitor representing her deceased uncle, and have undertaken all of the man's duties. There is a matter of a small inheritance I wish to speak to her about."

"What is her name?"

Seigneur Richard smiled. "Emilie Basseaux."

Recognition flashed in the nun's eyes. "Have the goodness to wait," she commanded.

"Outside?" inquired Richard, as the little shutter began to close.

"Of course," answered the nun, opening the aperture again and shutting it as soon as she had spoken.

Long moments passed. The sun seemed to blaze down on him, even though it was early morning. Richard grew hot and wiped his forehead with a handkerchief, folding it before returning it to his pocket. A slight bout of nausea arose then passed. In the heat, the stench of death became almost unbearable. He could not wait to get Emilie and leave this cesspool of death. What was it about her that drove him to face such risks? To put himself in the midst of an epidemic in search of her was beyond even his own understanding. The need to acquire her had become his sole desire. With regard to the girl, he was no better than a drunkard who could not turn away from a wine bottle. Soon, she would be his. At last, he heard the sound of steps again, and a few seconds later, the aperture slid open.

"You must speak to a woman named Emmanuelle at the Hôpital Général," the portress said. "It is not far from here. She may know more about the woman you seek."

The woman's answer confused him and he pondered its meaning. The nun drew back a little from the loophole. Just as he was about to ask for clarification, the shutter slammed shut and he heard her walk briskly away.

Fatigue burdened his every step, but when he arrived at the Hôpital Général, he stopped in the street to take in the chaos that greeted him. People lay sick in rows on the front lawn. Nuns skittered between patients as priests prayed over some of the afflicted. The moans of the ill and dying resounded like a mournful cadence, drowning out the sounds of carts that hauled away the dead. To see such death, in its most brutal form, shook him to the core. All he wanted was to leave this God forsaken settlement and return to the safety of his home.

With his handkerchief to his mouth, he approached one of the nuns. "Please, sister, I am here to speak to a woman named Emmanuelle."

"You can find her at the back in one of the tents."

"*Merci*," he said, but he doubted she heard it, for she had already turned away to tend to a patient.

Without removing his handkerchief, Richard walked to the side of the building where he stooped low to enter through a small arched gate. At the rear, a long line of open sided tents shaded numerous rows of cots laden with the stricken. Nuns, priests, and physicians moved about, carrying bedpans, bowls of broth, linens, or prayer books. He stopped one nun and inquired about Emmanuelle. She pointed to a woman who sat on a three-legged stool holding the hand of an old man.

A warm, but gentle breeze blew through the tent as he approached the nun and made a low bow. "*Excusez-moi*, are you Soeur Emmanuelle?"

She jerked her head up to look at him. "Who wishes to know?"

Not a smidgen of warmth existed in the depths of her dark eyes. It was as if the eyes of death looked hard upon him.

"I am a solicitor searching for a young woman you may know something about," Richard said gravely and stood still. He gazed at her beautifully shaped white hands in which she held a rosary of brown beads and thought he had never seen such lovely hands before, so highbred and attractive. Richard did not know what else to say, and because nothing seemed to be expected of him, he kept silent and waited for her response.

"And who would that be?" she asked, her voice guarded.

"Mademoiselle Emilie Basseaux."

Emmanuelle turned away and brushed a damp lock of hair from the sick old man's forehead. "I've never heard of her."

"It's urgent that I speak with her about an inheritance," Richard said, hoping to recapture her attention.

She glanced at him. A glimmer of suspicion burned in her tapering eyes. "I've already told you I don't know anyone by that name." Her tone was cold and dismissive, but Richard sensed she lied. Another pause followed, during which neither moved. Then Emmanuelle cast him an angry look. "Why are you still here? I have already said I don't know her."

"I believe you do."

"Then you believe wrong. *Au revoir, monsieur*. May God send you light." Emmanuelle rose to her feet and walked away.

Convinced he had struck a nerve, he fought the temptation to chase after her. Judging by her reaction, Emilie must be here somewhere. Richard swung around and hastened away from all the oppressive illness, but each step felt laborious. He hurried around the building and down the street until he was at a safe distance from the hospital.

Despite the warm sun and the perspiration that dripped from his forehead, he shivered. By now, Thomas would be awake. He needed to speak with him so they could formulate a plan and return to the hospital before the woman warned Emilie. His excitement soared and he congratulated himself on his extraordinary good fortune. He knew Emilie was nearby. He sensed it. By this time tomorrow, Emilie would be tight in his clutches.

Walking home, he experienced a strange languor, a weakness in his limbs. Breathing became more difficult and an inward burning heat came to life inside of him, which he attributed to last night's late hours when he imbibed too much wine. Even though his body yearned for rest, the moment Richard arrived at the inn, he pounded on Thomas' door and ordered him to follow him to his room.

Thomas frowned and studied him with suspicion. He kept himself at a distance and hovered near the door.

"What are you afraid of? I'm well, as you can see," Seigneur Richard said. "I might have drunk a little too much wine last night. Come in and sit, I think I've found the girl."

"Where?" Thomas did not move any further into the room.

"She is at the hospital, I'm sure of it."'

"You're sure? Did you see her?"

"No, but I spoke to a nun who behaved suspiciously and reacted strongly when I mentioned the girl's name. I am certain she is there. We must make a plan and fetch her." Seigneur Richard sat on the edge of his bed and rubbed his forehead.

"You don't look well," Thomas said, still keeping his distance. "Lie down and rest. I will go to the hospital myself and have a look around. Have a short sleep; it will do you good. You'll need your energy for later."

Richard flopped back onto the bed. "You're right; I should get some sleep. By the time you return, I will be refreshed. Before you go, close the shutters; there's a chill in the breeze today."

Thomas crossed the room to the window, but did so nervously while keeping as much space as possible between them. "I'll return soon," he said, his voice void of emotion.

Richard gave a slight moan and buried himself under the bedclothes. The quilt seemed to smother him and he threw it off. He tried to relax and closed his eyes to satisfy the urgent need for sleep. Richard drifted off into the darkness of rest and had scarcely closed his eyes when he awoke again, his body aflame with heat, his mind tossing with delirium. His thoughts turned to his obsession for Emilie, which had driven him into the midst of pestilence, to last night's wine, even to the debaucheries of his past. He blamed them all for his current state. He had never felt so poorly before.

After a long battle, he fell asleep, and began to dream gloomy and disquieting dreams.

Richard walked through the world until he found himself inside a large church amid a great crowd of people. How had he arrived there, for he rarely went to church? Vexation weighed upon his chest. The bystanders were pale, emaciated, with hollow eyes, and drooling lips. Their tattered garments fell to pieces and through the rips and slits appeared livid spots and swellings.

'Make room, you rabble!' He accompanied the cry with his harshest expression then glanced at the church door, which was far, far away. Yet, he could not move and flee the polluted creatures that crowded him on every side. None of the senseless beings heeded his command. Instead, they pressed against him even more. One of them elbowed him on his left side, pushing against the space between his heart and armpit with a painful, heavy pressure. When he tried to writhe away, another being pricked him in the same place.

Enraged, he reached for his pistol. The throng grabbed it from him, turned it around, and pointed it at his chest. The barrel pressed so hard against his flesh that he experienced an even sharper jab. He cried out, but all the faces turned away. He looked too, and saw a pulpit, and the upright figure of a Jesuit priest arose from behind it. Père Marc-Mathieu fixed his gaze harshly on him. The priest raised his hand in the same manner he had done when in his home. Richard lifted his own hand in fury, and made an effort to throw himself forward and grasp the priest's arms. The priest began to utter his curse.

Richard's own screams burst forth in a great howl, jerking him awake.

He lowered the arm he had lifted and strove, with great difficulty, to make sense of everything. His eyes opened and struggled against the dimness. He recognized the bed and the chamber and understood that he had been dreaming. The church, the people, the Jesuit priest, all had vanished- all, but that pain in his left side. His heart raced and pounded. A noise and hum rang in his ears. Fire raged within his body, his limbs as heavy as anvils.

The terror of death seized him. He had seen the carts full of the dead and the mass graves and feared the same fate. How could he avoid this same horrible outcome? His thoughts grew obscure. Unconsciousness drew nearer and he suffered a sense of despair. He called out for Thomas, repeatedly until he lost all sense of time.

Then, as if his prayers had been answered, Thomas returned. He stood at some distance from the bed, gazing at him.

"Thomas!" Richard croaked with difficulty, raising himself in a half-hearted attempt to sit, which failed. "You've always been my trusted servant."

"*Oui*, Seigneur."

"I have always treated you well."

"Not always."

"I trust you..." He paused to inhale a deep breath. "I am ill, Thomas."

"It appears as if you are."

"If I recover, I will heap upon you more favours than I have ever yet done."

Thomas waited.

"There is no one I trust more than you," Richard resumed. "Do me a favour, Thomas."

"Command me," replied Thomas.

"Do you know of a good physician in Québec?"

"I know of a few."

"I need a quiet man, who, if he is paid, will not speak of my illness. I do not wish anyone to know I am ill. Go and find him; tell him I will give him four, six Louis; more, if he demands it. Tell him to come here discreetly, so that no one sees him."

"I will go and return soon," Thomas said.

"Listen, Thomas; give me a drink of water first. My throat is so parched. I can't bear it."

"No water," Thomas replied, his expression bland and cold. "At least not until the physician sees you. There is no time to be lost. Lay still and keep quiet and I'll return soon." Thomas turned around and left, shutting the door behind him.

In his mind, Richard accompanied Thomas in his search for

a physician, counting the steps, calculating the time. After some time, he listened for their arrival; and this seemed to suspend his sense of illness and kept his thoughts in some semblance of order.

All of a sudden, he heard footsteps. He threw his legs out of bed and looked at the door. It opened and Thomas entered the room, alone, his eyes cold with malice, burning with hatred.

Richard thrust one hand under his pillow, grasped his pistol, and drew it out. Thomas rushed to the bed and wrenched it out of his hand, flinging it across the room.

Richard's fury mingled with contempt. "God rot you!"

Thomas walked over to the trunk at the foot of the bed and forced open the lock with a kick of his heel.

"You bastard!" Richard howled, frustrated at his own weakness. "I'll kill you, Thomas! Help! Someone help!"

"Save your breath," Thomas said. "I sent everyone away."

"You'll pay for this!" Richard roared.

Thomas ignored him and tossed clothes out of the trunk until he found the bag of coins, which he dropped into his pocket.

"Thief! Fiend of hell! When I recover, I'll come after you!"

Thomas stared at him with a smirk. "You're a dead man. Look at your chest. It's the black pox."

Richard glanced at his chest, the black pustules already threatened to burst and spread the contagion to every part of his body. No one survived the black pox. What remained of his strength drained away as he stared at Thomas. Richard heard himself moan. He breathed as heavily as he could, then expelled the breath with all his effort in the hopes the contagion would seize Thomas. In a misty haze, he watched as Thomas gathered up the clothes he had been wearing when he had fallen ill and emptied them of money.

Richard grinned at Thomas's folly.

A strange peace came over him when Thomas yanked the pillow from beneath his head. His mind conjured up the curse that Père Marc-Mathieu had begun to utter against him in his home so long ago and again in his recent dream. It was coming true. A shot of intense pain exploded in his skull. He could not move.

With a hand on either end of the bolster, Thomas lowered it over his face.

Richard closed his eyes and waited for the blackness to consume him.

125

As Thomas sat at the far end of a long table in a public house, he was seized by a sudden cold shiver. He felt ill. Thomas cursed his own stupidity. By grabbing Richard's garments and emptying them of money, he had touched the foul contagion. Now, he could not stop thinking about his foolishness. With each passing second, his sight became clouded and his strength failed him. He grew delirious and could not recall falling to the ground; obviously, he had. Someone rolled him out into the street and lifted him into a cart after stealing his money and valuables. He lost track of time, minutes, hours, days. Soon death would come to him bearing an evil face, the being's laughter eager and wild, as it would pull him into a dark, fathomless void. There was nothing to do but wait for death to take him.

126

In the spring, Robert left the sugar shack and returned to work in Bastien's mercantile. Bearded, and with a moustache, his altered appearance provided him with a sense of security, sufficient to permit him to venture back into society. Eager to be active once more, he took on clerical duties in the back room of the store.

Smallpox soon stretched its deadly tendrils into their village. Because of his contact with sailors and dockworkers, Robert was one of the first to be struck down.

Fearful, Bastien closed down the mercantile. He hired a native woman who had survived the pox to nurse Robert, who lay sick on a cot in the back room, and hurried home where he remained behind locked doors with his family.

For weeks, Robert suffered, feverish and debilitated, but made a full recovery. While Bastien continued to remain sequestered in his home to avoid contagion, Robert kept busy stocking the store and then reopening and operating the mercantile.

Spring turned to summer, then to early autumn. Because of all the added responsibilities, it took Robert some time to realize he had not heard from Ada. He sent numerous letters to her, but received not one response. Alarmed, he decided to leave Saint-Anne-de-Beaupre to search for her and his beloved Emilie.

Robert broke the news to Bastien when he brought him the ledger with the week's accounts.

"Now? With the pox still rampant? Who will look after the mercantile?" Bastien slammed shut the ledger and leaned forward.

Bastien's home looked more like a continuation of his store than a residence. Crates of supplies and bolts of cloth lay stacked against two walls. Cured hams and sausages hung from lines strung across the beams over the head of his wife as she tended a pot on a crane over the fire.

"Gilles Dubeau survived the pox too. He has minded the store before. Pull him from the docks and warehouse. I know he'd welcome the change."

"If you're caught, you'll be hung like the rest of the rioters," Bastien argued.

Robert flopped onto the chair opposite his friend and stared at him from the other side of the table. "I have to find them, Bastien. Something is wrong, I can sense it." A year of frustration simmered inside him, but when he noticed the concern on Bastien's face, he softened. "You would do the same, and you well know it. Besides, I have lived off your charity long enough. It's time to get my life in order. After I find them, I want to find a way to clear my name."

"And how do you propose that?"

"If I can find a way to speak with the Governor, I'm sure he'll understand the charges against me are unfounded. He witnessed how I helped him."

"I think you're taking a big risk."

"Perhaps." Robert retreated into his own thoughts. Like a tiny ship tossed about on a tumultuous sea, his life was a mess and his future uncertain. He had to start somewhere to set things right again. "Whatever happens, know that I'm grateful to you for all you've done. With your help, I've been able to put enough money aside to start a new life."

Bastien shook his head. "You should wait; time will work in your favour. It's foolish to go back to Québec where your troubles are worse."

"I'm going to Pointe-du-Lac first; that's where Ada sent her letters from. The thought that Emilie and Ada are nearby and beyond my help is more than I can bear. What kind of man would I be to allow my future wife and her mother to suffer? Now that I've survived the pox, I am safe. I must do what I can to make them safe." Robert knew it wasn't that simple. Even if he found Emilie, her vow hung between them like a stone wall. He needed to see her, to hear her explanation in her own words, and then he would do everything in his power to convince her to change her mind.

"When are you going, Robert?"

"In the morning."

"Heaven protect you." Bastien folded his hands before him. "Whatever you do, don't get caught. Find the women, and when you return, everything here will be waiting for you. We'll be business partners, just like we planned."

"If all is well, I'd like that. I'm leaving most of my belongings here."

"Your things are safe with me, whatever you decide, whatever happens."

Choked with emotion, all Robert could do was nod. Bastien's kindness had known no bounds. "I'll send word as soon as I can. We shall see each other again soon, my friend. I promise."

Bastien rose, walked around the table, and gave Robert a manly embrace. "I'll hold you to that promise, *mon ami*."

127

Robert awoke before dawn and rummaged through the trunk at the foot of his bed for the items he needed to take with him. Beneath a neatly folded pile of shirts, he came across the bag of money Ada had sent him. It remained intact, untouched. He had not told anyone about it either, not even Bastien and decided to leave the money here where it would be safe. When he found Emilie, he would return it to her. Instead, he pulled out a leather purse that contained the silver coins he had saved over the past months. He slipped some coins into a money belt, which he tied around his waist beneath his shirt and breeches.

After removing a change of clothes, he tucked them into a leather sack, which he slung over his shoulder. He locked the trunk and tucked the key into his pocket. From beneath his pillow, he removed a folded paper that identified him as Simon Germaine and slid it into the pocket of his trousers together with a sheathed dagger. One never knew when danger would present itself. With the newly risen sun at his back, he set off.

Everywhere he went, he encountered signs of the pox. Like him, those fortunate enough to recover would forever bear the scars of their illness. Signs of those who languished or perished existed in every *habitant* farm he passed. With so much sickness, what would happen at harvest?

When darkness fell, Robert slept beneath an overturned abandoned cart at the side of the road, safe from wild animals or rogues that might stumble upon him during the night. After another full day of travel, Pointe-du-Lac came into view. Hard to believe a year and a half had passed since he had last set foot here. His heart beat rapidly as a host of memories assailed him, the strongest of which was the tolling of the church bells that pealed relentlessly on the night they fled. Yet this evening, the settlement lay before him in deathlike silence. Not a person ventured anywhere and every window and door was closed to the world.

When he neared Ada and Emilie's cottage, he experienced a profound sense of loss. A chill wind blew, even though the sun shone. *Please let me find them in good health.* The cottage's shutters were closed and there was no sign of habitation. He knocked, waited, and knocked again, but there was no answer.

Disappointed, he turned away. After a few paces, he noticed a man wearing only a shirt and breeches sitting on the ground, resting his back against a hedge, repeatedly tossing something into the air and catching it again. From a distance, and the strange behavior of the man, Robert thought it might be poor, dim-witted Gervaise, but as he drew nearer, he saw it was his friend Denis, the scars of the pox having laid waste to his face. He tossed a rag doll into the air by its head and caught it by its legs, oblivious to Robert's presence.

Robert stopped before him. "*Salut* Denis."

Denis raised his eyes, without moving his head and gave him a blank stare.

"Denis, don't you know who I am?"

"Whoever has got it, has got it," responded Denis, gazing at him with grief-stricken eyes.

"It's me. Robert. Don't you recognize me?"

Denis looked up, eyes wide with recognition. "Robert? Is it really you behind that beard? I thought you were dead."

Robert stepped back with a grin. "As you can see, I'm alive and well."

Denis made no move to stand and greet him, but his slight smile reassured Robert that he had not lost his mind altogether.

"Where is everybody?"

Pain glazed Denis' eyes. "Dead."

Cold fear clutched Robert's gut and his knees nearly buckled. "Everybody?"

"No, but almost. Those who are well are looking after the sick, but remain locked in their homes."

"And you?"

Tears glazed Denis' eyes. "In my house, I alone survived."

"I am sorry."

Denis nodded and looked away, staring into the distance at the Saint Lawrence River whose waters glimmered against the setting sun.

"Have you any news of Ada and Emilie?"

"Gone."

Panic ran rampant through his body. "Gone where?"

Denis shrugged then returned to flipping the doll and humming, dismissing Robert.

Disheartened and more fearful than ever, Robert walked away.

A man wearing a black cassock turned the corner and advanced towards him. It was Père Jean. He walked slowly, and as he approached, Robert discerned his pale, emaciated countenance, as if he too had passed through a storm. He looked askance at Robert; at first not recognizing him, but then he came to an abrupt halt. Père Jean's eyes bulged as he sucked in a breath and raised his hands in the air, his glance darting about as if he intended to flee.

Robert hastened to meet him and nodded his head in greeting. Père Jean seemed to have aged since he last saw him. He had also lost weight and what little hair remained on his head was white. His face bore the scars of the pox.

"Robert, is that you?" Père Jean asked.

"Yes, it's me. I am looking for Emilie. Have you heard anything about her?"

Père Jean clutched his hands together and raised them to his chest. "Last I heard she was in Québec, but who knows if she's still in this world."

"And Ada? Is she alive?"

"She may be, but who knows for certain. All I know is that she's not here."

"Where is she?"

"Gone to find Emilie."

"And Père Marc-Mathieu?"

Père Jean shrugged. "He's been gone for some time."

Robert pushed back his annoyance. "I know. Ada wrote and told me as much; but I want to know if he's returned."

"No, no one's heard anything about him."

"What of Seigneur Richard?"

Père Jean shrugged again. "Some believe he went to Québec."

The words sent a fury of shock through Robert's gut as anger settled in his heart. Seigneur Richard must have gone after

Emilie. There could be no other reason for his going there.

"And you, Robert? What are you doing here? Don't you know the authorities are looking for you everywhere?"

"What does it matter anymore?" Robert cast him a hard gaze. "My life is in shambles because of you. Everything would have been different if you had married me to Emilie that day."

Père Jean looked at the ground and said nothing.

"But I'm determined to set things right."

Père Jean looked up. "Hard to do that now. Is it wise for a wanted man to return to the wolf's mouth? Take my advice; leave before anyone sees you. Go back to wherever you came from. The authorities have been here looking for you. They've ransacked everything, turning your house upside down."

"I'm not surprised, but I don't care! All I want is to find Emilie and her mother."

"I have already told you they're not here. The pox is everywhere; it's best not to go look for them."

"I see you've recovered from it, Père Jean."

"*Oui*, I had it! Obstinate and bad enough it was! I am here by a miracle. It has left me in an awful state. Now, I need a little quiet to set me to rights again. In the name of Heaven, go back to where you came from lest the authorities find you."

"Not until I find them."

Père Jean made the sign of the cross and shook his head.

Robert looked around. "Have many died here?"

Père Jean wrung his hands as he entered upon a long enumeration of the dead.

Robert had expected something of the kind, but, on hearing the names of acquaintances and friends, grief overcame him and he hung his head in sorrow, unsure of what to say.

"You see what I mean?" exclaimed Père Jean. "And it isn't over yet."

"Don't worry about me. I've no intention of remaining here."

"Ah! Thank Heaven, you've come to your senses and will leave."

"No, not yet, I have something I must do first."

"What folly! It's not safe here."

"Never mind about me," Robert said as he waved him away. "At any rate, don't tell anyone you've seen me. You are a priest; I am one of your flock. If you betray me again, you'll be sorry." Robert studied the face of the old, broken man before him.

Père Jean's face reddened and he sighed petulantly. "You would ruin both of us. You haven't gone through enough already, I suppose; and neither have I. I understand, I understand." Muttering to himself, he went on his way.

Robert stood there, chagrined and discontented. So much had happened. Fury burned through him at the thought that Seigneur Richard might have kidnapped Emilie. What if she was already in his clutches? That would explain Ada's absence, for she would not hesitate to go to her daughter's aid, no matter the danger. Something was not right and he had to hurry to Québec. He prayed it wasn't too late to find Ada and Emilie alive.

128

Robert stood on the crest of a hill overlooking Québec. A dense column of black murky smoke curled upwards and dispersed into the grey, motionless atmosphere. A crowd encircled a bonfire. People tossed clothes, bedding, and other infected articles into the flames. Thick, heavy air hovered like a sluggish cloud of mist that veiled the entire sky, forbidding the sun from peeking through.

Solitude and silence added consternation to Robert's disquietude, keeping his thoughts somber. The sun would set soon. Robert knew he must hurry. He set off down a path towards the right and came to a sentry box. A guard stood in the doorway, leaning on his musket languidly watching the road leading in and out of the colony.

Now was as good a time as any, and with eyes focused on the ground, Robert advanced. The sentinel stopped him. "No one enters because of the pox."

Robert drew out a silver coin. "It's a matter of great urgency." With a wink, he showed it to the sentry.

The fellow held out his hand and Robert tossed it to him.

"Go on then."

Without hesitation, Robert passed through the gate and entered the colony. At first appearance, everything looked deserted. Then, in the distance, he saw a man walking towards him. As he drew closer, the man stared at him suspiciously then crossed the street. He raised his knotty walking stick and pointed it at Robert. "Keep away from me."

The man's reaction seemed extreme, but Robert reminded himself that the pox was worse here than anywhere else. To keep his anonymity, he had no intention of going near anyone and continued on his way.

On each corner, on every street, few people walked about. Morose sadness existed in the air, linked to the many deaths, which Robert knew left no family untouched. He glanced about. Somewhere amid this misery, he hoped to find Emilie.

He turned to the left following a road that led to the lower part of the colony. He heard someone call out to him and he glanced upwards in the direction of the sound. A woman surrounded by a group of children stood on the balcony of an isolated dwelling. Large, thick boards covered windows and doors. She beckoned him to come closer. "Please help me. My husband is dead and they've nailed up the doors and windows. No one has brought us anything to eat since yesterday. I've stood out here for many hours, but no one is willing to help us.

My poor children are hungry and cold. Please tell the authorities to release us."

Robert reached into his pocket and withdrew two coins. "I have no tools or food with me, but if you can direct me where to go, I'll get you something to eat."

She pointed to a nearby bakeshop down the street. Inside, the baker maintained his distance and placed two loaves in a basket with a long handle jutting out of its side. He slid it over the counter to him. Robert took the loaves and dropped his money into the basket to pay for it. He thanked the baker and returned to the woman.

"God reward you! Wait a moment." The woman disappeared inside. She returned with a small basket and cord by which to lower it down to him. Robert placed the loaves in the basket. In that instant, he remembered the loaves of bread he had discovered on the ground the first time he had come to Québec so long ago. He experienced a sense of relief and satisfaction, for this act was one of restitution. His heart swelled at having done a good deed for the helpless woman. "I'm not sure that I can help you in requesting the authorities to release you." He could not take the risk. At least not until he found Emilie and Ada and knew they were safe.

Her face sank with a combination of fear and disappointment.

A pang of guilt struck Robert. "Please don't worry. Somehow, I'll find a way to help you." He paused and an idea came to him. "Perhaps you too can do me a kindness. I am looking for two women who go by the family name of Basseaux, Emilie and Ada Basseaux. Have you heard of them?"

She shook her head. "I've never heard of them, and who knows where they could be now, amid all this sickness? Perhaps if you go a little further into the colony, you may encounter someone who has heard of them. And please don't forget to tell someone about us."

"I won't." Robert turned and walked away.

From the corner of a church, a man drove a two-horse cart laden with the dead; the bodies pitifully entwined in tattered sheets. At each obstacle and jolt, the cadavers quivered about in a horrible manner, heads dangling, and women's long tresses disheveled. Robert shuddered at the wretched sight. As he whispered a silent prayer for the unknown souls, a horrible thought flashed in his mind – what if Emilie was in that cart, or one similar? He shook off the notion and continued past.

The cart disappeared down the deserted street and he walked in the opposite direction. A priest carrying a small stick stood near a half open door with his head bent and his ear at the opening, and then raised his hand to pronounce a blessing and left the doorway. Robert strode towards him, keeping to the middle of the road.

When he came within four or five paces of the priest, Robert took off his hat and stopped to help him understand he would not come any closer. "Father, may I speak to you?"

The priest planted his stick on the ground, leaving a good space between them, and waited.

"Mon Père, I am looking for two women by the name of Basseaux from the settlement of Pointe-du-Lac."

The priest shook his head and shrugged his shoulders. "A third of the population has been lost already; many more are ill. We are all at God's mercy, my son."

"If they have taken ill, where would they be brought?"

"The Hôpital General or the Hotel Dieu." The priest pointed out the directions.

"God keep you in good health," Robert called out. As the priest began to walk away, Robert remembered the woman. "May I ask a favour of you, *mon Père*?"

When the priest stopped and nodded, he told him of the

forgotten woman and children.

"Thank you for telling me. Rest assured, I will inform the appropriate authorities and see what can be done to free them," the priest said and continued on his way.

As Robert walked, he struggled. Not because the directions were too complex or the way he went was too onerous, but because uneasiness rose in his mind. The priest had provided little information other than the directions to the hospital. Soon, he would learn the fate of Emilie and Ada. All hope would either be dashed or renewed. Regardless of what happened, the troubles that had trapped him these past two years would soon be over. No more doubts. Emilie was living or Emilie was dead. It had come to that and nothing more. The idea struck him with such force, that for a moment, he did not want to know, but gathered his resolve and continued on his way.

Robert passed through an unsightly quarter of the colony. The virulence of the contagion sweeping through this neighborhood had been so destructive; any survivors must have abandoned their homes. Doors swayed open, some off their hinges, their interiors ransacked. The spectacle of solitude and desertion that greeted Robert stunned him, and he quickened his step, consoling himself with the thought he was close to his destination.

Everywhere he walked, black crosses drawn with coal marked some houses. Rags and corrupted linens, infected straw, clothes, and sheets thrown from the windows littered the street. A haunting silence lingered. The cries of vendors, the clatter of carriages, and the chatter of neighbors that once rose like a cacophony of sound the last time he wandered through this quarter no longer existed. Only the occasional lament of a widow or the wail of a sick child broke the stillness of the air.

The last ray of sun slipped beneath the horizon and darkness grew thick. Church bells tolled in the distance; a call for prayer to those who needed solace from their desperation. The knowledge that somewhere amid the devastation, Emilie waited, alive or dead, drove him on. In her arms she carried love and hope for the future. He had lost her once already because of the manipulations of an evil man who cared little whose life he destroyed in order to satisfy his own greed and lust. Robert refused to lose her again. If she lived, he would embrace her, love her with every shred of passion he possessed, and share with her his life, love, and wealth. He would cling to her with all his might and treat her as the treasure he believed her to be. No vow would stand in their way.

Another death cart entered the street and Robert lowered his head then hurried past. When he looked up again, a beautiful middle-aged woman came down the front steps of a home with a weary gait. Her face bore scars, but not recent ones. She too was a previous survivor. Although red from recent weeping, no tears fell from her eyes. There was something peaceful and profound in her sorrow as she carried a child of approximately nine years in her arms. Although the girl's poxed face was lifeless, her hair had been parted, and she wore a clean white gown. The child lay with her breast resting against that of her mother's. Still with death, her delicate hand, as white as wax, hung from one side, and her head rested upon her mother's shoulder.

The death cart approached the woman and the driver hopped down. Respectfully, the man attempted to take the child from her arms. The woman drew back. "No! Don't take her from me. I must place her on the cart myself." She opened her hand and displayed a small purse, which she placed into the driver's hand. "Promise me you will not take anything from her, nor let anyone else attempt to do so, and to lay her in the ground just as she lays in my arms now."

The driver laid his right hand on his heart then hastened to make room on the cart for the dead child. The woman kissed her daughter on the forehead, laid her tenderly on the spot, and arranged her as if she lay upon the finest funeral bier, covering her with a pure white linen cloth. "*A bien tot, ma chère Cecile.* Soon, your brother will join you, and you can rest together forever." She turned to face the driver and pointed at her home. "When you pass this way again, check on us, for my entire family is ill.

Robert watched with bewilderment as she re-entered the house, and, after an instant, reappeared at the window. In her arms she held an even younger child, a boy, still living, but with the black marks of pox on his flesh. She stood still as death, her gaze never leaving the cart until it disappeared from sight. Then Robert saw her turn sadly away. Oppressed at heart, sadness weighed his every step. He reached the end of the road and beheld a small group of young men. Drunk, they weaved about. Robert stopped to let them pass.

The largest of the four spotted him and stopped. "And where might you be going?" he slurred as he steadied himself. A wide gap separated his two front teeth so that he resembled a beaver.

"Don't come any closer. I'm ill with fever," Robert said, eager to avert any trouble.

"Like hell you are," said the ugliest of the four. This youth was slight of build with bulging eyes and a wide crooked nose that looked as if it had been broken more than once.

"What have you got there?" The shortest of the four stared at Robert's leather pouch and took a step forward. In one swift movement, he reached into his pocket and pulled out a knife.

"I'll give you the pouch as long as you promise to let me by." Robert slid it from his shoulder and let it dangle from his hand. Let them have his clothes. His money was safe in the leather belt he wore around his waist hidden beneath his clothes.

The youth with the knife gave a quick nod and the fourth

young man stepped forward and snatched it from Robert's hand.

"There, you have what you wanted. Now I'll be on my way." Robert tried to swing past the group.

The beaver-toothed boy blocked his path and glared at him menacingly. "Not so fast. We haven't checked your pockets yet."

The youths circled him. Robert reached for the knife in his pocket, but beaver boy kicked his hand away. From behind, someone kicked at the back of his knees and he fell forward. A flurry of fists and boots assailed him.

Robert fought and kicked, but there were too many of them. Then came the horrific pain of the knife as it sliced across his lower belly. Robert ignored the searing flash of pain hoping the wound to be superficial. He groaned and clutched his stomach. Blood soaked his shirt and seeped through his fingers.

"Run," yelled one of the youths as they tore down the street. In his haste, the fellow carrying the pouch accidentally dropped it.

Thoughts of Emilie surfaced and a strong determination took hold. Robert rose to his feet and steadied himself. The hospital was not far.

He picked up the pouch. Ignoring the pain, he took one stumbling step after another until he passed through the hospital's front doors and fell mercifully to his knees.

129

Emmanuelle crossed the hallway carrying a tray laden with a pitcher of water and several cups. She was thinking of Emilie and the male visitor who came to see her two days ago. She had not told Emilie about him yet; there had not been time for they had both been busy tending to the sick. She didn't want to cause any alarm, but she would warn Emilie at the first opportunity so she could be vigilant of anyone around her. It was her fault that she fell into danger the first time, and Emmanuelle vowed not to let it happen again. She did not know who the man was, but suspected him to be either her betrothed or the man who blighted her troth. Regardless of which of them it was, she must warn Emilie.

A young man, his shirt bloodied, stumbled through the front doors and fell onto a bench in the waiting area. Emmanuelle lay the tray on a hallway side table and rushed to his side. He looked to be no more than twenty-five years, of slim build, tall, with a handsome countenance. His breath came in short rasps and the blood on his shirt centered on his abdomen.

"What happened?" Emmanuelle asked, as she leaned over him, her eyes fixed on that crimson stain.

"I've been stabbed, but I think it's only a flesh wound," the young man said, his face puckered in pain.

"Wait here. I'm fetching a cart to take you into the infirmary."

"I can walk," he said already rising.

"Are you certain?"

He nodded and she assisted him to his feet. One step at a time, she guided the young man into the nearest room where she eased him onto on a cot. He lay white-faced and panting from the exertion.

Emmanuelle reached for a pair of scissors on a nearby table. With practiced hands, she cut off his bloodied shirt. A tear across the front of his breeches just below the navel exposed part of the wound.

With care, she loosened the breeches and pulled them down to expose the wound. A long red slash ran from his left lower abdomen, across, and past the point of his navel. She reached for a clean cloth and positioned it across the wound to absorb some of the blood. Even beneath her lithe touch, he inhaled a sharp breath.

Cuts, even superficial ones like this, imparted much pain. Now that the cloth sopped up some of the blood, she examined the wound more closely. It was a slash that would require stitches. With care, she eased the breeches down a little more. She froze and sucked in a breath at the sight.

A birthmark in the shape of a horse's head caught her eye. She could not tear her eyes from the sight of it. A scream caught in her throat as her hands began to shake. She stepped back, her eyes roaming from the birthmark to the young man's face.

Memories of her son flooded her mind. The same fathomless eyes gazed back at her. The unmistakable upturned nose, similar to hers and that of her own parents, rested between the high cheek bones of his face. His hair color and the shape of his face and hands matched those of his father. Tears blurred her vision as she fought the desperate desire to clutch him to her breast.

She had dreamed of this moment every day of her life, visualizing the tearful embrace, the joy in her son's face. Now that the moment had arrived, however, she experienced only a profound terror that he might reject her, anger at the fate forced upon him, which her actions had wrought. And, if he did dismiss her, she would not wish to live. Her legs trembled and her heart raced. Any attempt to compose herself failed.

"What's that matter? Is it my wound?"

She shook her head. "I will send someone else to tend you." Overcome with emotion, she fled the room in search of solitude, to think, to pray. She had one chance to regain her son and must not err. The never ending chain of broken lies and failures haunted her now, more than ever.

When Emilie entered the receiving room in the convent, Ada rushed to embrace her. To feel her mother's arms around her filled her with joy. When they parted, she noticed Seigneur Claude smiling at her from where he stood near a window gazing out at the gardens. A muscle twitched in his jaw and his eyes did not waver from her, but today they seemed distant, pensive, as if his thoughts were somewhere else.

Alarm replaced the initial look of joy in her mother's face. With the back of her hand, she grazed Emilie's cheek, over the small scars that now marred her once perfect complexion. "Dear God, you've been ill." Her mother's eyes roamed from her head to her toes. "You've lost so much weight and there are dark circles beneath your eyes; my poor Emilie, how you've suffered." The words flew from her mother's mouth; the pain evident.

Tears of joy cascaded down Emilie's cheeks. With a thumb, her mother brushed her tears away. "I was ill, but I'm recovered now. Only fatigued from the long hours of work in the hospital."

Seigneur Claude stepped closer and took her hands in his. "I'm so happy to see you, and I'm glad to see you well recovered."

Emilie looked away, self-conscious about the scars still evident on her face. "There is nothing to worry about now. I was one of the fortunate ones. Too many weren't spared. It is rewarding to spend my days caring for others who are afflicted."

"Most generous of you." Seigneur Claude smiled at her. "But you mustn't work too hard. You're still pale and need your rest."

"My daughter is of a most generous spirit," Ada said. "But Seigneur Claude is right - you must look after yourself foremost. You are all I have. When your letters stopped coming, I feared something bad had happened to you and I would never forgive myself if I wasn't nearby if you needed me." She frowned. "My instincts were correct, I see."

"You look well, *Maman.* And you, Seigneur Claude?" Emilie asked.

"I accompanied your mother. Because of fear over the epidemic, your mother couldn't find anyone to bring her here. So I offered."

"Something for which I shall always be grateful," Ada added.

Warmth filled Emilie's heart over the generosity and kindness of this man who had changed so remarkably.

"No need for thanks. It is the least I could do. Besides, I promised you both that should you ever need anything, I would be there to offer my assistance. And I mean it with all sincerity."

Gratitude formed a lump in Emilie's throat. Raising a daughter had not been easy for her widowed mother. To have someone to rely upon in times of need would ease any future worries.

After a brief silence, Seigneur Claude cleared his throat. "Well, I hope you will forgive me if I leave you in each other's company for the time being. I have a matter I must attend to."

"Of course. Emilie and I have much to talk about," Ada said.

"I'm happy to see you reunited." Seigneur Claude bowed his head to replace his hat and left the room.

Emilie raised an eyebrow.

Her mother shrugged. "I don't know, but whatever it is, it must be something of importance. I've never seen him so pensive." Ada paused and ran her hand down Emilie's cheek. "Now, tell me all that has happened since we parted."

131

Seigneur Claude stared up at the gatehouse that loomed above him. A generous stipend paid to the Ursuline Sisters kept Gaston employed here. In return, Gaston provided him with reports of Emmanuelle's comings and goings. He knew the man controlled her through guilt and that she had suffered since he banished her from his life. The thought that her life became one of depravity added to the cloud of remorse hanging over him. Regret pressed upon his conscience at the knowledge that he caused Emmanuelle so much pain. Now he must make things right between them. Until he did, his soul would remain black and his own guilt would grow until he found a way to atone for his misdeeds.

He opened the door, made his way up the stairs, and entered the room at the top.

"Gaston?" he called. But the room was empty save for a bed and a small table with two wooden chairs near the window. A whip lay coiled on the floor as did some rope and a mask. Realization set in. What kind of man was Gaston to indulge in such things?

He seethed with anger as he picked up the whip and allowed the lashes to run through his fingers. Gaston had always confidently assured him that he had Emmanuelle under his full control. Was this how he did it? Seigneur Claude sat in a chair and waited, the whip coiled on his lap. Before long, he heard the sound of footsteps in the stairwell.

Gaston entered the room, his face full of surprise at the sight of him sitting there. "Monsieur Prudhomme, I wasn't expecting you."

"No, I found myself in Québec and decided to stop by for a visit."

"Can I offer you some refreshment? A glass of wine perhaps?"

"No, I'll be brief and then I'll be on my way. Sit, please." Seigneur Claude gestured to the opposite chair.

Gaston pulled it out and sat a comfortable distance from him.

Seigneur Claude removed a leather pouch from an inside

pocket of his coat and tossed it to him. "For you. Payment for the entire year. It should provide for you until you find other work. I have no further need of your services."

Gaston turned the pouch over, weighing its heaviness in his hands. Then he looked back at Seigneur Claude. "Is something wrong? You don't look pleased?" He looked at the whip in Claude's lap and swallowed.

Seigneur Claude narrowed his gaze and fixed it on Gaston. "Is this how you controlled her?"

"She wanted it."

"Not anymore." He pressed his lips tight together and shot him an icy stare.

Gaston swallowed and looked at his feet.

"Where is she now?"

Gaston looked up in surprise. "Isn't she in the convent?"

"No."

"Then she's at Hôpital General tending to the sick."

"You have till the morning to leave." Claude rose and strode to the door. His hand on the latch, he turned back around.

Gaston looked up at him, his countenance pensive, confused.

"Gaston, take it from one who knows, find God, let him into your heart and ask for forgiveness. Then pray like hell it isn't too late."

132

The afternoon light shining through the stain-glassed window cast a tranquil glow in the chapel where Emmanuelle knelt in the first pew before the altar. Her tears had long since ceased. Her life played itself out in her mind, and along with it, she weighed her every action. Peace eluded her, happiness always beyond her grasp. But as she prayed before the statue of the

Virgin Mary, a profound love began to warm her soul. It was as if a sunburst extinguished the darkness in her heavy heart.

Her son lived. Emmanuelle's heart soared with elation and renewed hope. She could never change the past, but the future glowed bright with promise. Determination now replaced despair. Emmanuelle knew she must face each of her failures and atone for them. She sensed a presence behind her and turned her head.

A man stood motionless in the shadows at the rear of the nave and she could not make out his features. He took a step forward into a ray of sunshine. Her breath caught in her throat when she saw his face. Claude stood still, tall and lanky as she remembered, only now, deep lines marred his once handsome face.

Panic possessed her and she glanced about for an escape, but he stood between her and the only exit. Her heart hammered a frantic cadence in her chest. He approached slowly, as if measuring each step. Cold fear gripped her. Her eyes fell upon the tricorne held in his hands. Cruel hands that nearly killed her.

"Emmanuelle," he said, his voice echoing in the vast emptiness beneath the vaulted and beamed ceiling.

From somewhere deep inside of her, courage arose, and along with it came the fortitude to face the demons of her past.

His gaze swept over her, and she tried to disguise her trembling hands in the folds of her habit.

"Do not be afraid," he said. "I mean you no harm."

"Why are you here?" The words flew courageously from her throat.

He searched her face, his eyes sorrowful. "I came to see you, to right a terrible wrong."

Emmanuelle fought back the cry that threatened to escape from her throat and stood before him speechless.

"Please, I have alarmed you. Come and sit." He spoke with gentleness and an underlying tone of sincerity.

When she sat, he slid into the pew beside her and stared ahead at the Virgin Mary. Emmanuelle slid a little further away from him; the added distance easing the discomfort a little of having him so near.

Disquietude fell over them like a pall. Fear kept her from breaking the silence.

He turned to look at her and she read the torment in the creases of his face. "Emmanuelle, I have lived a wretched life with sin as my constant companion. There is much I must atone for." He paused. "You and the boy are my greatest regrets"

Like a great void, the path towards truthfulness stretched before her. She knew which path to take. She nodded and composed herself. "I, too, have regrets, Claude."

He studied her then, as if seeing her for the first time. "I destroyed lives. It is what I did best and I admit, I relished every moment." He swallowed and looked at his hands. "I was wrong, so very wrong. I can never change what I did, and God knows, I do not deserve forgiveness. What I did to you and your son, has been my greatest burden."

Your son. The words echoed in her mind like a bell that refused to cease tolling. "He is your son, too. I swore it then, I swear it now." Her words seemed to send a jolt through him.

"If I could, I would take it all back. The loss is more than I can bear. Oh, Emmanuelle, I don't deserve your forgiveness, but I am here to do what I can to make amends, to better your life." His tears fell freely now.

For years, she had dreamed of this moment, but it had been only a dream, a wish that would never come true. And yet now, it seemed as if it had.

"I regret my lies, too." She looked him squarely in the eye. "It's true, I was a married woman in France, but my husband was cruel and he beat me for no reason except for the pure pleasure of it. If I had stayed, I would have one day died because of it. When I learned about *Les Filles de Roi,* I saw it as a means of escape, a new start. Hope for a better life. And so I came. At first, I wanted to tell you, but I feared you and what you would do to me when you found out. It turns out, I was right."

His eyes closed at the memory. "Did you know the man you were once wed to in France is now dead?"

She sucked in a breath at the news. "No, I did not."

"I learned about it recently. Because he was still alive when wed, our marriage was never valid. So you are free to do as you wish."

Emmanuelle let the news wash over her. Freedom, an unencumbered future. Hope again opened itself to her.

"What will you do now? Will you take your final vows?" he asked.

"Perhaps one day, but not now."

He looked at her with puzzlement, but didn't question her any further. "I am sorry for all the harm I have done to you and our son. Were I able to take it back, I would. Whatever it is you need or wish to do, I will give you the means to do it. You need only ask."

She studied his face and saw sincerity there. "And you?"

His face turned serious and his eyes clouded over with pain. "I am alone, with no one to share the empty shell of my life. If I can, I will find our son and beg his forgiveness. As my heir, he shall have all that rightfully is his."

She wavered, unsure. Could she believe him? Had he really changed into someone she could trust? The peace and forgiveness that renewed her moments before resurfaced. The opportunity to restore shattered lives presented itself like a golden road before her. Their son had been deprived of his true parents his entire life. He had a right to know his father, his mother, and if he so wished, to reject them altogether. Together she and Claude must stand before their flesh and blood and reveal all.

"I know where he is." She expelled the words breathlessly, as if she could not believe them herself.

Claude froze and his mouth fell open as a look of shock on his face turned to one of confusion. He seemed at a loss for words.

"A man came into the hospital not long ago with a flesh wound on his abdomen. When I stripped away his clothes to cleanse the wound, I saw the birthmark."

"The horse's head? You are certain."

"Without doubt. A mother would never forget such a thing. But I said nothing to him, so he does not know."

"Then we must tell him. Together." Claude offered her his hand.

She recoiled.

He kept it extended, as if he expected such a reaction. "We have much to talk about, much to do, but for now, we cannot squander what fate has put in our paths."

Emmanuelle's heart soared at the same time that anxiety took hold. She rose to her feet and looked him in the eyes. Slowly, she placed her hand in his. It felt warm, strong, and in that moment, she no longer feared him. Side by side, they walked down the aisle. When they reached the doors, Claude put his hand on the latch then hesitated. "Thank you," he whispered.

Emmanuelle's eyes welled with tears. A slight smile graced her lips and he swung open the door to let her pass through first.

133

The slash across Robert's abdomen had not pierced him beyond his flesh, but because of its length, it took a physician and a nurse nearly an hour to stitch it. Only the cadence of a resolute throbbing remained to remind him of his ordeal. He had been lucky. Robert lay back in his cot and contemplated what to do next.

A Jesuit priest walked into the ward – a Jesuit, who, even at a distance, had all the bearing and motion of Père Marc-Mathieu. He walked from one cot to another blessing the ill, and as he drew near, Robert saw it was indeed the good priest. He became painfully aware of how much Père Marc-Mathieu had changed since he last laid eyes on him. The priest walked with a stooping, laborious carriage and his wan, shriveled face bore the signs of exhaustion. His hair seemed longer, but thinner and greyer. Most alarming of all, deep yellow tones tainted the whites of his eyes and tarnished his skin.

He raised a hand over Robert and began to speak a blessing, but stopped. “Robert, is that really you behind that beard?”

Robert looked about and raised his index finger to his lips to silence him. “It's good to see you again,” Robert replied in a soft voice.

“It is you!” A smile lifted the corners of the priest's mouth.

“How are you, *mon* Père?”

“Better than many of the poor creatures you see here,” he replied. His voice was feeble, hollow, and as changed as everything else about him was.

“How did you come to be here?”

“After you left Pointe-du-Lac, I was transferred to La Prairie de la Madelaine. When news of the epidemic ravaging the town of Québec reached my ears, it afforded me the opportunity I desired, of devoting my life to the service of others. I entreated my superiors to send me here to attend the sick. My request was granted without difficulty. I have been here for a few days." Père Marc-Mathieu pulled out a handkerchief and wiped his forehead. "But enough talk about me. Tell me about you. I heard about your trouble."

"I'm sorry to tell you, Father, but since I last saw you, I have suffered one disaster after another."

Père Marc-Mathieu frowned and pulled up a chair. "Tell me everything."

Speaking in a low voice to avoid being overheard, Robert described the day he spent in Québec, and his flight; of the price on his head. He explained how he had lost track of Emilie and later learned of her abduction from the Ursuline convent.

The priest seemed to shrivel at the news. "I'm sorry, I thought it would be safe for her there."

"So here I am, back in Québec, to look for her; if she's alive and will have me."

"At the risk to your own life."

"Risk worth taking," Robert assured him.

"But what brought you here to the hospital?"

"I heard Emilie was here, and on my way, I was attacked by some scoundrels. One slashed me across the belly, but it's been stitched and should heal."

"Have you any information as to where she might be lodged?

"None, Father, except that she is here somewhere. I thought you might know."

Père Marc-Mathieu shook his head. "As I said, I arrived only two days ago. If she's here, I haven't seen her yet."

Robert clenched his fists. "Emilie should have been my wife by now. For nearly a year and a half, I've borne our separation. I've come this far and faced great risks, one worse than the other; and still, I cannot find her."

"I don't know what to say." Père Marc-Mathieu rubbed his chin. "Your intentions are good, and God blesses your perseverance in seeking Emilie." Père Marc-Mathieu rose to his feet. "Are you well enough to stand?"

"I think so," Robert said as he accepted the priest's hand and carefully pulled himself to a sitting then standing position. He waited for the pain to subside then straightened.

Père Marc-Mathieu led him out into the corridor. He raised his thin, tremulous hand and pointed to the left. "I will be holding a mass in the Église de Notre-Dame-des-Anges soon. There is to be a procession. God willing, Emilie might be there with the other sisters, and if she is not, then prepare yourself, for many have died."

Robert could not bear to think of her as dead. If she died, it would all be because of Seigneur Richard. His anger surfaced. "I must find her!"

"And if you don't?" Père Marc-Mathieu gave him an admonishing look.

Robert's anger had been swelling in his bosom and now overpowered his thoughts. "If I don't find her, I'll find Seigneur Richard instead. Either in Québec, or in his detestable palace, or at the end of the world, or in the abode of the devil himself, I'll find that spawn of Satan who separated us. If not for him, Emilie would have been my wife months ago; and if we had been doomed to die, we would at least have died together. If that villain still lives, I'll find him and make him pay."

"Robert! Do not speak like that in my presence." Père Marc-Mathieu grabbed him by one arm and stared at him severely.

"If I find him," Robert continued, blinded by rage, "if the pox hasn't already wrought justice upon him, I'll make sure the coward no longer mocks people or drives them to desperation. I'll meet him face to face and get my own justice!"

"Robert! Have you not learned your lesson yet?" Père Marc-

Mathieu's voice assumed its former full and sonorous tone. He raised his sunken head, his cheeks flushed with their original colour. Fire flashed from his eyes. "Look about you!" He grasped and shook Robert's arm with one hand, and with the other, pointed to the mournful scene around them. "Justice! You would get justice? You! Do you know what justice is? I hoped that before my death, God would give me the comfort of seeing you and Emilie reunited, that you would both pray upon the grave where I shall be laid. But God will not reunite you if there is such hatred in your heart. I do not wish to hear anymore babble from your mouth." He threw Robert's arm aside and walked away.

"*Mon* Père!" Robert followed him with a supplicating air. "Wait, please."

The priest turned back around, relaxing nothing of his severity. "Dare you steal my time away from these poor afflicted people only to listen to your propositions of revenge? I listened to you when you sought consolation and direction, but now you have reprisal in your heart. What do you want with me? Everyone who is dying longs for forgiveness. They are the ones who deserve my attention, for they understand. Not you, with your desire for retribution blotting your soul, unable to show any signs of forgiveness." He shook his head. "What am I to do with you?"

"You want me to forgive him?" Robert's voice rose.

The priest looked at him with tranquil sternness. "You must. Search your heart and I know you'll find forgiveness there."

Robert scowled and said nothing.

Père Marc-Mathieu inhaled a deep breath and expelled a sigh. "Do you know why I wear this habit?"

Robert hesitated.

"You know why! You've heard the rumours about the man I once killed, so admit it," resumed the old man.

"I do," Robert answered.

"I too have hated, and that's why I rebuke you for your thoughts. The man whom I long hated, I killed and I've spent my life repenting it."

"But I heard it was an accident. You were defending yourself."

"If I had forgiven him, there would have been no need to defend myself and the man would be alive today."

"It is not the same thing. Seigneur Richard is a despicable tyrant, one who-"

"Hush!" Père Marc-Mathieu interrupted. "Murder can never be justified. If only I could instill in your heart the regret I have had, and still have, for the man I hated! I can't, but maybe God can. You dare to meditate revenge; but He has power and mercy enough to prevent you. You can learn from my mistakes. God can arrest the hand of the oppressor as well as that of the revengeful. Do you think that God will not defend this man against you and your vengeance? Whatever troubles befall you, rest assured it will feel like punishment unless you learn to forgive."

A deep shame burned through Robert. "I don't know if I can forgive him."

"What if you were to see him?"

Robert opened his mouth then closed it again, unsure. Could he suppress his anger and forgive?.

"The Lord commands us to not only forgive our enemies, but also to love them."

The priest's words held merit. Robert wearied of the hatred and anger that had consumed him for so long, and the futility of it. All this time wasted, nearly two full years, and for what? Thoughts of revenge held him entrapped as if he were tethered with chains. Forgiveness was the sole way to free himself. Only then could he look to the future. "With God's help, I will try."

"Well, come and see him. You have said you wanted to find him, and so you shall. Come and see the man against whom you harbour so much hatred; upon whom you wished so much evil."

Robert reached for his bag, removed a clean shirt, and slipped it on, wincing at the discomfort. He grabbed his coat and donned it gingerly.

The priest took Robert's hand and pulled him onward.

Robert followed him out of the building without daring to speak another word. Every step pained him, but he endured it.

After a short walk, Père Marc-Mathieu stopped near the entrance of a tent at the rear of the hospital. He fixed his eyes on Robert with a mixture of gravity and tenderness, and drew him in.

Several men lay upon sheets on the ground. Père Marc-Mathieu led him to the last man in the row, a nobleman's cloak laid over him as a quilt. Robert gazed down at Seigneur Richard and shrank back in horror.

Père Marc-Mathieu nudged him closer and pointed to the man. Seigneur Richard lay motionless. His bosom heaved from time to time with short respirations. His eyes were open, but blank. The black spots of the deadliest form of the disease covered his pale face. His black and swollen lips twitched, revealing his tenacity for life. The right side of his face drooped.

"You see," said Père Marc-Mathieu in a low and solemn voice. "If the smallpox won't kill him, the apoplexy will. This may be a punishment, or it may be mercy. For four days, he has lain here, just as you see him, without any signs of consciousness. Perhaps this man's salvation depends upon you and your ability to forgive." He made the sign of the cross over Seigneur Richard.

Robert stood frozen with shock as he looked at the pitiful sight of the once powerful man reduced to nothing more than a mass of flesh. When they heard the tolling of the church bell, they left the tent.

"Go now and search for Emilie," said the priest. "Prepare yourself for the worst. Whatever the outcome, find me and tell me."

Without another word, they parted ways. Numb with shock, Robert set off for the church.

134

Emmanuelle led Claude through the corridors until they reached the room where she had left her son, but he was not there. Emmanuelle glanced about at all those who lay sick or motionless near death, but he was not among them. She stopped a nun who hurried past with a tray piled with cloths and a small basin. "Please, can you tell me where to find the young man with the flesh wound on his abdomen?"

The nun barely glanced at her. "We moved him into the men's ward." She tilted her head in the direction of the ward across the hall then hurried past without another word.

Emmanuelle and Claude exchanged a look of encouragement then entered the room together. Ten cots lined either side of the long, narrow room. Again, her eyes roamed over each man, but he was nowhere to be found.

135

The haunting vision of Seigneur Richard near death, coupled with the berating by Père Marc-Mathieu, agitated Robert more than words could express. He could never make sense of the ordeal he and Emilie had endured because of that man's whim. The knowledge that it had been all for nothing was more than he could bear. His raw anger had boiled to the surface. Now that Seigneur Richard was no longer a threat, he should have experienced some relief, but he had suffered too much. The overlord and destiny had woven a treacherous path for him and Emilie, forcing them apart. Would they find their way back to each other? And if so, what of their love? Had it survived? His love for Emilie burned even stronger, but as for her feelings for him, he no longer knew for certain; but he had to find out.

Robert stood in the street and watched Père Marc-Mathieu appear at the entrance of the church and face those assembled. When the priest began to preach, Robert circumvented the crowd until he stood at the back. In the centre of the crowd, he distinguished veiled heads, but could not make out any of the nun's faces.

Père Marc-Mathieu's voice boomed a solemn address. “Let us remember the thousands who have died.” He pointed to the cemetery. “Bless all who survived and now live with uncertain futures. Life is a gift to be cherished and we must make the most of each moment. Remember all you have suffered that it may make you compassionate towards others. We must begin new lives with love as the foundation. Lend a brotherly arm to the feeble. Those who are young must sustain the old. Those without children must look for children without parents and form a family. Only in this way can we alleviate our sorrows.”

The crowd became silent when he hung a rope round his neck, and knelt, his head bowed. Everyone waited. He stretched his arms out to the side and looked to the crowd. “I implore your forgiveness. If something rendered me less attentive to your needs, less ready to answer your calls; if impatience or weariness sometimes made me severe or dispirited; if I have somehow failed to treat you with humility; if, in my frailty, I have caused you offence, please forgive me! And may God forgive you all your trespasses and bless you.” He made the sign of the cross over the assembly and rose.

A lump formed in Robert's throat and he fought the sadness

that threatened to erupt in a cascade of tears. The words so eloquently expressed with such sincerity were this good man's final adieu to the people he had served so generously; true words of forgiveness and hope.

Many fell to their knees sobbing, but Robert could not move. Transfixed, he watched as Père Marc-Mathieu took a large cross, which rested against the wall, elevated it before him, and proceeded into the mass of people who made way for him.

Robert followed the crowd. Soon, he found himself near a group of tents for the sick next to the hospital. Père Marc-Mathieu walked with the rope round his neck; the heavy cross elevated before him. His face was pale and haggard, inspiring both sorrow and encouragement, and he walked with slow, resolute steps. Immediately behind him came the women and children, their languor filling Robert's heart with pity. He studied each tragic face that filed by, glancing over the crowd as it thinned.

At the rear of the procession, carts bore convalescents not yet able to walk. Hope renewed itself inside him, for the nuns walked among them. The procession passed so slowly, Robert could study each nun or postulant or novice, but Emilie was not among them.

His hope dissipated. Maybe she was among the ill. He walked round the church to its rear garden and passed through a dilapidated gate at the back. He paused in a narrow passage between two little tents. Stooping to loosen his shirt to check the bandages, he heard a familiar voice from inside. It brought him to a sudden stop. Could it be possible? He held his breath and listened again.

"Fear of what?" asked a woman, her voice gentle. "We've passed through the worst of the illnesses."

Robert could utter no cry because his breath lay trapped in his lungs. His knees threatened to fail him. No sound existed in the entire world except for that melodious voice. He straightened, alert, more vigorous than ever. In three bounds, he moved around the tent and stood at the opening. A woman wearing the habit of a novitiate stood with her back to him.

A tear in the roof of the tent allowed a tiny ray of sunshine to pour inside. It bathed her in a golden light as rich as the precious metal. The world beyond him ceased to exist as she turned ever so slowly around.

136

A scant inkling of intuition swept over Emilie. She held herself taut as a statue. A silence, charged with verve and spirit, urged her to turn her head. A man stood in the doorway, but she looked away again, dismissing him as a stranger. The power of his unyielding presence refused to fade, so she straightened and turned around again.

Behind a beard, Robert stared unwaveringly at her, his eyes aglow as if they were fire itself. Her hands flew to her mouth. "Robert," she whispered, her voice smothered by her elation.

Robert advanced towards her, his hands trembling. "Emilie! You're alive!"

Emilie grew cold with shock then almost as quickly, her body trembled. "Robert!" She reached out a trembling hand and touched his arm.

As if parched from so long an absence, her eyes swept over him, taking in his beard and moustache, and the tiny scars that pocked his cheeks. Tears brimmed and blurred the sight of him. "Is it really you, Robert? You're alive."

"I survived the pox." He paused as his face lost some of its brightness. "I see you have too."

She nodded, at a loss for words, unsure. The air seemed suddenly oppressive. The distance between them seemed hauntingly insurmountable.

Robert inched closer and raised a hand to her cheek. A deep sadness seemed to wash over him. "How pale you are, how gaunt you've become."

"There has been much to do here and little time for rest." Emilie turned to the ill woman in the cot. "I'll be back soon to check on you," she said with a smile to reassure her patient. Then she turned and gestured for Robert to follow her outside.

"Why are you here?" she asked.

The question seemed to stun him. "What do you mean? You are all I've thought about night and day."

"Didn't my mother write to you?"

"She did, but I refused to believe what she told me in her letter."

"What she wrote was the truth. I made a vow and all is over between us."

"Why is it over? We are betrothed!" Pain glazed his eyes. "What has changed?"

"Everything has changed. I hoped that by now you would have forgotten me."

"I could never forget you or the love we once shared."

His words resurrected a long buried ache in her heart. "So you came all the way here, to this place of death to find me?"

"Do you think it's right that we who have survived should live in despair?"

"I made a vow I cannot break." She looked away. Her desperate pleas to God had been answered and she could not renege on such a vow.

He tilted her chin with his fingertips and forced her to look at him. "A promise that isn't worth anything."

"It is a promise to God."

"It's my belief that God does not hold people to promises that will cause pain to everyone around them."

"You don't know what I went through; you've never found yourself in the same circumstances." She turned away from him, but he grabbed her arm and spun her back around.

"Tell me one thing. If this vow of yours didn't exist, would you be with me?"

Emilie faced him again, struggling to restrain her tears. "What does it matter now? What is there to gain by making me answer that? It's too late for us. You must go, and think no more of me. After all that has happened, it's clear we are not meant for each other."

Her words seemed to turn him to ice. He did not attempt to move closer to her. "Emilie, please."

"No, go away, please!" The pain of his nearness was more than she could bear.

"Listen, I just spoke with Père Marc-Mathieu."

"He's here?"

"I spoke to him a few minutes ago. He asked about you."

Fear raced through her. "Is he sick?"

Robert hesitated. "Yes, but not with the pox. I fear he has not long to live."

So much sadness, so much death. It seemed like a never ending stream that refused to stop. "Where is he?"

"He led the procession to the cemetery, but afterwards, I suppose he'll be here somewhere attending the sick." Robert took hold of her arms. "We talked about you. He told me I did the right thing in returning to look for you; that God approved and would help me find you. And he was right. I'm here now with you, aren't I?"

"He doesn't know all that has happened."

"How could he know? How could anyone know? This vow of yours, which no one knows about, is all that stands between us. Seigneur Richard is no longer a threat."

"What do you mean?"

"Père Marc-Mathieu took me to see him. Seigneur Richard is dying, Emilie. He may be dead as we speak."

Emilie listened as Robert told her about his visit to the man's bedside. Accustomed as she'd become to death, she was overwhelmed at the news. "The poor man." Although he had been the cause of all the destruction in his or her lives, no one deserved to die in such a horrific manner.

"There is nothing to stand between us now, nothing to prevent us from marrying."

Emilie shook her head, walked to a nearby bench, and sat. The sense of hopelessness refused to leave her. "No, we are not. I prayed for my life that night, and my prayers were heard. In exchange I made a vow, which I must keep."

"And your mother, that poor woman who strove so hard to see us married. Did she not argue against this vow of yours?"

"My mother! Do you think she would encourage me to break a vow?"

He sat beside her and looked at his hands. A long silence ensued. "Père Marc-Mathieu told me to tell him whether I had found you. I will go fetch him, then you can hear what he thinks about your vow from his own mouth."

"Yes, find him. I want to see him." She turned to look at him. "For your own sake, Robert, do not come back and tempt me to go back on my word. Once Père Marc-Mathieu knows about my vow, he will bring you to your proper senses and will set your heart at rest."

"My heart will never be at rest without you! You had that abominable letter sent to me. Do you have any idea how I suffered because of it? You want to forget me, but I don't want to forget you. I'll go mad. You're all that I've thought of every waking moment since we last set eyes on each other. Consider all we have suffered. None of it was my doing. Do you doubt your love for me because I was persecuted? Because I've spent a time from home, unhappy, and far from you? Because I came in search of you as soon as I could?"

She glanced away, her face bathed with distress.

"Why do you believe that God will make us suffer for words that escaped your lips at a moment when you did not understand what you were saying? If you don't love me anymore, if I have become hateful to you, then tell me, but don't hide behind this vow of yours."

"I don't hate you, Robert. I can never hate you. Go find Père Marc-Mathieu. He will help you understand, but don't come back here." She rose and began to walk away.

"Emilie," he called out to her.

She stopped at the entrance of the tent, but didn't turn around.

"I'll go, but even if I found myself at the other side of the world, I will always return to you."

When she heard him walk away, she ducked her head and slipped back inside the tent. Emilie sunk to the ground by the side of a cot. Resting her head against it, she wept bitterly.

137

Every step he took, every move he made, aggravated Robert's painful wound, yet it was nothing compared to the ache in his heart brought on by Emilie's rejection. He hadn't told her everything about his struggles or his wound because he didn't want to influence her. If she returned to him, he wanted her to do so with an open heart.

Robert found Père Marc-Mathieu administering last rites to a dying woman who lay on the ground on a sheet. Robert waited in silence. He saw him close the poor woman's eyes, raise himself upon his knees, and after a short prayer, rise.

"Ah, Robert," Père Marc-Mathieu smiled. "Well? Did you

find her?"

"She's here," Robert said grimly.

Père Marc-Mathieu studied him for a moment. "In what state?"

"She has recovered."

"The Lord be praised!"

Robert stepped closer. "There's a problem."

"What is it?"

"After all that has happened, she tells me she can't marry me. In a moment of terror she made a vow to God in exchange for her life."

"Where is she now?"

"A few yards beyond the church."

"Give me a moment," Père Marc-Mathieu said, "and we'll go to see her together."

"Will you help make her understand?"

"I know nothing about it, my son; first I must hear what she has to say."

"I understand." Robert watched the priest leave. With his eyes fixed on the ground and arms crossed over his chest, he waited in stark suspense.

Père Marc-Mathieu returned with a basket on his arm. "Let's go."

An icy chill and a dark sky forewarned of an autumn storm. A shrill breeze blew, threatening to topple tents. Robert's spirit roiled with uneasy expectations and he walked deep in thought. He looked behind him and saw that Père Marc-Mathieu lagging behind, suffering under the pressure of his malady. Robert slackened his pace. Père Marc-Mathieu walked with difficulty, occasionally raising his pale face to heaven, as if seeking more air to breathe.

When they came to stand outside of the tent, Robert stopped. "She's in there."

Père Marc-Mathieu put his hand on Robert's shoulder as if to give him strength. Then he entered the tent. Robert followed him inside.

138

As soon as they entered, Emilie sprang up and greeted Père Marc-Mathieu. His appearance shocked her, but she disguised any reaction. “How good it is to see you.”

“It's good to see you too, child. Look at how many troubles the Lord has delivered you from. You must indeed rejoice that you have always trusted in Him.”

“Oh yes, indeed! But you, *mon* Père? How are you?”

“As God wills, I will soon be delivered.” He gave her a placid look and drew her to one side. “I can stay for a few moments. Are you able to confide in me like you used to?”

“Of course, you will always be *mon* Père.”

“Then, my daughter, what is this vow that Robert has been telling me about?”

“It's a vow that I made with God. If he saved me from the peril I faced, I promised to give my life to His service.” Emilie clasped her hands together.

“When you made the vow did you recall that you were already bound by another promise?”

She frowned. “No; I didn't.”

“My daughter, the Lord approves of sacrifices and offerings when we make them of our own free will, but you cannot offer up the will of another, particularly someone to whom you had already pledged yourself.”

“Have I done wrong?”

“No, my poor child, but tell me: have you never consulted anyone about this?”

“I didn't think I needed to.”

"Is that all that hinders you from fulfilling the promise you made to Robert?"

"There is nothing else," Emilie said with hesitation, her cheeks hot. She glanced at Robert who stood unmoving. Beneath a frown, his eyes never wavered from hers.

Père Marc-Mathieu lowered his eyes. "Do you believe that God has given me the authority to purge the debts and obligations that men may have contracted to Him?"

"Yes, I do."

"You understand that I can free you from the obligation of your vow?"

"Is it not a sin to renege a promise made? One I made with utmost sincerity?" Emilie shook her head in confusion.

"A sin? It is my duty to guide you through this. See how you and Robert have been re-united? Regardless of the troubles you both have faced, you have been brought together again. It is written in your destinies. If you need me to absolve you from this vow, I shall not hesitate to do so."

Emilie noticed the hopeful look in Robert's eyes. She gave the priest her warmest smile. "Then... I do request absolution from you."

Père Marc-Mathieu beckoned to Robert. When he drew near, the priest smiled at Emilie. "By the authority vested in me, I declare you absolved from the vow and free you from its every obligation."

As if the vow had burdened her painfully, lightness lifted Emilie's spirits. A shard of happiness sprang to life within her.

Père Marc-Mathieu turned to Emilie. "Love each other as companions in a journey. If God grants you children, inspire them with love. Has Robert told you whom he has seen here?"

"Yes, he has."

The priest's face darkened with sadness. "Pray for Seigneur Richard Tonnacour. And pray for me also, my children. I hope you will remember me."

From his basket, he pulled out a little wooden box, turned and polished it with priestly precision. He raised the lid and showed its contents to Emilie. Inside lay a golden necklace upon which hung a cross pendant embedded with rubies. "When my mother died, this was sent to me. It is all that I have left of her and my once happy family. They have all died, except for me, but that day, too, draws near." He smiled at her. "My mother would have liked you very much. It would please me if you would keep it and wear it. Let it be a symbol of love and family to you. Your children will be born into a harsh world and they will live amid evil as you and Robert have. My mother taught me to forgive. Teach your own children always to forgive." He paused and swallowed hard. "Pray for me, Emilie." With a trembling hand, he handed the box and jewel to her.

She received it with reverence and kissed the priest on both cheeks.

"I must go now," he said softly.

"Oh, Père!" said Emilie. "Shall I see you again?" She could barely utter the words.

Père Marc-Mathieu's face remained void of expression, but his eyes glowed with warmth as he pointed to the heavens. "Above, I hope. Give Ada my blessings, and beg her, and all those who are left, to remember Père-Marc-Mathieu and pray for him. God go with you both and bless you forever!" Then he turned and disappeared from sight.

A brutal wind swirled and howled and a pure white snow fell in a flurry of whiteness from the skies.

139

Emilie turned to Robert and wept as he took her into his arms. The press of her body against his pained him and he inhaled sharply. She pulled away from him and her eyes studied him. Fear scoured Emilie's face. “Robert, you're bleeding!”

Robert looked at the growing stain of crimson seeping through his shirt. His hand flew protectively over his injury. “Don't be alarmed. It's only a flesh wound.” He glanced at her.

“It needs to be tended to. Come and lay down.” The panic in her tone bespoke her love, and a surge of joy filled him.

“It has already been cleansed and stitched, but all this walking hasn't helped.”

“What happened?” Emilie asked.

“I was accosted by some rogues on my way here to find you. One of them drew a knife and during the scuffle, sliced me. If it weren't for the girdle of money I wore at my waist, it could have been far worse.” The sudden remembrance of his money belt sent a quiver of worry through him. Where was it? The woman who tended him had removed it and cast it aside. “My money. I must go back and make certain it's still there. Come with me.” Robert took her by the hand and led her from the tent back into the hospital.

The pain in Robert's abdomen ached more than ever, but his anxiety urged him on.

When they entered the ward, Robert noticed two people standing near the bed where he had lain. Robert tensed and stopped. The woman was the same one who had fled when she uncovered his wound. What if she had recognized him and she fled to call the authorities, and the man with her was here to arrest him?

Robert tightened his grip on Emilie's hand, ready to run back out of the ward, but Emilie held him back, her face confused.

“Wait, please!” The man's voice boomed across the room, rousing several of the sleeping patients.

“Robert, what's the matter?” Emilie said. “I know those

people."

He hesitated, glancing between Emilie and the couple. Their countenances were strained, their bodies taught with tension. He sensed something was amiss, but what? For all these months, he had been forced to run and hide; but no more. With Seigneur Richard dead, he was determined to put an end to all the troubles of the past. Warily, he advanced towards them. The woman held his money belt in her hands, and as he came near, she raised it to him. Her cold, trembling fingers accidentally grazed his and he forced himself not to recoil.

"*Merci.*" Judging by the weight of the belt, he doubted any of it was missing. Robert hung it protectively over his arm. The man's intense, unwavering gaze made Robert uncomfortable.

"Have you come to fetch me?" Emilie asked the man.

Robert stared at Emilie. "You know this man?"

Emilie smiled. "Of course, I do. He is Seigneur Claude Prudhomme, a good man, my protector." She gestured at the woman. "And this is Emmanuelle, my friend who lives at the Ursuline convent, and who cared for me during my illness."

Robert relaxed a little, but he could not shake off the foreboding that settled in his gut. It was the way the man stared at him, assessing and sorrowful, a pained, haunted look, that disturbed him the most. As for the woman, her pale demeanour and trembling limbs revealed her distress. Robert could not fathom why she seemed scared and vulnerable. An urge to take her into his arms and console her swept over him.

"Robert," the woman whispered tremulously. "You're bleeding. Let me help you."

The pain in her voice shook him to his core. "How do you know my name?"

The woman held herself straight. "I knew you when you were born."

Excitement blossomed inside him. This woman might know

who his parents were and what had become of them.

Her face contorted with confusion, Emilie turned to Emmanuelle. “You know Robert?”

Emmanuelle nodded, her eyes brimming with tears.

“But, he is my betrothed, the one I told you about,” Emilie said.

Emmanuelle's eyebrows rose and her eyes widened. The tiniest of smiles curled her lips then disappeared. “Please lay down, so that I may examine your injury.”

Robert complied, allowing Emmanuelle and Emilie to remove his coat and bloodied shirt. “I'm afraid that's the last of my shirts.”

“I'll have some clothes brought to you,” Seigneur Claude stated.

“Why are you doing this? Who are you?”

Emmanuelle stopped her ministrations to exchange a look with Seigneur Claude who gave her a nod of encouragement.

She inhaled a breath and in a gentle voice said, “You are our son.”

“Your son?” His voice rose an octave as his eyes shifted between Emmanuelle and Claude, searching their features for similarities to his, his mind unable to keep pace with the resemblances his eyes processed. He had his father's build and facial features; his mother’s eyes and chin matched his own. These were the people who had abandoned him. A thousand questions surfaced. “How can this be? What proof have you?” He felt the press of Emmanuelle's hand upon his arm.

“Our son was born with a distinct birthmark, the color of blood in the shape of a horse's head.” She placed her hand on the right side of her lower abdomen. “Here,” she demonstrated. “I recognized it earlier when I removed your shirt to tend to your wound.”

Robert's breath caught in his throat. Now he understood

why she reacted so strongly and fled. Only the people who had raised him knew of his birthmark, but they were dead, and he had never mentioned the mark to anyone, not even to Emilie. He closed his eyes, consumed with confusion, anger, and the pain that came with abandonment after his parents had discarded him like flotsam. In his mind, one question arose, mightier and more prevalent than any other, and he summoned the courage to ask it. "Why did you forsake me?"

Emmanuelle seemed to crumple at his words. She looked helplessly at Claude then at the hands she wrung at her waist.

"I am to blame, for all of it, for everything that happened to you," Emmanuelle said.

"No, I am to blame," Seigneur Claude said as he took her hand and squeezed it. "It is I who treated you badly, casting you both out of my life." He swallowed hard. "And I regret it with all my heart."

Tension, clogging and slow, cleaved the air.

"I want to know," Robert said, decades of hurt pressing hard on him.

Seigneur Claude straightened and held himself still. "I have many regrets in my life, but the greatest of all is what I did to you and your mother." His voice carried a mournful tone as he relayed the history of his life, of their once happy family, and of the terrible anger that had caused him to tear a babe from its mother. With each word he spoke, his body seemed to shrivel.

Robert saw how the devouring guilt of his sordid past had robbed Seigneur Claude of joy. He looked old and pitiful as he confessed; a man whose soul was buried beneath years of transgressions and who now raced against time to make right his wrongs.

While he spoke, Emmanuelle worked in silence. When her delicate hands removed the bindings, all eyes fell upon his mark. Silence hung over them and no one moved or spoke.

Then slowly, Emmanuelle took up a cloth, dipped it in warm water, and cleansed the wound, her eyes flooded with tears. Each touch graced his flesh with tenderness.

When her turn came to tell them about her life, she did so stoically, her voice poised, but tinged with remorse, the pain of her past contorting her face. Robert's heart broke at the knowledge of what she had endured.

A mother's caress. Robert delighted in the feel of her hand whenever it touched his; a balm to his soul. In their honesty and suffering, a vast chasm was being breached; a family reunited again under improbable circumstances. The words of forgiveness Père Marc-Mathieu had spoken, reverberated in his mind again and again. If there was anything Robert had learned during the past year and a half was that life was short and it could change as fast as the wind. One had to reach out and grasp life whenever and wherever one met it. His heart softened and opened to this man and woman who had brought so much pain to themselves and others. Robert stilled his mother's hands and pressed them to his cheek.

She sucked in a sharp breath. Then her head fell against his chest as she sobbed; the sound of relief a tidal wave of unburdening.

Emilie placed her arm around Emmanuelle. Robert looked at them both. In their eyes he saw a future filled with family and hope. All he needed to do was forgive, for with forgiveness came the freedom to partake of life unimpeded by the failures of the past. A rich life lay before him in all its glory, tempting, promising, luring him like a lustful courtesan. Again, they fell into a silence. Again, it was Claude who ended it.

"Robert, nothing can atone for the past and for all the pain I have caused you and your mother." Claude looked strongly at him. "You are my son and I am your father. I have failed you in the past, but I will not fail you now, or tomorrow, or for what remains of my sorry life." Next, Claude faced Emilie. "And you, beautiful child, I hope you will forgive me. I already think of you as a daughter. To know that you are betrothed to my only son, and to have a family again, when for so long I have been alone, brings me great joy. Robert, you are my sole heir; all that I have will be yours – home, lands, and all."

As Claude spoke, Robert noticed his mother grow tense. "What of my mother?" he asked.

Seigneur Claude rubbed his chin as Emmanuelle turned her dark eyes upon him. He took a step toward her and took her hand in his. "I loved you the moment I laid eyes upon you, and you cannot know the happiness I felt when you gave birth to our son. From the day I forced you from our home, my life was plunged into misery. Loss and emptiness filled my every waking moment. Torment has been my just reward. If I am given another chance, I will spend the rest of my life proving to you that you can trust me again. You don't need to answer me now, but if you can forgive me for the evils I have done to you and our son, please become my wife again, and reunite our family."

140

Emmanuelle looked into the eyes of the man who was once her husband with utter disbelief. Although the words Emmanuelle had longed to hear for all these years soothed like a balm upon a raw wound, apprehension gripped her. All her life, with golden words, guileful men had uttered their promises to her. Each one had failed her – her father who had promised to wed her to a good man, her first husband who had promised to love and honor her, Claude who had beat her to within a breath of death only to cast her away like refuse, and Gaston who had exploited her guilt and pain.

Now, Claude stood before her professing to be a changed

man, making promises of a good life surrounded by family. Dare she open her heart and trust again? Even if she dared, could she forgive?

She glanced at Robert, flesh of her flesh, blood of her blood, and mourned all the years lost. A mother deprived of nurturing her child into adulthood. A son never having known his mother's love. Her arms yearned to hold him, her lips yearned to kiss his cheek, yet she dared not do so.

As for Emilie, the young woman whom she had betrayed, but grown fond of, she and Robert represented the future. The fates had conspired to bring them all together in this room after being torn apart by lies and betrayal. However, Emmanuelle knew the past could not be washed away with one stroke. Time must pass before they could all bridge the torrents of trouble that had separated them. Wounds could not heal overnight.

She looked back at Claude, emotion forcing her voice to waver. "All these years I dreamed of hearing these words. There is nothing I want more than to reunite our family."

He studied her face. "Yet you cannot." Claude spoke the words with disappointment.

"Not yet, but perhaps one day. There is much we must share with each other. The years have changed us both, Claude. I am not the same person you once knew. Let us become reacquainted with one another first and permit ourselves the time we both need to heal. There is nothing I want more than to know my son again, and his new bride. Then, if God wills it, we can marry."

She read the disappointment in his face and laid her trembling hand on his cheek. "Can you wait?"

He took hold of her hand and pressed it against his face, his eyes closed. "I will wait a lifetime for you." He kissed her hand.

Emmanuelle's heart pattered with joy.

Claude released her hand and smiled back. "In the

meantime, I insist that you allow me to provide for you. Please, come home with me. You'll have your own rooms."

Emmanuelle searched his face then nodded, rejoicing in the happiness that appeared when she agreed.

Claude then turned and looked at Robert. "My manor house is large, with plenty of land for all of us. My home is your home. Nothing would make me happier than to have us all together. There is a large, but quaint, cottage next to my manor house that I think would suit your new bride. Plenty of room for Ada too. What do you say to my suggestion that both of you come to live with me?"

Robert exchanged a look with Emilie. Her eyes were bright with excitement. He looked over at Emmanuelle, who seemed to be holding her breath. "I promised my friend Bastien I would move to Saint-Anne de Beaupre and enter into business with him."

Emilie's eyes lost their lustre and his mother's body seemed to slump. He cast them both his most heartfelt smile. "But I know he will understand."

Emilie gave a shriek of delight.

"What of your mother?" Robert asked her. "How will she feel about living with us?"

"My mother! She knows none of this. But she'll be happy to learn all that has happened. And I know she'll be happy as long as we can be together."

"Splendid," said Claude, his grin wide. "Everything shall be arranged."

141

The day after they arrived at his father's manor house, Robert set off with Emilie and their parents to the church. He and Emilie wanted the wedding to occur with all haste. They had already lost far too much time.

Despite the winter snow and cold winds, Robert was filled with warmth. Nothing could dispel the joy he experienced as their sleigh pulled by two majestic bay geldings glided over the snow. They bundled beneath furs, hot stones at their feet to keep them warm. With his father beside him, Robert looked across at Emilie who sat between Ada and Emmanuelle. Of the two mothers, Emmanuelle was the enigmatic one. An aura of sadness tinged with caution surrounded her. A wall of protection seemed to shield her. If eyes were the windows of the soul, deep within hers, he could envision her pain, much of it wrought by his father, who now worked tirelessly to heal the wounds he had once caused. All his life Robert had believed he was an orphan. Now, on the eve of his marriage, he would have a real family by his side.

Anger had been his first reaction when he learned his parents lived and the roles they played in his abandonment. Now, he sensed their remorse as well as their sorrow. If Père Marc-Mathieu could teach him to forgive Seigneur Richard, he could do no less for his own mother and father.

Now that he and Emilie were to be married, he wanted nothing to stand in their way. Especially not their parish priest.

The sleigh pulled up in front of the rectory. Robert and Claude helped the three women dismount. Together they braved the extreme cold and walked through the small gate to the front door. Robert gave three brisk taps on the knocker and waited. No one answered.

"Let's go around the back," Claude said.

"Perhaps he's in the kitchen and can't hear our knock," Ada suggested.

At the rear of the house, they knocked again. Père Jean swung open the door. His eyes grew wide and he dropped the breviary in his hand. He looked like a deer trapped by hunters, desperate for escape, but not knowing which way to turn. A fire burned in the hearth and a bowl of partially consumed soup rested on the table.

"Père Jean, how good to see you again," said Robert as he entered last. He shook the priest's sweaty hand.

"Robert! Seigneur Prudhomme!" Père Jean snatched the book from the ground, and rubbed the snow from its cover as he straightened.

"Père Jean," Robert smiled. "This is my mother with whom I was reunited in Québec."

"Your mother?" A confused look crossed the priest's features.

"And Seigneur Claude is my father."

Père Jean's jaw dropped and he stood speechless, pale, his hands clasped over his chest.

Robert slapped him on the back. "I hope you've lost that headache, which prevented you from marrying me and Emilie many months ago." Robert decided to take advantage of the priest's speechlessness to press his case. "We've returned home now, and with our parent's approval, we are eager to marry."

Père Jean opened his mouth to say something, but Robert pressed on. "I have checked and there aren't any religious holidays like Lent to interfere this time. So, the earlier you can perform the ceremony, the better for all of us."

Père Jean hesitated. "Robert, are you sure? It would be foolish to call attention to yourself when there is a proclamation for seizure still out against you. To marry you, I will have to publish your name." He scratched his head and continued with his sundry excuses. "Why get married here in Pointe-du-Lac when you can get married just as easily elsewhere? I will have to read the banns again because too much time has transpired, and I'll need to complete all the searches again."

Père Jean was about to utter another excuse when Claude interrupted him. "There is nothing for you to fear. If we can convince you that you will come to no harm, surely you can marry my son to this beautiful young woman." He flashed a quick smile and a wink at Emilie who watched with a worried expression.

"The banns have already been read and the searches done," Robert said in a tone that would brook no argument. "There was no impediment then and there is no impediment now."

Père Jean stared at his hands and shook his head. "Now that you know who your parents are, the process must be repeated."

Claude pulled an envelope from his vest pocket. "I had the searches conducted while in Québec. I'm sure you'll find everything in order."

Père Jean opened the envelope and his eyes moved over each word. His Adam's apple bobbed as he swallowed hard.

"You have nothing to fear. Seigneur Richard is on his death bed," Robert said. "I saw him with my own eyes; the deadly black pox covered his entire face and body. He lay in an incoherent state upon a small cot at the Hôpital Général, struggling to breathe. I am certain he is dead by now. May the Lord have mercy on his soul."

"You cannot know for certain that he is dead. As long as a man has breath in his body there is hope. I've also been ill. I was close to entering Paradise myself, and yet I survived." Père Jean glanced at Emilie as if to solicit support. "I will not bring any more trouble upon myself."

"You are well now," said Seigneur Claude. "In fact, I've never seen you look so hearty and aglow with good health."

Père Jean picked at a thread from his cassock. "I do not recommend proceeding until the order for Robert's arrest is lifted." He turned to Emmanuelle. "You, Madame, who come from Québec, will know the course these matters take." He smiled as if an idea came to him. "Why not marry in Québec? There are plenty of priests and far grander churches than this."

The more spoke, the more courage he seemed to gather. "To tell you the truth, Robert, with you being sought by authorities, to proclaim your name from the altar is something I can't do with a quiet conscience. It would not set a good example. I wish you and Emilie well, but I am afraid I can't marry you."

"We are a long way from Québec," Ada interjected, her face reddening. "No one from there will hear about a small wedding in a tiny settlement so far away."

"It is not difficult to perform a wedding at short notice," Emmanuelle added, her voice calm. "I have encountered many priests who have done so."

Robert could not help but smile at her motherly intervention.

At that moment, someone knocked at the door. As Père Jean flung it open, a blast of cold air blew into the room. A finely dressed nobleman with a black armband around his right sleeve stood on the other side, his cheeks wind reddened, frost on his moustache. At Père Jean's urging, he stepped inside and stomped the snow from his boots. "I'm sorry to disturb you, but I knocked on the front door and because there was no answer, I came round the back. I have come in the hopes that you can direct me to the home of one of your parishioners."

"Who is it you seek, Monsieur?" Père Jean asked.

"I seek a man named Robert Lanzille."

Père Jean turned pale and everyone became still.

"May I ask who is inquiring?" Seigneur Claude said as he took an imposing step closer to the man.

A wounded look darkened the man's features. "I am Count Georges Le Barroy, uncle to Pierre Robillard and Richard Tonnacour who both held seigneuries nearby. My nephews were struck down by the pox and I've come to settle their estates."

Ada gave Père Jean a pointed look as if to reinforce what

they had already said about Seigneur Richard's probable death.

"You have my condolences," Claude said, the sincerity in his voice clear. "I conducted some business with Richard not long ago. I benefitted from it in many ways."

"That is heartening to know," said the Count. "It doesn't seem right for someone of my age to survive young men, but God works in mysterious ways."

"Indeed he does," said Père Jean looking relieved, but he recovered and his features became serious. "I'll say a mass in their honor."

"I would be most grateful," the Count said.

"What business have you with Lanzille?" Seigneur Claude asked.

The Count withdrew an envelope from his waistcoat and held it in his hands. "Bishop Laval asked me to deliver this to him. Does anyone know where I can find him?"

Père Jean opened his mouth to speak, but before he could utter a word, Seigneur Claude interrupted him. "He's not here, but I'm looking for him myself. If you leave the envelope with Père Jean, we shall see it safely delivered."

The Count hesitated. "My instructions from the Bishop was to deliver it to Robert Lanzille."

"I shall send a letter to the Bishop on your behalf advising him that it is in our possession here in the parish until Lanzille returns. The Bishop knows me well," Seigneur Claude said.

"Very well." The Count handed him the letter. "It's for the best. I'm not certain how long I will be here in Pointe-du-Lac. As my nephews' only living heir, I came to close up their homes, see to the servants, and to sell their land and holdings."

"It just so happens that I've been thinking of purchasing some more land," Seigneur Claude said. "The Tonnacour land borders mine on one side and that of your other nephew, Monsieur Robillard, on the other. Perhaps we can discuss the matter in a day or two?"

"I would be most grateful."

"Perhaps you can dine with me tomorrow evening?"

"You are very kind. I shall be there, *merci*," the Count replied. He tipped his hat to the women and took his leave.

"There is no longer any doubt," Claude said as he handed the letter to Robert. "Seigneur Richard is dead."

"Is it really true?" Père Jean asked.

"Surely you do not doubt the man's own uncle? Did you not notice the band of mourning he wore?"

Père Jean sank back onto his bench and pressed his palms over his eyes. "Ah! He's dead, then! He's gone!" He looked up at them, his eyes glittering with relief. "You see how Providence works. What a great relief it is! The speckled death has been a terrible scourge, but it has also been a good broom; sweeping away our problem. He will no longer bother us and he'll never threaten a poor priest again."

"I've forgiven him from my heart. You should too." After Robert narrowed his eyes at the priest, he broke the seal on the envelope.

"Why yes, of course, it's our duty to do so," replied Père Jean. "But we can also be grateful that we have been delivered from the problems he brought down on us." He paused and watched Robert as he removed three papers from the envelope.

Silence fell on them all as Robert glanced over the first letter. "It's from Père Marc-Mathieu."

Emilie drew closer to him.

He handed the letter to her. "I'm too nervous, *cherie*. Please read it for us."

Emilie cleared her throat and began.

Cher Robert,

By the time you receive this letter, I might be well in my grave.

Do not grieve, for I have led an amazing life and go into the next world with a grateful heart. I have known for quite some time that my death was imminent. In many ways, it is a blessing to know one's hour of death, for it provides one with the opportunity to complete many things. I once urged you to trust in God for he would make all things right. And for you and Emilie, He has done this.

Emilie paused, caught up with emotion.
Robert put his arm around her and she continued.

After our encounter in Québec where you told me all that had happened to you there, I sought an audience with his Excellency Bishop Laval. Although he would not reveal his sources, he had learned of my decision to help you and Emilie resolve the matter of your blighted troth. Upon confirmation that your presence in Québec on the fateful day of the bread riot was because I had sent you there with a letter by my own hand to seek refuge at a monastery, he took me to see the Governor. After listening to the story of all your troubles, and describing you, the Governor recalled you clearly and was most appreciative of your help in escorting him to the door of the Intendent's house and afterward by clearing a path for his carriage. As for the lieutenant who was assaulted in the street, the Governor assured me no charges will be laid and that you had no hand in what happened. He signed a proclamation absolving you of all charges, which I have enclosed with this letter. Further, I have enclosed a letter by his Excellency Bishop Laval giving Père Jean Civitelle immediate dispensation to marry you and Emilie. My only regret is that I cannot be with you on that joyous day to see you and Emilie wed, but I shall be with you in spirit. May you and Emilie enjoy a loving fruitful life together. You have my blessings now, and for all eternity. Pray for me as I shall for you.

Père Marc-Mathieu

Robert glanced first at the documents then at Emilie.

Tears rained down her cheeks. "Oh, Robert, I knew we could trust in Père Marc-Mathieu. He promised us that he would take care of us, and he did. You are free, your name has been cleared. We can begin our new life with no burdens from the past."

Robert scowled at Père Jean and handed him the document from the Bishop. "No more excuses."

Père Jean gave a nervous laugh. "Why of course, I shall be happy to conduct the wedding ceremony."

142

Emilie wed Robert on a magnificent morning replete with a fresh covering of sparking white snow beneath a sunny azure sky. Church bells pealed as the entire settlement of Pointe-du-Lac crammed the church to witness the long awaited event of a blighted troth set right. To the people, their wedding proved that perseverance, good intentions, and forgiveness conquered all.

In the carriage on the way to the church, Emilie fingered her mantua gown made of golden silk brocade with a large scale pattern of pink roses and leaves. She was delighted with the gown made from a single length of silk, which was open down the front of the skirt to reveal a satin and lace petticoat. On her head she wore an elegant, but modest, fontange with furbelows of lace, her hair piled into layers of elaborate curls and locks. Two long silk streamers hung behind the fontange and draped along both her shoulders as cornets. Emilie had never worn such beautiful garments before. Seigneur Claude had presented her with the items after purchasing them from a newly arrived ship from France.

Her heart skipped a beat at the sight of Robert, her beloved, waiting for her at the altar. How handsome he looked in his tan coloured, knee-length coat with over-sized turned-back cuffs over a dark brown waistcoat. A fine gold braid and embroidery in a fleur-de-lis pattern trimmed its edges. Emilie admired his ivory coloured silk stockings and brown leather shoes fastened with gold buckles. On his head, he wore a high parted white wig. In his finery, he looked as resplendent and handsome as any young man of the French court.

She walked towards him, prolonging the exquisiteness of the moments. Her love for him filled her.

He stood tall, hands clasped below his waist, unmoving except for the nervous tapping of his shoe. A generous smile graced his clean shaven face as he watched her every step while she made her way to his side.

When she neared, she locked her gaze to his; penetrating, ardent, merry. A flood of love filled her heart. When she lay her tremulous fingers on his coat sleeve, he reciprocated by placing his warm hand over hers. He looked at her with glowing affection, squeezing her hand in encouragement as the ceremony began.

Père Jean made the sign of the cross over them. "In nomine Patris *et Fillii et Spiritus Sancti.*"

She yearned to hold Robert's gaze, but, as required, he reverently faced Père Jean. The stability of his hand over hers, was more than adequate for now. She stood by his side before Père Jean, obeying the rituals of the ceremony and Mass, standing, kneeling, praying. Finally, the priest asked them to join their right hands and she could gaze into his eyes.

Their hearts and souls in accord, they each recited their vows. Emilie spoke with deliberate clarity to make certain he understood she harboured no reluctance. With each word she spoke, he tightened his clasp of her hand and his smile brightened. Tears formed in her eyes when he spoke his vows, his voice tremulous with emotion.

Père Jean made the sign of the cross over them. He blessed them with incense and holy water.

Emilie experienced inexplicable warmth and knew without doubt that Père Marc-Mathieu's spirit watched from above, sending them his blessings.

Throughout the Mass, Emilie knelt beside Robert, serene but attentive each time his elbow touched hers or her mind wandered to the night to come. She was now a wife, Robert's wife. Married at last! After the reception, they would be alone together for the first time and in the morning would attend mass together, this time as husband and wife.

Finally, the Mass concluded. They made their way arm in arm down the nave along the central aisle.

When they burst into the snow blanketed world, Robert took her into his arms and kissed her, respectfully, his eyes aglow with ardor. When their lips parted, he took her chin in his fingertips. "Madame Lanzille."

"*Oui*, that is my name now and it is the most beautiful name in all the world."

The first of the villagers exited the church, and within moments, they found themselves engulfed in embraces and joyful exclamations.

Followed by their guests and parents, Emilie and Robert led the way to a large barn, emptied, swept immaculately clean, and heated by several braziers. Numerous tables and chairs had been set up for their wedding banquet.

A never ending stream of dishes were prepared and served by the women of the settlement; spicy tourtières, pork terrine, and blood sausage all interspersed with plenty of roasted vegetables and loaves of fresh bread and *fromage*.

With great pride, Ada presented Robert with a bowl of

peeled carrots. "Eat," she insisted. "The entire bowl. I'm not getting any younger and I've waited long enough for grandchildren." She stuck one in his mouth and he bit off a chunk. Everyone laughed till tears fell from their eyes. Afterwards, they enjoyed hefty servings of sugar pie and ripened apples.

After the last of the dishes was served, Emilie's tears knew no bounds when Seigneur Claude presented Robert with the deed to the Seigneurial mill of Pointe-du-Lac and the entire estate that once belonged to Seigneur Richard, which he had purchased from the Count.

Soon after the tables were cleared away, men pulled out their fiddles and harmonicas and the music began. The rhythmic clacking of spoons against muscular thighs and the tapping of feet provided the percussion to the lively rigodons, gigues, and reels that followed. Vocalists sang *'À Saint Malo'*, a tale of ladies and sailors who argued over the price of grain until the women won the grain for nothing. With tankards of ale and cups of wine in their hands, the guests sang the rounds of *'Alouette'* until their voices were hoarse.

"Look, Robert." Emilie pointed to the bench where Seigneur Claude sat beside Emmanuelle. They both smiled as they secretly witnessed Claude take Emmanuelle's hand and raise it to his lips to kiss it. Emilie knew in her heart that with time, all would be well with Robert's parents.

Robert did his best to find a free moment and sneak Emilie away for a kiss or two, but there were too many guests and too many eyes upon them to make it possible. They spent the entire day swarmed by felicitations and embraces from friends and family. The festivities continued until night fell and the guests dispersed.

Tears glazed Ada's eyes as she kissed Emilie on the cheek and held her for a few brief moments.

Emilie gave her mother a reassuring look, then went to Robert. He led her to the seigneurial mill of Pointe-du-Lac where Seigneur Claude had ordered a room prepared for them in the upper story. A crackling fire blazed in the stone hearth. A bed with a hand crocheted coverlet and numerous plump pillows beckoned. Robes for each of them hung from hooks on the wall and their bed clothes were laid with care at the foot of the bed.

Emilie came to a stop just inside the door, overcome with emotion at the thoughtfulness of their parents who arranged everything at such short notice. Robert's arms enfolded her and she turned round in his embrace. As he lowered his head and kissed her, she indulged in the touch and taste of his lips.

Robert reacted as if her lips seared him. He fell against the wall, pulling her to him, her body tight against his. She fitted against his burly perfection and she pressed against him, reveling in the new sensations.

He raised his head, his eyes ablaze, and lifted her into his arms as if she were a precious treasure. "Come to bed," he whispered, and carrying her across the span of the room, laid her across the pillows. He lowered his head and kissed her anew. This time, his hand roamed to her breast and he stroked her with unhurried enchantment.

His touch stilled her, captivated at the sensations that quavered through her body. Her lips fell open and her breath grew shallower as his hands explored her flesh.

He kissed her breasts, first one then the other, through the gown before freeing them from its restrictive bodice.

She whispered his name, but with a kiss, he silenced her.

His hands trembled as he struggled to release her from her complex garments.

She helped him with each item until she lay splendidly unclothed before him. Then, with wonder, she watched him as he undressed against the firelight.

Gently, he lay upon her. She learned the feel of his arousal and the lowering of his body atop hers for the first time. He allowed her to explore his body at ease, accustomizing her to his touch, as he familiarized himself with hers. His hands explored the length of her back and when he ran his hand over her stomach, she inhaled a sharp breath of uncertainty, but he let her relax and his hand remained faithful to the act of love that awaited them.

Together they experienced the beauty of lovemaking.

Outside, the cold and snow glistened against a bright moon, but inside, the blaze of a fire kept them warm. After their joining within the comforting confines of the seigneurial mill, they emerged the next morning aglow with love and blissfully happy, their hearts and souls united for their entire lives.

The End

Reading Group Guide

1. How important is the theme of forgiveness to this story? Are there lessons to be learned from Robert and Emilie's plight? If so, what are they?

2. Emilie sacrificed much because she defied Seigneur Richard. Do you know women who have made sacrifices to exercise mind, heart, and spirit for the love of a man? Do you think such sacrifices are justified?

3. At various times throughout the story, Emilie makes promises she regrets keeping. Is she accurate in holding to her promises?

4. Each character is faced with the need to forgive, whether it be themselves or someone else. Discuss the role forgiveness plays for Emmanuelle and Seigneur Claude.

5. Emilie at first seems to be a young woman with simple needs. Does that make her someone with whom it's hard to sympathize?

6. Robert is at first obsessed with revenge. How does this influence his state of mind, his actions, and his relationship with Emilie?

7. At the end of the book, Emilie believes that she and her new family have found happiness. Do you think this is true? Is it possible for Claude and Emmanuelle to truly forgive and find

happiness after all the pain and suffering they endured at each other's hands?

8. What was unique about the setting of the book and how did it enhance or take away from the story?

9. Do the characters seem real and believable? Can you relate to their predicaments? To what extent do they remind you of yourself or someone you know?

10. How do characters change or evolve throughout the course of the story? What events trigger such changes?

11. Did certain parts of the book make you uncomfortable? If so, why did you feel that way? Did this lead to a new understanding or awareness of some aspect of your life you might not have thought about before?

About The Author

Books are one of Mirella's obsessions, especially those that pertain to medieval eras and with Italy as a backdrop. To fulfill a life-long dream, she began writing several years ago and has never looked back. Since then she has published several short stories and completed three novels with several more novels in various stages of completion. Her fascination for women of history and Italy is often reflected in her work, blogs, and websites. She writes from her home in Alberta surrounded by her husband, Richard, a notorious polygraph examiner nicknamed Darth Vader (for good reason), her two successful and beautiful daughters, Amanda and Genna, and a rambunctious little grandson Joseph, who, with his mighty Nerf shooter, fiercely protects her against marauders while she peels potatoes in the kitchen. His unanticipated interruptions and humorous calamities and disasters provide much fodder for her writing and a ton of daily joy. To learn more about Mirella Patzer and her work, please visit:

http://historyandwomen.com
http://mirellapatzer.com
http://historicalnovelreview.blogspot.com

7756811R0

Made in the USA
Charleston, SC
07 April 2011